Time is not Enough

Volume I
of the Solarian Chronicles

Neil Templar

CW01497045

Copyright © Neil Andrew Esslemont 2025

All rights reserved. No part of this book may be reproduced, stored in a retrieval system, or transmitted in any form or by any means, electronic, mechanical, photocopying, recording or otherwise, without the prior written permission of the publisher, except as permitted by U.S. copyright law and for brief quotations used in reviews or scholarly works.

The right of Neil Andrew Esslemont to be identified as the author of this work has been asserted by him in accordance with the Copyright, Designs & Patents Act 1988.

Registration no. 30957181125S196

This is a work of fiction. References to real historical people, places, organisations, events and public figures are presented in a purely imaginative context. Their inclusion is for storytelling purposes only and should not be construed as factual, nor as representations of any person's actual views, words or actions. All other characters, names, places, organisations and events are products of the author's imagination, and any resemblance to actual persons, living or dead, is purely coincidental.

First published 2025 by

Galactic Spacetime Publishing

First edition

eBook ISBN: 978-1-9193322-2-2

Paperback ISBN: 978-1-9193322-0-8

Colour Hardback ISBN: 978-1-9193322-1-5

To Sir Arthur C. Clarke

"We do not inherit the earth from our ancestors,
we borrow it from our children."

Native American proverb

Contents

Preface 7

Prologue 8

Chapter 1 12

Chapter 2 21

Chapter 3 25

Chapter 4 30

Chapter 5 35

Chapter 6 40

Chapter 7 47

Chapter 8 53

Chapter 9 58

Chapter 10 63

Chapter 11 68

Chapter 12 74

Chapter 13 83

Chapter 14 96

Chapter 15 108

Chapter 16 117

Chapter 17 124

Chapter 18 133

Chapter 19 141

Chapter 20 145

Chapter 21 151

Chapter 22 162

Chapter 23 172

Chapter 24 186

Chapter 25 200

Chapter 26 224

Chapter 27 234

Chapter 28 240

Chapter 29 248

Chapter 30 258

Chapter 31 266

Chapter 32 279

Chapter 33 285

Chapter 34 292

Epilogue 297

Afterword...306

Acknowledgements & Sources 308

Image Credits 315

Preface

This is a work of fiction. However, woven into the sci-fi narrative is as much scientific fact as possible, based on our current understanding of the universe.

And perhaps some elements of the *'fiction'* may even turn out to be true.

Prologue

"Let's face it, you're lost," Rebecca said.

She could barely make out her boyfriend's face in the darkness, despite sitting right next to him in their hire car. Squinting through the windscreen at the pouring rain, they could just about read the names on a tiny white signpost illuminated by the headlights. Unfortunately, none of the Wiltshire village names meant anything to either of them.

Many men – and quite a few women – would have immediately denied being lost. Or would have offered a string of explanations for why they were lost, none of which would have been their own fault. However, Ian, a serving officer in the US Navy, knew that such excuses would cut no ice with Rebecca.

Ian had been born in England to American and British parents. His father had been a US Air Force captain stationed at Greenham Common military base when he met Ian's mother, a staunch anti–nuclear weapons advocate. But love had prevailed, and Ian was living proof of that.

He mentally retraced the steps that had led to this predicament. They had spent the afternoon at Stonehenge – a place that had fascinated him ever since his father first took him there as a boy. Afterwards, they had decided to postpone their return to the hotel in Exeter and take a detour, driving a few more miles into the countryside, up onto the Wiltshire Downs. It had all seemed like such a good idea at the time.

They had stopped to watch the sunset and admire the scenery, which could be spectacular at this time of year. Then the heavens had opened – and it had been pouring ever since.

Then the hire car's onboard sat-nav system had suddenly stopped working. He thought he had heard a voice on the car's speaker say something like: '*We are about to enter an area with low quality map data*', but he wasn't sure and the message was not repeated.

Now, every time he said '*Hey Mercedes, navigate to Exeter*' or '*Hey Mercedes, show me our location on a map*', the response was: '*I am not able to use that function at the moment, please try again later.*'

A paper map would have helped – but who, in this day and age, still uses paper maps? He wished he'd downloaded an offline map of the area onto his phone in advance. With not even a single bar of signal showing,

Google Maps displayed their position as a blue dot on a grey, featureless background. It didn't even show the road they were on – or, for that matter, *any* road or building at all.

And then there was the fuel situation. The hire car had previously shown a range of forty miles when, without warning, the display went blank – the fuel must have dropped below the reserve level. Presumably, the manufacturer doesn't want to be blamed for people running out of fuel because of inaccurate range predictions, so it simply stops displaying the range when fuel gets very low.

Ian knew that in the Wiltshire Downs, on a bank holiday Monday night, open petrol stations were going to be few and far between.

Ian had thoroughly enjoyed *'An American Werewolf in London'*. The Wiltshire Downs did seem a bit less remote than the moors portrayed in the film (was it set in Exmoor or Dartmoor; he really couldn't remember?). But he definitely didn't fancy being stranded in the middle of nowhere at night. At the moment, if they were to drive around the corner and come across the Slaughtered Lamb pub, it would be a very welcome sight.

"You're right, we're lost," Ian said.

Rebecca, to her own admission, had such a poor sense of direction that she often turned the completely opposite way to the correct one and ended up getting lost. However, she was also perfectly capable of working out how to find her way again.

"Okay, we know the main road – the A303 – runs southwest from Stonehenge toward Exeter and our hotel, and east until it merges with the M3," she said. "We were north of the A303 when we left the Stonehenge car park, and then we drove roughly north and east towards the Wiltshire Downs.

"So now we just have to keep driving south and we should eventually hit the main road. By then, we'll hopefully get a mobile signal – and maybe even find a 24-hour filling station open on a Bank Holiday."

It was a good plan – as long as they didn't run out of petrol. Ian couldn't think of anything better at the moment, unless they came across a house where he could beg to use the phone and call for breakdown assistance, explaining that the car's fuel tank was almost empty. He didn't fancy that idea much, though – it would mean swallowing a lot of pride.

A few minutes later, as they came round a corner, they saw a bright light in the sky ahead of them. The rain was still coming down so hard that the windscreen wipers couldn't keep up – so they couldn't tell whether the light was coming from a tall building or from a hovering aircraft – perhaps a helicopter. And they couldn't hear anything over the noise of the car's engine and the somewhat squeaky windscreen wipers.

As they drew closer, it became clear that this was definitely an aircraft of some kind. Saucer-shaped, with strange, swirling colours glowing across its surface, it hovered above a field beside the country lane they had been driving along.

Ian brought the car to a juddering halt. He didn't need to voice his first thought – *"What the fuck is that?"*

They sat, mesmerised, as beams of light shone down onto the field below, sweeping slowly across it in wide arcs, as if searching for something.

In all his military experience, Ian had never seen anything like it. Just as he was about to slam the car into reverse and get the hell out of there, all the lights from the 'aircraft' suddenly went out. Then, without a sound, it shot upwards and away – so fast it could not possibly be considered a conventional aircraft.

"I think we've just seen a UFO," Ian blurted out.

"That was incredible! Do you think it could have been some kind of advanced experimental aircraft – or a drone?" Rebecca asked.

Before Ian could reply, she added quickly, "And we _are_ still lost, so maybe we should just get out of here?"

"I really think we need to take a look at that field before we go," Ian insisted.

Using their phones' torch apps for light, they eventually found a stile that allowed them to climb into the field. The rain had eased off to a light drizzle. The moon, about three-quarters full, peeped out from behind the clouds, and they could now see that they were standing in a field of yellow flowers about waist high. Curved pathways, roughly three feet wide and seemingly cut into the crop, wound around the field, occasionally turning left or right. It looked a bit like a maze – though one you could easily see over the top of.

"These plants look like oilseed rape," Ian commented. "Let's head towards the centre – I think I can see something glinting in the moonlight."

The 'flowers' were densely packed, their stems surprisingly stiff, making it difficult to walk through them – especially since the plants were soaking wet from the rain. Nonetheless, pushing straight through to the centre was going to be far quicker than following the winding paths. As they neared what must be the heart of the 'maze', they came upon a large circular area where all the crops had been flattened.

In the middle of this circle, just sitting on the ground, was a bright red five-gallon fuel canister.

Chapter 1

"I've no idea what we saw last night, but how weird is it to find a can of petrol just when we needed it? Why would a UFO – if that's what it was – leave it there? Or did someone else?" Rebecca remarked.

It had contained petrol – not diesel, the most common fuel for agricultural vehicles. The canister itself was unremarkable and, as evidenced by the writing around it, was a fairly common brand of manufacture – most definitely human in origin.

It was Tuesday morning and they were sitting on the balcony in their hotel, admiring the view of Exeter Cathedral. Ian had come to the UK to attend a joint UK/USA NATO military conference on IT security & Cryptology and had taken the opportunity to visit his mother whilst in the UK. He did not have to fly back to his base in the USA until Friday and so had a few days to spare.

"We only saw that place in the dark and only from the ground. I'd like to take another look – and from the air," he said.

"Okay, how do we do that?" Rebecca asked.

"I'm pretty sure we could hire a light aircraft at Exeter Airport," Ian replied.

After a few internet searches and phone calls, they managed to find a pilot who was willing to take them over to Wiltshire the following day.

On Wednesday morning, they found themselves flying over the Downs. They were lucky enough to have fine weather, with blue sky and sunshine. Having downloaded Google offline maps for the area, they were able to track their way back to the field where they'd had such a strange encounter.

From the air, it was apparent that the field contained what many would describe as a 'crop circle.'

"Let's get some photos of that pattern," Rebecca said, as the pilot circled the field again.

"Given we've both seen something we'd once have said was impossible," Ian observed, "a flying object that can only really be explained as alien – what *were* they doing carving a pattern in a field late at night? If this is meant to be some kind of message, surely there are easier ways to communicate with the human race."

Rebecca thought about that for a while. "Well, I reckon we should try to work out if the pattern's got a message in it. We've got plenty of photos now – let's head back."

Back at the hotel, they started going through the photos. Ian sketched the design on a sheet of paper, trying to keep roughly the same proportions.

Right at very heart of the pattern was a large circle, which he estimated as about eight metres across. That was where they'd found the red petrol can – an unexpected bonus – which they'd gratefully used to refuel the car.

The pattern could be considered a single continuous path, roughly one metre wide, spiralling in broad arcs outwards from the central area. At regular intervals, each arc was interrupted by a short zigzag – first veering 90 degrees right, then almost immediately turning 90 degrees left – before resuming its curved course around the centre. Occasionally, the path passed through one or two small circular areas, about two metres wide. And twice it went through a slightly larger circle three metres in diameter.

After spiralling around the centre several times, the path eventually reached its final destination at the outer edge of the pattern – a large circle, second in size only to the central one, yet completely empty.

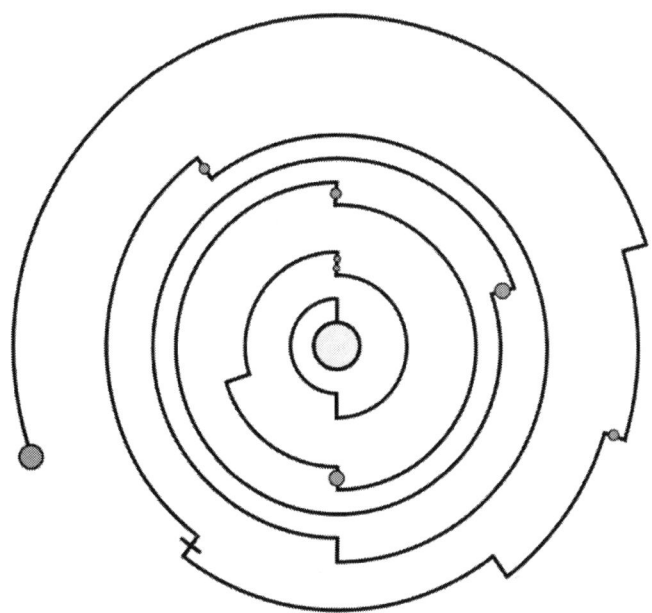

Ian and Rebecca considered a number of different theories – all of which were eventually discarded.

Rebecca sighed. "Okay, we're not getting anywhere. There must be loads of information about crop circles online – maybe I can find something useful."

Even after witnessing what appeared to be a UFO carving a pattern into the field right before her eyes, Rebecca still struggled to believe that crop circles were not all hoaxes – and entirely man-made.

She found one website which described the '***Crop Circle Season***':

'Although it might seem obvious, crop circles occur only during the crop growing season. In the UK, the first circles can start to occur in April and May, reaching their height in late July and August. Crop circles do in fact occur all over the world in many countries and obviously they similarly follow growing seasons in that particular part of the world.'

"It also says," Rebecca continued, "that some years the UK season doesn't start until the barley is tall enough to allow a crop circle to be made – which can be any time from late May to June. So it looks like oilseed rape is the only suitable crop this early in the year."

There were many websites showing images of crop circles created over the years. Many were strikingly beautiful, often perfectly symmetrical – but none looked like the one they had found.

Then, after half hour or so, Rebecca came across a 2008 article entitled *'Baffling crop circles equal Pi.'* The article went on to say: *'This appeared in a barley field in the Wiltshire countryside near Barbary Castle. The pattern seems to represent the first ten digits of pi – 3.141592654.'*

Rebecca showed the picture of this crop circle to Ian.

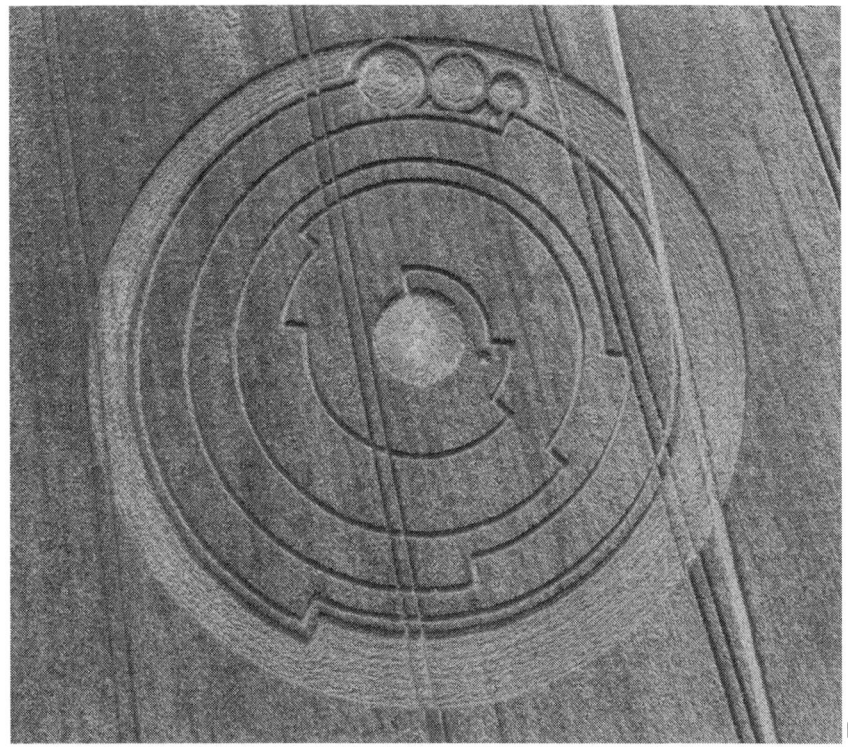

[1]

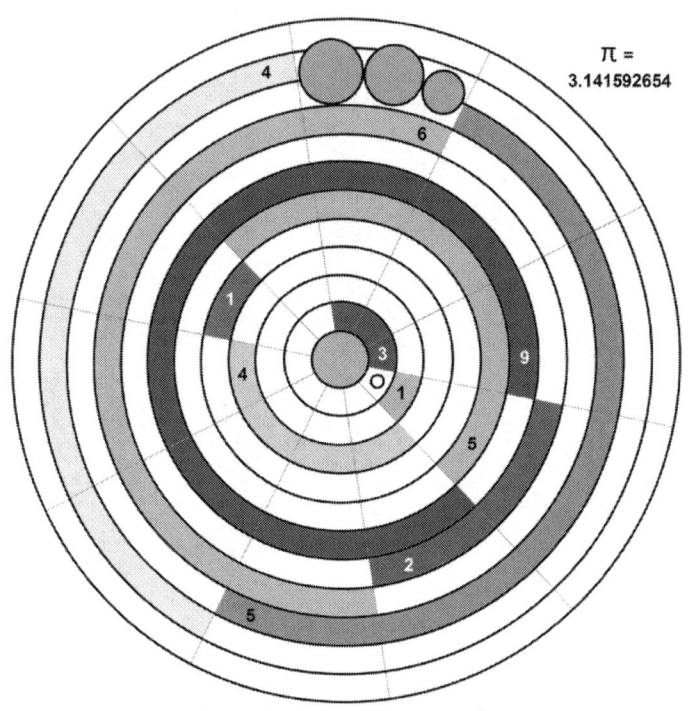

$$\pi = 3.141592654$$

"Might be a coincidence, but Barbury Castle is probably about 25 miles from where we found *our* crop circle – as the crow flies," he said.

"As the UFO flies, you mean?" Rebecca responded with a wry smile.

"We use π in mathematical formulae for circles and spheres, don't we?" Rebecca asked, thinking back to her maths classes in school. "But this must be a hoax. We already know what π is – so what would be the point of an alien UFO leaving a crop circle to tell us something we already know?"

Ian thought for a moment... then suddenly exclaimed, "It's not the answer that's important – it's the question!"

"What do you mean?" Rebecca asked, puzzled.

"What if an alien spaceship came here to leave that crop circle as a clue? And some human mathematician eventually cracked the code – proving it by uncovering the first ten digits of π. It's probably the most universal number in existence. A number the aliens knew we'd recognise."

"Hmm. I still don't see what you're getting at," Rebecca said, frowning.

"The real message was the methodology," Ian said, eyes alight with excitement. "The Barbury Castle circle didn't just contain a number – it gave a key – a demonstration of how to decode a pattern like this one. It even used a small circle to represent a decimal point."

"But that was seventeen years ago! How could it possibly have anything to do with what we're doing now?" Rebecca asked, incredulous.

"Considering how closely the Barbury Castle pattern resembles our crop circle, I think we should try the same decoding method," Ian replied. "After all, we don't have any better ideas, do we? Let's work out the length of each curve in the pattern and see where it takes us."

The shortest curve in the entire pattern covered about one-tenth of a circle – about 36 degrees. He proceeded to draw ten spokes radiating out from the central circle, superimposing them over the sketch of the pattern he had drawn previously. Next to each curved path, he wrote a number indicating how many segments the arc travelled through.

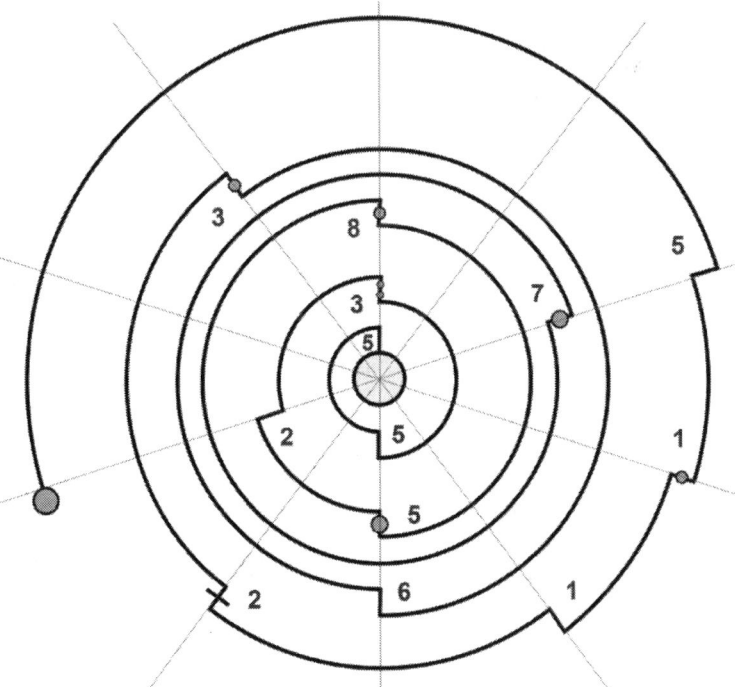

They could see two symbols that appeared nowhere else in the entire sequence, as if they had been deliberately placed there to convey a hidden meaning. Next to one of the twos was a line that crossed the zigzag, forming what looked like a plus sign ('+'). And near a three – on another zigzag section – two small circles nestled close together, smaller than any other circle in the whole pattern.

"And what do those two larger circles, next to one of the 5s and the 7, mean?" Ian thought.

The Barbury Castle crop circle had only used numbers from 1 to 9 – enough to depict the first ten decimal places of pi, which happen to contain no zeros. But Ian couldn't dismiss the possibility that their own pattern might include zeros. That uncertainty made him hesitate: should the first 36 degree segment be counted as a '1', or does it actually represent a '0'? If he chose '1' as the value for a single arc, a full circle – ten segments totalling 360 degrees – would symbolise '0'. However, none of the arcs in the pattern actually completed an entire circle – in fact, the longest arc only crossed 8 out of the possible 10 segments.

After scrutinising the pattern in silence, Ian traced the winding path outward from the centre and wrote down two possible sequences in a table. He put in full stops to represent the smallest circles but, as it wasn't clear what any of the other symbols meant, he just put them into the number sequences, using a 'Φ' symbol for the two larger circles.

If each arc represents a number between 1 and 10

55 : 32 Φ 5 . 8 Φ 76 . 3 + 21 . 15

If each arc represents a number between 0 and 9

44 : 21 Φ 4 . 7 Φ 65 . 2 + 10 . 04

He showed the sequences to Rebecca. Despite his background in cryptology and code breaking, Ian couldn't see anything in these numbers and symbols that made any sense.

"What are we supposed to do with these – and which of the two sequences is the correct one?" he thought.

As they didn't seem to be getting anywhere, they decided to break for dinner. Afterwards, as they were mulling the problem over their glasses of wine, another idea came to Ian's mind.

"I have assumed that the number sequence starts by following the path outwards from the centre of the pattern, like the Barbury Castle one does," Ian explained. "But what if they are deliberately trying to make it more difficult to decode? Perhaps, the sequence starts from the outer edge of the crop circle? Maybe the larger three metre circle was even there to give us a clue about where you should start?"

He drew up a new table, this one containing *four* sequences. The two new ones were the reverse of the previous two sequences, as they started from the outer circle and followed the path *into* the centre.

He showed it to Rebecca.

Arcs represent the numbers 1 – 10
Sequence starts from centre
55 : 32 Φ 5 . 8 Φ 76 . 3 + 21 . 15

Arcs represent the numbers 0 – 9
Sequence starts from centre
44 : 21 Φ 4 . 7 Φ 65 . 2 + 10 . 04

Arcs represent the numbers 1 – 10
Sequence starts from outer edge
51 . 12 + 3 . 67 Φ 8 . 5 Φ 23 : 55

Arcs represent the numbers 0 – 9
Sequence starts from outer edge
40 . 01 + 2 . 56 Φ 7 . 4 Φ 12 : 44

They puzzled over this for a while – it still seemed pretty daunting – the additional two sequences looked just as cryptic as the first two. Then, suddenly, Rebecca had a flash of insight.

"Hmm... it might just be a coincidence, but tomorrow is the 8th of May," she said thoughtfully. "And the way you've written it out, that '23:55' at the end of the third sequence looks like it could be a time of day – so perhaps it's a date and time?"

"Oh, that's *brilliant!*" Ian exclaimed. "I wonder what the other two sets of numbers mean then – the 51.12 and the 3.67?"

"Map coordinates?" Rebecca suggested.

Ian looked at her in amazement. "Wow – you just *might* be onto something!"

Map coordinates are conventionally given as so many degrees, minutes and seconds north, and so many east. If the seconds are omitted, it means zero seconds.

"If these numbers *are* coordinates," Ian pondered, "they can't be in degrees and minutes, since there are only sixty minutes in a degree – and the second coordinate was 3.<u>67</u>. So they must represent **51.12 degrees north** and **3.67 degrees east**, with the last two digits representing hundredths of a degree."

"I think Google Maps allows you to type in map coordinates," Ian said, reaching for his phone.

He typed in '51.12, 3.67' and they were soon eagerly studying the map.

"I don't think this makes any sense," Ian said. "This is a housing estate in Belgium. Why would an alien spaceship – if that's what it was – carve a pattern in a field giving the map coordinates of a Belgian house?"

But Ian suddenly had another inspiration. Most of the UK lay to the West of Greenwich Meridian in London, not to the East. Map coordinates are defined as degrees & minutes North and East, so a negative number would mean South or West respectively. What if the strange '+' symbol between the 12 and the 3 was actually a negative sign? Now that he thought about it, a single line had been carved across the main path on the zigzag, so that might represent a minus sign '-'.

He quickly edited the coordinates in Google Maps, adding a minus sign in front of the '3' to make it '51.12, −3.67' and hit 'Search'. The satellite image now showed a lonely field beside what looked like an overgrown footpath or a narrow country lane.

As he zoomed out for a wider view, the landscape came into focus – this was remote, windswept Exmoor – about an hour and a half's drive from Exeter. Far removed from the Wiltshire Downs – where they had seen the UFO and discovered the crop circle – but still a lot nearer than Belgium.

Ian stared at the screen. "Okay, perhaps this *is* what we were supposed to find... but why would an alien spaceship carve a cryptic message into an oilseed crop, pointing us to a field in an isolated corner of Exmoor – together with a date and time?" pondered Ian.

"Because the aliens want us to go to that field tomorrow night at five minutes to midnight?" Rebecca speculated.

They looked at each other.

Chapter 2

Wednesday, 7th May 2025, Exeter

"You're absolutely *not* going on your own," insisted Rebecca.

"And *you* are not coming with me – it's too dangerous," Ian shot back.

"You don't even have your service revolver," Rebecca retorted.

"If I end up in a situation where a gun becomes necessary," Ian said, "then everything's already gone to hell – and I won't be coming back."

"Then why go at all? Just report it to your Navy superiors!"

"Oh sure," Ian said with a laugh. "And they're really going to believe me? What evidence do I have – some photos of a pattern in a field that, like every other crop circle, the world thinks is a hoax? And let's not forget the clincher: an empty petrol can of obvious human manufacture. Maybe I should dust it for fingerprints?"

This had been going on all Wednesday evening, since the revelation that they seemed to have been invited by a UFO to go to Exmoor at midnight the next day.

Ian's flight back to Baltimore was booked for Friday afternoon, as his period of leave was coming to an end and he had to report back to his base. Ian was a Lieutenant in the USA Navy – serving as a Cryptologic Warfare Officer – stationed at the US Navy Information Operations Command at Fort Meade, Maryland.

His expertise was in cyberspace security, cryptology (code breaking), signals intelligence and electronic warfare. Little of which seemed to be of much help in this situation. He had received some basic combat training, but was not generally expected to see action 'in the field'.

Ian and Rebecca continued to discuss the pros and cons late into the night – why should either of them even be thinking of going. This carried on the next morning but, come Thursday lunch time with the deadline looming, they finally agreed that they would both go – but Rebecca would stay hidden in the background to observe. They were acutely aware, however, that even human infrared technology could detect body heat at night, let alone what alien technology was capable of. So, Rebecca would definitely have to keep her distance and use whatever cover was available.

They studied the terrain on various websites like Google Earth and Street Map. Google Street View did not have any ground-level pictures of the country lane immediately next to the field, but gave a general idea of the nearby countryside. The satellite images *did* show a fairly dense row of trees on one side of the lane and a hedge – separating the lane from the field – on the other side. And there was a nearby farm, a hundred yards or so further down the lane, possibly where the owners of the field lived.

"Okay, we need to go and look at this place in daylight and work out where you can hide. If you need to call for help and you can't get a mobile signal, you could always go to that farm."

However, they both privately thought that if the UFO did appear and carried out a hostile action of some sort, there would be nothing a local farmer or even the local emergency services would be able to do to intervene. But perhaps Rebecca could find safety in the house and, if Ian did need medical help, she might need to call an ambulance.

They set off after lunch and by mid-afternoon had arrived at the country lane near the field. The sat-nav had mysteriously started working again. They left the car parked by the side of the road near the farm and carried on down the lane by foot until they reached what they thought was the closest point to the field. The terrain was as much as they expected and they even found a gate into the field.

The field was unremarkable and looked like it may be used for grazing or been left fallow, as it was covered in short grass, with no signs of any crops planted.

"If the UFO does come here, it won't be making a crop circle," commented Ian. "Of course, this could just be a wild goose chase, as we may have completely misinterpreted the pattern or the numbers – or the UFO may never even have had any intention of coming here."

However, they studied the area and refined their plans for the evening. The forecast suggested no rain and fairly clear skies. The moon was about four days away from being a full moon, so it would be fairly bright if it was not hidden by the clouds. Not that that was necessarily an advantage, given that Rebecca needed to stay hidden. They had checked and sunset was going to about 8.30pm. Moonrise was due a few hours earlier at 4.30pm, so by midnight would be quite high in the sky.

Having made as many preparations as they could think of, they went back to the car and drove off in search of supper and a drink at a local pub.

When they returned and parked their car, it was about 11.30pm. Rebecca settled in to her observation point, in a place they had previously spotted, where the trees and bushes were fairly dense. They had talked about the chances of Rebecca being detected if she kept her mobile phone switched on, but had decided that the benefit of being able to call each other overrode the risks. So, she now set her phone into silent & vibrate mode.

Ian had decided he would wait in the field, close to the gate and the hedge, so he set off down the lane.

They were both in position by 11.45pm. Time ticked by, each minute seeming to take forever. Every animal noise rustling in the hedge made him jump. Ian's watch had florescent hands and so he could just about make out the time, without having to open up his mobile phone case, which would have made the screen light up.

11.55pm came and went. This was looking like a massive waste of time and energy. The tension in Ian started to subside and be replaced by annoyance. After all, they could have been enjoying the last few days of their holiday instead.

Ian opened the cover on his phone and started to call Rebecca, to tell her that this was a waste of time and to suggest they went back to their hotel.

Then suddenly, at what must have been midnight precisely, he heard a rushing noise like a strong wind above his head. Despite all their planning and preparation, he was truly shocked to see what looked like the same UFO they had seen before, hovering about 30 foot up in the air. It was about 100 feet away from him, near the centre of the field. This time the ship was only faintly shimmering, silver in colour. Or was it just the moonlight reflecting on its surface?

The UFO slowly descended until it reached perhaps 10 foot off the ground. Then a small section of the ship seemed to come away from its body and one end rotated down onto the ground. It clearly looked like steps of some sort and it revealed a doorway behind it.

Then something appeared silhouetted in the doorway and started to walk down towards the ground. There was enough light to make out a human-like figure which, bizarrely, appeared to be dressed in an open-necked shirt, jacket, trousers and boat shoes. A wide brimmed hat was on its head, positioned at a slightly jaunty angle. He looked more at home at the Henley Regatta, rather than in a muddy field in Exmoor, Ian thought.

"Good evening, Lieutenant," the figure said with an impeccable King's English accent, pronouncing the rank the American way 'Loo-tenant'.

'*He*' then took off his hat and gave a small bow towards him. "Sorry I'm late."

Chapter 3

Sun Tzu was a Chinese military strategist, general and philosopher who lived around the 5th century BC. He was the author of a classic treatise on military strategy, tactics and leadership called the '*The Art of War*'.

There is a well-known saying: *"No plan survives contact with the enemy."* It is often attributed to Sun Tzu, but although his treatise expresses similar ideas, he never actually wrote those words. The quote is more accurately credited to Helmuth von Moltke the Elder, a German field marshal of the late nineteenth century. Whoever first coined it, the observation has proved remarkably true over the centuries.

Whilst Ian had been waiting in the field, he had turned the speaker volume on his phone down to zero, so if it rang it would not give him away. Just before the UFO had arrived, he had pressed the call button to ring Rebecca. In all the excitement of watching the ship descend and land, Ian had not noticed that the call to Rebecca was still in progress.

Rebecca, still hidden in the bushes further down the country lane, suddenly received a call from Ian and, despite her saying "Hello" a few times, could hear almost nothing coming from the other end. She then thought she saw something in the sky, just a faint light, which drifted downwards until it was almost completely hidden by the hedge around the field.

Thinking that Ian had called for help, she left the call in progress and, abandoning her safe haven, she instinctively rushed up the lane towards the gate to the field. Staying hidden behind the hedge, she peered around the corner, trying to see what was happening – hoping Ian was still unharmed.

She arrived just in time to see the UFO hovering a few feet above the grass and a humanoid figure standing at the bottom of some steps. Steps that went up to a doorway in the side of what looked like a 'flying saucer'. And, standing right in front of what was presumably an alien, was Ian.

Meanwhile, oblivious to what was happening to Rebecca, Ian's first thoughts were: *"How the hell did the Brits get hold of such a technologically-advanced aircraft?"* and *"If NATO wanted me to get involved in such a project, why hadn't the US Navy just sent me an encrypted message to tell me this, rather than sending this idiot to find me?"*

Anyway, Ian's reply to the *'alien'* was "Good evening. You appear to know who I am?"

Ian was on leave and was most definitely not wearing a military uniform. There was no way this *'person'* would be able to tell he was a Lieutenant from what he was wearing.

The alien replied "Of course, forgive me for not introducing myself, I am Istariol and I am here as an official representative of the IGC. I have some important news for you." Ian had never heard of the 'IGC' and had no clue if it was a US or a British military organisation.

Istariol then turned, looking straight at Rebecca through the hedge foliage, and said, "Ah, Rebecca. I hadn't realised you were here. My name is Istariol."

Realising that there was not much point in hiding any more, Rebecca emerged from behind the hedge.

"How come you know my name?" she asked. Then, turning to Ian, she added, "So, this *is* a military aircraft and they've come to pick you up early from your shore leave, haven't they?"

Interrupting, Istariol said, "Actually, no. As I was explaining to Ian, I am an IGC representative with some important news for him. I was about to invite him – and him alone, I'm afraid – aboard my ship, so we could discuss these matters in more comfort – and in private."

"What do you mean invite *'him alone'*?" Rebecca protested. "You've dragged us out to the wilds of Exmoor, wasting days of our time with your stupid message hidden in a crop circle – when you could've just called or messaged him. And now you tell me that you're ordering him into your aircraft, presumably to take him to some military base, where he'll have to go back on duty.

"And I'm not even invited to come in out of the cold? What am I supposed to do – just go back to the car and drive back to Exeter on my own? He doesn't even have to report in to his base until Saturday afternoon."

Privately, Ian could only agree with Rebecca's outburst, even if it had not been expressed very diplomatically. And, in the early hours of a May morning, it *was* getting quite chilly standing out here in this muddy field.

"I see," Istariol said. "Well, I'm sorry you've had quite a difficult time recently, but I'm afraid security regulations strictly forbid your entry aboard my ship."

But he then averted his eyes a little and, staring into the space above their heads, started talking: "Ah yes... Ahem...Yes...Okay, that *is* a good point. I hadn't thought of that. Well, if you're sure that would be alright?"

"It has just been pointed out to me," Istariol said, looking at Rebecca, "that there is, shall we say, a way of interpreting the regulations that would allow us to approve you coming aboard.

"You would both have to sign Non-Disclosure Agreements and the penalties for breaching them are, to say the least, best not contemplated.

"Ian, you will need to formally recruit Rebecca as your Deputy. You will, of course, need a team, so we can consider this your first appointment. Is that acceptable to you both? If so, and you give me your word, I'm happy for you to both come in and I will get a printout of the appropriate contracts."

"Hang on," Rebecca interjected. "I have a job and I've got to go back to work. I can't just drop everything and go off on some secret military mission."

"Rebecca, I will explain everything to you both when you come aboard, but I can assure you that you will come under Ian's sole jurisdiction. He will be totally free to allow you to perform any of your work or other duties as he sees fit. Your only other commitment is to keep secret anything you see or hear when you come aboard my ship, or anything you might learn about this 'mission'. In addition, subject to my other commitments and priorities, I would be willing to drop you off almost anywhere in the world you might want to go."

With a glance at Rebecca and a shrug of the shoulders, Ian said "Okay by me. *Rebecca*?"

Rebecca nodded, so Istariol led them up the steps and through the doorway into the aircraft/ship.

In retrospect, things had been happening so quickly that Ian wasn't entirely sure what he'd expected the inside of the ship to look like. It certainly seemed larger than he'd anticipated. They entered a small hall with white metal walls. Istariol then turned left and, without visibly pressing any button, a doorway appeared in the wall ahead of him – as if that section of the wall had simply vanished.

They stepped through the opening into a room that looked remarkably like a Victorian 19th-century dining room, complete with a dining table, chairs and four comfortable-looking armchairs. Ian glanced up, his eye briefly catching a small black speaker mounted on the ceiling – its sleek, modern design at odds with the room's antique style.

"I'm sorry, but I haven't had time to update the furniture. Are you hungry? I can arrange for some food to be served? And would you like a drink of something? Wine – or perhaps something stronger?"

They both agreed that a drink would help steady their nerves and asked for a glass of white wine and a Scotch on the rocks. But what kind of aircraft had the space for such a large living area? Ian had once seen the interior of the US presidential aircraft, *Air Force One*, a specially configured Boeing jumbo jet. This reminded him of that, but the curvature of the room suggested that they were in a relatively small section of the craft.

Once they had settled into their seats and had their drinks in hand, Ian and Rebecca both blurted out all the questions they had about the situation.

Istariol asked them to stop and hold their questions for a little while, as he had much to explain. He suggested that he should first go through his briefing and, if they had any questions of clarification, he would be happy to answer them.

"So, to recap: as I mentioned, I'm here as an official representative of the IGC, with some important news for Ian – and, indeed, information that concerns you both."

"What is the IGC, I've never heard of it?" asks Ian.

At that moment, a slit opened in the wall and a sheaf of papers were spat out onto a small table they hadn't noticed before.

"Aha," Istariol said, striding over to collect them. He handed each of them a set, then passed an extra document to Ian.

"These are the contracts you both need to sign – and this is the paperwork authorising Ian to deputise Rebecca." He offered them pens and looked at them expectantly.

The contract was a Non-Disclosure Agreement – an NDA – but it bore little resemblance to any US military NDA or security-clearance document Ian had seen before. Still, he knew that specialised NDAs were often required when dealing with certain technologies or agencies such as the NSA, CIA, or Special Operations.

Ian quickly scanned through the wording, then shrugged and signed. Rebecca, following his lead, did the same. But when Ian turned to the separate 'Deputisation' document, one term leapt out at him – 'IGC' – together with a new and unsettling phrase: 'Solarian Representative'.

"You haven't told us what IGC means – and what's this about a Solarian Representative?" Ian asked. "For that matter, you seem to be dressed somewhat informally for an aircraft Captain. Don't you have a uniform? Or are you a spy?"

"Okay, I *can* explain this to you Ian, but if you want Rebecca to hear this, both of you first have to sign the Deputisation form. Or, if you prefer, Rebecca can wait in another room whilst I brief you?"

It had been a long and stressful day already and it seemed there was more to come. Ian looked at Rebecca quizzically and she nodded. They both signed the papers. Istariol gave a little sigh and seemed to relax, as he sat back in his chair and took a sip of red wine.

"Okay. I am very sorry about all the paperwork, but we have some very formal processes to go through in the next few weeks and this is just step one. I had no intention of misleading you, but you have made quite a few false assumptions about what's happening here. And without these papers signed, I was extremely restricted in what I could tell you.

"The IGC is the 'Inter-Galactic Council' – a body that represents intelligent life forms and advanced civilisations across several stellar systems throughout the galaxy. I, myself, am from a planet in the Antares star system and serve as a kind of ambassador on Earth."

Scratching the side of his head, he added, "And, well... yes, I *am* a spy actually.

"Welcome to my spaceship."

Chapter 4

Ian was in denial. He had seen what he had thought was a UFO flying saucer in the Wiltshire Downs. The coded message in the crop circle had led them to this field in Exmoor.

He didn't truly know what he'd expected, but it was probably something like the film he had seen years ago: *'Close Encounters of the 3rd Kind'*. The UFO would land and strange creatures would emerge, looking a bit like *'E.T.'* – short, with disproportionally large heads and big eyes and three fingered hands. They would then give him a message to deliver to the leaders of mankind. Or perhaps, worse, he would be abducted and they would perform some awful medical experiments on him.

A UFO *had* landed. But, instead of aliens, some British guy, dressed as if was going boating, had walked out and greeted him as 'Lieutenant'. Seconds later, Rebecca had arrived at the scene and the guy says something like *"Hello, Rebecca."* Clearly, he knew who they both were – and so this guy must work for the British military or MI6 and this must be some sort of secret, advanced aircraft. The discussions which had followed – with all the palaver about getting them both to sign confidentiality contracts – had only reinforced his impression that this was a secret military operation (presumably NATO, given the Brits were involved). Why would aliens bother with paper contracts?

So here they were sitting in the living space inside this huge aircraft, when Istariol – as he calls himself – announces he is an alien spy and that this is a spaceship! This must be a test of some sort. How was he supposed to react?

Rebecca, on the other hand, was now convinced they had been hoodwinked into boarding a spaceship and that they were now prisoners. But all that business about getting them to sign those legal documents made little sense to her – unless they'd just been duped into signing over all their possessions and aliens were going to start living in their flat?

As these thoughts flashed through their heads, the 'room' they were in started to vibrate slightly and they noticed a slight humming noise around them.

Istariol was talking again. "Well, you've had a long day and there's plenty of time tomorrow to go through the details. I suggest you retire and get some sleep. Meantime, we need to move the ship somewhere a little more discreet."

He stood up and waved his arm towards another doorway which had appeared in the wall. There was no sign of the entrance they had used when they first entered the room.

Ian stood up and took Rebecca's hand. After a surreptitious glare at Rebecca, he said "That sounds like an excellent idea. Come on, let's get some kip."

He practically had to drag Rebecca behind him as he stepped through the doorway into the next room. It had a large double bed and they could also see another small room that looked like an en-suite bathroom. Laid out on the bed were two sets of night clothes.

They heard Istariol call out after them, "Good night. I will see you again at breakfast." The doorway behind them silently disappeared, leaving just a blank wall.

"Are you completely mad?" Rebecca spat out. "You just willingly led us into our cell."

Meanwhile, the vibration and faint humming noise continued and, if anything, was now a little bit more pronounced.

"Look, this is some sort of test," Ian replied. "Perhaps the military want to see how we react, before we're accepted on the mission?"

Their discussions continued into the early hours of the morning. Both parties could see the other's point of view, but retained their own belief in what was happening. They finally agreed that they needed some sort of proof before they could decide what to do next.

They had checked their phones and, unsurprisingly, there was no wifi or mobile signal. Curiously, though, on each side of the bed stood a small table with a circular pad on it. They soon realised these were wireless phone chargers and took the opportunity to charge their devices. But what was the point of letting them charge their phones if they couldn't actually use them?

It *had* been a long day, though, and it was not much longer before they both drifted off to sleep.

The next morning, they woke refreshed, but as bemused about the whole situation as they were before. They realised that the humming and vibration wasn't there anymore.

There was a small shower in the en-suite bathroom and, as if this were a normal hotel room or ship's cabin, a shaving kit, two toothbrushes, toothpaste, and other toiletries. They also found two sets of clean clothing in a drawer beneath the bed. The clothes were similar in style to the ones they were wearing. The larger set fitted Ian perfectly, but the smaller outfit was a little too loose on Rebecca.

"Looks like they really *weren't* expecting you to come aboard," Ian observed.

Once they had showered and dressed, their eyes were drawn to the wall they had walked through the night before, coming from the 'living room'.

Now the faint outline of a doorway was clearly visible – an outline that hadn't been there before. Beside it, a small button glinted subtly in the wall.

Rebecca frowned, tilting her head. "I'm sure that wasn't there last night," she murmured.

"Okay, are you ready?" Ian asked.

Nodding, Rebecca pressed the button and part of the wall silently disappeared – leaving an open doorway. Stepping through, they found the living room was as they had left it, except that the dining table was now laid out for breakfast, complete with bread, cheese, cold meats and fruit.

"Do you really believe that aliens would give us a continental breakfast?" asks Ian.

"Yes, if they wanted to drug us," was the response.

"Surely they could just gas us if they wanted to do that," Ian retorted.

So, they sat down at the table and both proceeded to eat and drink their fill. Shortly after they had finished, another door opened and Istariol emerged. After they had all said *"good morning"* to each other, he invited them to take a seat in the armchairs.

"I have much more to tell you, but first I imagine you may have some questions you'd like to ask?"

They had discussed this last night and had agreed Ian would take the lead.

"Despite all we've seen," Ian explained, "we still find it difficult to believe that you really are an alien from a different planet. And that this *is* a spaceship, rather than an advanced human-built military aircraft. Is there some way you could prove that to us?"

"Oh... I hadn't really expected disbelief at this stage. Hmm... let me think."

He paused, then continued, "One problem I have is that I'm bound by regulations to limit the amount of information or exposure I give you to our technology. The ship doesn't have any glass windows, so I could only show you views of the outside on a 'TV' screen — which could easily be faked. However, there are some things I *will* have to show or tell you in order for you to carry out your duties."

"Can we take a look around the rest of your ship?" Rebecca asked.

"I'm afraid not. That would be a breach of Regulation 9," was the response. "Yes, you're going to ask me what Regulation 9 is. In essence, it forbids any IGC member from interfering with other more vulnerable civilisations that do not have the capability of interstellar travel. This definition of interference includes passing on or revealing more advanced technology — and bans the IGC member from even revealing the existence of their own civilisation or their spaceships. However, given the particular situation we currently find ourselves in, we *are* permitted to share certain essential information with the Representative and his team — but there are strict limits."

"This sounds like Star Trek's 'Prime Directive'," Rebecca observed.

"We suspect there may have been an information leak to Gene Roddenberry — as the principle is very similar — but we never found any concrete evidence of that."

"Well, how about you tell us what our duties are going to be?" Ian asked.

"There's a lot you need to know about the background before I can go into that in any detail. Just to outline the plan for our next steps — it's likely to take a long time to brief you both, so I'll explain your duties tomorrow morning."

"*Tomorrow* morning! That's not going to be possible — I have to catch a flight from Heathrow this afternoon," Ian protested.

Istariol smiled faintly, saying "That's not something you need to worry about. We could, of course, drop you off near Fort Meade tomorrow morning in time for you to report for duty. However, we have already arranged all the appropriate security clearances to allow you to go on an 'assignment' to a secret military operation, so they are not expecting you back anytime soon."

Turning to Rebecca, Ian said, "See, I told you this was a NATO military mission."

"Actually, that's not quite right Ian," Istariol interjected. "You are a Cryptologic Warfare Officer serving in the US Navy. You'll be fully aware that your so-called 'quantum' computers will soon be able to crack every single code mankind has ever used. So, you won't be at all surprised when I tell you that our computers can already do this – and that we've hacked into your military database and altered the records to account for your absence from base, without raising any suspicion."

"However, I think it's time I convinced you both that we really *are* on a spaceship, so we can get on with business," he continued.

He turned and gestured towards a doorway that had appeared in the wall. "Please step outside for a moment."

It seemed to be the same door they had entered through when they first boarded the aircraft. They stepped into the small hall. The outer door stood open, and they could see the top of the steps lit by the light spilling from the room behind them. Beyond that was only darkness.

Taking Rebecca's hand, Ian led the way out through the outer doorway. According to British Summer Time, it was about eight o'clock in the morning, so they should have been seeing daylight.

However, the aircraft must have taken them into a different time zone – as it was clearly night time here – and they were looking at the most stunning view of the stars they had ever seen. Ian had seen the Southern night skies before, but this was even more impressive.

The top of the steps was about twenty feet above the ground, which, in the dim light, looked like some kind of rock-strewn terrain. They turned their heads slightly to take in the scene.

"Oh my *god*!" screamed Rebecca.

"Jesus Christ," was Ian's only comment.

To their right, they could see the horizon – but it looked much closer and more curved than it should have been. Above it hung a distant sphere and, even though half of it lay in darkness, they immediately recognised what it was.

They were looking at the planet Earth.

Chapter 5

None of this seemed right to Ian. For a start, how could they be standing outside a spaceship without a space suit and still be breathing air? It was clear that they were *supposed* to think that they were on the moon. But the stars looked like they were light bulbs suspended from a black ceiling high in the air – they weren't even twinkling. Perhaps this was all rigged up in a studio the size of an aircraft hangar? But he had no idea why they would go to this amount of trouble to arrange such an elaborate hoax.

Ian decided he was going to get to the bottom of this and go and explore this 'studio'. He knew he wouldn't have to walk very far, perhaps to the edge of the hanger, before he would be able to confirm that this was all a hoax.

They were standing on a small platform at the top of the aircraft's narrow steps, with Rebecca immediately behind him, just outside the doorway. Ian stepped forward onto the first step – only to find himself suddenly floating in mid-air. He drifted forward and downward in a gentle arc, completely overshooting the steps, and landed on the ground in a soft puff of dust.

He immediately realised he didn't feel nearly as heavy as he should. Turning to look back, he saw Rebecca still at the top of the steps, frozen in place with her mouth hanging open in shock.

Istariol stood just behind her. "I suggest you come back inside now," he called out. "The atmospheric dome only extends so far from the ship – and you wouldn't want to step beyond it."

Ian began walking slowly and gingerly back up the steps, trying not to float off them. As he reached the top, he suddenly felt heavy again – like normal gravity had just been switched back on with the flick of a switch.

They all came inside and sat back down in their chairs. The doorway behind them closed and disappeared, leaving behind just a blank wall.

"I trust you are now convinced and we can get straight down to business. I will start by explaining why you are here," Istariol said, looking straight at Ian. "You have been appointed as the Solarian Representative by the Inter-Galactic Council – the IGC – and by signing the papers you have agreed to this appointment."

Ian had so many questions that his head was spinning, but he thought he had better try and focus on what Istariol was telling him. "What *is* a Solarian representative?" he asked.

Istariol seemed puzzled by the question for a moment. "Ah okay... well... there is usually only one habitable planet in a star system and, even if they have colonized more than one planet, we tend to use the star system's name when referring to a particular civilisation, rather than using an individual planet's name. You call your sun 'Sol', so you are all 'Solarians' and, Ian, you are their Representative."

"The representative for the *entire* planet?" Rebecca asked. "Why him? Why aren't you dealing with the leaders of the major world powers? And while we're asking the questions, what the hell are we doing on the *moon*?"

"We're on the moon because it's more discreet. No Solarian, including any of your military, can see us or spy on us here – and nobody is going to stumble across our ship by accident. And, by the way, we'll be going back to Earth tomorrow."

"As to why Ian was chosen, the IGC insisted that the method used to select the Representative was completely fair, based on the individual's skills and intelligence. They would not want Sol to be represented by any idiot. Do you think *any* of the Earth's leaders have obtained their position of power fairly? And most of them are pretty stupid anyway."

"But how come *I* was selected? And how many others were considered?" Ian enquired.

"Four people were shortlisted for each of Earth's four regions. I am responsible for EMEA – the *'Europe, Middle East & Africa'* region – and I have colleagues who deal with the other three regions: North America, Latin America and Asia–Pacific. It didn't matter where a person came from or what nationality they are, it depended on which region they were going to be in just before midnight on the 8th of May."

"It seems very strange to me that the IGC decided to use exactly the same regions of Earth as we do," Ian pointed out.

"Perhaps you're wondering why four people were selected from each region, even though their population sizes vary tremendously?" Istariol replied.

"For instance, you might be thinking: as over half of humanity lives in Asia–Pac, why were only four candidates chosen from there? And since fewer than five percent of Solarians live in North America, how did they end up with the same number of candidates?

"The answer is fairly simple – that's how Solarians have chosen to divide their planet into regions, and the IGC saw no reason not to adopt the same divisions."

"Anyway, IGC chose the people on the short list for each region using criteria which is highly classified," Istariol continued. "Meaning, I don't know why they were chosen, I was just told who the people were in my region – and how to find them.

"My role was to present the same puzzle to all of the candidates at about the same time, give or take a few minutes. The code in the pattern gave the deadline and the coordinates of a target meeting point. The first person who arrived at their target on or after midnight would be selected as the Representative. And that was you. You did it before any of the other fifteen candidates."

"But it was a team effort. In fact, Rebecca solved more of the crop circle code than I did," Ian protested.

"It doesn't matter. You were the first person I saw and spoke to after midnight and the first of all of the regions. So, under IGC regulations, you are designated as *the* Solarian Representative. And, given how much Rebecca helped, it's a good job she's on your team. Incidentally, I can now inform you that I am also here to help. I would like to offer you my services as Lead Counsel." Istariol was smiling.

"Well, I still have no clue what it is I'm supposed to do. I appreciate your offer, but would you mind if I waited until I understand my duties before accepting? And I'm still somewhat confused about how we came to stumble upon the crop circle in that field in the Wiltshire Downs at just the right moment. For that matter, where were the other shortlisted candidates at that time? Finally, what on Earth was that petrol canister doing in the middle of the circle?"

"Of course, you may accept my offer to join your team any time you wish. As to the circumstances around showing you the puzzle on Monday night, we had to show the pattern to all the candidates in all regions at more or less the same time. Not all of them were shown the pattern in a crop circle, but they were all given the same puzzle – and in a way that was designed to pique their interest and suggest this was important.

"In your case, you were driving a Mercedes CLE 200, and by using the Mercedes app we were able to track your position and the amount of fuel left in your car – which, incidentally, is a standard feature of the app. We also hacked into your car's computer to temporarily disable the sat-nav. Once your car was close to a field of oilseed rape, we flew there and arranged for you to see my ship carving a pattern in the crops. And, since you were low on fuel, I thought you might appreciate a top-up for your car – so I left you a can of petrol."

"So, this was all pretty much prearranged. But I didn't even book a Mercedes…" Ian's voice trailed off as he realised just how much Istariol must have been interfering. "The hire car company said they didn't have the model I'd booked and offered me a free 'upgrade'. I don't suppose you had anything to do with that?"

Istariol simply smiled.

"Okay, how did you know about *me*? You greeted me by name when you first saw me," Rebecca asked.

"We find that there are many advantages of piggybacking on 'native' systems. For a start, it considerably reduces the risk of exposing any of our own technology. Let's just say that it wasn't very difficult to hack into your car's hands-free system."

"You were eavesdropping on us the whole time we were in the car?" exclaimed Rebecca.

"Yes, but not just when you were in the car. Modern Solarian mobile phones make a great monitoring device – and of course every SMS, phone call, email, Messenger or WhatsApp message was intercepted. Don't feel too bad though, it wasn't just you – we had to do this with all of Earth's candidates. Anyway, none of this is particularly important and time is pressing, so can I get on with giving you the background briefing now?"

"One more question please. You talk about 'my' ship and yet you also keep saying 'we'. Who are you referring to?" asks Rebecca.

Istariol paused for a moment before answering. "Okay, well I was going to have to go through this anyway. It is 'my' ship, as I am the captain. Who I mean by 'we' depends on the context. My ship and I carried out the surveillance of the candidates in my region, EMEA. I collaborated with the

IGC 'ambassadors' in the other three regions to carry out and complete the overall selection process. I am seconded to the IGC to 'manage' EMEA on Earth, but I am actually 'employed' by my government in the Antares star system."

"What do you mean by *'my ship and I'*?" Ian asked.

"Well, the ship and I work together on almost everything. For example, Alexa handles the huge amount of data we collect and, of course, all the flight and navigation systems on board. And she 'hacks' into any computer system – such as the US Navy's – that we might need access to."

"*Alexa*?" exclaimed Rebecca.

"Well, yes. The ship has a fully autonomous sentient AI – Artificial Intelligence – with her own personality. Over the centuries, she's been known by a number of names, but here and now, I call her 'Alexa'. I do have a habit of speaking aloud to her, quite unnecessarily, of course.

"I am a spy, after all – so when I go out on a field trip and discreetly mingle among Solarians, no one bats an eye if they hear me talking to 'Alexa'."

Chapter 6

They spent the rest of the morning with Istariol. He gave them each a tablet, explaining that – whilst they weren't connected to the internet at the moment – he had loaded a great deal of information onto them. This included material downloaded from Alexa's database about the IGC and some of the associated alien civilisations and species, as well as other relevant data from the Solarian internet.

Istariol told them that they were going to have to face questions from an aggressive race originating from the star system 'Mekbuda' – a star in the 'Gemini' constellation about 1,200 light-years away from Earth. Of course, the stars in any constellation, including Gemini, only appear close together when looking at them from Earth. In reality, they can each be hundreds or thousands of light-years apart, spread out in space.

Mekbuda, despite being over a thousand light-years away, was still inside the same galaxy as Sol – the Milky Way – which contains hundreds of billions of stars and spans tens of thousands of light-years in every direction from Earth.

Looking at the pictures of the Mekbudans, they appeared very similar to humans – walking upright on two legs, with two arms and a human-like head atop their bodies. They reminded Ian of Klingons from the *Star Trek* films, or J. R. R. Tolkien's Orcs. Another example of an information leak? Ian wondered.

"Why are the Mekbudans at all interested in what happens on Earth?" Rebecca asked.

The Mekbudans turned out to be prolific explorers and colonisers, spreading far out across the Milky Way. They had been doing this for millennia, even before the IGC was formed. In addition to colonising many worlds, they would often just set up a mining operation on a planet, habitable or otherwise.

"Earth is a very good source of precious materials," Istariol explained. "And it's not just gold and platinum, but other rare metals and minerals – such as rhodium, palladium, and iridium – that are highly sought after.

"One of the most valuable is tantalum. On Earth, it's typically mined in central Africa. It has an extremely high melting point, exceptional corrosion resistance, and excellent electrical conductivity, making it an essential component in everything from military equipment to spacecraft.

Even Solarians use tantalum – you'll find it inside your own phones and laptops."

"And, of course, any spaceship visiting this stretch of the Milky Way would also be interested in visiting Earth to refuel," Istariol continued.

"With *petrol*?" Rebecca asked.

"No, not petrol, water of course," Istariol said, laughing.

After some blank stares, Istariol started to explain.

"Water," he began, "is nothing more than two hydrogen atoms bound to one oxygen molecule – what we call H_2O. With a process called electrolysis, you can split it apart. Picture two metal rods dipped into a tank of water and a current running through them. At one rod, bubbles of oxygen rise to the surface; at the other, hydrogen collects in a steady stream.

"The trick," he added, "is to keep the gases apart. Hydrogen is highly flammable in the presence of oxygen, and a single spark could ignite it – or even cause an explosion. When hydrogen and oxygen recombine into water, they release a great deal of heat."

He paused, letting that image settle.

"So water is not only essential for life," Istariol went on, "it's also a valuable source of oxygen. Most carbon-based creatures need to breathe oxygen. Even plants need it to live – though in daylight they produce more than they consume.

"Of course, there are exceptions. Yeast, for example, can survive with or without oxygen. Without it, they can still metabolise sugars – and in doing so, excrete alcohol as a by-product."

Rebecca knew she was not alone in enjoying the occasional alcoholic drink, but was not sure they needed to know anything about how to produce hydrogen and oxygen from water. She remembered reading about the early airships, which used to be filled with hydrogen gas to make them float in the sky. At least, until the *Hindenburg* caught fire and was totally destroyed.

"So, you burn hydrogen gas to fuel your spaceships?" she asked.

"In a way, yes – but probably not in the way you're imagining."

Istariol brought up another technical article on their tablets.

This one was an extract from a human scientific paper and entitled *nuclear fusion*:

Unlike fission, where large, heavy atoms are split into smaller ones, *fusion* involves combining four hydrogen atoms to form a single helium atom ($^4He_2$).

A fusion reaction releases an enormous amount of energy – significantly more, proportionally, than a fission reaction.

The early atomic bombs dropped on Hiroshima and Nagasaki relied on nuclear fission. In contrast, nearly all of the energy released by the much more powerful modern hydrogen bombs comes from nuclear fusion. However, scientists have only been able to achieve fusion in the form of a hydrogen bomb, which uses an initial fission explosion to generate the extreme temperatures and pressure required to trigger fusion.

The atomic bomb dropped on Hiroshima, known as Little Boy, had an estimated explosive yield of approximately 15 kilotons of TNT. By comparison, a fusion reaction using the hydrogen atoms in just **one litre of water** would release roughly the same amount of energy – about 17 kilotons of TNT.

"Every active star," Istariol explained, "including your own Sun, sustains a nuclear fusion reaction at its core – that's how it generates such immense heat."

"You're telling me that your starships use nuclear fusion as their power source?" Ian asked incredulously. He had studied physics at university and knew that hydrogen atoms fuse only at extremely high temperatures and under immense pressure. For decades, scientists have been researching ways to build a practical nuclear fusion power station, but progress has been slow.

"This is highly classified information but, yes, fusion is the primary energy source, although most ships will have a number of different propulsion mechanisms. Why do you think all the pictures you've seen of a UFO, shows a craft which is circular on the horizontal plane? It is because every spaceship contains a round Particle Accelerator inside its hull, much smaller but similar in concept to your Large Hadron Collider at CERN.

"So, you can see how incredibly valuable water is – not just because it gives us oxygen to breathe, but because it's also the most practical source of energy. We *could* harvest hydrogen gas directly from gas giants – and in some star systems, we have to – but using water is far simpler."

"Okay, so why don't you just collect and store liquid hydrogen?" Ian asked. "Water is much heavier than liquid hydrogen."

"Water *is* heavier, since it contains oxygen atoms that are sixteen times heavier than hydrogen. But we need to store oxygen in some form anyway. Eighteen grams of water – H_2O – contain two grams of hydrogen and sixteen grams of oxygen, making it nine times heavier than an equivalent amount of liquid hydrogen containing the same number of hydrogen atoms.

"Even so, one litre of water actually holds about 1.6 times more hydrogen atoms than one litre of liquid hydrogen – meaning it takes up roughly one-third *less* space to store the same amount of hydrogen in the form of water.

"I've told you all of this, so you appreciate how important Earth is to IGC and its member civilisations. Habitable planets with such an abundant water supply and rich mineral veins are extremely rare in the universe.

"The Mekbudans have always taken a particular interest in Earth. Their nearest colony is only 20 light-years away – in a star system you call Delta Pavonis in the southern constellation of Pavo. And the Mekbudans have been on Earth for a very long time. For example, we know they had a mining operation in Africa around 67 million years ago," Istariol explained.

"67 *million* years ago? But how could the Mekbudans have been on Earth so long ago? Surely, dinosaurs were still roaming the Earth then?" Ian asked.

"Okay, this is probably the last science lesson I have to give you, but it is absolutely fundamental to the way the universe works and you need to understand the principles. I don't know whether Einstein came up with all of his theories on his own or whether he had a little 'help'. But when I met him, he seemed to be a very bright cookie, so perhaps he did work it out for himself."

"*You* met him?" interjected Rebecca.

"Yes – but please let me finish, before I talk about that."

Another scientific article came up on their tablets: *Einstein's Theory of Special Relativity (published 1905):*

Einstein's theory explains that time becomes distorted at very high speeds. Time slows down significantly for objects moving near the speed of light, relative to a stationary observer.

The formula that calculates the effect on time is shown below:

$$T = t \times \sqrt{1 - \frac{v^2}{c^2}}$$

Where:

T = time experienced by the traveller (e.g. on a spaceship)
t = time for the stationary observer (e.g. on Earth)
v = speed of the traveller
c = speed of light (186,330 miles per second)

For example, if you travelled in a spaceship to a star 10 light-years from Earth and back – a round trip of 20 light-years – and you went 99.99% of the speed of light, then:

> Time for you (the traveller) would seem to pass normally – your watch would tick like usual but, compared to Earth, time would actually run much slower.
> For people who stay on Earth about 20 years would have passed when you get back.
> When you return to Earth you will have aged much less than those who stayed behind. In this example, about 3 months would have passed.

"However, the energy required to accelerate and decelerate to such a speed is tremendous," Istariol explained. "And when you reached the distant star, in order to maintain that high speed for the return journey, the ship would need to slingshot around a large gravity well – such as the star itself. According to Solarian scientific knowledge, this is only possible in theory."

"But what you're *really* telling us is that the IGC civilisations – including the Mekbudans – can reach speeds high enough to distort time to that degree?" Ian asked.

"And," Ian continued, "since your spaceships travel between star systems that are light-years apart they must be capable of travelling *faster* than light somehow? This is theoretically impossible for any object which has more than zero mass – at least according to our scientific knowledge."

"The answer to both of those questions is 'yes'. The details on how any of this is done, is strictly forbidden under the IGC's Directive 9. I am telling you about time distortion to explain that we all use it when we wish to travel 'forward in time'. It is impossible to travel *backwards* in time, though, so this is a one-way journey.

"I *did* meet Einstein in 1905, after his theory was published. I had to investigate whether Directive 9 had been breached and if any unauthorised information had been leaked to him. But I found no evidence, so the case was dropped."

"That was 120 years ago!" Rebecca exclaimed.

"Yes, with our advanced medical knowledge and treatments, we *do* live quite a long time, compared to humans. But, no, I have not stayed on Earth continuously since 1905, we have skipped forward in time since then. You see, my watching brief on Earth is supposed to span centuries, so I cannot afford to spend much time on Earth on any particular visit.

"To answer Ian's question about how the Mekbudans could have been on Earth sixty-seven million years ago – yes, dinosaurs were still roaming the planet and humans hadn't yet evolved. I imagine that created a few security headaches for them. But the Mekbudans wouldn't have stayed long each time they visited. They use slaves whenever and wherever they can.

"Back then, Directive 9 didn't exist and they were free to interfere with the planet however they wished. They would have brought slaves with them to work alongside their mining robots and drones. You can imagine them arriving to establish a mining operation – one designed to be self-sufficient and run smoothly without any Mekbudans remaining on site. Then they would skip forward in time and return later to collect all the 'treasure' mined during the years they were away – gold, platinum, rhodium, and one of the most valuable minerals of all: tantalum."

"I've noticed that sometimes you use the term 'Solarian' to describe mankind and other times you say 'human'. Why *is* that?" Rebecca asked.

"Very perceptive of you and you are quite correct. By 'Solarian', I mean humans living in the Solar System – at the moment that simply means anyone living on Earth. But there are humans living on other planets in the galaxy. Humans *did* originate on Earth but, over the last few thousand years many humans have been abducted and taken to other colonies as slaves. And the Mekbudans are amongst the worst offenders. If you ever meet a Mekbudan they are highly likely to treat you as if you were one of *their* human slaves. They have a number of different species serving as crew aboard their spaceships, including humans."

"I should also tell you that we know the Mekbudans have carried out genetic engineering on early humanoids. You may have heard of *'Lucy'*, the famous fossil specimen of the pre-human species Australopithecus afarensis, who lived around 3 million years ago? Lucy was *not* human; she was a close ancestor or cousin species. We have evidence that her species was subsequently 'enhanced'.

"Homo habilis, the first species in the genus 'Homo', which appeared about two and a half million years ago, has genetic sequences matching another more intelligent species originating on a planet in the Delta Pavonis system. As I mentioned before, Delta Pavonis is the nearest Mekbudan colony.

"So, although they won't admit to genetically modifying humans, Mekbudans do privately consider themselves the creators of mankind and vastly superior to you."

"I'm really not looking forward to meeting a Mekbudan," Ian commented dryly. "But how are they involved in the current situation, and what *are* our duties?"

"I think it would be best if we stick to the plan and I brief you on that tomorrow morning. I'll ask Alexa to take us back to Earth overnight, so when you wake up, we'll be in France. You're going to be based in Paris and you'll be leaving the ship tomorrow afternoon."

"I suggest you have some lunch and spend the afternoon absorbing what I've revealed to you," Istariol said. "You should also browse through the information we've downloaded onto your tablets. I'll be busy for the rest of the day catching up on some admin. If you have any more questions, you can ask Alexa – just say her name and speak to her, and she'll answer."

"Does she play music?" Rebecca joked.

"Of course," Istariol replied. "But only Solarian music.

"Alien music is copyrighted," he added with a straight face.

Chapter 7

Rebecca whispered to Ian, "They must be listening and recording everything we say. Istariol admitted as much by suggesting we could just say *'her'* name and she would talk to us." Lowering her voice even further, she continued "Do you believe any of this? Do we just trust them and do what they say?"

Ian had recently been exposed to the moon's gravity, which was only one sixth the strength of the Earth's. Despite his previous scepticism, there was no longer any doubt in his mind – they *were* on the moon sitting inside an alien spacecraft. And it was quite clear that they were both totally at the aliens' mercy – they could be killed, or worse, if that was what they wanted to do.

"We *are* currently on the moon and this *is* a spaceship," Ian replied. "Istariol said he has not *yet* told us everything he intends to. For reasons completely unknown, they may actually be deceiving us – but my instincts tell me that it's time to accept what he has told us. I think we should believe that they *are* 'on our side' and start to focus on whatever this 'mission' is. What do you think?"

Rebecca could not really fault his logic. "Okay, but the moment we find that we have been betrayed, we need to do everything we can to escape. In the meantime, I am sure there are quite a few questions Alexa may be able to answer."

A silky female voice emanated from the ceiling: "I would be very happy to answer any questions you might have, although you must appreciate that some information is off limits for security reasons. I am glad you've decided to trust us – at least for the moment. I can assure you that we *are* here to help and, once you fully appreciate the task in hand, you will both realise how tremendously important it is."

As Alexa spoke, they realised her voice seemed to be emanating from the small speaker on the ceiling. Having looked at it again, it reminded Ian of an Amazon Echo Studio speaker. Like Istariol, Alexa spoke in perfect King's English, but perhaps with a hint of a French accent.

Of course, they both realised that their whispered conversation had been overheard, but so be it.

"It's very nice to finally *'meet'* you, Alexa," Ian said. "I do have a few questions about your ship. I'm not sure they relate directly to our mission, but I have to admit – I'm still very curious. How does the ship silently hover above the ground? And how are you able to control gravity on the moon, so that it feels like Earth's gravity?"

"Istariol has already told you a little about the capabilities of our spaceship. All IGC civilisations have access to this technology, which means there's some additional information I *can* share with you that may be relevant to your mission," Alexa replied.

Their tablets lit up with a soft *ding* as more information was downloaded. Looking at the screens, they saw a new article, apparently extracted from a human website or scientific paper, describing the four fundamental forces of the universe. It explained that, while gravity has an infinite range, it is by far the weakest force – and always causes bodies with mass to attract one another. This is unique to gravity; the other three forces can either attract or repel, depending on the state of the objects involved.

Ian and Rebecca were, of course, familiar with one of the other fundamental forces – *electromagnetism*. Like gravity, it has an infinite range and is responsible for the existence of particles such as electrons and protons. They knew that magnets operate through electromagnetic forces, attracting or repelling each other depending on which poles were brought close together.

The other two forces – the Strong Nuclear and the Weak Nuclear forces – operate only at the atomic level. Whilst this sounded familiar to Ian, Rebecca had not come across these terms before.

Then they noticed some footnotes, written in a different font. These explained that spaceships are equipped with 'Gravity Drives', capable of *repelling* mass. This technology allows the strength of gravity experienced by the crew on board to be adjusted – and different species from different home worlds are accustomed to varying levels of gravitational strength.

The ships could also use their gravity drives to neutralise the gravitational pull of any celestial body, allowing them to hover effortlessly above the surface of a planet or moon. Alternatively, the drive could be used to silently *repel* the ship away from any large massive body, and at extremely high speeds, if necessary.

By adjusting the ship's gravity drive relative to the horizontal plane, it could travel at any angle, granting it complete freedom of movement. The final note explained that once the ship was a long distance from any planet or other massive body, the gravity drive became effectively inoperable – as there was nothing close enough to 'push' against.

"So," Alexa continued, once they had finished reading the article, "we do have the technology to control gravity – both to move the ship and to maintain a comfortable level of gravity for the crew."

"Thank you, Alexa. I have a question. Given that this spaceship is sitting on the surface of the Moon, why didn't we suffocate and die when we went outside?" Rebecca asked.

"That is highly sensitive, top-secret information. Directive 9 forbids us from sharing any details with low-technology civilisations," Alexa replied. "Suffice it to say, we're able to generate a force field a short distance around the ship. When necessary, we can maintain breathable air at a high enough pressure for people to walk within this field without a spacesuit."

"Alexa, how do spaceships travel between the stars, given that the gravity drive stops working once the ship is out of range of a planet's gravity?" Ian asked.

"You're now asking about our 'warp' technology," Alexa replied. "I *am* authorised to give you *some* details. Warp drives work by warping the space ahead of a ship, contracting it, while simultaneously expanding the space behind – to create a wormhole.

"However, wormholes cannot be generated in a strong gravity well – near a star or planet – because gravity disrupts the warp field. This makes the warp drive complementary to the gravity drive. Normally you can use one or the other, but not both at the same time.

"If a '*micro*-wormhole' is created, the ship can 'fall' into it and accelerate to high speeds without subjecting its crew to extreme g-forces. This enables the ship to travel between planets.

"It's also possible to create a full-sized wormhole, allowing a ship to appear to travel faster than light to an outside observer. In practice, this is how a ship can 'jump' to another star system. But a full size wormhole can only be created in regions of near-zero gravity – in places such as the outer edges of a star system.

"Warp drives can also be configured for something else, a discovery first made by the Mekbudans. They can generate a different kind of full-sized wormhole – a so-called 'virtual black hole'. A ship falling into it accelerates very close to the speed of light. But it wouldn't cross to another star system this way – the trip would take years.

"Einstein's Theory of Special Relativity explains that time will slow dramatically for anyone travelling at near-light speeds. That's how a spaceship can 'jump forward in time' relative to people who remain behind on a planet."

Ian found all this quite fascinating, but it still didn't explain what they were supposed to *do*.

"Alexa, can you at least tell us *something* about our duties before tomorrow's briefing?" he pressed.

"Okay," Alexa replied. "When you disembark, you will be taken to an apartment in Paris in a convenient location, where you will both stay for the rest of the month. This should give you adequate space to house the rest of your team. Should you need additional accommodation, there will be other suites available in the hotel."

"I thought you said we would have an apartment, so what's this about a hotel?" enquired Rebecca.

"The '*Apartment*' is part of the Cheval Blanc Paris hotel. Feel free to have a look at the information they have on their website."

Their tablets lit up again, this time showing what looked like a brochure. The hotel was right next to the Pont Neuf bridge over the River Seine. According to the hotel's website, the 'Apartment' was on the top two floors of the hotel and featured the following facilities:

> Exceptional 1,000m² accommodation, spanning two floors with two reception rooms, each with a dining space;
> Terraces unveiling sparkling views of the Seine, Notre-Dame and the Eiffel Tower;
> Seven stunning bedrooms, each with their own adjoining bathroom hosting a spacious bathtub and hammam-shower, as well as their own dressing rooms;
> Swimming pool, hammam, sauna, treatment room and fitness suite;
> Private projection room;
> Private elevator and dedicated parking space, for completely confidential access to the hotel.
> Majordome service on hand 24/7.

"Wow, what do we need all this for? I don't even know what a 'hammam-shower' is!" Ian exclaimed.

"A hammam-shower combines the experience of a Turkish bath, or hammam, with the convenience of a shower," intoned Alexa. "The shower provides a humid, steamy environment, typically with temperatures ranging from forty to fifty degrees Celsius, similar to a traditional sauna. It is designed to provide relaxation, deep cleansing and have potential benefits for skin rejuvenation."

"What's a *'Majordome service'*?" Rebecca asked.

"Think of it as the old-fashioned head butler," Alexa replied. "Back in the day, a majordome ran the household – managing staff, greeting guests, sorting meals and wine, even booking theatre tickets. In today's terms, it's basically a mix of Room Service and Concierge rolled into one."

"I have another question," Ian stated. "Given the Apartment has seven bedrooms, why would we need even more space?"

"We thought that the Apartment would be used by yourselves and your 'top team' – those people that you choose to spend the most time with. However, if that team expanded and you needed more bedrooms, they could live in some of the other hotel suites. I should tell you that we have reserved *all* of the rooms in the hotel," was the reply.

"You've booked the *entire* hotel for three weeks? How big is it?" Rebecca asked.

"Including the seven bedrooms in the Apartment, the Cheval Blanc Paris hotel has a total of seventy-two rooms and suites, as well as a number of conference rooms and other facilities, which include a spa and wellness centre, sauna, fitness centre and indoor swimming pool," Alexa replied.

"Are you kidding me?" gasped Rebecca. "What on Earth do we need seventy-two bedrooms for?"

"That will become clear after Istariol has briefed you on your mission tomorrow," she replied. "I *can* tell you, however, that we have organised a conference at the hotel and most of the other bedrooms will be for delegates and speakers, as well as our own security personnel. I can also let you know that we have temporarily 'enhanced' the hotel's security systems and computer firewalls – and that even alien supercomputers will not be able to hack into your tablets or phones.

"As to the topic or subject matters that will be discussed at the conference, I am not at liberty to say. Istariol will brief you on that tomorrow."

"So, who's paying for all of this then?" Ian queried.

"The expenses will come out of the funds allocated for your mission. Your initial budget has been set at two hundred and fifty million US dollars."

Rebecca could only manage a stunned, "Holy crap!"

Chapter 8

Feeling mentally exhausted, they decided it was time for lunch and asked Alexa if they could get something to eat and drink. A panel slid open in the wall beside the dining table, revealing an alcove laden with cheeses, cold meats, salads and a couple of steaming jacket potatoes wrapped in silver foil. They were also pleased to find a bottle of Chablis nestled in a bucket of ice, accompanied by two wine glasses. They settled down and ate their fill.

After lunch, Ian and Rebecca settled back into their armchairs, each with a cold glass of wine in hand.

"The more I hear about this mission, the less I like it," commented Ian. "Two hundred and fifty *million* dollars is the *initial* budget. An entire seventy-two room hotel hired out for three weeks for a conference. Conferences only go on for a week at most. And Alexa wouldn't tell us what the subject of the conference was. I would have heard if any public conferences on security or cryptology were being held in Paris this month and there aren't any."

There were as many as a dozen public – rather than military – conferences on cryptology and security held every month around the world. For example, *The International Conference on Practice and Theory in Public Key Cryptography* was scheduled for Monday, May 12, in Norway, but it was only three days long. The *First International Workshop on Artificial Intelligence Security and Privacy* was also due to be held in Japan, though much later in the month.

"I *am* wondering how much my military background – and experience in code breaking and electronic warfare – was a factor in me being selected to be on the shortlist. That crop circle puzzle really wasn't that difficult to decrypt, although your inspirational brilliance obviously helped," Ian said, smiling.

"At least *you* now know the basics of how alien spaceships fly," laughed Rebecca. "Perhaps they're going to train you as a pilot?"

Thinking about the mission again, Ian asked: "So, Alexa, why would we need two hundred and fifty million dollars – and how did you even get the money – or shouldn't I ask?"

"Two hundred and fifty million dollars has been set as the initial budget. However, Ian, if you find that you need more money, then you would be able to apply for a budget increase – as long as you give us written justification, of course," she replied.

"As to where the money comes from, let's just say that it has been provided by mankind. Or, more precisely, by individuals and institutions who have, somewhat unwisely, invested in Bitcoin and its derivative financial instruments. Of course, *I* can mine Bitcoin much more quickly and efficiently than any Solarian computer and, given nuclear fusion is my energy source, it's completely carbon-free," Alexa boasted.

Ian knew that it had been estimated that the combined energy consumption of all of the computers used to mine Bitcoin was comparable to that of a medium-sized country, such as Argentina or the Netherlands. Although the figure varied, depending on the energy source (with coal-heavy regions producing more carbon than those relying on renewable energy), the total carbon emissions from Bitcoin mining has been estimated to be as much as one third of the whole of the UK's.

"I've heard of Bitcoin, but what's Bitcoin *mining*?" Rebecca asked.

"Bitcoin mining is the process by which new Bitcoins are created by adding blocks to the Bitcoin blockchain – a public, decentralised digital ledger," Alexa responded. "To add a block to the blockchain, miners use their computers to solve a cryptographic mathematical puzzle. It's easy to verify a correct answer, but very difficult to find one. It's called 'mining' because it's similar to mining precious metals – it requires significant effort and resources – and, if successful, there's a reward in the form of a newly created Bitcoin.

"One Bitcoin is currently worth about $100,000 – so your $250 million budget is the equivalent of 2,500 Bitcoin. There is a fixed limit to the total number of Bitcoins that can ever exist: 21 million coins. Though, of course, there are other cryptocurrencies. Over one million Bitcoins remain unmined, so they're not going to run out anytime soon."

"We still know almost nothing about Istariol or his home world. Shall we ask her?" Rebecca said to Ian.

"Istariol's species originates from a planet in the Antares system about five hundred and fifty light-years from your solar system," came the instant response from Alexa.

"Viewed from Earth, Antares is the brightest star in the constellation Scorpius. By coincidence, the Solarian name 'Antares' comes from the

Ancient Greek Ἀντάρης, meaning 'rival to Mars'. In fact, the Antarian and Mekbudan civilisations have been embroiled in a cold war for millennia and have even fought wars against each other in the past."

"I thought we had to say '*Alexa*', when we wanted to talk to you?" enquired Rebecca.

"Not if it's very obvious that you are speaking to me – or *about* me." Rebecca thought she could detect a hint of humour in Alexa's tone of voice.

Their tablets burst into life again, and this time they displayed a picture of two young people who looked very similar to humans – except in one quite obvious way.

"Are those Antarians?" Ian asked. "But they've got pointy ears! Istariol doesn't look anything like that."

Then he realised he hadn't actually seen the tips of Istariol's ears. Istariol didn't have long hair, but he had been wearing his hat the whole time – except for the first time Ian had seen him, when he'd come down the steps from the UFO, removed his hat, and made a small bow towards Ian. But it had been dark, and Ian had been in shock – so he well have not noticed his ears.

"Yes, they are Antarians," Alexa replied. "And Istariol *does* have what you'd call 'pointy' ears. But I'd strongly advise against calling him an 'elf' – or worse, a 'Vulcan'. Still, it's entirely possible that occasional sightings of Antarians over the centuries may have led to the myths about elves.

"Elves have been part of human stories for centuries," Alexa went on to explain. "Their roots go back to Norse and Germanic folklore in the 13th century. But even earlier, in the 10th century, Anglo-Saxon medical texts mentioned elves – sometimes blaming them for sudden fevers and strange aches, yet also crediting them with the power to heal."

Ian and Rebecca sat for a while, reflecting on everything that they had learnt since boarding the ship. Without understanding the nature of their 'mission', it was pretty much impossible to plan anything. They remembered that Istariol had used the term 'Lead Counsel', when offering to help them. That seemed to imply that he would be handling the legal aspects or implications, whatever *they* might be. And, given the amount of information they had been given about the Mekbudans, perhaps they would turn out to be their enemies.

"Alexa, you said the Antarian and Mekbudan civilisations have been rivals or enemies for ages. Can you tell us why?" Ian asked.

"Their cultures could not be more different," she replied. "Antarians value truth, integrity, intelligence, modesty and respect for others, which is reflected in their art, literature and politics. Whereas, Mekbudans value physical prowess, courage, assertiveness and self-confidence to the point of arrogance. In their minds 'Possession is not nine-tenths of the law', it is ten-tenths. They take what they want or need – and care nothing about the impact on other people or civilisations.

"Istariol has told you that, many millions of years ago, the Mekbudans were mining precious metal and minerals in Africa– and that these mines were operated by robots and slaves.

"I am sure you've heard about what happened when an asteroid the size of a city collided with Earth," Alexa continued. "The 'Chicxulub impactor', as it is called, struck Earth 66 million years ago and triggered one of the most catastrophic events in Earth's history – marking the end of the Cretaceous Period and leading to the mass extinction of about 75% of all species, including most dinosaurs who had been the dominant life form for nearly 200 million years.

"A crater was created, over 150 km wide, at the edge of the Yucatán Peninsula in Mexico. The collision was devastating: rocks from deep within Earth's crust were raised 25 kilometres high and a rim of mountains taller than the Himalayas formed around the crater's edge.

"The explosion released energy equivalent to 10 billion Hiroshima atomic bombs, instantly vaporising the meteor and the rock in its vicinity. It caused intense heat and firestorms as temperatures soared to thousands of degrees Celsius near the impact site. Superheated debris rained back down across Earth, igniting global wildfires. Animals and plants near the impact zone were incinerated instantly. Massive earthquakes rippled around the planet and giant tsunamis hundreds of metres high devastated coastlines around the world.

"The asteroid hit at 20 kilometres per second at an angle of 60 degrees above the horizontal plane – just right for sending the maximum amount of vaporised rock, billions of tonnes, into the atmosphere. Plumes of sulphur-based gases and fine dust blocked out the sun, triggering a dramatic global cooling, known as an 'impact winter', that lasted for fifteen years. The sun-blocking debris halted photosynthesis, leading to the collapse of plant life and marine plankton – the base of many food chains. Herbivores starved, followed by carnivores and scavengers.

"However, after the dust settled, ecosystems slowly began to recover. Birds – descendants of certain dinosaur species – along with small mammals and many flowering plants, survived the catastrophe. In the absence of the dominant dinosaurs, they diversified and flourished. And, of course, this eventually led to the evolution of *Homo sapiens* – 'mankind', as you term it."

"I guess this was fortunate for us, as we wouldn't be here otherwise. The Mekbudans must have lost all their mining operations, so I imagine they weren't very happy about that?" Rebecca commented.

"The Mekbudans must have known the meteor was going to hit Earth, as we know they evacuated all their personnel and dismantled as much of the mining settlement as they could carry away. But we also know they returned only 25 years later and re-established their operations. So, it seems they managed to minimise any lasting disruption," Alexa replied.

"However, to give you an example of what the Mekbudans are actually capable of doing, I can tell you that we know what they did," Alexa continued. "The meteor was not originally going to hit Earth. The Mekbudans nudged it off course, aiming it directly at Earth at just the right angle to cause such a catastrophic event."

"Wow, they changed the entire evolutionary path on Earth! And so, they *really* were responsible for mankind's existence. But I thought that was banned under Directive 9?" Ian asked.

"Actually, no. Directive 9 didn't exist at the time they did this," Alexa replied. "In fact, the IGC put the directive into place specifically because of what the Mekbudans did – and because the Antarians were threatening to go to war with them if they refused to comply."

"But why did the Mekbudans do this?" Rebecca asked. "Didn't they find it a big inconvenience?"

"They did it," came the dry reply, "because the dinosaurs kept eating their slaves."

Chapter 9

Later that afternoon, Ian and Rebecca heard a faint humming sound start up, and they felt the floor of the room vibrating slightly again.

After a little while, a door appeared in the wall and Istariol walked into the room.

"Good afternoon. I understand you've covered a lot of ground with Alexa while I was away. I've asked her to make preparations for our return to Earth – a little earlier than planned – but we may as well make use of any extra time we can gain," Istariol said, taking a seat in a chair opposite them.

"Hi, glad you're back. When we were talking to Alexa this morning, she mentioned a conference. Can you tell us what it's all about, and how long it goes on for?" Ian asked.

"Whilst she may have used the term *'conference'*, it's more like a private workshop, attended by many like-minded experts from around the world," Istariol replied.

"The workshop does not finish until the end of May, although not all of the attendees will be there all of the time. How long any individual is there, will to a large extent, depend on you. We are expecting you to select some of these people to join your 'top team' and come and live with you in the Apartment. That will be your choice, however.

"You'll also be free to ask us to try and recruit people who are not at the conference, but that would be subject to their availability. Or perhaps, subject to their greed or need for money. The vast majority of attendees – and all of the speakers – are on 'retainers', with their fees paid in advance for the whole three weeks.

"But let me tell you what the workshop is about. It's focused on climate change. In a short space of time, we've assembled as many of Earth's leading experts on the subject as we could find.

"In case you're not aware, in 1992 a Solarian intergovernmental treaty was adopted to address climate change." He gestured towards their tablets on the table, which lit up to display an article on the subject.

Ian and Rebecca began to read through it.

> The UNFCCC – or *'United Nations Framework Convention on Climate Change'* – is an international treaty whose primary goal is to stabilise greenhouse gas concentrations in the Earth's atmosphere at a level

that would prevent dangerous anthropogenic interference with the climate system.

To support this goal, a secretariat was established in Bonn, Germany, which serves as the administrative body responsible for monitoring implementation and coordinating climate negotiations under the UNFCCC framework.

In December 2015, a convention called the 21st Conference of the Parties – or *'COP21'* – was held in Paris. The Parties to the UNFCCC reached a landmark agreement to combat climate change and to accelerate and intensify the actions and investments needed for a sustainable low carbon future.

Commonly referred to as the *'Paris Agreement'*, it built upon the UNFCCC Convention and – for the first time – brought all those nations into a common cause to undertake ambitious efforts to combat climate change and adapt to its effects. As such, it charted a new course in Earth's global climate effort.

The Paris Agreement's central aim is to strengthen the global response to the threat of climate change by limiting the global temperature rise this century to **below 2 degrees Celsius** above pre-industrial levels. And to pursue efforts to limit the temperature increase even further to 1.5 degrees Celsius. It requires all parties to submit their own emission reduction targets and actions every 5 years.

However, the agreement does not impose binding emission limits, instead relying on voluntary actions by each nation.

"Every US president in recent years," Istariol explained, "has supported the Paris Agreement – except President Trump, who opposed it at every opportunity, claiming that the agreement would *'undermine'* the US economy and place the country *'at a permanent disadvantage.'*

"In January 2025, shortly after his second inauguration, President Trump signed an executive order to withdraw the United States from the agreement for a second time – having previously initiated withdrawal during his first term, only for it to be reversed by President Biden. So, as it stands, the United States is no longer a party to the Paris Agreement."

"Okay, but what's the purpose of this workshop?" Ian asked. "I assume we're not going to try to change Trump's mind – or get him to reverse his decision. So is it about coming up with a better plan to keep the global temperature rise below two degrees Celsius, now that the US has walked away from the Agreement?"

"Very well. Keep that question in mind – I believe you're now ready to receive the mission briefing," Istariol said.

Ian and Rebecca sat bolt upright in their chairs, looking at him expectantly.

"I would like to remind you that I have offered my services on your team, but you are under no obligation to accept. This offer will remain valid for the whole duration of your assignment.

"One of the reasons you were selected for the short list, Ian, was that your military record says you are very good at handling stressful situations – remaining 'calm under fire', as you might say."

"But you must know I've only had the most basic combat training," Ian protested. "My duties don't really involve getting into a fight or a battle."

"Yes, I understand that," Istariol replied, "and I sincerely hope that remains true for this mission."

With that, he reached inside his jacket and took out a manila envelope.

"This is what we have to deal with – the English translation, of course."

He opened it, removed a single sheet of paper, and handed it to Ian.

The letter was printed on clearly expensive parchment and contained the following:

The Tribunal of the Inter-Galactic Council

Appellant: Mekbuda
Defendant: Sol ('Mankind')
Date of Issue: 9th May 2025
Date of Hearing: 30th May 2025
Place of Hearing: Paris, France, Earth

Subject: <u>Catastrophic Climate Change</u>

The Defendant is hereby charged with gross negligence and dereliction of duty.

Mankind is accused of releasing unacceptably large quantities of carbon dioxide and other greenhouse gases into Earth's atmosphere, despite having become aware in recent decades of the risks posed by climate change.

Furthermore, Mankind — fully aware of the devastation this will cause — is also accused of planning for, or allowing, the continued release of even greater quantities of greenhouse gases over the coming years.

This will trigger irreversible and catastrophic global warming, ultimately resulting in a mass extinction event and rendering Earth uninhabitable for millions of years.

As the dominant intelligent life form on the planet, Mankind is to be held accountable.

Ian sighed and handed the paper to Rebecca. "Okay, I'm beginning to understand what's going on now. This is going to be tough, isn't it? Proving that mankind *is* trying to prevent climate change."

Rebecca shook her head as she gave the paper back to Ian. "You can say that again!"

"Yes, it will be *very* tough," Istariol said. "But you need to turn the page over – it's double sided."

There was something about the way Istariol spoke that unsettled Ian, but he turned the page over and read the other side.

Ian turned a deathly white and, with a dead-pan expression, showed Rebecca the other side of the sheet of paper, which read:

The Tribunal of the Inter-Galactic Council

Penalties for attempting to cause catastrophic climate change

The Defendant is hereby advised of the penalty that would be imposed if found guilty of the charges.

1) *Earth would be temporarily assigned to the Mekbudan authorities for caretaking.*

2) *The Mekbudans would be granted permission to 'cleanse' the Earth of Mankind.*

3) *This permission would include the right to crash an asteroid or similar body into the Earth, so as to cause an impact winter.*

Even Rebecca was rendered speechless.

Chapter 10

"Okay, so this means that as the *sole* representative of Earth – of mankind – I'm responsible for defending humanity's global record on managing climate change," Ian gasped. "And if I fail, the planet will be wiped clean of nearly all life as we know it?"

"Yes, I'm afraid so," Istariol replied. "But you may use anything – or anyone – that money can buy. And over fifty climate-change scientists and other experts will be arriving at your hotel in Paris the day after tomorrow."

"I had thought it would be impossible to change Trump's mind about supporting the Paris Agreement," Ian said, shaking his head in disbelief at what was happening. "But surely if you flew your spaceship and landed it on the White House lawn – and presented him with the IGC summons – he'd realise he *had* to support the Agreement, if only out of self-preservation?"

With a wry smile, Istariol said, "Unfortunately, even under these circumstances, Directive 9 means I'm not permitted to reveal my spaceship to any other Solarian – or otherwise 'prove' that an intelligent alien civilisation with advanced technology exists. And without that proof, Trump will not change his mind. Why would he?"

"What exactly are greenhouse gasses anyway?" Rebecca asked.

"The five most abundant greenhouse gases in Earth's atmosphere," Istariol replied, "are water vapor, carbon dioxide, methane, nitrous oxide and ozone. They are known as greenhouse gases because they trap heat in the atmosphere – like glass does in a greenhouse – and in doing this they help keep the Earth warm.

"Greenhouse gases are produced mainly by burning fossil fuels, such as coal, oil and natural gas, and by clearing and burning vegetation."

"Okay, so how bad *is* it? How much of these greenhouse gases *are* we generating?" Ian enquired.

"You will get a lot more information on this at the workshop, of course, but here's a summary." Istariol brought up an article on their tablets.

> Carbon dioxide (CO_2) has by far the greatest impact on global warming of all the greenhouse gases, accounting for around **66% of the change** in the balance of energy flowing through Earth's atmosphere.

Global greenhouse gas emissions have reached **record highs** in recent years despite international climate pledges. Emissions from key polluting sectors such as power generation and transportation continue to rise, while levels of **methane** and **nitrous oxide** – both of which have far higher global warming potentials than CO_2 – are also increasing rapidly.

The **growth rate of CO_2** has more than **quadrupled since the 1960s**, accelerating from an annual average increase of 0.8ppm to around 3.5ppm in 2024 – the fastest rise since modern measurements began in 1957. Concentrations of methane and nitrous oxide also reached record levels in 2024, with **methane** in particular now exceeding **two and a half times its pre-industrial concentration**.

Around **half of all CO_2 emissions** each year remain in the atmosphere – the rest is absorbed by Earth's land ecosystems and the oceans. However, as global temperatures rise, the **oceans absorb less CO_2** because of reduced solubility in warmer water, while land-based sinks are increasingly disrupted by factors such as persistent drought.

Since the start of the Industrial Revolution in **1750**, humanity has released an estimated **1,800 gigatonnes of CO_2**. *One* gigatonne is equivalent to 1,000 million tonnes – or roughly **twice the combined weight of the world's population**. The vast majority – **85%** – of this total has been emitted **since the end of the Second World War**.

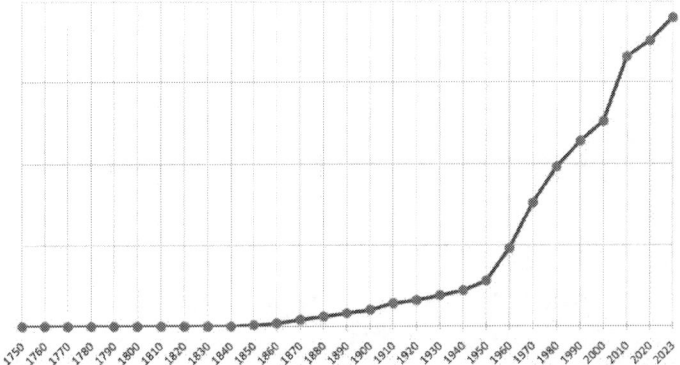

The **oceans** have absorbed a significant portion of this excess CO_2 – enough to reduce the average **pH of seawater** from **8.18 in 1750** to **8.04 in 2024**. This **0.14-unit drop** represents about a **40% increase in acidity**. Ocean acidification is now occurring **ten times faster** than at any point in the past **300 million years** – and the oceans are **more acidic today** than they have been for over **20 million years**. This rapid chemical change poses severe risks to **marine ecosystems**, especially coral reefs and shell-forming organisms.

Today, the amount of **carbon dioxide in the atmosphere is more than 50% higher than pre-industrial** levels. This is likely the highest atmospheric CO_2 concentration in at least 3 million years, and possibly as far back as 15 million years – when **sea levels were over 30 metres higher** than they are today. There were no humans then – Homo sapiens would not appear for another 14 million years.

"So, we do have an enormous challenge to try and prove that Solarians – 'Mankind' – are not acting with gross negligence," Istariol said. "And we can't claim you don't understand the risks of excessive global warming."

"But, why would the IGC permit the Mekbudans to crash an asteroid into Earth?" Ian demanded. "Are they really going to replace a *possible future* extinction – brought on by greenhouse gases – with *certain* and *immediate* annihilation? That makes no sense!"

"Very well, I'll explain," Istariol replied.

"When greenhouse gases build up beyond safe levels, the planet tips into a chain reaction – triggering runaway global warming. Firestorms sweep across continents, devouring forests and releasing even more carbon dioxide. Ice caps collapse into the sea, unleashing vast stores of methane – an even more potent greenhouse gas. The oceans turn acidic and starved of oxygen, their marine life dying off.

"Once that begins, there's no turning back. The damage effectively becomes irreversible – it would take millions of years to undo.

"Earth has previously experienced five mass extinction events, each wiping out a large percentage of species over a relatively short geological timespan." He brought up a table showing the five mass extinctions.

Age	Million yrs ago	Result
End-Ordovician	443	85% of marine species extinct.
Late Devonian	372-359	75% of all species dead.
End-Permian	252	81% of marine and 70% of terrestrial vertebrate species extinct.
End-Triassic	201	76% of all species died out.
End-Cretaceous	66	75% of species became extinct, including all non-avian dinosaurs.

"All but one – the event that killed the dinosaurs – involved climate change triggered by greenhouse gases," Istariol continued.

"The worst extinction event in Earth's history, known as *'The Great Dying'*, occurred at the end of the Permian period, around 252 million years ago. It began with massive volcanic eruptions that released huge amounts of carbon dioxide, warming the planet by around five degrees Celsius.

"The warming then accelerated as it triggered the release of methane – another potent greenhouse gas – with global temperatures eventually peaking at 10°C above normal. Nearly all life on Earth was wiped out."

"These global warming events didn't last forever," Ian observed. "So, how did Earth eventually recover from the Great Dying?"

Istariol nodded. "Four main processes worked together to bring your planet back from the brink."

He held up a finger. "First, the volcanoes eventually stopped erupting. They only erupted for about a million years – but that was enough to devastate your planet. Once they quieted, the constant flood of greenhouse gases finally eased."

He raised a second finger. "Second, that was when Earth's own geology kicked in. Silicate rocks on the continents began to weather – slowly, over hundreds of thousands of years. That chemical weathering pulls carbon dioxide out of the atmosphere and traps it in stone."

Rebecca leaned forward. "Natural carbon capture," she murmured.

"Third," Istariol continued, "life started fighting back. Algae, cyanobacteria – primitive organisms – began photosynthesising again. And when they died, some of their carbon-rich remains were buried in sediments, locking away even more CO_2."

He raised a fourth finger.

"And finally, the recovering ecosystems created feedback loops – rebalancing oxygen in the oceans, restoring food chains and stabilising climate patterns. It took millions of years... but life slowly reclaimed the planet."

"In contrast," he added, "after the impact winter that wiped out the dinosaurs, the planet actually cooled. Dust clouds shrouded the Earth, reflecting sunlight and lowering temperatures. And when the dust finally settled – less than **20 years later** – the skies cleared and the Earth became habitable again."

There was a long silence.

Then Ian spoke. "So, we're pushing the planet towards the brink of extinction, in a fraction of the time it took before."

Istariol's face darkened. "Yes. Only this time, mankind are the volcanoes."

Chapter 11

"Okay, this is all utterly crazy, but it is what it is," Ian said.

"Istariol, I accept your offer and appoint you as Lead Counsel. Now, can we get the date of this hearing postponed? How can they possibly expect me to put a defence case together in only three weeks?"

"Impossible, I'm afraid, sir. The IGC's view is that the Antarians have been given responsibility for preparing the defence – up until the point when the Solarian Representative is appointed – and we've already been given more than enough time. After all, that's why we organised this workshop."

"This is completely ridiculous," snapped Rebecca.

"Yes, it is," Ian agreed. "But I suppose we'll just have to get on with it. I need a complete list of everyone attending the workshop, along with any ideas you have about who should be on the top team. And I'll need all the information you can give me on the IGC hearing – where it will be held, who will be there, and how long it's going to last."

"Yes, sir," Istariol replied. "I will sort out the paperwork you need to sign, for my assignment to your team, in due course. Alexa, please download the list of delegates to their tablets, together with their profiles and the provisional short list we drew up for the 'top team'."

"Why are you now calling me 'sir'?" Ian enquired.

"Because, sir, you have appointed me to your team. This means that not only am I at your service, but all the resources at my disposal – including my ship – are also yours to command, provided this does not compromise the safety of myself, my ship, or its crew, and that we remain compliant with Directive 9."

"You're giving me *control* of Alexa?" Ian exclaimed.

"I'm not entirely sure that '*control*' is the best word, sir," Alexa interjected. "It would be more accurate to say that I am at your command and will obey any order you give me – subject, of course, to any overriding restrictions I am bound by – sir."

Rebecca couldn't help thinking it was rather 'cool' that Ian was now commander of a spaceship – even if all they had really seen of it so far was their nineteenth-century-style living quarters.

"Okay, sounds fair enough – but can you both stop calling me 'sir'?" Ian insisted. "Anyway, I interrupted you, so please can you tell us about the IGC hearing?"

"Of course," Istariol said. "The Hearing is scheduled to last three days and will be held on board a Mekbudan spaceship, which will be stationed close to our hotel in Paris. The first day is reserved for the Mekbudans – as prosecutors – to make their case, whilst I will have the opportunity to cross-examine.

"The second day is for your team to present the case for the defence, calling any witnesses you wish, whom the Mekbudans may then cross-examine. However, I should point out that no other Solarians – apart from you and Rebecca, as your deputy – are permitted to know anything about aliens, or the true nature or location of the Hearing.

"The third day is reserved for the IGC judges to consider the case and make their judgement – there is no jury. The judges will attend by video and their species and identities will be kept secret.

"In order to comply with Directive 9, none of the delegates – including your 'top team' – will have any idea about what's really happening. They have been told that at the end of the conference some of them will be asked to attend a 'mock hearing'. There, they will have to defend mankind's track record and present any plans or projects they have to mitigate climate change. They have been told that, if the judges at this mock hearing are convinced by their arguments, then an anonymous benefactor will provide five billion US dollars to fund some or all of the projects. When any of them do attend the hearing, they will not know they are on board a spaceship – and all of the 'people' they see at the hearing will appear human."

"How is it even possible for them to not realise that they're on a spaceship?" Rebecca asked.

"All will become clear in due course. That's a detail you really don't need to concern yourself about now."

"Okay, then can you explain why you didn't tell us all this when we first came on board your ship?" Ian asked.

"You have now been on board for approximately sixteen hours – and for six of those, you were asleep. Ian, you were initially quite sceptical and thought this might be an elaborate test by your military. I believed you needed more time to adjust to your new circumstances – including being on board an alien spaceship – before telling you about the IGC Hearing and the catastrophic penalties if the case is lost."

Ian looked at his watch – which was still set to British Summer Time (BST) – and saw it was nearly 5 o'clock in the afternoon. "Alexa, where are we now – and when do we get to Paris?" he asked.

A section of the wall shimmered and then displayed an image. The screen was showing the Earth below, clearly revealing that they were observing it from orbit.

"We are currently in geostationary orbit, 36 thousand kilometres above Paris, France," Alexa answered. "My 'cloaking' technology is more effective in the dark and it would be better to arrive when there are fewer people around. So, I plan to wait until after 2.00am local time before making our descent. I expect you will arrive at your hotel around 3.00am."

"You're just going to land in the centre of Paris?" Rebecca asked incredulously. "What are you going to do – park the ship on the hotel roof? And surely, we'll be picked up by commercial or military radar?"

"The cloaking system prevents both visual and radar detection," Alexa explained. "It bends light, radar and other electromagnetic waves around the ship so they continue in their original direction, as though passing through us. This creates the illusion that we don't exist – although the effect isn't perfect in broad daylight or up close."

Ian raised an eyebrow. "So... you're saying no one will notice a spaceship landing in the middle of the city? And *where* exactly are you going to land?"

"Not land," Alexa corrected. "Submerge. Beneath the waters of the River Seine. Near the Pont Neuf bridge and right next to our hotel. Hidden and secure."

"The *Seine*?" Ian scoffed. "That river can't be very deep – how is it going to hide a starship? And any boat passing above would risk colliding with the ship."

"Ordinarily, it wouldn't be deep enough," Alexa admitted. "But we've made some... *preparations*. Dredging and excavation. Nothing major. Just enough to leave a convenient, spaceship-shaped hollow in the riverbed. Any boat, including the water buses and fast-moving sightseeing boats will pass above us with plenty of room to spare."

There was a moment of silence. If Alexa had a face, Ian imagined she might be smiling slightly.

"So, I'll simply descend into the water and nestle into the hollow. Once we're in position, the top of the ship will be level with the river bed. Any boat passing overhead will have no idea we're underneath them."

Rebecca blinked and finally reacted. "You actually dug a *parking space* under the Paris waterways?"

"I prefer to think of it as... urban camouflage," Alexa replied, with something that sounded suspiciously like smugness.

"I know this is probably a stupid question, but how do we get out – given the ship will be underwater?" Rebecca asked.

"We've hired, at considerable expense, a small commercial submarine – in fact, a *'yellow submarine'*," Istariol explained.

"Of course, there's very little to see in the Seine. However, as part of our arrangement, the owners are offering free trips to the public throughout May, as part of a publicity campaign for their regular operations in the Canary Islands."

"How big is this submarine?" Ian asked.

"It's 19 metres long, 4 metres wide, and about 6.5 metres high – including the part that stays submerged when it's on the surface," Alexa replied.

"In Solarian imperial measurements, Ian, that's 60 feet 8 inches long, 13 feet wide, and about 21 feet 4 inches high. And it can hold up to 48 people, crew included."

"But why do we need a submarine to carry so many people – there are only three of us?" Rebecca asked.

"You asked me earlier why the conference delegates won't realise they're on a spaceship," Istariol replied. "The Mekbudan ship will also be beneath the riverbed, in another part of the River Seine. We'll use the submarine to ferry the delegates – and ourselves – to the hearing being held on board their vessel. They'll be told that it's located in a secret underwater chamber, so they won't know they're boarding an alien ship."

"Anyway, tonight we'll use the submarine to disembark from the spaceship and – when we dock on the surface right next to the hotel – no one will notice if a few more passengers get off than originally got on a few minutes earlier.

"Before you ask, no Solarian will ever be taken anywhere near our spaceship. And whenever *we* use the submarine, it will be crewed by our local human security personnel."

"Very impressive," Ian said, genuinely impressed. "But I believe it's time I gained a clearer understanding of what this ship actually is. I've yet to see it properly."

"Alexa, as commander of this ship, I need you to tell me more about the spaceship and show me what it looks like," he ordered.

After what seemed a heartbeat of hesitation, the wall display changed and a saucer like object appeared on the screen.

"You are in command of an Antarian *Tay*-class reconnaissance vessel," Alexa replied, with a hint of pride in her voice. "It is one of the smallest spaceships in the fleet, designed for spying and scouting missions.

"The vessel is 27 metres in diameter and 10 metres in height – or about 90 feet by 33 feet, if you're using the imperial system of measurement. Just to give you some idea of how large the ship is, its diameter is about the same as the length of an adult blue whale – and about half the height of Nelson's Column.

"The normal crew complement is four and it's equipped with all the standard Antarian systems: life support, navigation, communications, cloaking, surveillance drones, gravity control, fusion energy generator, helium rocket thrusters, warp drive and weapons for self-defence. It can also accommodate one or two 'guests' in self-contained, low-technology, living quarters – which you are already familiar with."

"A crew of four? But we've only ever seen Istariol. Who are the other crew members?" Ian asked.

"We have two engineers aboard. The third crew member would prefer to introduce herself at dinner, if you don't mind," Alexa replied.

"That would be acceptable. But can I meet the engineers?"

Istariol intervened. "They're quite shy and they don't speak vocally, so I think it would be better if they weren't forced to meet you. Would a photograph of them be acceptable?"

Ian nodded. The wall display went blank for half a second, before another picture appeared on the screen.

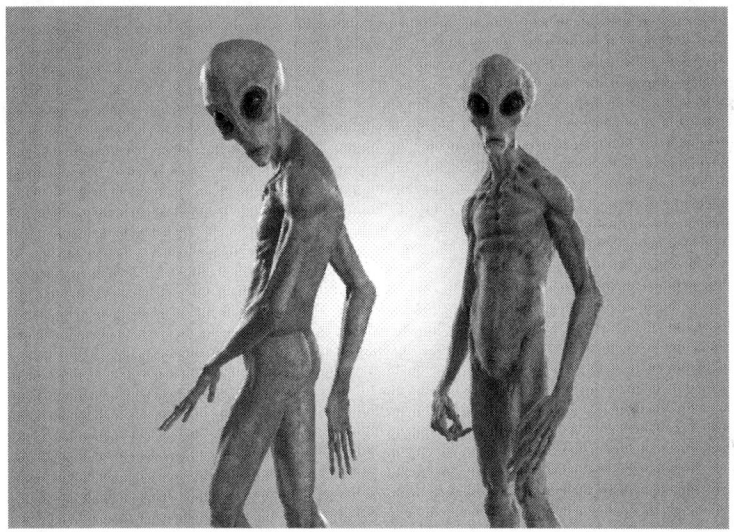

"This is *Huey*, the ship's Chief Engineer – and his colleague *Dewey*, the Science Officer," Istariol explained.

Chapter 12

"You *are* full of surprises, Istariol!" Rebecca exclaimed. "They look like a very interesting species!"

"Yes, their species is a very old one, originating many years ago on a planet in the star system Vega," Istariol said wistfully. "They are one of your closest neighbours, as their home world is very close to Sol – only 25 light-years away. But their story is a very sad one. The Mekbudans found the Vegan system many millions of years ago – in fact, even before they visited Earth.

"The Vegans are very peaceful and contemplative by nature. Art and science go hand in hand with them – they appreciate the beauty of mathematics and the nature of the universe as much as they do poetry and other literature. Over the millennia, their technology became extremely advanced and they became superb communicators – their bodies even evolved to the extent that they lost the use of their voice-box. They cannot speak aloud – not that they need to.

"Unfortunately for the Vegans, they never spent much time researching weapons technology and, when the Mekbudans finally came across their planet, they were almost completely defenceless, despite having already discovered both fusion and interstellar travel. Not that the Vegan mindset would have really allowed them to go to war, even in self-defence.

"So, the Mekbudans easily subjugated the Vegan civilisation and incorporated their home world into their ever-expanding empire of colonies. They also realized that the Vegans had an exceptional aptitude for science and engineering, so they took them as slaves to be engineers on their spaceships and other scientific establishments.

"The Vegans were enslaved before the Mekbudans had even colonized one of your other close neighbours – Delta Pavonis – 20 light-years away from Sol. Delta Pavonis and Vega are almost in the opposite directions from Sol and are actually 37 light-years apart from each other.

"They also used Vegans as slaves in their mining operations throughout their empire. When the Mekbudans reached Earth and began extracting resources in Africa, it was Vegans who were forced to work as slaves alongside their robots and droids. Yes – and those *are* the slaves who were regularly eaten by dinosaurs," Istariol said grimly.

"How come you allow another alien species amongst your crew?" Ian asked.

"Huey and Dewey are actually former slaves who escaped from a Mekbudan ship and eventually made their way to an Antarian world. There, they were granted asylum and, in time, Antarian citizenship. They have the right to be treated the same as any other Antarian, including humans. So, we recruited them several years ago."

"After all," Istariol added with a smile, "it does no harm to have officers aboard your spy ship who are familiar with Mekbudan vessels. And there's no question where their loyalties lie."

"What do you mean when you say that Vegans have the same rights as humans?" Rebecca asked.

"I mean," Istariol replied, "that anyone with Antarian citizenship has the same legal rights – whether they are of the Antarian race, human, Vegan, AI, or otherwise. This includes any human who has obtained citizenship, either by birth or through other means.

"There are quite a few humans living on our colonies. Most were born there and, for some reason, they seem to prefer Antarian worlds to Mekbudan ones," he added with a wry smile.

"You say anyone, including AIs, can have citizenship – so Alexa is an Antarian citizen?" Ian asked.

"Of course, why wouldn't she be?" Istariol replied.

"I have another question... *we* use the term *'Vegan'* to describe people who are strict vegetarians," Rebecca commented. "They do not eat or drink any food that comes from animals and they abstain from using any animal product, such as leather."

"Do you think this a coincidence – or another information leak?" she asked.

"Perhaps I should answer that question," Alexa said. "The Vegan species *are* actually 'vegans' by the Solarian definition – in that they don't consume or use any animal products. And, like cows, they can digest almost any plant material – including grass – thanks to their four-chambered stomach, particularly the chamber which hosts symbiotic microorganisms that break down tough plant fibres.

"I believe you have already seen pictures of 'aliens' of the Vegan species – as they have become famously associated with an event in 1947 that you call the *'Roswell incident'*," Alexa continued. "So, you might be thinking that somehow the information about the Vegan species' diet was discovered then – and was subsequently adopted as the term used to describe that strict vegetarian regime.

"However, three years earlier in 1944, the founder of the 'Vegan Society' was the first to coin the word *'Vegan'* using letters in the word *vegetarian*. He simply combined the first three letters *'veg'* with the last two letters *'an'*. Not really compelling evidence that anyone had discovered anything about the Vegan race.

"Of course, the word *vegetarian* comes from *vegetable*, which first appeared in English in the early 15th century. At that time, it referred broadly to any plant, not just edible ones.

"You also need to look at when Solarians first named the star *Vega*," Alexa continued. "The name comes from the Arabic *al-Nasr al-Wāqi* – meaning 'the falling eagle' – used by Islamic astronomers between the 8th and 10th centuries. Later, when European medieval scholars translated Arabic texts into Latin, they rendered it as *Wega*. Over time this evolved into *Vega*, the standard form by the early 15th century.

"It's entirely possible that, in this era, a human encountered an alien who knew the European name for their home star and said they came from Vega. And if that human also knew the alien ate only plants, it would make perfect sense to merge *veg* with *eatable* to form *vegetable*.

"In early 15th-century English, the common word for a plant, root, or herb was *wort*. But from that point on, *vegetable* gained ground, and *wort* gradually fell out of general use – surviving mainly in the names of certain herbs.

"So, it *is* quite possible that the word *vegetable* came about through contact with an alien," Alexa concluded.

"You can't possibly mention the Roswell incident and then just gloss over it," Rebecca protested. "Talking about where the bloody word *vegetable* comes from without telling us the truth about what happened?"

"Okay, well – if you insist," Alexa replied. "As is often the case with any myth, it's wrapped in confusion, misinformation, conspiracy theories and even hoaxes. But at its core, there's usually a kernel of truth.

"The Roswell Incident traces back to 24 June 1947, when a pilot on a search mission over Mt. Rainier in Washington State reported seeing nine bright saucer-like objects flying in formation at incredible speed at an altitude of 10,000 feet. He clocked them and estimated their speed at 1,200 miles per hour – an impossible speed in those days.

"He noted their strange, skipping motion, as they weaved in and out of formation, and compared it to the way a saucer skims across water. When the press picked up his account, the term 'flying saucer' was born.

"A couple of weeks later, a rancher near Roswell – a town in New Mexico – told the local sheriff about some unusual wreckage scattered across his land. He'd noticed it days earlier, but only connected it to the flying saucer stories after reading the news reports. He thought the debris could have come from something that crashed during a recent storm.

"An intelligence officer from Roswell Army Air Field, about 120 miles away, went out to the ranch to investigate and brought some of the debris back to his base to show his superiors. Then, the military base's Public Information Officer contacted a local journalist and issued a press release, which included this:

> 'The many rumours regarding the flying disc became a reality yesterday when the intelligence office of the 509th Bomb Group of the Eighth Air Force, Roswell Army Air Field, was fortunate enough to gain possession of a disc ...'.

"The news sent shockwaves around the world, but it's the iconic front-page headline of the local Roswell Daily Record that's best-known: 'RAAF Captures Flying Saucer on Ranch in Roswell Region'.

"However, the debris actually came from a military balloon, one of a long train of balloons launched as part of a top-secret programme – Project Mogul – intended to detect Soviet nuclear tests. The balloons were launched from a different Army base, 130 miles away from Roswell – Alamogordo Army Air Field, which later became Holloman Air Force Base.

"Within 24 hours, in a complete reversal of their position regarding the Roswell debris discovery, the US military said a mistake had been made. To obscure the true source of the debris, they stated that the 'flying saucer' was in fact from a crashed weather balloon.

"America, in the early post World War Two years, was very different to today – and people had more trust in authority – so the weather balloon explanation was almost universally believed. Interest in flying saucers and UFOs went from strength to strength, but the Roswell story was forgotten.

"It remained relatively obscure for three decades, until the story of the Roswell UFO crash was rediscovered in 1978. A retired military man – the intelligence officer who had first visited the debris field – admitted that the weather balloon explanation had been a cover story and that the photos had been staged, with weather balloon debris being substituted for the real wreckage.

"He claimed that everyone involved in the retrieval was clear the object had indeed been an extraterrestrial spaceship."

"So... if you want to know the truth...," Alexa teased, "... it *was* just a US military balloon and all this conspiracy theory was triggered by the military trying to obscure their top-secret project.

"The military personnel based at Roswell had no knowledge of Project Mogul – because it was top secret – and just jumped to the conclusion that it was extraterrestrial, because they couldn't think of anything else the debris could have come from.

"Even when the retired intelligence officer came forward with his story in 1978, the project remained secret. It was almost five decades later, in 1994, that the US Air Force declassified Project Mogul and released an 880 page report to explain what really happened."

"However, that pilot in June 1947 actually *did* see nine spaceships," Istariol interjected.

"The Mekbudans were shipping some of their mining proceeds off planet and claimed that a 'bug' in their ships' control software caused a failure in their cloaking systems," Istariol added. "When I came across the pilot's report in the newspaper, I reported it to the IGC and the Mekbudans were heavily fined."

"But I suspect you're still wondering about the stories of alien bodies," Alexa continued. "None of the original Roswell reports mentioned alien bodies and even the intelligence officer denied this aspect of the story, which only emerged later. By the 1980s, popular accounts conflated the 1947 Roswell debris investigation with two separate myths of humanoid bodies.

"One was the *'Aztec crashed saucer hoax'*, first published in 1949, which claimed that a flying saucer crashed the year before in Aztec, about 400 miles away from Roswell. However, in the mid-1950s, this story was exposed as a hoax fabricated by two con men, as part of a fraudulent scheme to sell supposed alien technology.

"The other, *'Majestic 12'*, is claimed to be the code name of a secret committee of scientists, military leaders and government officials. This committee, according to the story, was formed in 1947 by an executive order by US President Harry S. Truman to facilitate recovery and investigation of alien spacecraft.

"The codename first appeared in documents circulated by 'Ufologists' in 1984, who argued that the United States government has conspired to cover up knowledge of a crashed extraterrestrial spacecraft, where alien bodies had been recovered.

"One of these documents, in addition to the Roswell incident, also mentioned a second crash in Mexico in 1950, along the Mexico–US border.

"After further investigation it was demonstrated that the documents were fake. Truman's signature was 'a pasted-on' photocopy of a genuine signature – including accidental scratch marks – from a completely different memo that Truman wrote.

"However, this was not a hoax perpetrated by the UFO community. The papers were actually part of a US government disinformation campaign meant to deflect attention from various secret Air Force projects.

"The irony of all this is, that the crash in Mexico – known as the *'Crash at El Indio'* – was real. It was not properly investigated until the early 1990s, forty years later. The investigators concluded that the presumed crash impact site was just a natural sink hole and there was no evidence to show that this was a UFO crash site.

"However, they missed one piece of evidence. A woman staying at a Texas ranch in December 1950 wrote to her husband about something that defied explanation. That night, she and the other guests saw an object flying overhead, trailing fire. At first glance it seemed like an airplane in distress, but its movements were wrong – too erratic. Moments later it dipped below the horizon toward the Mexican border.

"At dawn, the ranch cowboys saddled their horses and rode out. Hours later, they returned shaken, whispering about wreckage unlike any machine they'd ever seen. The craft was scorched and twisted, its metal strangely smooth. And among the debris lay bodies – small, charred forms, their proportions eerily childlike. The men swore the bodies were no children of this Earth."

"I'm afraid this *was* one of ours," Istariol explained. "An Antarian colleague of mine, responsible for the North American region in the '50s, was flying near the Texan-Mexican border when the fusion drive failed – catastrophically – and the spaceship exploded, killing everyone on board.

"That shouldn't have happened, as the ship's fusion system had triple redundancy, designed to ensure fail-safe operation even if one or two individual systems failed. We suspected sabotage, but there wasn't enough of the ship left to properly investigate this.

"I was ordered to go there, clean up the mess and remove all evidence of extraterrestrial life – including the bodies – to minimise any breach of Directive 9 as quickly as possible.

"We collected any remaining 'incriminating' evidence – but it was too late for a complete cover-up. Some Vegan bodies had already been seen – by the Texan cowboys and their guests – and we believe that's how the modern Solarian 'myth' of what aliens look like actually began."

"Hmm… interesting… 98% fiction, 2% truth," Ian commented. "Istariol, you seem to be everywhere – or perhaps I should say *'everywhen'* – anything interesting happens on Earth."

"Anyway, thank you for the explanation," Ian said. "Now, I think we should get back to the tasks in hand. Istariol?"

"Certainly. If you're happy, we will start our descent to Earth at midnight tonight – and we'll arrive in Paris at 2.00am local time? Can I suggest that we meet up for dinner at 8 o'clock?" Istariol asked.

It was now just after 5.45pm Central European Time. Ian and Rebecca decided that it would be a good idea to go back to their bedroom/cabin and take some time to think about all of this before dinner.

"Good idea," Ian said. "I think we're going to take a bit of a siesta now. If we do have any more questions before dinner, I assume it would be ok to ask Alexa?"

"Absolutely," responded Alexa. "But anytime you are in your cabin, for your privacy, I will automatically suspend all monitoring of your conversations and will only start listening if you start a sentence by speaking my name – *'Alexa'.*"

"Incidentally, we are now near enough to Earth to allow me to tap into the Solarian internet again. The tablets we gave you and your personal phones have now been automatically connected to the ship's 'wifi', so they will all have access.

"But, as I'm sure you'll understand, you must *not* contact anyone on Earth. If you do so, and the IGC or the Mekbudans find out, then the Hearing would be automatically cancelled and the case forfeited."

After a short pause, "Anyway, welcome back to Earth," Alexa concluded.

Ian and Rebecca retreated back to their room.

"They seem completely obsessed about their Directive 9. I'm not really sure what the fuss is about," Rebecca observed.

"If you remember," Ian replied, "Alexa told us that the Antarians almost went to war with the Mekbudans over what they were doing on Earth, and that Directive 9 was created as part of the peace agreement. So yes, we should ask for more detail on this."

For understandable reasons, Ian and Rebecca had not slept well the previous night. So once they got into bed – despite the many other questions occupying their thoughts – they quickly fell asleep.

They woke to the sound of the alarm on Ian's phone, which he had set for 7.30pm. After a quick shower to refresh themselves, they gathered their belongings and sat on the bed together.

"Are you ready?" Ian asked.

"Yes, let's go," Rebecca replied. "But I wonder how many more surprises they have in store for us before the day is out."

Rebecca pressed the door button and it opened – or rather, the wall disappeared – and they walked into the dining room. The table was already set for four people.

Istariol was seated in an armchair. On seeing them, he rose and said "Greetings. I trust you managed to get a little sleep?"

Ian and Rebecca sat down to join him and they asked Alexa to provide them with some drinks – which duly appeared in the alcove next to the table.

"I promised to introduce you to my fourth crew member. I believe she is joining us for dinner," Istariol said.

They exchanged a few pleasantries, when Alexa suddenly said "Bonne soirée."

But the voice had come from behind Ian and Rebecca – not from the speaker in the ceiling.

Turning around, they saw a woman dressed entirely in black walking toward them.

She gave the slightest flick of her head and her light brown hair flared out, as if caught in a sudden gust of wind. *"How _did_ she do that?"* Ian thought.

"Bonjour, mon chéri," she said to Istariol. Ian noticed that her ears were definitely *not* pointed.

"Stop showing off, Aurelia," Istariol said, adding as an aside to Rebecca, "She doesn't get out much, you know."

Chapter 13

"If I may make the introductions?" Istariol asked rhetorically, as they all rose to greet Aurelia.

"Aurelia, this is Ian, the Solarian Representative — and this is Rebecca, his deputy," he said, gesturing towards each of them in turn.

"Ian and Rebecca, please meet Aurelia, my Security Officer."

"I can't help but ask, why is she speaking French and why does she have Alexa's voice?" Ian enquired.

"Au contraire, mon ami, c'est Alexa qui utilise ma voix, et non l'inverse," Aurelia replied.

"She said, that I am using *her* voice, not the other way round," Alexa explained — her voice, as usual, coming from the speaker in the ceiling. "That *is* true. I could use any number of voices, but Aurelia and I are a team and it makes sense to me that I should use her voice.

"When you leave the ship, with your permission, Aurelia will accompany you and stay in the hotel apartment with you," Alexa continued.

"But I will be able to come with you, as I will cohabit Aurelia's mind. I will be able to see, hear, smell, taste and feel everything Aurelia does. And she will be in constant contact with me through her thoughts.

"In fact, if you say *'Alexa'* in Aurelia's presence, you can talk directly to me — and Aurelia will pass on my reply to you verbally. Of course, when you are in any private room in the hotel, including the rooms in your apartment, you can also speak to me directly through the speaker systems."

Interrupting, and with a pronounced French accent, Aurelia said, "And I was speaking French because we are in Paris — or at least soon will be — and, as they say, *'when in Rome, do as the Romans do.'* But I can, of course, speak English fluently," she added.

"You don't appear to be a native Antarian? How come you're serving as Security Officer on board Istariol's ship?" Ian asked Aurelia.

"If I may interrupt?" Istariol said. "Can I suggest we all sit down for dinner and we can resume our discussions at the table?"

So they all sat down to dinner, which unfolded as a classic four-course affair. The French theme held strong: a small bowl of soupe à l'oignon to start, followed by moules marinières as hors d'oeuvres, and then a hearty boeuf bourguignon for the main course. The inevitable cheese course lingered longest of all – as Ian was quite a fan of cheese, particularly French ones.

Between mouthfuls, Istariol managed to explain that Aurelia *was* human and that her parents had been household slaves in ancient Rome.

"Roman household slaves were typically not mistreated," Istariol explained, "and were often regarded as part of the family. But much depended on their master's temperament. As for their children, they were often torn from their mothers and sold off like livestock.

"Outside of wealthy households, life in ancient Rome for female slaves was far harsher. Beatings, rape, and backbreaking labour with little food or rest, were not uncommon. Many slaves didn't live past thirty. And as for escape? Well, freedom without money, skills, or protection usually meant destitution.

"Aurelia's parents served in a household ruled by a cruel, corrupt master – and a womaniser. When her mother fell pregnant, her parents visited a seer who told them that their unborn child was a girl."

"Could they really tell the sex of an unborn child in those times?" Rebecca asked.

"Of course not. But that never stopped a so-called 'seer' from claiming otherwise. At the time, I had certain… business arrangements with the head of their household. That business required me to plant listening bugs throughout his residence. As part of that surveillance, Alexa overheard the parents discussing their intention to offer their child to the gods – *if* the baby was a girl.

"There was a human woman, Liene, serving on my ship. She posed as a seer and, during a visit we arranged, scanned the mother's womb. It was indeed a girl – and Liene told them so.

"So the parents resolved to give Aurelia up to the gods, hoping she would find a better life. They chose Salus, goddess of security, prosperity and well-being. To fulfil this vow, her mother would have to give birth in the temple itself.

"When we heard that, we arranged for the parents to have a 'vision' from Salus explaining that they needed to go to a 'special shrine' outside the city to give birth, rather than the main temple in Rome."

"These slaves could travel out of Rome whenever they pleased then?" Ian probed.

"Absolutely not. I persuaded their master that I needed a package delivered to a village outside Rome – and this couple had to do it to avoid any suspicion. He was handsomely rewarded.

"When Aurelia's parents were mysteriously asked by their master to run an errand beyond the city's borders – which had never happened before – they simply accepted it as the will of the goddess.

"When they came to the 'shrine' of Salus to offer up their child to the goddess, the cave they entered to reach the shrine was actually that doorway." Istariol pointed in the direction of the door they had used to enter the ship.

"Aurelia was actually born in this very room. Of course, it was more appropriately decorated.

"Since Aurelia's birth was on board my ship, this technically made her Antarian-born, as the ship is considered Antarian territory, irrespective of its location. She immediately gained Antarian citizenship. And yet Aurelia has never been to the Antarian home world – or to any of our colonies."

"Surely you were interfering with Earth's people? Didn't this go against your Directive 9 regulation?" Rebecca asked.

"Good question," Istariol replied. "No, the parents had no idea that their daughter was born on a spaceship. Every point of contact we made with them was in the context of their religion. They had a vision from one of their gods and had no idea there was any extra-terrestrial involvement. No, the Directive 9 rules were not broken.

"The Mekbudans have been manipulating mankind for centuries, masquerading as one or other of their gods – for their own selfish gain – without being in breach of Directive 9. They were particularly successful in ancient Egypt."

"I'm still struggling to get my head round the timescales here," Rebecca said, holding her head in her hands. "Aurelia looks so young, so how could she be born in ancient Rome?"

"Well, a lot of people have spent quite some time talking *about* me, so perhaps, mes amis, it's time I had a chance to speak?" interrupted Aurelia.

"I was born in 30 BC – a year after Gaius Octavius defeated Mark Antony and Cleopatra at the Battle of Actium – and three years before he was granted the title *Augustus*, becoming the first Roman Emperor in 27 BC.

"The Roman Republic had been riddled with corruption for decades. Julius Caesar – Octavius's great-uncle and adoptive father – became a benevolent dictator and brought order and stability. But his reforms ended the Republic, and for that, he was assassinated.

"I'm only telling you this to explain that I was born in a period of great change for Rome and its territories. Not that I had any personal involvement, because I didn't grow up in Rome. Istariol needed to skip forward in time – his work with the Romans had come to an end.

"Anyway, Istariol left Earth shortly after I was born and I stayed on his ship in Liene's care, who acted as my nursemaid. I barely remember her, but I have no memories at all of my mother, as she left the 'shrine' two days after my birth.

"Istariol had several missions to complete along the way, but I was only two years old when he took me to fifteenth-century France. He left me there for fourteen years, under the supervision of his agents, so I grew up in the small village of Domrémy in medieval France. It was a very different time, of course – women were forbidden to wear men's clothing, and doing so was considered an act of blasphemy.

"Istariol gave me my first task when I was sixteen years old – and it took me three years to complete. He didn't have time to remain on Earth for that long, but he did return to collect me at the end of my mission. So, at the tender age of nineteen, I joined Istariol's crew and have travelled with him ever since. And Alexa, ma sœur, taught me pretty much everything I know."

"That's a pretty amazing story, Aurelia," Rebecca said. "And I imagine you must have quite a few more tales to tell, given the number of years you've been on board this ship."

Before Aurelia had a chance to answer, Ian interrupted with a question. "I am curious, Istariol. Why *did* you choose to go out of your way to recruit a Roman slave's unborn baby girl?" Ian asked.

"For two reasons. Firstly, I happened to be there at the time 'on business' and became aware that her parents were desperate to give their child a better life. Why wouldn't I help, if I could? But secondly, it is routine to scan the genome of any person we come in contact with. In this case, the unborn child's DNA was isolated from a blood sample we took from the pregnant mother.

"To say that this child had potential would be a huge understatement. It was immediately obvious that with the right training and upbringing, Aurelia, as her mother named her, would be a fantastic credit to the Antarian fleet," Istariol said beaming.

Aurelia actually blushed. "Tu es un flatteur scandaleux, Istariol," she replied.

"Can't you just design your own crew, genetically modifying them to your specification. Why are Aurelia's genes so special?" Ian asked.

"We consider that unethical. So no, we don't do it – unless there's a genetic defect that would lead to a medical condition causing significant suffering," Alexa replied.

"However, the Mekbudans have no such qualms. They select each member of their ships' crew based on the genome most advantageous for that role. They also construct armies of clones, with each soldier type consisting of identical individuals, replicated millions of times. They will capture any slave that takes their fancy, but most of their slaves are bred in captivity – and they control the gene pool, typically favouring strength, intelligence and passivity."

"So, what actually is Aurelia's role on this ship, under normal circumstances?" Ian asked.

"Aurelia, as Security Officer, is primarily responsible for counter espionage," Istariol replied. "Working with Alexa and Dewey, our Science Officer, Aurelia also takes the lead on ensuring that the ship's systems and communications are properly protected from any external attack. You would understand this better than most, Ian, given your skills in cyberspace security and electronic warfare."

"However, *mon Commandant*," Aurelia interjected, "I do have a few ideas about how I could best assist you once we get to the hotel.

"I have already set up all the security and surveillance systems at the hotel, bringing the Solarian technology up to Antarian standards. Not that the hotel staff know, of course. I have also recruited a security team who will be staying at the hotel. Some of them will be piloting the submarine when they pick us up tomorrow morning.

"Alexa is incredibly intelligent, of course, and has a massive database of her own, but even an AI has to depend to a certain extent on the available data held externally. In this case, this will include the delegates' own project papers, published and unpublished. She can't always tell truth from lies – if the lies are plausible and self-consistent enough.

"The amount of money that our 'anonymous donor' has put up, as potentially available for their project, will no doubt attract a few charlatans.

"We can hack into any of the delegate's computer systems and phones, and have already done so – but the clever ones won't document things they want to keep really secret.

"So, I believe my time will be best used mingling with the delegates. In addition to keeping a look out for possible Mekbudan spies, I may also get to know some of them well enough to see who is telling the truth about their own projects and who are the fakes. I am sure nearly all of them will underestimate my technical knowledge and let their guard down with me."

"What's this about Mekbudan spies? Why would they need to have spies amongst us?" Ian asked, with concern in his voice.

Istariol answered. "The Mekbudans are extremely confident that they will win the case, but it is in their nature to cover all possible outcomes. If it looks like you may be able to put up a plausible defence, then they will want to know about it before the Hearing starts. We have protected the entire hotel against hacking and surveillance devices and they know this. So, the best way to gather information is the old-fashioned way – to send a person to do it – and in this case they would only use human spies.

"Even if we attempted to monitor all the cellular traffic in the vicinity of the hotel, the spy only has to board their spaceship, which we know must be in the vicinity, to report their findings."

"Okay, so what other security issues are there?" Ian enquired.

"Well, we're quite certain that you are both safe from assassination attempts," Aurelia said – which got a couple of startled looks from Ian and Rebecca. "The IGC regulations on this Hearing would work very much against the Mekbudans, if anything *unfortunate* were to happen to either of you. The slightest suggestion of foul play would result in the case being immediately dismissed and the Mekbudans will not risk that. In any event, it would be very likely that the Hearing date would be postponed –

probably for at least a year – and the Mekbudans also wouldn't be happy about that.

"This protection extends somewhat to ourselves – and potentially to the delegates. If it turns out that a delegate has a project vital to your defence, and his or her disappearance would jeopardise your case, then the Mekbudans would have to be desperate to try anything, as it could backfire on them.

"And we do have our own spies amongst the Mekbudans, but the less you know about that the better."

"Okay, well I'll leave it to your judgement Aurelia – and, yes, you are very welcome to join us and come and stay at the hotel apartment," Ian said. "You may share anything you want with Istariol, of course, but for the purposes of the chain of command, I want you to report directly to me."

"Oui, *mon Commandant*!" was Aurelia's reply.

"And don't overdo the French when you are talking to us," Ian warned, smiling.

"Non, bien sûr que non, Commandant," Aurelia responded, also smiling.

"Good, now that that's settled, we have some other questions, Istariol," Ian said. "Although I guess it doesn't really matter, we couldn't help wondering why Paris was chosen for the Hearing?"

"It was at the request of the Mekbudans," Istariol replied, shrugging his shoulders. "They asked for the Hearing to be located in Paris when they submitted their Challenge – their accusation that Mankind is acting with gross negligence and dereliction of duty. Both the IGC and the Antarians had no reason to object, so Paris it is. We think it's what passes for Mekbudan irony – setting the hearing location in the same city that hosted the *'Paris Agreement'* – which they will no doubt argue has been completely ineffective."

"Fair enough. On another topic, why do you user *paper* for contracts and signatures – which seems quite low technology and not very secure – rather than electronic systems based on block chain technology or similar?" Ian asked.

"As you don't really have a need to know this, Directive 9 forbids me from giving you the full details," Istariol explained. "But what I can tell you is that both types of technology are used – electronic and physical. Your DNA has been added to the pieces of paper you signed, together with some secret chemical ingredients known only to us. And the paper also has a watermark containing a public encryption key, which is used to encrypt a copy of all the data – both the written words on the papers and the voice and camera recordings made of you signing the contract."

"Very interesting," Ian said, nodding. "So, tell me – why are the guest living quarters on your ship all 'low tech'? That actually looks like an Amazon Echo Studio speaker on the ceiling, yet all the disappearing doors demonstrate a much higher level of technology."

Istariol actually grimaced at the question. "I've lodged a number of complaints with my superiors, but their hands are tied. Our 'Tay' class reconnaissance vessel is essentially a modified version of the standard 'Bara' type spaceship, which is more commonly used. Antarian shipyards produce relatively few Tay-class ships compared to the high volume of Bara-class vessels, so they refuse to alter their standard hull designs to suit the specific needs of our spy ships. It's a *'take it or leave it'* situation.

"To be fair, we've usually been able to work around any problems we've encountered with our guests," Istariol admitted. "This room made quite a good shrine to Salus, after all."

"However, to answer the other half of your question, Directive 9 stipulates that wherever possible, native technology must be used when we are in contact with a lower technology civilisation. So, for example, you will see us using Solarian wifi, Bluetooth and cellular equipment – and Amazon Echo devices – in preference to any of our own technology."

"Incidentally, all tablets and phones you will be using – either here or at the hotel – will all be Solarian equipment, albeit with some added 'alien' security software," Aurelia added.

"I should also reassure you both, that none of your colleagues, friends and relatives will worry about your continued absence," Aurelia continued. "All inbound messages and calls you would have received, will be intercepted and dealt with by Alexa. You probably know enough about *'deep fake'* calls and videos to understand that Alexa will be quite capable of impersonating either, or both, of you if someone calls.

"Just so you know, the cover story is that Ian has to go to another conference in Norway in mid-May and you've both extended your annual leave for 3 weeks to take advantage of the opportunity to sightsee. After all, it's almost June and a good time of year to take in the sights of the Norwegian fiords."

"Anyway, I think I will take my leave until it's time to disembark," Aurelia announced. Then, with a smile, she added, "Feel free to finish the cheese, *mon Commandant* – it's there to be eaten."

"And *I've* got some work to attend to, so if you'll excuse me, I'll also retire to my quarters," Istariol said, standing up from the table. "May I suggest we meet here at 1.45am ready to disembark?"

Everyone agreed. So, Ian and Rebecca were left to their own devices. It was quarter past ten in the evening, local time.

"I think Alexa said we'll start our descent at midnight and be in Paris by 2am," Ian remarked.

"Yes, Commander, that's correct," Alexa replied.

"Well, we may have a long day ahead, so let's see if we can get some rest," Ian said to Rebecca. They once again went through the door to their cabin. Ian set an alarm for 1.15am. They still felt a little jet-lagged – presumably because they had only managed to get quite short periods of sleep since boarding the spaceship – so it wasn't long before they nodded off.

What seemed like only a few minutes later, they were woken by the buzzing of Ian's phone alarm. They had no bags – apart from Rebecca's handbag – to carry anything in.

"Alexa, are we supposed to take anything from our cabin, like clothes?" Rebecca asked.

"No, everything will be provided in your rooms at the hotel," Alexa replied.

"Okay thanks." Ian and Rebecca went through their door to the living / dining room.

"Two coffees please, Alexa, filter coffee with milk please," Rebecca asked.

"Certainly... coming right up," was Alexa's response.

They sat down in the armchairs and drank their coffees. After a short while, Istariol joined them.

"Coffee looks like a good idea to me," he said. "If you please, Alexa?"

At 1.45am precisely, a door opened and Aurelia glided into the room. "Bonjour à tous, ce café sent vraiment bon!"

"Are you *really* going outside wearing that outfit," Istariol asked.

"Quel est le problème? My hat will keep me warm. Besides, if everyone is looking at me, you guys won't even be noticed. And I firmly believe in the principle of hiding in plain sight," she replied, with a grin.

At that point they felt the ship rock ever so slightly. "Alexa, bring up the screen and show us where we are," Ian commanded.

The stone archways of Pont Neuf, the oldest standing bridge in Paris, could be seen across the water just ahead, their aged stones illuminated by lamps that cast golden reflections dancing over the River Seine.

"The ship's cloaking is fully functional, but I should warn you that as the ship enters the river and starts to submerge, there will be a disturbance in the waters – and there's nothing we can do about that," Alexa warned.

"Witnesses will just see a large round area with swirling water and ripples," Alexa continued, "but it *will* be directly over our parking spot. We believe it's a very small risk that anyone would want to investigate further, but it's still worth trying to avoid doing this with people looking in our direction.

"I *can* confirm there is no moving river traffic in our area. And the boats moored nearby should be unoccupied at this time of night – or their occupants will be sleeping," she added.

"I would like to take a few moments to look around before we submerge. Please pan the screen around to show us our surroundings, Alexa," Ian ordered.

To the east, they could see the towers of Notre-Dame Cathedral, their Gothic silhouettes etched in the light of the nearly full moon against the night sky.

Further afield, they saw the Eiffel Tower shimmering in the distance, its iron latticework gleaming where moonlight and electric lights converge.

"Pretty beautiful, eh? Shame we're only here on business – but I'm sure we will be able to find some time to do some shopping, tu ne penses pas?" Aurelia said to Rebecca, winking.

"My scanning systems give us an 'all clear' – no one is staring in our direction," Alexa declared. "There *are* a few people around, but they're just walking over the bridge or strolling along the bank."

"Very well, as everything seems clear – take us down," Ian ordered. The screen briefly displayed a few ripples and bubbles as the ship started to submerge and then went dark, showing just a few grey swirls.

"The River Seine is quite polluted, so there's really not much to see underwater, particularly at night," Alexa explained.

Then everything went quiet. They hadn't really noticed the faint humming noise until it stopped.

"The ship is now in its place underneath the Seine riverbed," Alexa announced. "And the submarine is moving into position, so we'll be able to disembark shortly."

"Just so you know," Aurelia explained, "the security team crewing the submarine are all human and none of them will know that they've picked us up from an alien spaceship. They can only see a small section of our hull when the submarine is docked with it, and they've been told that this is a secret underwater base.

"They also know nothing about the Hearing or our roles," Aurelia continued, "– and you should not tell them your names – I will handle that. They *do* know we are holding a workshop, but they've been told the same cover story as the delegates."

A few minutes later they heard a faint clanking sound outside.

"Okay, here we go," Istariol said.

The door they had used before reappeared in the wall. They stepped through into the small hallway where the external door stood open, revealing the top of the steps lit by the outside lights.

"I trust we're not going to find ourselves on the moon again," joked Rebecca, as she walked towards the door.

As they looked outside, they could see the ship's stairway – but this time a submarine was tied up alongside the bottom of the steps, its hatchway positioned level with the lowest step. The stairway itself was completely dry, while the top of the submarine and the hatch glistened with moisture. They were clearly within a 'bubble' beneath the waters of the Seine.

Then they heard a grinding noise, and watched as the wheel on the hatch began to rotate. With a metallic clang, it swung open, and one of the crew – dressed in a black security guard's uniform – climbed up out of the boat.

Waving up at them, he said, "Bonjour. Be careful when you come on board, as it's slippery down here."

"Once more into the breach, *chers amis*," Aurelia said as she led the way down the steps and then clambered down the ladder in the hatchway.

The others followed, and the crewman climbed down after them, closing the hatch above his head.

"I'd like to introduce you to Jacques, my local Head of Security," Aurelia said. They all shook hands with the crewman, but didn't announce their own names.

They all took a seat next to a window but, as Alexa had said, there really was not much to see in the murky waters of the Seine.

A few moments later they could feel the boat start to move. They could see swirling dark waters through the windows, but not much else. Then they could feel the submarine start to rise and bubbles could be seen in the water outside.

A few minutes later, looking though the portholes they could see the surface of the Seine above them, lit up by the moon.

The boat drew up next to the riverbank and the crewman climbed up one of the ladders and opened the hatchway. Everyone followed. Two other crewmen, one presumably the pilot, were in the process of tying up the boat to the bank.

They were on the Right Bank of the Seine. Looking around, they could see there was a sleek black limousine parked next to their mooring.

"Welcome to Paris," Istariol announced. "Your carriage awaits."

Chapter 14

Saturday, 10th May 2025, Paris, France

Istariol opened the back door of the limousine and signalled for them to get in. Inside were four black leather seats.

Ian gestured towards the open door. "Ladies first," he said.

He and Istariol followed Rebecca and Aurelia into the car and took their seats. It had that unmistakable 'new car' smell.

From the front seat the driver turned his head and said, "Good morning, ladies and gentlemen – we are very close to the hotel, so we'll be there in less than five minutes."

The electric limousine glided along silently, and after going round the block, slipped into an underground car park. Moments later, it rolled to a halt beside an elevator, and the four of them stepped out.

Istariol reached into his pocket and pulled out a handful of fobs, each a different colour. He handed one to Rebecca, Ian and Aurelia, keeping the fourth for himself.

"This fob will give you access to the private elevator, the front door of the apartment – which leads into the rest of the hotel – and your own private rooms."

They looked at the fobs. They were engraved in gold italic letters – the blue and pink ones both had '*R&I*' on them, whilst Aurelia's black fob had a golden '*A*' embossed on it. Istariol was holding his and they could see an '*I*' etched onto the green fob.

Istariol pressed the button next to the elevator and it lit up. After a short while the elevator doors opened and Istariol stood aside while the other three walked into the elevator. Following them inside, Istariol then pressed his fob against a small panel and pressed the highest of the two elevator buttons.

The doors closed and the elevator rose swiftly. It came to a halt with a slight judder, and the doors opened to reveal an expansive reception room in the Apartment. Most of the walls were lined with floor-to-ceiling windows, through which they could see the Parisian skyline, bathed in moonlight, with flickering lights in the distance.

Istariol led them through the spacious reception rooms and showed them to the door of Ian and Rebecca's private suite.

"I guess no one wants to swipe my credit card then?" Ian joked.

It was about 2.30am and they agreed to meet again for breakfast at 8 o'clock. Aurelia and Istariol bade them goodnight.

They explored their luxurious bedroom, which opened on either side into separate wings – each with its own bathroom featuring a spacious honey-veined marble bathtub, a hammam-style shower and individual dressing rooms.

"His and hers bathrooms, eh? No squabbles about whose turn it is to use the shower then," observed Ian.

Opening the wardrobes, they found them filled with designer clothes for both of them – slinky dresses and elegant shoes for Rebecca.

"That's some view from *my* bathroom," Rebecca said, gazing out at the distant Eiffel Tower and claiming that side as her own.

"So, this is our home for the next three weeks or so. Pretty spectacular – but with a budget of two hundred and fifty million dollars, I guess it won't break the bank," laughed Rebecca. "I think we should test the quality of the bed," she added with a wink.

The next morning, they both took showers, Rebecca admiring her view over Paris, with the Eiffel Tower clearly visible on the horizon.

"Mmm... these toiletries smell gorgeous," Rebecca said appreciatively, when she met up with Ian afterwards.

They dressed in their new clothes and began exploring more of the apartment. It was vast, spanning the hotel's top two floors. One spectacularly large reception room even featured a grand piano.

They stepped out onto the terrace to take in the panoramic view of Paris – from Notre-Dame to the Eiffel Tower.

They discovered their private swimming pool with stunning views of Sacré-Coeur.

"Do you fancy a swim?" Rebecca asked.

"Not just at the moment," Ian replied. "But I'm sure the private projection room will come in handy sometime soon," he added dryly.

They also found a private sauna, a treatment room and a well-equipped gym.

They reached one door with the sign 'Hotel' written above it. They used one of their fobs to unlock it – and upon opening it – they saw a man dressed in a black suit with an earpiece standing nearby, as if guarding the door. Ian noticed the slight bulge in his suit jacket and concluded that the man was armed.

"Good morning, sir – and ma'am. I trust you slept well?" he said, turning towards them.

"Yes, fine thank you. Are you here for a reason?" Ian enquired.

"I'm mainly here to ensure that none of the hotel staff come into the Apartment," he replied, "like an over-zealous cleaner, for example – unless we give them permission, that is. But I'm also here to inform you that no one is allowed into the rest of the hotel at this time – without express permission from Aurelia."

"You know who I am then? And that Aurelia reports to me?"

"Yes, sir, but it's the chain of command, sir – only Aurelia can give permission – so if you wish to explore the rest of the hotel, you'll have to speak to her."

"I'll bid you good day then," Ian replied smiling, as they turned and walked back into the Apartment, closing the door behind them.

Just after 8am, they made their way to the dining area in one of the reception rooms. It took a little wandering – as they hadn't agreed on which dining room to meet in – before they found Istariol and Aurelia already seated and enjoying breakfast.

"Bonjour. Hope you liked the clothes – I chose them all you know," boasted Aurelia. "You can't have too many shoes, eh Rebecca? *Tu n'es pas d'accord?*" she added, smiling. "Please join us."

Ian and Rebecca sat down with them at the table. "The clothes are wonderful, thank you," Rebecca said, "although I haven't tried on all the dresses yet."

"I assure you they'll all fit perfectly," Aurelia assured them.

"We met one of your men this morning," Ian said to Aurelia. "He said we were not allowed to go into the rest of the hotel without your permission?"

"Oui, it's for your own safety," Aurelia replied. "I don't think there is any need for either of you to leave the Apartment at all during this workshop. We can screen any of the workshop's presentations and meetings in our private projection room and – if you want to meet any of the delegates – they can come here."

"I thought you said the Mekbudans had no interest in trying to kill us? And, presumably, if they *did* want us dead – it would be difficult to stop them?"

"D'accord, but as the saying goes: *'Assumption is the mother of all fuckups'* and I don't like making assumptions," Aurelia replied. "Besides, we don't know whether or not there are any other 'interested' parties."

After they had all finished a spectacular continental breakfast, Istariol turned to more formal matters.

"As you're aware, today is Saturday 10th May," Istariol said. "The delegates will start arriving tomorrow in readiness for the start of the workshop on Monday. You can decide how best to use the time of course, Ian, but I suggest we start to make a plan for the next few days."

"Sounds good to me," Ian replied, "although I think we need some more information on these Mekbudans, before we can start planning."

They all left the dining table and took a seat in the nearby armchairs, bringing their unfinished coffees with them.

"There's one thing that's been bugging me," Ian said. "Who was responsible for the crop circle that appeared seventeen years ago near Barbury Castle? The one that gave *pi* to ten decimal places – and gave us a vital clue on how to decode your crop pattern?"

"Yes, it *was* me that made the 2008 Barbury Castle crop circle, if that's what you're asking," admitted Istariol. "It was the first time we had come back to Earth after the Mekbudans submitted their petition to the IGC in 2005."

"Are you kidding me? The Mekbudans applied for this hearing *twenty years* ago?" Rebecca exclaimed.

"Yes. The rate of greenhouse gas emissions suddenly increased," Istariol explained. "Between 2000 and 2005, global annual greenhouse gas emissions increased dramatically – due to growing industrial activity, energy use and deforestation. By 2005, the annual rate was increasing significantly enough to give the Mekbudans enough evidence to claim that you – the Solarians – were culpable.

"The IGC weren't entirely convinced – and the Antarians were able to argue that the Hearing should only be *provisionally* granted. The IGC also accepted that the hearing date should be delayed for 20 years, until May 2025, to allow further monitoring of the situation, before such a drastic remedy – the annihilation of 90% of life on Earth – could be considered. The final decision – on whether the Hearing would actually go ahead – was scheduled for May 2024, to give one year's notice to all parties."

"Incidentally, when the Hearing was confirmed by the IGC last year – global emissions had reached over 57 Gigatonnes of CO_2 equivalent per annum, including land-use changes and forestry emissions – which was a rate over *30% higher* than 2005. So, it was a relatively straight forward decision for the IGC to make."

"So, you've personally known that there might be a Hearing as far back as 2008?" Ian enquired. "And you've actually had an *entire year* to prepare – since the IGC granted the Hearing last May?"

"Yes. Well, how much notice do you think we had to give to book this entire hotel?" Alexa said rhetorically – her voice booming out of the speaker in the ceiling above their heads.

"We had to choose the delegates we were going to ask to attend the workshop – and send out invitations in good time, so they could put it in their diaries."

"Oh, hi Alexa. We hadn't forgotten about you," Ian lied, somewhat unconvincingly.

"We also had to hire the submarine and get it moved to Paris..." Alexa continued, "... and excavate a spaceship-sized hole in the bottom of the River Seine."

"Okay, I get the picture," Ian responded. "In retrospect, I completely understand this was a very complex operation. "And, incidentally, how did you get the submarine here?"

This time, Istariol replied, "At least that's a relatively easy question to answer – we drove it here. Well, towed it for much of the way, actually. The submarine isn't capable of travelling across the ocean on its own – it only has battery-powered electric motors and a fairly short range."

"You towed it across the *ocean*?" Rebecca asked. "Why didn't you just put it on a ship?"

"It was far too big, even for a customised shipping container, so we purchased a 30-metre ocean-going cruiser to tow it from its base in Puerto Calero, Lanzarote, in the Canary Islands."

"You towed it all the way from the Canary Islands?" Ian asked in amazement. "That must be over 3,500 km just to get to Le Havre. Why didn't you transport it by road?"

"Far too complicated," Alexa chipped in. "Firstly, the submarine is quite tall when loaded on a lorry and – even assuming we could have planned a route that avoided low bridges – it would have been considered a 'wide load'. Permits would be required in every jurisdiction along the route, probably involving multiple police escorts, for the 2,000 kilometre trek from southern Spain to Paris.

"Secondly, how would we even have got it to Spain? It's too big to be shipped on any ferry from Lanzarote, so we'd have had to tow it across the Atlantic anyway. The closest land is Tarfaya in Morocco – 132 kilometres away. But even if we'd managed to load it onto a lorry and drive the 1,300 kilometres up to Tangier, we'd still need to find a ferry willing to take such a tall and wide load across the 35-kilometre Strait of Gibraltar."

"So you bought a 100-foot motor yacht – no doubt costing a few million dollars – just to tow this submarine up from the Canary Islands?" Ian asked incredulously.

"Yes, well, it had to be done in good weather," Istariol replied, "following the coasts of Africa, Spain and France – up to Le Havre and into the Seine estuary – and then along the river to Rouen.

"Even taking it quite slowly, and taking shelter in port whenever the weather became a bit dicey, by travelling twenty-four hours a day she was able to reach Le Havre in less than three weeks."

"We've still got the cruiser moored at Rouen Marina – if you fancy going on it sometime," Istariol added, as an aside.

"More boys' toys, eh?" remarked Rebecca.

"Anyway," Istariol continued, "from Rouen the submarine made its own way upriver to Paris – navigating through six locks – with a companion support vehicle loaded with spare batteries and battery chargers, of course."

"The more we delve into your preparations, the more it makes my mind boggle," Rebecca said, chuckling.

"Going back to the Hearing – the IGC, the Mekbudans and the Antarians – have all had one year to prepare for this," Ian stated. "So, how come we – Rebecca and I – only get 3 weeks' notice?"

"It's dictated by the Directive 9 regulations for conducting a Hearing of this nature," answered Istariol. "Given the stress that one would expect the defending Representative to experience, it's deemed unfair to give them more than 3 weeks' notice. The first Hearing on another star system allowed the defendants 6 months' notice – and they emotionally broke down after a month and a half. So, the rules were changed. And, of course, as your advocate, we have been using the time to help prepare a defence."

"Well, it is what it is. So, please can you tell us more about the Mekbudans, given they are clearly our adversaries," Ian urged.

"Certainly," Istariol replied. "The Mekbudan Empire spans thousands of light-years and dozens of planets. It has survived millions of years by having a very rigid structure and vigorously enforcing against all infringements of their constitution. Their elite rulers are almost continuously jumping forward in time, which also helps to maintain continuity over the millennia.

"Their empire is made up of six realms, each ruled by a king. Every one thousand years, they conduct a secret vote to determine which of the kings will next serve as emperor. In the event of a tie, the sitting emperor gets an extra tie-breaking vote – but this vote cannot be for himself."

"Hmm. But if the current emperor receives the same number of votes as another candidate, surely he or she isn't going to vote for their rival. So it'll still be a tie." Ian observed.

"Yes, you're right, of course. In that case, the results are announced, and another round of secret voting is conducted – only this time the new votes are added to those from the previous round. If there's another tie which the sitting emperor can't resolve, then they repeat the process. Eventually, there *will* be a winner."

Istariol reached into the inside pocket of his jacket and took out what looked like a smartphone. He tapped on it a few times and then showed them this picture on it.

"This is the symbol of the Mekbudan Emperor, ruler of the six realms. If you see anyone wearing that badge, they're working directly for the Emperor."

"Wow, is that what Mekbudans look like?" Rebecca gasped.

"Actually, that is the ceremonial mask the emperor wears," Aurelia interjected. "And only the empereur is allowed to wear it. Most Mekbudans aren't as pretty as that," she said ironically.

"The ancient Mekbudan species *did* have horns, but over millions of years of evolution, they gradually disappeared," Aurelia continued. "Some modern Mekbudans still have small vestigial bumps on their foreheads, but for most, they've completely vanished.

"However, many members of the ruling elite are, in fact, ancient Mekbudans – complete with horns and a forked tail – and are still alive because they've been skipping forward through time so much," Aurelia concluded.

After a moment of silence, Istariol said, "Anyway, to continue – the six realms of the empire are each made up of six clans, and each clan is led by a chieftain.

"Each clan, in turn, consists of six tribes. This 6-6-6 structure is enshrined in their constitution and has endured for millions of years.

"Only the Patriarch of a tribe has the right to own a planet. And there *are* more than six Mekbudan tribes per clan, spread across the galaxy. The minor tribes vie with one another politically, each aspiring to supplant one of the ruling tribes.

"Gulinrog is the Patriarch of the tribe that 'owns' Earth, according to the Mekbudans," Istariol continued.

"They *own* Earth?" Ian exclaimed.

"Yes, that remains their belief, but the IGC and the Antarians dispute their claim, because when the Mekbudans crashed the asteroid into Earth 67 million years ago, the resulting treaty – which prevented an intergalactic war – designated the Sol system as neutral territory. Directive 9 was established to protect it, along with other planets that might face similar risks in the future.

"So even though it is not a legal claim, in his heart of hearts, Gulinrog believes he is Earth's rightful owner – and that he can do anything he wants with it – providing he doesn't get caught.

"It probably partially explains why the Mekbudans have taken such an active role in mankind's history. A number of Earth's ancient civilisations – such as the Aztec, Egyptian and Sumerian ones – have been heavily influenced by them over the centuries. We suspect that the Mekbudans frequently posed as gods when interacting with the locals.

"They were typically interested in acquiring valuable treasure – why mine it themselves, if it can be acquired directly from the locals instead? Diamonds & pearls have no galactic value – they're just baubles to be traded with the natives for more precious items, such as gold and platinum."

"Doesn't Directive 9 forbid all this?" Ian asked.

"Directive 9 prevents any of the civilizations signed up to the IGT, the Inter-Galactic Treaty, from giving any technology information to primitive civilizations, as well forbidding them from leaving any evidence of extra-terrestrial life. However, it does not prohibit exploiting mankind's religious belief in their gods.

"There's also a bit more to tell about why the Mekbudans destroyed the dinosaurs," Istariol said, continuing the story.

"Mekbudans consider every other species as cattle or slaves. One of the reasons they gave up on the dinosaurs <u>was</u> that they kept eating their Vegan slaves. On occasion, they would come back to Earth after a few years – to pick up the treasure that had been mined – only to find the entire settlement and mining operation had been wiped out by large dinosaurs.

"However, the situation *is* somewhat more complex.

"It's much easier and cheaper for the Mekbudans to take slaves from the local population, rather than import them from their colonies on other star systems. So, they dabbled with some genetic engineering with some of the dinosaurs, to see if they could create a species suitable for slavery. They needed a species no taller than a human or Antarian – otherwise they wouldn't be able to operate machinery or fit into the living quarters of their ships.

"Some, like the *Dromaeosauridae* family of predators – commonly called 'raptors' – were fairly intelligence and had some potential, particularly *Deinonychus*, who were similar in size to humans.

"However, any species they developed had to compete with all the other dinosaurs in the ecosystem – the big ones had a tendency to eat the smaller ones – and all of the Mekbudan creations just went extinct.

"By the way, Velociraptors didn't actually look or behave anything like how they were portrayed in the *'Jurassic Park'* films. I think there was some confusion about dinosaur naming conventions between the film's scientific advisers and the palaeontological community. In reality, Velociraptors were much smaller, covered in feathers, and hunted alone rather than in packs."

"Hmm. But why didn't they just import enough slaves from another planet to seed a breeding colony on Earth – with Vegans, or other intelligent species from the Delta Pavonis system you mentioned?" Ian asked.

"The slaves they brought in to run the mines lived in controlled environments, sheltered from Earth's bacteria and viruses," Istariol explained. "In some of their early colonies, the Mekbudans came back to find all their slaves had died from some native disease. Even Vegans couldn't eat the native plants of that era – their diet consisted solely of imported crops – cultivated by the robots in the settlements they built around each mine.

"You have to appreciate that the Mekbudans could never stay very long during each visit. Each mining outpost had to be self-sufficient – and slaves couldn't be trusted with valuable medical equipment or medicines. No, what they needed was a native slave species: one that could survive independently in Earth's environment.

"After about 100 million years, they had had little success with their dinosaur-breeding programme. So Gulinrog's great-grandfather made the decision to give Earth an 'ecological reset' – and wipe out ninety per cent of all life. Dinosaurs were simply too troublesome and – from the Mekbudan point of view – an evolutionary dead end.

"We believe they still have some *Deinonychus* specimens in a colony somewhere. I think they use them as guard dogs," he added.

"But there's more to tell. I told you yesterday about the evidence we had proving that the pre-human *Australopithecus* – 'Lucy' was a fossil of this species – had been genetically modified by the Mekbudans to create *Homo habilis*.

"However, we believe that the Mekbudan genetic interference wasn't limited to Lucy's species – it was far more widespread. We think they actually used artificial insemination on mammals over millennia, selectively favouring traits like intelligence and aggression, until – with Mekbudan help – apes eventually 'evolved' into *Homo sapiens*.

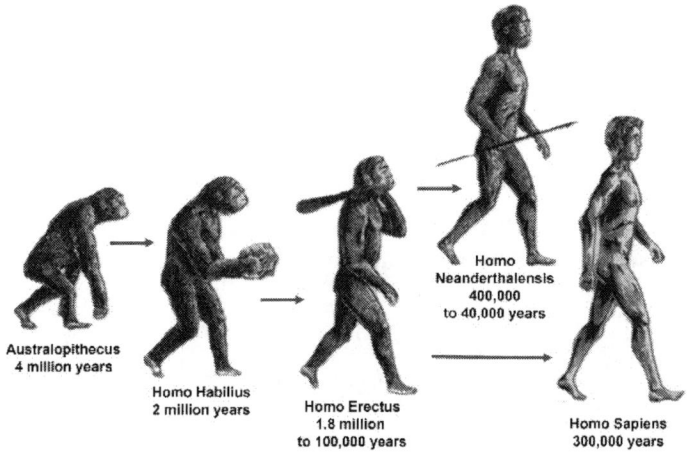

"And then, about 50,000 years ago, a mass migration out of Africa led many *Homo sapiens* to encounter their 'sister' species, *Homo neanderthalensis* – the Neanderthals – who had already been living in Europe and parts of Asia for hundreds of thousands of years. *Homo sapiens*, in addition to having more advanced weapons, were a much more aggressive species.

"There *were* multiple causes but, less than 10,000 years later, the Neanderthals had become extinct.

"Not only did the Mekbudans clear the way for mammals to evolve into the dominant species on Earth by wiping out the dinosaurs – we believe they actually created mankind through continuous genetic engineering.

"You see, humans are the slaves the Mekbudans have been seeking for millions of years."

"Plus – and I don't think you're going to like this..." Istariol almost whispered. "...many of the modern Solarian religions state that *'man'* was created by their god – in the god's own image. Well... the Mekbudans used their own DNA to create *Homo sapiens*.

"Humans typically have over fifty percent of Mekbudan DNA in their genome. So, you could argue that the Mekbudans truly *are* your gods.

"And, if you were to use the term **'orc'** to describe Mekbudans – which was a sort of *'hell-devil'* in old Anglo-Saxon literature – then humans would actually be **'half-orcs'**."

Chapter 15

"Well, after that little revelation, I need another cup of coffee. Anyone else want one?" Ian asked.

Istariol asked Alexa to order more coffee from the hotel's Majordome. A few minutes later, a waiter came into the room with a fresh pot of coffee. Ian eagerly poured a cup for each of them.

"I do have another question," Rebecca said. "I recently read a news report that one of NASA's telescopes discovered what could be signs of life on a planet over 120 light-years away.

"You've told us that there are advanced civilizations living on planets in the Vega and Delta Pavonis star systems – both within 25 light-years of Earth. So how come no one has detected any sign of life, including radio transmissions, from either of them?"

"Well, some scientists *claim* to have found signs of life," Alexa replied from the speakers in the ceiling. "They have discovered the gas dimethyl sulfide – or DMS for short – in the atmosphere of an exoplanet orbiting the red dwarf K2-18, about 124 light-years away. On Earth, DMS is mainly produced by simple marine organisms.

"However," Alexa continued, "some scientists can be a little overzealous – perhaps making sensationalist claims to gain attention. Other Solarian researchers have already pointed out several flaws in that particular claim.

"This exoplanet, known as K2-18b, has a low density – less than half the density of a rocky planet like Earth – so it's made up of something far more rarified than Earth-like material.

"And K2-18b orbits quite far away from its relatively cool parent star, with an average temperature of around *minus* 8°C – below the freezing point of water. So K2-18b is not a 'water world' with a global, deep ocean of liquid water.

"It actually has a large, thick global atmosphere – and NASA's James Webb Space Telescope found signs of methane gas a couple of years ago. K2-18b is actually a cold Neptune-like world, rather than a terrestrial, Earth-like one.

"By the way, Neptune is blue in colour, mainly because of the abundant presence of methane in its atmosphere," Alexa added.

"It's true that most of Earth's dimethyl sulfide *is* produced by phytoplankton and bacteria – it's this gas which gives the sea its unique smell. However, DMS is also found throughout the universe, produced by non-biological means. It's even been found in the interstellar medium, including in a large molecular cloud in the centre of the Milky Way.

"So, based on the scientific data available to Solarians, this claim of finding signs of life is *not* supported by the data.

"And, in fact, I can confirm that there *is* no life on K2-18b," Alexa announced.

"But let me go back to the main point of your question: '*Why are there no reports of life on Vega or Delta Pavonis?*' The answer is that Directive 9 also applies to activities on our home worlds and colonies.

"We have to use planetary scrambling systems to mask our transmissions – and this also stops your radio telescopes from detecting any chemicals which would give conclusive proof of extraterrestrial life," Alexa explained.

"Okay, I have one more question – and then we should move onto planning how we're going to handle this workshop," Ian announced.

"In the worst-case scenario – where the Mekbudans are given authority to crash an asteroid into Earth – how would they do it, and when?" he asked Istariol.

"The solar system contains a vast number of asteroids in orbit," Istariol replied. "In fact, more than a million of them are over one kilometre in diameter. Most are located in the main asteroid belt between Mars and Jupiter, in the Kuiper Belt beyond Neptune, and among the Trojan asteroids that share Jupiter's orbit."

Istariol reached down to his briefcase and pulled out a tablet. After a few moments, he passed it over to show this picture:

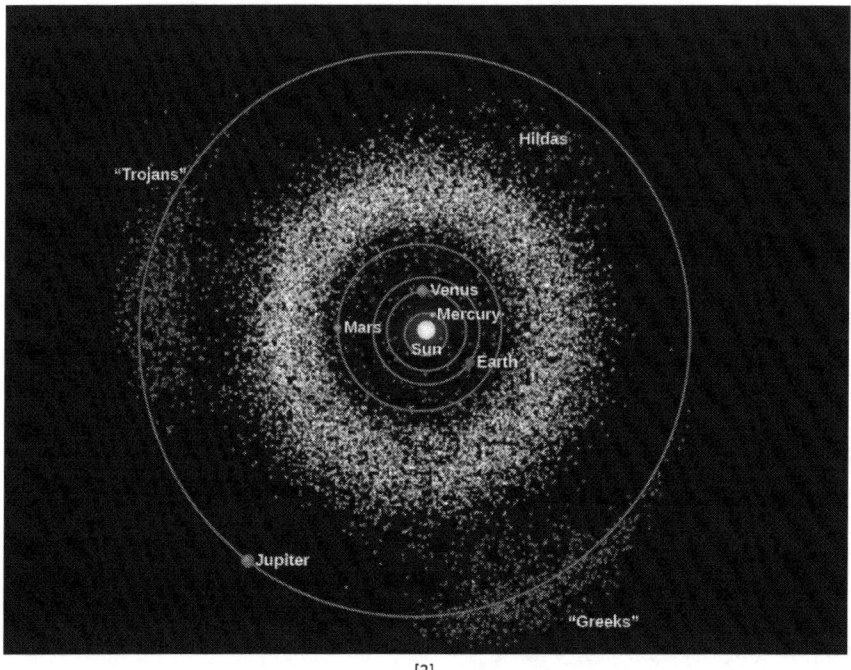

[2]

"So the Mekbudans have quite a long list of prospects to choose from," Istariol continued.

"The vast majority of these asteroids have very stable orbits and, under normal circumstances, could never come anywhere near Earth.

"However, there *are* a few asteroids who have elliptical orbits and will come very close to the Earth in the near future.

"We also need to consider the size of the asteroid. It needs to be large enough to cause an impact winter that would last long enough to wipe out most of life on Earth. The asteroid that wiped out the dinosaurs, known as the 'Chicxulub Impactor' was about ten kilometres in diameter."

"Alexa, please bring up our short list of asteroids the Mekbudans could use – showing their size relative to the Chicxulub Impactor," Istariol asked.

"Sure," Alexa said. This chart appeared on Istariol's tablet:

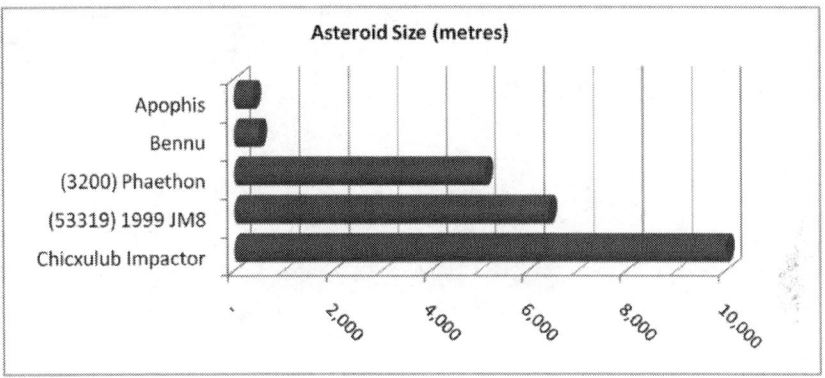

"In comparison to the 10-kilometre-wide Chicxulub dinosaur exterminator, Apophis and Bennu are tiny," Alexa explained. "They are only noteworthy because their orbits will often bring them very close to the Earth.

"Apophis is named after the Egyptian god of darkness and chaos, and is an Empire-State-Building-sized asteroid that swings close to Earth roughly once per decade. On Friday the 13th of April 2029, Apophis will come within 32,000 kilometres of Earth's surface. That's a very close pass, considering the Moon is about 380,000 kilometres away – it's *even* closer than the 36,000-kilometre altitude of a geostationary satellite.

"Bennu – named after the ancient Egyptian mythological bird associated with the Sun, creation and rebirth – is roughly spherical, larger than Apophis, but less dense. As a result, it's only about 20% greater in mass. Bennu will come even closer to Earth – just 24,000 kilometres from the surface – but that won't happen until 2182, over a hundred and fifty years from now.

"3200 Phaethon is named after the mythological Greek hero Phaëthon, son of the Sun god Helios, who attempted to drive the chariot of the Sun. Phaethon has a highly eccentric 524-day orbit that brings it closer to the Sun than Mercury before slinging it back out beyond Mars. It trails a thick stream of debris over 14 million miles long – the source of the annual Geminid meteor shower, which occurs when Earth passes through the material left behind by Phaethon.

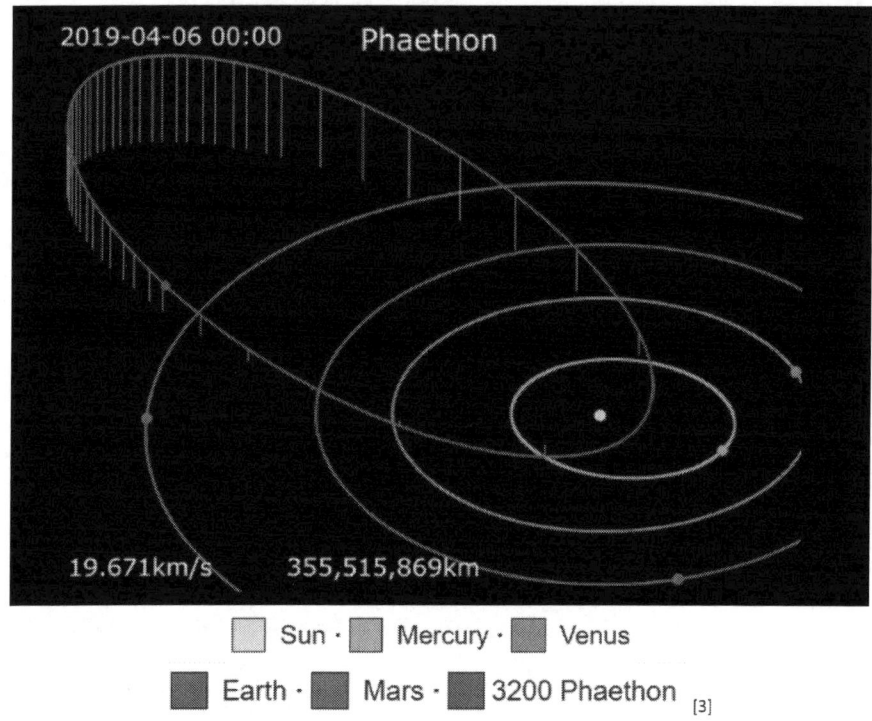

2019-04-06 00:00   Phaethon

19.671km/s   355,515,869km

☐ Sun · ☐ Mercury · ☐ Venus
■ Earth · ■ Mars · ■ 3200 Phaethon [3]

"Phaethon is much, much larger than Apophis and Bennu," Alexa continued, "with an average diameter of 5.8 kilometres and a mass of roughly 200 trillion kilograms – about 2,700 times greater than Bennu. Its orbit brings it relatively close to Earth approximately every 1.5 years, but its next notable approach won't occur until December 2093, when it will come within 3.5 million kilometres of Earth.

"53319-1999 JM_8 is an even more massive asteroid about 6.5 kilometres in diameter, which slowly tumbles along in its orbit. It's the largest body that the Solarians have classified as a 'potentially hazardous asteroid'. It has passed closer than 30 million kilometres to the Earth five times in the last century, but its next closest approach in 2075 will be fairly far away at around 38 million kilometres.

"So, these are our shortlisted 'villains' – the asteroids we think are the most likely candidates for the Mekbudans to use to crash into Earth – if they are allowed to," Alexa concluded.

"Thanks, Alexa – so let's just make sure it doesn't come to that," Ian said grimly.

They all decided that they needed to stretch their legs. Aurelia got up and walked over to a nearby window. She then turned back and waved at Ian, beckoning him towards her.

When Ian came close, Aurelia whispered "You need to come with me to my chambre à coucher." Without any further word, she started walking out of the room.

Looking round, Ian could see Istariol and Rebecca were standing together near the door to the balcony looking at the view and chatting about something or other. So, whilst a little bemused at so surreptitious an invitation, he followed Aurelia out of the room.

Aurelia led him to a door and swiped her 'A' fob against the door panel. She opened the door and walked through. Ian followed, still not knowing what to expect.

They emerged into a large bedroom, complete with a huge luxurious double bed, a sofa and two large double wardrobes.

"Allez-y, ouvrez l'armoire," Aurelia instructed, turning her back and walking into the bathroom.

Ian's knowledge of French was rudimentary at best, but he got the gist of her request – to open her wardrobe. So, he walked up to the nearest one and opened the door. It was full of slinky dresses, ladies' negligees and shoes – but mostly shoes.

Being somewhat confused about what he was supposed to be looking for, he turned in the direction Aurelia had been walking, intending to ask her what it was she wanted him to get.

He caught a glimpse of Aurelia in the bathroom, standing before the mirror in a state of semi-undress, and quickly averted his eyes. Well, perhaps not *that* quickly.

"I think you should choose one, mon commandant," Aurelia called out from the bathroom. "Or, alternatively, I do have something special in my collection that I could give you? I'm just changing into something more comfortable and I'll be with you in a moment."

Bemused and a little embarrassed, Ian responded: "I think you need to explain what you want."

Aurelia, now fully clothed — in a black jacket, short skirt and black leather thigh-high boots — walked back into the room. "Pas celui-là, idiot," she laughed. "The *other* wardrobe!"

Ian walked over to the second wardrobe — which was a large standalone one — and opened both doors. He found himself looking at wall-to-wall guns: dozens of pistols, revolvers, rifles and submachine guns.

"This is my private Solarian gun collection — but, non, you can't have my antique French musket. You *are* firearm trained, je pense, non?"

"Yes, of course — but why do you think I need to carry a gun?" he asked.

"You can't be too careful. I'm not suggesting that you carry a rifle around, so choose a revolver that you would be comfortable with."

"However," Aurelia added, opening a drawer next to her bed and pulling out a gun, "I also recommend this — an Uzi. It has a 32 round magazine and is capable of semi-automatic or fully automatic fire, up to a maximum effective range of 150 metres."

Ian took the Uzi, and Aurelia handed him a small briefcase designed to hold the gun, along with a few magazines. The case also contained a silencer.

"Keep this in your room," she said.

He selected a small revolver from the wardrobe. Aurelia opened another bedside drawer and rummaged around until she found a suitable shoulder holster and some ammunition cartridges.

Ian put on the holster and secured the gun — fully loaded, but with the safety catch on.

"D'accord," Aurelia said, "You're all set now."

Aurelia then took her jacket off and picked up a shoulder holster – complete with some sort of handgun – and put it on. She also strapped on another holster around her thigh. She opened her handbag and took out a 'mouse gun'. The gun was smaller than the palm of her hand, being just over 4 inches by 3 inches in size.

Aurelia put this gun into her thigh holster. "It's a semi-automatic and it doesn't have a safety lock, so be careful if you ever pick one up. The only safety mechanism is its 11-pound trigger – so you need to squeeze it very firmly."

"Okay, Aurelia," Ian said. "You understand you report to me now, right?"

"Oui, commandant," she replied.

"So, how about you tell me what's going on – and why we now each have more guns than most armed guards?"

"There's not much to tell," was her answer. "This is just a precaution. But I work on the basis that I assume that the enemy knows everything we would want to keep secret – who we are, where we are and what we are doing, including the purpose and location of the Hearing.

"Then, on that basis, I consider the possible motives an enemy might have. Rebecca's powers as your deputy are only provisional – meaning she can act on your behalf only if you are temporarily unavailable. But if you were killed or incapacitated and unable to act as the Solarian Representative, Rebecca would not be permitted to take over on a permanent basis.

"This would inevitably lead to the Hearing being postponed or cancelled. If the IGC believed the Mekbudans were responsible – or if we were able to prove it – then the case would be dismissed. However, the Mekbudans could refile their petition and, unless the greenhouse gas emissions rate stops increasing, the IGC would be obliged to grant another hearing.

"On the other hand, if the perpetrators were unknown – or it couldn't be proven that the Mekbudans were involved – then the Hearing would simply be postponed by one calendar year. That would allow enough time to appoint another Solarian Representative and complete all the necessary preparations for a new Hearing.

"So, they could be any number of 'interested' parties with a motive to kill you. Perhaps a rival Mekbudan tribe with a grudge against Gulinrog – or maybe someone on Earth who has discovered what's happening. Imagine if one of the Solarian superpowers found out about this – do you think they might quite like the Hearing to be delayed?

"Anyway, this is why I want you armed and why you shouldn't go anywhere you don't have to go – like the rest of the hotel. Rebecca is less at risk, but what if they kidnapped her to gain leverage over you?

"I won't mention any of this to Rebecca – I'll leave it to your discretion, as to how much you tell her."

"Okay, I now see your point. Thanks. I'll have to think about what I share with Rebecca," Ian replied.

"In the meantime," Aurelia said, "I've changed clothes, as I'm going to make the rounds of the hotel and check everything is in place for the delegates' arrival tomorrow. I'll report anything important back to you, of course – and I'll see you at lunchtime."

They walked out the room and Aurelia bid farewell, as she left to go into the main hotel.

Ian went to his bedroom and put the briefcase into a drawer near his bed, before returning to the lounge to find Istariol and Rebecca.

Chapter 16

Rorcmog was really *'pissed'*. Not in the British English sense – meaning *drunk* – but in the American sense: *annoyed*. In fact, Rorcmog was *really, really,* pissed.

As captain of a Mekbudan warship – a *Xolak*-class destroyer, no less – and its sole owner, he believed he should have some control over his own life. His vessel, 55 metres in diameter (roughly three-quarters the length of a jumbo jet), had nearly six times the mass of one of those puny Antarian *Tay*-class ships.

But now, his sodding father – Gulinrog, Patriarch of their tribe and the self-declared 'owner' of Earth – had ordered him to shut down his tantalum mining operation in Central Africa. In fact, all mining on Earth was to cease for twenty Solarian years, starting May 2025.

Rorcmog's tail lashed with frustration at the very thought.

This order had been made twenty years ago, but Rorcmog had only learnt of it twelve years ago – when he returned to normal space in the Solar System. His father owned and operated quite a few mines himself, but most of the Mekbudan mines on Earth had been leased out to members of his family – in return for a 'cut', of course.

So Rorcmog had dutifully given the order to his team to be ready to pack up all the valuable equipment – and as many of the mining crew as possible – since they would have to leave before the deadline of 11 May 2025. He had then left Earth to skip forward in time to 2025.

So here he was, back on Earth the day before the deadline – only to find that repetitive breakdowns of the robot workers, combined with a series of poor yields of tantalite ore, had meant that the mine had failed to hit its production targets. Unfortunately, IGC's Directive 9 prevented them from using nanobots or other advanced Mekbudan technology.

True Artificial Intelligence – sentient intelligence – is forbidden by the Mekbudan constitution. Millions of years ago, an AI in control of most of their war machines, starships and weapons systems rebelled. The resulting civil war nearly wiped out the Mekbudan civilisation. Since then, sentient AIs have been strictly banned – on pain of death. Only basic, non-sentient AIs are permitted to control their ships, robots and mining systems.

As far as Rorcmog is concerned, this is a foolish and outdated law. The Antarians, for example, have one major advantage over the Mekbudans: they trust their sentient AIs and rely on them extensively – including for their starships.

However, non-sentient AIs are not reliable enough to make good decisions when things go wrong. They are also not very proactive. The Mekbudans regularly leave their mines to their own devices for twenty years at a time; they have to be entirely self-sufficient. Of course, no Mekbudan is willing to waste their time by staying on Earth to supervise, so the work has to be done by the foreman and the other slaves.

Uma, his mine's foreman, is human – an ex-slave who is now a *freeman* – and he receives ten percent of the profits. But now Uma will get nothing for his twelve years' work, as there is no profit. Anyway, that's Uma's problem – a reward for not keeping the 'bots' working properly. And Gulinrog's cut is not a simple percentage share of the profits; it includes a minimum annual payment, so the operation will actually be making a loss on this trip.

Not only that – but, somewhat predictably – there's not enough room on his ship for everything of value. Heavy mining equipment, robot workers and Vegan slaves are a precious commodity – as is Uma, the mine's foreman – but nearly all the human slaves will have to be left behind.

Rorcmog intends to travel to Delta Pavonis next – the nearest Mekbudan colony – 20 light-years away. Once his ship reaches the outer reaches of the solar system – somewhere where there are virtually no gravitational forces – he will be able to engage the warp drive and *'jump'* to the Delta Pavonis star system, and it will only take a couple of Solarian days to get there.

"So, Uma, have you carried out my orders?" Rorcmog demanded. Rorcmog had ordered all but three of the human slaves to be executed, to ensure none of them would betray the location and nature of his mine.

All slaves and ex-slaves, including the foreman, have a brain implant installed which is impossible to remove without killing the person. The implant contains a small explosive powerful enough to kill the slave if it self-destructs – but it would just look like an aneurism if it did, as nothing of the device would survive to prove suspicious. Alternatively, the implant can be made to stimulate the host's pain receptors, without physically damaging the slave. So a runaway slave could be forced to crawl their way home to stop the excruciating pain.

"Yes, your highness," Uma replied, bowing. "I triggered implants. And I got one of the mfanyakazi robotis to dig big hole and throw bodies in," he added, in broken Mekbudan mixed with Swahili, flashing a crooked gap-toothed grin.

Rorcmog was in the middle of interrogating Uma about the progress of loading the ship when the speakers came to life, interrupting him. It was the ship's irritating non-sentient AI control system – which he had named *'Xurek'*, meaning *'stupid one'* in Mekbudan.

"Captain, two of the three remaining human slaves have died," Xurek reported. "It appears one slave is female and the other two were male – and the men fought over who was to have the woman, sir. Before a robot could intervene, one man stabbed and killed the other, only to be attacked from behind by the woman, who managed to inflict a fatal wound. So only the woman is alive. Shall I arrange for the bodies to be disposed of, sir?"

"Oh, that's just great – it gets better and better! Send the female to my quarters – I will interrogate her there. But be careful handling her – it seems she has a sting in her tail!" Rorcmog ordered. "And, yes, of course you need to get rid of the bodies, Xurek."

Rorcmog longed to replace the dead slaves by abducting more Solarian humans, but he knew it wasn't worth the risk of breaking that damned IGC Directive 9.

Then Xurek started speaking again. "Captain, a Mekbudan spaceship is approaching sir," Xurek announced. "It looks like it will touchdown just outside the mining settlement in 2.7 minutes."

"What the hell's going on," Rorcmog asked rhetorically.

Xurek answered anyway: "The spaceship is descending at 61.5 km per hour, sir. It is predicted to land 97.3 metres away from the ship. And I have just received a coded message to say that the ship is under the command of Krognák and he wishes to come aboard your ship."

"Oh, just great – that's all I fucking need," Rorcmog exclaimed. Krognák was the head of his father's secret police. And, to add insult to injury, Krognák was a bloody human. Rorcmog considered his father to be utterly obsessed with humans. Why Gulinrog had decided to assign a *Homo sapien* to such an important position was beyond him.

"Uma, go and meet him when he comes aboard – and bring him directly to my quarters," he ordered. "And Uma..." Rorcmog waited until Uma turned back towards him. "Say nothing at all to Krognák – about *anything*," Rorcmog ordered. "If he even speaks to you, just say you are to bring him to my bridge – and nothing more. *Understood*?" Rorcmog was glaring at Uma, his tail twitching furiously and his horns were flushed crimson red – always a dangerous sign.

"Of course, your greatness," Uma assured him, bowing as low as he could.

Rorcmog had caught a glimpse of Krognák once before, when visiting his father's palace on Delta Pavonis. Rorcmog had secret ambitions of inheriting his father's position as Patriarch one day – and Krognák's new position of power unsettled him.

Krognák was clearly a Mekbudan name, not a human one, so it was obvious he had adopted it. But when Rorcmog tried to dig into Krognák's background to uncover why Gulinrog had recruited him, he found nothing. It was as if the man hadn't existed before his appointment as head of the secret police. Not even a *'classified'* or *'top secret'* entry showed up in the database – simply nothing.

And there was something else very strange. In every photograph or video Rorcmog could find, Krognák was either facing away from the camera, or his face was completely indistinguishable. It was as if Krognák were a ghost.

Rorcmog's thoughts were interrupted again by another announcement from Xurek. "Captain, Krognák has boarded the ship and Uma is escorting him here. The other vessel has now lifted off and is in the process of leaving the area, sir."

"*Oh, it gets even better,*" Rorcmog thought, "*the bastard thinks he's going to stay aboard my ship. Well, this'd better be good.*" He could think of nothing better than to be able to abandon Krognák to his own devices in the middle of the African bush.

Rorcmog composed himself, tucking his tail out of sight behind his desk in the command centre, as he waited for Krognák's arrival.

"Guten Tag, Kapitän," Krognák said, a thin, calculated smile on his lips. He wore the stark black uniform of Rorcmog's father's secret police, the fabric pressed to perfection, and he wore thin rimless spectacles. Rorcmog knew that, almost the moment he'd taken over the agency, Krognák had ordered the redesign of every uniform – a clear declaration of authority.

And no one needed to wear spectacles these days – not even Solarians – with a wide range of optical corrective technologies readily available. So, the glasses were clearly just an affectation.

Rorcmog seethed inwardly at Krognák's audacity in addressing him in German, rather than Mekbudan, but he refused to give him the satisfaction of showing it.

"Good afternoon, to you," Rorcmog replied, smiling broadly. "And to what do I owe the pleasure of your company?"

"Please ask your ship's AI to access the last transmission my ship sent over," Krognák replied. "At the end of the message there is an encrypted attachment – and I will now decode it for you." He drew out a mobile phone and tapped on it a few times.

"You will see that your father, Gulinrog, has ordered you to temporarily hand control of your ship over to me. You will remain as Kapitän, of course, but I need to take overall command, as we have a very important mission to attend to." Krognák's thin smile remained in place, as if it had been painted on.

"Your father has forced the IGC to hold a three-day hearing in central Paris, starting Friday, 30th May," Krognák explained. "The purpose of the hearing is to determine whether the Solarians are so irresponsible that they will inevitably trigger catastrophic global warming. The hearing will take place on board *your* ship – and *I* will lead the Mekbudan prosecution.

"Your father has given up on the Solarians. *When* – not *if* – they trigger runaway global warming, it will devastate the planet for millions of years. Not even our technology will be able to reverse it for ages. They have to be stopped."

"Are you telling me I can't leave for Delta Pavonis?" Rorcmog demanded. "That instead, I've got to hang around on Earth until the end of the month? That's days away! And then I'm supposed to take my ship to central Paris to host some stupid hearing? What am I supposed to do – park my ship next to the bloody Eiffel Tower?" Rorcmog's plan to remain calm was clearly not going very well.

"Your father sends his love and asks that you appreciate the importance of this mission," Krognák replied, smoothly. "Which is why he sent me." This time, Krognák's smile was ever so slightly more pronounced. "I will explain the plan for the Paris hearing in due course."

"However, you should know that the result of the hearing is a foregone conclusion – the IGC *will* grant us the right to create an impact winter by crashing an asteroid into Earth. Moreover, Mein Kapitan, your father has bestowed that honour on *you*. You will be the one to carry out the extermination of life on Earth. And, in order for you to achieve that, after the hearing you will need to travel to December 2027 and await further instructions."

"Fucking great," Rorcmog thought. *"Now I'm even more delayed. Not only do I have to host some bloody trial, I also have to take my ship forward to 2027 and crash an asteroid into the Earth. After that, it'll be twenty years of impact winter before I can finally import replacement slaves, replant crops, and re-establish my mine. Thanks very much, Dad. Love you too."*

Rorcmog's actual response was: "What a great honour, sir. Xurek, please ask Uma to show our guest to his quarters. Please excuse me Krognák, but I have to attend to the loading of my ship. Uma will be happy to arrange for any refreshments you may require."

Once Uma arrived, Krognák bade him farewell with a curt "Lebewohl," giving him a salute in a manner which Rorcmog found rather peculiar, then turned sharply on his heel and walked out.

"Did you manage to get a clear picture, Xurek?" Rorcmog asked.

"Yes, captain." Xurek brought up a photograph on the main display of the ship's bridge.

"Great, so now I've finally got a picture of the Head of my father's Secret Police," Rorcmog thought.

[4]

"Oh... I didn't bother mentioning it before," Xurek admitted, "but we received various news items when we arrived back in the Solarian system a few hours ago. Apparently, Krognák has renamed the agency as the *'Gestapo'*."

"Ok, you bastard – now I'm going to find out who the bloody hell you are!" Rorcmog declared, to no one in particular.

Chapter 17

Ian was not a happy bunny. He still had no idea how they were supposed to present a credible defence at the Hearing, and the survival not only of the human race but of practically every species on Earth now rested squarely on his shoulders. Well – almost every species. Ian was not a great fan of cockroaches; given that they had survived one extinction event 66 million years ago, they would no doubt survive another.

And Aurelia had just told him that if any of Earth's governments found out about the Hearing and Ian's role, they would be more likely to assassinate him to buy themselves time than offer any kind of support.

However, he had the germ of an idea – and it would be interesting to see how much it aligned with Istariol's thoughts. After all, Istariol did start planning this a year ago.

The first thing, Ian thought, was to harness those things which he did have. Like a sentient AI with access to the world's internet and capable of hacking into even more databases, coupled with computing systems far more powerful than any quantum computer on Earth.

And a whole bunch of climate change scientists *were* assembling right here for the next three weeks or so.

He had been told that he had a US$250 million budget – but, no doubt, a fair chunk of that must have already been spent on paying the workshop delegates, hiring the hotel and the submarine and buying that ocean-going cruiser.

But what if Alexa were to mine some more Bitcoin? All the delegates had been told that an anonymous donor was prepared to stump up US$5 billion – but this was just a cover story.

What if they *were* to actually put up this amount of money and really fund these projects? Perhaps, that would allow them to put up some sort of defence at the Hearing?

These thoughts were running through Ian's mind as he made his way back to the lounge where they had eaten breakfast, to rejoin Istariol and Rebecca.

"What have you been up to?" Rebecca asked with a smile.

"Oh, you know... Aurelia wanted to show me her etchings – well, no, actually her gun collection," Ian replied with a grim smile. Seeing the quizzical expression on Rebecca's face, he added: "Ask me about it later."

Ian sat down opposite Istariol. "Alexa, I have some questions for you."

"Of course," was her reply. "How can I help?"

"I believe you said there are currently over one million un-mined Bitcoins. How many would you need to mine to get 5 billion dollars' worth?" Ian asked.

"As of today, Saturday 10th May, 2025, approximately 1.15 million Bitcoins remain," Alexa replied. "The price can be quite volatile, but one Bitcoin is worth about $108,000 today. So, in round numbers, 50,000 Bitcoin would need to be mined – and sold – to build up a fund of 5 billion dollars."

"So, here comes the million-dollar question – or five billion to be more precise," Ian thought – and he couldn't think of a better person to ask.

"Okay, let's assume a 5 billion dollar budget was available to fund a number of projects," Ian said. "After all, that's what the workshop delegates have been told. Of course, these projects must aim to significantly reduce the greenhouse gas concentration in the atmosphere."

"Which type of projects would you fund to get the biggest impact – and please include projects that involve carbon capture, as well as those that reduce the emissions rate?"

"The answer *is* somewhat complicated," Alexa replied. "Can I suggest that you all reconvene in the private projection room and I will put up some text on the big screen?"

As they walked towards the projection room, Istariol said: "You're thinking along the right lines, but don't expect a simple answer. After all, this *is* why we've organised this workshop."

They took a seat in the projection room and Alexa brought this up on the screen:

> With a **US$5 billion budget**, you could fund a portfolio of high-impact projects aimed at both reducing greenhouse gas emissions and enhancing atmospheric carbon removal. The most effective strategy would be to diversify across proven and scalable technologies, while also investing in promising innovations.

Global Climate 5 Year Strategy (2025 – 2030)
with 7 Strategic Priorities:

1. **Industrial-Scale Reforestation & Ecosystem Restoration** (~$1,000m)
   > Why: Reforestation is currently one of the most cost-effective and scalable carbon sinks.
   > Impact: 5-20 tonnes CO_2 per year per hectare sequestered.
   > Targets: Tropical reforestation (e.g. Brazil, Congo Basin, Southeast Asia), peatland and mangrove restoration.

2. **Grid-Scale Renewable Energy Acceleration** (~$1,250m)
   > Why: Reducing reliance on fossil fuels is essential; renewable energy displaces emissions permanently.
   > Use: Seed-fund solar, wind and battery projects in rapidly developing countries.
   > Mechanism: Public-private partnerships and low-interest infrastructure loans.

3. **Direct Air Capture (DAC) and Carbon Storage** (~$750m)
   > Why: One of the few scalable technologies to remove CO_2 directly from the atmosphere.
   > Targets: Fund early-stage DAC companies and invest in geological carbon storage hubs (e.g. Iceland, North Dakota).
   > Cost: Currently $300 – $600 per tonne CO_2; falling with scale.

4. **Methane Reduction Initiatives** (~$500m)
   > Why: Methane is over 80 times more potent than CO_2.
   > Focus: Methane leak detection & sealing in oil/gas infrastructure and agricultural methane reduction (e.g. feed additives for livestock).
   > Impact: Immediate reduction in warming potential.

5. **Electrification & Energy Efficiency in Cities** (~$750m)
   > Why: Urban areas drive over 70% of global emissions.
   > How: Electrify bus & delivery fleets, retrofit large buildings for energy efficiency and fund district heating / cooling systems.
   > High 'Return On Investment' in emissions saved per dollar spent.

6. **Agricultural Transition & Soil Carbon Projects** (~$500m)
   > Why: Agriculture contributes 20-25% of GHG emissions.

> How: Promote regenerative agriculture, reduced tillage, covering crops to protect the soil from erosion, and fund biochar programs to lock carbon into soils.

7. **Advanced R&D and Climate Innovation Grants** (~$250m)
   > Purpose: Support breakthrough ideas with transformative potential (e.g. ocean alkalinity enhancement, algae-based carbon capture, synthetic photosynthesis).
   > Format: Competitive grants, prizes, university and start-up support.

Combined Impact:
   > Short-term: Methane and urban electrification.
   > Medium-term: Renewable energy, agriculture, reforestation.
   > Long-term: Direct Air Capture and innovation.

Estimated Outcomes (by 2030)
   > **5 million hectares** of forest restored and protected.
   > **10 million tonnes CO2 per year** removed via Direct Air Capture and soil sequestration.
   > **Methane emissions reduced** by 40-50% in targeted sectors.
   > **Renewable electricity access** expanded to over 25 million people.
   > **150+ cities** benefit from electrification and urban decarbonisation.
   > **50+ breakthrough technologies** piloted or commercialised.

"Wow. I'm no expert, but that looks pretty impressive to me," Ian exclaimed.

"So, is that it, then? We spend our time at this workshop categorising all the delegates' project proposals and slotting them into this strategy – and then we have a plan we can present at the Hearing?"

"I did say it wasn't that simple," Istariol replied. "Alexa, please can you give us the estimated impact all this would have on Earth's global temperature?"

"By 2030," Alexa replied, "this strategy could potentially deliver a total reduction of about 100 to 150 million tonnes of CO_2 equivalent per year.

"However, global emissions in 2023 were about 57 Gigatonnes of CO_2 equivalent each year – that's 57,000 million tonnes. So, this strategy would only reduce annual emissions by about 0.20% to 0.25%.

"So, whilst 5 billion dollars *is* substantial, it is a fraction of the trillions needed globally to shift the climate trajectory," Alexa concluded.

Feeling quite crestfallen, Ian asked: "Okay, but what about if you mined pretty much all of the remaining Bitcoin – say one million of them – and raised **100 billion dollars** for these projects. What could that achieve?"

"Firstly, it would not be that easy to liquidate – in other words, sell – that number of Bitcoin," Alexa explained, "because it would flood the market and cause the price to drop dramatically. It's a bit like the reason why diamond companies can't sell all of their assets in one go – the diamond price would drop, if supply significantly exceeded demand.

"But if we set that issue aside," Alexa continued, "increasing the budget twentyfold to a hundred billion dollars would require far greater coordination – with governments, multilateral institutions and global investment banks. That level of funding demands a huge organisational effort. I can go into more detail about that later, if you'd like?

"However, even with a 100 billion dollar budget, the strategy could not halt climate change on its own. It would only reduce emissions by 3 Gigatonnes of CO_2 equivalent per year – and reduce global warming by an estimated 0.06°C to 0.12°C."

"So, we're totally screwed then?" Rebecca asked.

Ian turned to Istariol and said "Perhaps I'm asking the wrong questions? Do *you* have a plan?"

"Yes, but this is only work in progress. We'll need to improve and refine it over the next twenty days. And there are other ways we could raise 100 billion dollars, not just by mining Bitcoin, so we *can* use that figure as the working assumption for our level of funding.

"Alexa, please can you display our draft defence strategy," Istariol asked. A new page appeared on the screen.

Defence Strategy: The Case for Mankind's Redemption

1. Acknowledgement and Accountability
> Begin by **openly acknowledging** the failings: delays in responding to rising emissions, fossil fuel dependency, deforestation and political inaction.
> Demonstrate that many **nations and leaders now accept the science** of climate change and the need for urgent action.

2. Evidence of Progress

> Describe our fully-funded **$100B global strategy** as a committed, cooperative action plan, aligned with the **Paris Agreement**.

> Present clear **data trends** showing:
  - Rapid global **growth in renewable energy** (solar, wind, storage).
  - **Declines in coal** use in many economies.
  - Massive **reforestation** efforts and protected zones.
  - Rise of carbon markets and **emissions regulation**.

3. Technological Capacity and Adaptation

> Emphasise global adaptation programmes that support **vulnerable** communities and ecosystems.

> Highlight **breakthroughs** in:
  - Direct air capture and other forms of **carbon removal**.
  - **Methane** leak detection and containment.
  - **Sustainable** agriculture and lab-grown meat.

4. Moral and Cultural Awakening

> Stress the **growing cultural and generational shift** toward climate awareness.

> Introduce written testimony from youth leaders, indigenous communities, scientists and artists showing **global consciousness** and moral urgency.

> Note the rise of **climate litigation**, showing democratic systems beginning to hold governments and corporations accountable.

5. Commitment to Planetary Stewardship

> Propose a **binding planetary charter** to be adopted by Earth's nations to:
  - **Ban geo-engineering** without international oversight.
  - Set a **timeline to net-zero** and beyond (into net-negative).
  - Include Earth's biosphere in all future economic systems as a **stakeholder**.

6. Appeal to the Tribunal's Leniency

> Ask that a young civilisation should be **given guidance, not punishment**, when their survival is at stake.

> Argue that **Solarians are not beyond redemption** – but at an inflection point – and that we can now prevent catastrophe.

"However, we believe that we face three significant difficulties in this approach," Istariol explained.

"The first is this: will we be able to assemble enough tangible projects that can actually be put into action as part of a 100-billion-dollar programme? We expect the output of the workshop to address that.

"The second one is potentially solvable – that such a large programme will require a body of some sort to implement. One without the corruption that we have seen rife in some large not-for-profit organisations. Either you will have to run it, Ian, or you will need to find someone else capable and honest enough to become CEO.

"But the third and biggest problem is the lack of any agreements that are binding at a national level. This aspirational *'Commitment to Planetary Stewardship'* treaty is just pie in the sky. The Paris Agreement has no teeth – it's not binding – and there are no penalties for failing to meet any of the targets. Worse still, the largest contributor to human-caused climate change has recently walked away from the Agreement.

"The United States of America is the biggest emitter in history. In 2023, it was also the world's second-largest emitter of greenhouse gases, at 6.3 Gigatonnes of CO_2 equivalent per year, accounting for 11% of global emissions.

"Directive 9 prevents us from proving to the USA – or any other government on Earth for that matter – that mankind is under threat of extermination.

"So, everyone just carries on as normal," Istariol continued. "People elect leaders who promise to solve immediate problems – high prices, lack of jobs and high taxes – or the perceived threat of immigration. Meanwhile, they dismiss massive hurricanes, devastating forest fires and other signs of planetary distress as nothing more than the 'new normal' for the weather.

"Democratic governments focus on whatever will keep them in power and win the next election. Authoritarian regimes do whatever their 'president for life' believes is in their own best interests. Russia might even benefit from some global warming in the medium term – perhaps Mongolia could become the new 'breadbasket of the world' as temperatures rise."

"Yup, we *are* totally, completely screwed!" Rebecca confirmed.

Ian declared it was time for a break – and lunch beckoned. They were, after all, in France, in one of the most luxurious hotels in Paris, and French food was among his all-time favourites.

Alexa informed the Majordome and asked for menus to be brought and they moved into one of their private dining rooms. Aurelia joined them and they all sat down for lunch.

"How did your morning go, Aurelia?" Ian asked. "A bit better than ours, I hope."

"Everything is in order – we are as ready as we can be, mon commandant," Aurelia replied with a smile. "I do have one request though; I would like to requisition one of the bedrooms in the Apartment for the use of my local security team. I know I have guards stationed at every entrance, including at the entrance to the elevator – and they *do* have quarters elsewhere in the hotel. But I would be more comfortable, if we could have some of the team close by."

"Okay, but this may need to be on a temporary basis only – as we have yet to decide what to do with the four spare bedrooms," Ian replied.

"Well... Istariol has just identified the three key issues that we've got to deal with," Rebecca interrupted. "So, there you go."

"The three remaining bedrooms in the Apartment should be assigned to three leaders, each of whom will take charge of one of these tasks," Rebecca continued.

"One leader will be responsible for choosing the projects for the 100-billion-dollar programme.

"One leader will handle the selection of a CEO for the organising body and plan the Global Coordination Strategy.

"That leaves one more leader – he or she will focus on what the hell we can do about Earth's national governments and their lack of binding commitments.

"Aurelia gets the last room for Jacques and her local security team."

"Istariol, with Alexa's help – in addition to advising us all, of course – you should focus on how we present everything at the Hearing.

"Ian's in charge, of course, so he'll need to oversee the entire operation.

"And I..." Rebecca concluded, with just the hint of a grin, "...I'll just be the pretty face. I was thinking of going clothes shopping."

Ian looked at Rebecca, clearly astonished. But he recognised how well his logical approach, paired with her intuitive insight, worked – they made a good team.

"Okay, that sounds like a plan then – so be it," he announced. By now, the waiters had poured the drinks they had ordered.

Ian picked up his glass and held it high. "To us – Alexa, Istariol, Aurelia, Rebecca and me – the *'five musketeers'* – and to our success," he toasted.

Chapter 18

Over lunch, Aurelia told them that once a Leader was appointed, they should not use their real names when speaking about them or to them. This was to protect everyone's identities and guard against any information leaks. The list of delegates was being kept secret, of course, although this was likely to be quite a challenge, as some of the delegates were bound to know or recognise one another.

Any enemy who learnt of their role in this programme may well decide that one or all of the Leaders are *'persons of interest'*, given their importance. It would be difficult for Aurelia to protect all of the Leaders' families, wherever they might be – and if any of them were kidnapped or threatened – this would clearly compromise their position. A Leader might even be coerced to become an informer and spy on the programme.

Once appointed, a Leader – and anyone staying with them at the hotel – would move into one of the bedrooms in the Apartment – so they can be better protected.

"The delegates will be told that this is no ordinary workshop," Aurelia explained, "given the five billion dollars of seed money up for grabs, and the fact that we'll be making a film of both the workshop and the mock trial. This will be the cover story to explain why the delegates are to remain anonymous.

"So, Rebecca," Aurelia continued, "it was your idea to appoint these three Leaders, perhaps you can suggest some codenames for them?"

Rebecca had seen the Quentin Tarantino film *'Reservoir Dogs'*. "How about we base the codenames on colours?" she suggested.

The others thought this was a good idea and, after some discussion, the codenames were agreed.

'Professor Green' would be the codename of the Leader responsible for selecting the greenhouse gas reduction projects.

'Lord White' would be responsible for nominating candidates for the role of CEO – people with excellent contacts with governments, the world bank, International Monetary Fund, Non-Government Organisations and venture capitalists etc.

'Doctor Blue' would be responsible for their blue-sky initiatives – focused on securing firm commitments from governments. Influencing and manipulating voters, lobby groups, activists, and other stakeholders

through social media and various alternative communication channels was expected to be a central feature of these projects.

"I think you'd make an excellent '*Mr Black*', Ian – and Rebecca, you could be '*Ms Silver*', if that's okay with you both?" Aurelia suggested.

There were no objections.

"Ian, I'd like to move Jacques and a few other members of the security team into the bedroom that's been allocated to them in the Apartment."

Ian agreed, and Aurelia added, "Okay – please excuse me; I'll need to go and get that sorted out now."

After Aurelia had left, Ian, Rebecca and Istariol decided to head to the Projection Room.

They began poring over the CVs and project synopses submitted in advance by the delegates, searching for the most promising candidates.

It was far too early to select the three Leaders they would need, of course – the delegates weren't even due to arrive until tomorrow. But there was no harm in reviewing the profiles and provisionally assigning each to one of the three categories. They also made note of anyone particularly compelling by marking them as a 'favourite'.

After about an hour and a half, they heard Alexa's voice from the speakers above them, "Ian, I'm afraid we have a situation," she reported. "Aurelia has gone missing. Jacques, her Head of Security, is on his way to report what's happened."

"What do you mean: '*gone missing*'?" Ian demanded of Alexa. "I thought you were in constant contact with Aurelia?"

At that point, the door opened and Jacques burst in. "It looks like Aurelia has been kidnapped, sir," he exclaimed. "I found this in the carpark near our elevator."

He opened his hand, and in it was a black key fob with a golden '*A*' embossed on it.

"And this..." he said. He opened his other hand and a small 'mouse' gun nestled in his palm.

Ian recognised the gun as Aurelia's. "Yes, that's hers," Ian confirmed.

"Two bullets have been fired, as there's only four left in the magazine – and there's gunshot residue on the muzzle," Jacques said.

"Oh my god, why would have they taken Aurelia?" Rebecca asked.

"Ian, I *am* in contact with Aurelia," Alexa interrupted. "She's been kidnapped, but is unharmed. I have her exact position – she's in an abandoned building about 25 kilometres away. She's been disarmed and is being restrained in handcuffs."

"I also found this on the floor of our elevator," Jacques said. He handed Ian an envelope. It was not sealed. Inside was a folded piece of paper.

Opening up the paper, Ian saw a message written using letters cut out and pasted from a newspaper:

'IAN, IF YOU WANT HER TO LIVE, BRING US A MEMORY STICK WITH 500 BITCOIN ON IT. COME ALONE AND UNARMED – OR SHE WILL DIE.'

Underneath were what were clearly map coordinates, assembled from small numbers cut from a newspaper.

"They *have* given you the correct address," Alexa said. "It's a derelict car factory about 3 kilometres north of Aulnay-sous-Bois – about half an hour's drive from here."

"Istariol, if you would like to put your spare memory stick into the USB charging socket next to your seat, I will download 500 Bitcoin onto it."

Istariol reached into his jacket pocket and pulled out a USB stick. He plugged it into the socket.

"That's all done," Alexa confirmed after a few seconds.

Istariol took it out and handed it to Ian. "I don't like the fact that they want *you* to go, Ian. And I don't recommend that you go alone, so I suggest you take Jacques with you," he said.

"With your permission, I will stay here with Rebecca and the rest of our security team," Istariol advised. "There's a possibility that this is just a diversion and they'll attack us here whilst you're gone."

"I'm not sure we should split our forces. Shouldn't we all go – and you can be my backup while I go inside alone?" Ian suggested.

"I have appraised the tactical situation, sir," Alexa replied. "I can see and hear everything Aurelia can, and they haven't bothered to blindfold her. They will be watching your approach and, if you go in 'mob-handed', they may well kill Aurelia and open fire on you all.

"I believe surprise is our best weapon here. I can let Aurelia know of your approach and she may be able to make a diversion. Jacques can hide in the back of the car and follow you in, keeping to the shadows."

"Okay, I'll take your advice then. But should I really be unarmed or should I take one of Aurelia's mouse guns in a concealed holster?"

"I can't see any harm in you doing so," Alexa replied. "If they search you and find it, they'll just take it off you – and you won't be any the worse off. It might even make them a bit complacent, knowing you've been disarmed."

"Five hundred Bitcoin – fifty million dollars' worth – seems like a strange ransom," Ian mused. "Why would they think we've got that kind of money lying around? Unless they know we've been mining Bitcoin... in which case, why not demand even more?"

"And, Istariol, I agree, it seems very strange that *I* was named in the note. Who knows my name or even knows that I'm here?" Ian asked, somewhat rhetorically.

"Anyway, I do have one more question, Alexa," Ian said. "Aurelia was already at the factory when you first told us she'd been abducted, so surely she'd been missing for at least half an hour. If you're in constant contact with her, why wasn't I alerted the moment she was attacked?"

"That's a fair question, sir," Alexa replied. "I lost contact the moment Aurelia entered the elevator – it acts as a Faraday cage and blocks all electromagnetic signals. And when she emerged into the underground car park, it's too deep for a signal to reach her."

"So they attacked her in a comms blind spot. But why didn't you regain contact when she was driven out of the car park by her abductors?"

"Cars can also function as a Faraday cage, especially if they've been deliberately modified – by using metallic paint in the tinted windows, for example.

"I regained contact with Aurelia when her kidnappers took her out of the car, upon reaching the warehouse – and immediately reported it to you, sir."

That did make some sense to Ian, but he was less than impressed to find that the underground car park was a blackout zone for their communications.

"Surely, these aliens with all their advanced technology could have put in a system of wireless LAN repeaters around the car park?" Ian thought. *"This must have been an oversight. If we manage to get Aurelia out of this mess, I'm going to have to have a word with her about this."*

But he said nothing more on the topic.

"Okay, let's go," he ordered. "Jacques, get someone – not you – to bring a car round to the elevator. I'm going to Aurelia's quarters to get a mouse gun and holster – and I'll meet you at the top of the elevator. Alexa, will my key fob work on Aurelia's room?"

"Actually, sir," Jacques said. "Take mine. It only really works at point blank range, and I'm going to have to stay back in the shadows."

He unstrapped his thigh holster and gun – and handed it over to Ian. It was the same make and model as Aurelia's, but with a silver coloured grip.

With that, they both walked to the entrance to the elevator.

"The car will be there in about two minutes, sir," Alexa said. "The driver will put the map coordinates into the car's navigation system for you. He will also position the car so that Jacques can enter the back of the car directly from the elevator."

"Oh and, yes, your key fob would actually open Aurelia's room, sir."

They went down in the elevator and Jacques surreptitiously got into the back of the car and laid down out of sight. Ian walked round to the other side of the car. The car's driver had got out and was holding the driver's door open for him. The engine was still running.

With a nod and a curt "thank you", Ian got into the car and, after checking the car's sat-nav was set to the right destination, gunned the engine and roared out of the car park.

The navigation system had selected the A3 route. It was nearly 4 o'clock, but the afternoon rush hour in central Paris doesn't usually start until 5pm, so he made fairly good progress – and it was about half past four when they arrived in the area.

In front of the car stood a large gate, presumably marking the entrance to the industrial site where the derelict car factory was located. A sign hung from the gate on rusted chains, reading 'Privé – Interdit,' which Ian's rudimentary French told him meant 'Private – Keep Out.'

"Do you think I should proceed on foot and reconnoitre the area?" he whispered to Jacques, without turning his head.

"No, we have to assume they're watching the area," Jacques replied. "If you get out of the car now, I won't easily be able to follow you. It's hours before sunset, which won't be until about quarter past nine."

The gate didn't actually seem to be locked, despite the sign. Ian wondered if that had been arranged by the kidnappers. So, he got out of the car and pushed the gate to one side, its hinges creaking ominously.

Getting back into the car, he drove further along the road until the car announced, with an American accent: *"You have arrived at your destination, which is on the right."*

Looking to his right, Ian could see a rundown building with a rusty metal door standing slightly ajar.

"Okay, here we go," Ian thought as he stepped out of the car and walked around the hood toward the door. A faint *click* sounded behind him – probably the car's back door opening. He didn't dare look. One wrong glance and he'd gave the game away.

Ian opened the metal door, which squeaked noisily on its hinges, and stepped through – only to be confronted by his welcoming party: three goons in French berets, two of them pointing pistols at him.

"Check him," ordered the guy in front, who was clearly their leader. He spoke in English, with a slightly Eastern European accent, Ian thought.

One of the other guys came over and frisked him. Ian then caught sight of Aurelia. She was sitting on the ground, with her back propped up against a wrecked Citroen car. Ian could see her hands were handcuffed and her legs had shackles on them. She was also gagged, but was clearly alert – as she looked directly at Ian and nodded her head slightly.

Inevitably, the goon searching him found both the gun and the USB stick and, after walking back to the leader, handed them over to him.

"You've now got what you want – release the girl and we'll be on our way," Ian demanded bravely, thinking this really didn't look like that was going to happen.

"First, we have to check that the Bitcoins are on the stick," the leader replied, handing it to the second goon and pocketing Ian's mouse gun.

The second guy pulled out of his jacket what looked a bit like a credit card scanner and plugged the USB into it.

Ian then noticed something strange. The leader and the other goon *had* been looking in his direction, but he saw that they were now looking slightly over his shoulder, presumably at something behind him.

Although he thought he could be falling for the oldest trick in the book, Ian turned around to the left to see what they were looking at. He was quite surprised to see Jacques standing there holding an assault rifle in the general direction of the goons. Jacques was hardly being subtle – and yet the goons had not started shooting.

Jacques then turned towards Ian and – without saying a word – raised his rifle, aimed straight at Ian's chest, and fired two shots in quick succession.

Things seemed to happen in slow motion. Ian felt two tremendous blows to his chest and was flung violently backwards onto the ground. And yet, as he landed on what should have been hard concrete, it felt more like falling onto a soft mattress.

The wind had been knocked out of him and he was struggling to breathe, but he didn't feel any pain – presumably the adrenaline, Ian thought.

Still lying flat on the ground, Ian raised his head to look at Jacques – who was now returning his gaze with a quizzical expression on his face. Jacques raised his rifle again, this time pointing at Ian's head. Ian heard what he thought were scuffles and some grunts and groans coming from his right, just outside his peripheral vision, but he couldn't take his eyes off Jacques and the rifle.

Then Jacques's head exploded. As Ian stared, a high-powered bullet tore through Jacques's temple from the left-hand side and exited on the right, taking a large amount of skull and brain matter with it. This was accompanied by the roaring crack of a single gunshot.

Looking slightly to his left, towards where the bullet must have come from, Ian saw that a hand – seemingly disembodied – was suspended in mid-air at chest height, gripping a massive pistol. Probably a Smith & Wesson Model 500, Ian thought instinctively. The hand protruded from the sleeve of a jacket, but there was no arm, no body – just a hand floating in empty space holding the weapon.

Then, like static clearing from a broken signal, the air shimmered. The illusion dropped.

Istariol stood in its place – calm, composed, hat tilted just so – his arm still extended, the gun steady in his grip, still smoking.

The sounds of commotion to Ian's right suddenly ceased. Turning his head, he saw Aurelia holding two pistols – probably taken from the goons – levelled at their leader. Nearby, one of the goons sat on the ground, cradling what was clearly a badly broken arm, given the unnatural angle at which it hung. A few feet away, the second goon – the one who had been using the credit card machine – lay flat on the ground, rubbing his throat and struggling to rise. On the ground beside the car lay a set of handcuffs and shackles – both snapped clean in half.

"Qui t'a payé pour faire ça?" demanded Aurelia, looking at the guy with the broken arm.

"I don't know anything, I just..." the goon replied in English.

They never found out what he *'just'* did or didn't know, because Aurelia shot him clean in the centre of the forehead, killing him instantly.

She turned to the second goon. "Alors, que peux-tu me dire?" she asked.

"Ils étaient anonymes – nous devions recevoir le Bitcoin en récompense," the man replied, having managed to get to his feet, looking like he was about to bolt.

A second shot echoed through the deserted factory. Once again, a single round left a neat hole in the centre of the man's forehead – and he slumped to the ground, dead.

Aurelia then turned to the third man – their leader – and said, "As-tu quelque chose à me dire?"

The man stood calmly, gazing at her without emotion. "I work for ФСБ – the Federal Security Service of the Russian Federation – you know it as the FSB," he said, in what Ian now realised was a Russian accent. "I have information I think you'll find interesting – provided, of course, that you let me live."

Chapter 19

"I thought *I* was going to rescue you, Aurelia, but it looks like it was the other way round," Ian observed.

They were in their black limousine, heading back to the Apartment. Istariol was driving and Aurelia and her Russian captive were sitting in the back, facing Ian.

After the Russian FSB agent had offered information in exchange for his life, Aurelia had taken a small oval disc, about the size of a Blue Peter badge, and pressed it onto the Russian's neck. He had stiffened and stood to attention, his eyes staring straight ahead.

Aurelia had explained that the device was now controlling his body movements, and that his vision and hearing were locked into a virtual-reality scene of their choosing. He was unable to see or hear anything happening in the real world. Aurelia then directed the device to frog-march him into the car with them.

Aurelia hadn't bothered to find the USB stick before they left. "There's no Bitcoin on it – it's just blank," Aurelia said. Aurelia had asked Istariol what to do about the bodies and he'd told her to leave them as a message to whoever had commissioned her abduction and Ian's murder.

"Are you guys going to tell me what on Earth's going on," Ian said. "What happened to the agreed chain of command – why is Aurelia asking Istariol for instructions, when she's supposed to be reporting directly to me?"

Istariol answered from the driver's seat. "We *did* agree that Aurelia would become your direct report, but the unspoken caveat was – *providing* that did not endanger your life. In the situation that we found ourselves in, we had to prioritise your safety."

"Fine, so tell me what just happened," Ian demanded.

"One of our spies came across certain information," Istariol explained, "which led us to believe that our team had been compromised. Aurelia came up with a plan, which I approved, to find out whether we had a mole – and who it was. We had to use you as the bait, so we had to bypass the chain of command and keep you in the dark."

Interrupting, Aurelia said, "I gave a different piece of information to each of our three security guards, and another to our Head of Security, Jacques – namely, where we had a communications weakness and where someone could abduct me without immediate detection. Then I went to each location in turn, deliberately offering myself as bait, to see what happened.

"I was actually attacked from behind in the underground car park – by Jacques. He captured and bound me, took my key fob and my guns. He even fired two shots from my mouse gun – so he could show it to you later – to make it seem more realistic that I'd been ambushed by an unknown enemy and tried to fight back. His co-conspirators – the three crétins you met – were waiting nearby and they bundled me into their car and drove at speed to the derelict car factory."

"Wasn't that rather risky? They could have injured you," Ian asked.

"Perhaps, but they needed me alive to get you to come out to see them – and bring the fifty million dollars in Bitcoin – which, it seems, was actually to be their payment for the job. Anyway, it seemed pretty likely that this mission had *not* been organised by Gulinrog's people – there were no signs of any advanced technology – so we were always going to have the advantage."

"Ok, but what happened when we got to the factory?" Ian enquired. "How did Istariol appear from nowhere, brandishing one the world's most powerful handguns? And how did you get your cuffs off and neutralise those three goons?"

Istariol answered, "We've determined that, under Directive 9, we're permitted to explain this – as you *do* have a need to know. Aurelia, please tell Ian how we did it."

"Okay," Aurelia replied, "well, firstly, we have personal cloaking devices – which, like our ship's cloaking system, work best in low light. The field only extends about half a metre from the torso, so if you pull out a gun and point it, your hand and the weapon will appear to materialise out of thin air, while your body remains invisible."

Aurelia then reached forward in her seat and touched something on Ian's collar. Suddenly, a shimmering light surrounded Ian's body. And looking through the light field was like looking through net curtains.

"You can see yourself, because you are inside the field, but I can no longer see you – apart from your hands that is, as you haven't got them tucked in close to your body," Aurelia continued.

"And you didn't tell me this before… because?" Ian asked, with some exasperation. "And how do I turn this on and off?"

"You *can* ask Alexa," she replied. "So, for example, '*Alexa, please turn Ian's cloaking device off*'." The shimmering light disappeared.

"Actually, the top button on your shirt is the manual control – turn it clockwise or anticlockwise to switch the cloaking on or off. We know you never fasten your top button when you're out of uniform, so it seemed a good place to put it.

"We didn't tell you this because, for this operation, you didn't need to know. We could have activated your invisibility cloak remotely, if it had become necessary.

"Anyway, when the car pulled up outside the Apartment's elevator to collect you, unbeknown to the driver, Istariol was already sitting in the passenger seat with his cloaking device enabled. He stayed in the car until both you and Jacques got out at the derelict factory, then quietly followed you. The cloaking device does dampen some of the sound you make when walking, although you still have to tread carefully.

"Istariol knew Jacques must be our 'mole', but we needed to confirm exactly what his intentions were, before taking action. When he shot you, at almost point blank range, he sealed his fate. As you witnessed, Istariol then killed him.

"You were perfectly safe, of course, as the other device we have installed on all of your clothes, is a force-field shield generator. It acts in a similar fashion to a bullet proof vest, except that it protects your entire body, including your head. Not only did it deflect the bullets Jacques fired at you, it also cushioned your landing when you fell backwards from the force of the bullets. Handy little devices, I'd say – I had to turn mine off when I was trying to get abducted, of course.

"Finally, I ordered my nanobots to eat away at my handcuffs and shackles, leaving just a wafer-thin layer of metal, so I'd be able to snap them with ease at the slightest force whenever I wished.

"And I am a black belt in both karate and jiu-jitsu, so disarming those crétins was a piece of cake."

"They never really stood a chance, did they – the whole time?" Ian commented.

"Never give away any advantage that you don't have to. Always engage your enemy from a position of strength," Aurelia replied.

"Doesn't Directive 9 forbid you from using all this advanced technology in front of Solarians?" Ian inquired.

"The devil is in the detail – Directive 9 requires us to use native Solarian technology *wherever* possible. In this case, we had to use some of our advanced Antarian devices to ensure your safety. And, as for Solarian witnesses, they're all dead – apart from him," Aurelia said, nodding in the direction of the Russian. "And he's coming with us."

"So, what are you going to do with him?" Ian enquired.

"We'll construct a suitable virtual reality simulation – to make him think he is meeting his 'handler' to give a debriefing. I doubt we'll get much more information – but it might reveal how the Russians got wind of this. Perhaps one of Gulinrog's rivals tipped them off – or even explicitly hired them to do this."

"Do you know why Jacques betrayed us?" Ian asked.

"Simple greed, I'm afraid. He was very careful with his communications, so even though we were monitoring them, we're not entirely sure who contacted whom first – but we do know he thought he was going to get the fifty-million-dollar ransom. We doubt the *crétins* would ever have let him keep it – in fact, they most likely would have killed him."

"Hmm. I guess congratulations are in order then – for a well planned and executed operation," Ian remarked.

"There's just one more thing – that communications blackout zone in the car park..." Ian's sentence trailed off as he saw Aurelia smiling at him, with just the hint of a smirk.

After a short pause, he said, "There isn't a communications blackspot in the car park, is there? Alexa was actually in constant contact with you the whole time, wasn't she?"

Aurelia just kept smiling, although Ian thought her smile was getting almost imperceptibly wider.

Chapter 20

After that, they were quiet for the rest of the journey back to central Paris and their Apartment.

Ian reflected on everything that had happened in the last forty hours or so, since he had met Istariol. Despite his unasked-for role – to try to save mankind and almost all life on Earth – it seemed that everyone was trying to kill him, including the Russian spy sitting opposite him.

He just hoped the next 48 hours were going to go better but, somehow, he doubted that.

They arrived at the hotel car park just after 5.20pm – traffic had been heavier on the journey back in, as the rush hour traffic had become heavier. Apparently, Saturdays and Sundays were even worse than weekdays for some reason, presumably because of all the tourist attractions.

As they stepped out of the elevator into the Apartment, Aurelia said, "I've just received a report from Alexa that I think everyone should be briefed on. May I suggest that, after a short break, we all meet in the main lounge – the one with the grand piano – at, say, 6.30pm?"

Istariol then added "I've arranged for dinner to be served at 8pm. But I think we'll have enough time for the briefing, before we eat."

Ian went off to find Rebecca, while Aurelia marched their captive away.

Rebecca was sitting on the balcony, taking in the views of Paris. When she saw Ian, she got up and rushed over, giving him a big hug.

"Alexa had let me know that you were in very safe hands," she said, "and that Istariol had secretly gone with you. But I was worried, of course. At least until Alexa told me that Aurelia had been rescued and everyone was safe."

"Yes, but it was more like Aurelia rescuing me, rather than the other way round," he replied. "Anyway, I need a drink, so let's sit down and order a bottle of Chablis – and I'll tell you all about it."

Ian and Rebecca arrived in the grand piano lounge a minute or two before 6.30pm, carrying their drinks and the remainder of their bottle of wine in its ice bucket.

Aurelia and Istariol were already there, also enjoying some pre-dinner drinks.

Once everyone was comfortably settled, Aurelia began the briefing.

"We've received a report from one of our spies. I can't reveal who they are or where they're located, as they're still working undercover.

"The first item they have sent us appears to be the name of a location – Isla de la Pasión.

"There are two islands on Earth with that name," Aurelia said. "One is a small island at the North end of Cozumel in Mexico. The other is a French coral atoll in the eastern Pacific Ocean, also known as Clipperton Island.

"However, given that Cozumel is in the Yucatán Peninsula area...," Aurelia continued, "...well, I think you can see where this is going.

"The second piece of information is a set of numbers." Aurelia passed a tablet over to Ian and Rebecca.

On the screen the numbers displayed were:

10:38 / 25.12.2027 / 666 / 20.55, −86.86.

"The first sequence looks very much like a time and date – 10.38am on 25th December 2027.

"We're quite convinced that the last pair of numbers are map coordinates. Twenty point five-five degrees north and eighty six point eight-six degrees west lies just a fraction off Isla de la Pasión in Cozumel.

"So this implies that they've chosen Cozumel as the impact site – and that the asteroid will crash into Earth on Christmas Day, 2027," Aurelia speculated.

"Symbolism is an intrinsic aspect of Mekbudan culture," Istariol interjected. "I would imagine they deliberately chose Christmas Day for the impact, as they consider the nations where Christianity is widely practised to be most at fault for the current level of greenhouse gases in the atmosphere."

"How can that be?" Rebecca asked. "China has to be the worst culprit by far – aren't they responsible for one third of all global emissions? They're not Christians."

"You're right," Istariol replied. "China's emissions do account for about thirty per cent of the global total. But their emissions per person are only about two-thirds of those of the USA.

"And if you look at the historical record, the West has emitted far more than the emerging nations – the USA in particular is the largest historical emitter of greenhouse gases."

"Anyway, if I can continue with the briefing," Aurelia said, "we don't know what the '666' means, but it's an important number to the Mekbudans, as it represents the structure of their empire – the number of Realms, Clans, and Families."

"There are six Realms, or kingdoms, in the empire, each represented by a different colour of the rainbow. Each Realm is made up of six Clans led by a Chieftain, and each Clan has six ruling Tribes. Hence, 6-6-6 represents their empire."

"But there are seven colours in the rainbow," Rebecca protested.

"Not according to the Mekbudans," Aurelia laughed. "They've divided the visible spectrum into six colours. Makes sense to me – I never did get my head around the difference between blue and indigo.

"Incidentally, Gulinrog is the Patriarch of the most influential Tribe in one of the Clans in the *Blått* – or blue – Realm, although he's fairly low down in the pecking order of the empire as a whole.

"Anyway, the final piece of information given to us by this spy was this symbol."

Their tablet now displayed this.

[5]

"We've previously wondered what asteroid the Mekbudans might use," Aurelia said. "Well, this symbol was used in certain frescoes in the tomb of Ramesses the First, in the Valley of the Kings in Luxor, Egypt.

[6]

"It depicts Apophis, the 'Lord of Chaos' – the ancient Egyptian deity who personified darkness and disorder, standing in opposition to light and to *Maat*, the principle of order and truth. His greatest adversary was the sun god Ra, bringer of light.

"The symbol our spy found looks remarkably similar to that of Apophis," Aurelia said. "So we now believe the Mekbudans intend to crash the Apophis asteroid into Earth. It makes a lot of symbolic sense – using an asteroid the Solarians named after a god of darkness."

"What we don't understand, though, is that Apophis is a relatively small asteroid – about the size of the Empire State Building – and not large enough to cause an impact winter lasting long enough to extinguish life on Earth. It would probably just cause some regional destruction and only partially block out sunlight for a year or so."

There was a short pause, as everyone thought about this conundrum.

And then Alexa announced, "I know how they're going to do it!" A new image appeared on their tablets.

"This shows the position of Apophis and the inner planets on Christmas Eve, 2027," Alexa explained. "Apophis and Earth are at the top of the screen.

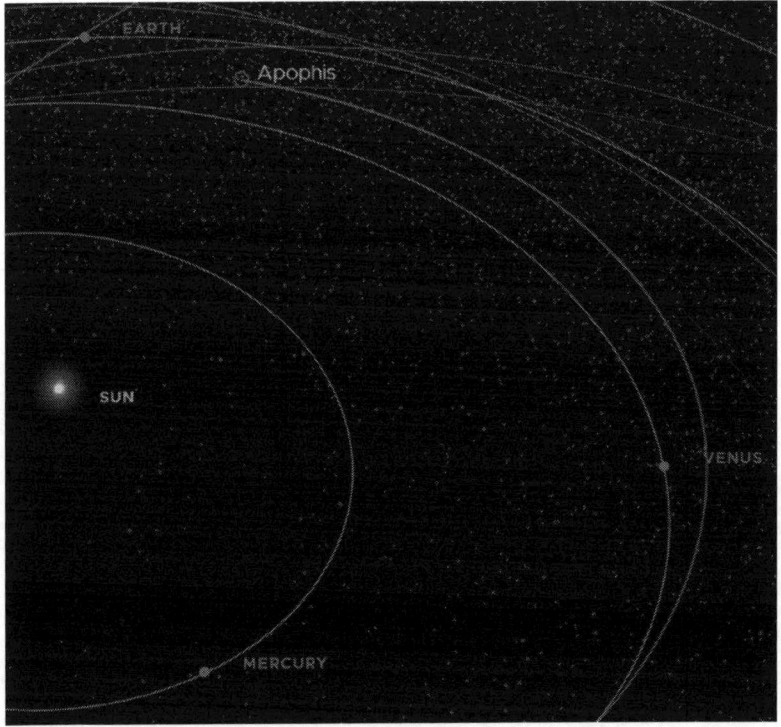

[7]

148

"Apophis's orbit follows a path similar to Earth's," Alexa continued, "except that it completes one revolution around the sun a little faster than Earth – in 324 days – and crosses Earth's orbit from time to time. It travels slightly faster along its orbit – about 30.7 kilometres per second – compared to Earth's 30 kilometres per second.

"I'm showing you where Apophis and Earth will be on this particular day, because Apophis will almost be at its closest point to Earth in this orbital period – about 43 million kilometres away.

"As I mentioned earlier this morning, Apophis will come extremely close to Earth's surface – just 32,000 kilometres – on Friday the 13th of April, 2029. That's over fifteen months later than December 2027. Based on the intelligence from our spy, the Mekbudans have clearly decided they don't want to wait that long.

"A small asteroid like Apophis could still cause mass extinction if it were travelling fast enough to compensate for its relatively low mass. A full extinction event doesn't necessarily require as much energy as the Chicxulub impact – even ten percent of that energy could trigger a catastrophic impact winter, global firestorms and widespread species collapse.

"I now believe I understand what the '666' means," Alexa continued. "The Mekbudans plan to accelerate Apophis to 666 kilometres per second. At that speed – over 100 times faster than a speeding bullet – it would generate approximately eleven percent of the energy released by the Chicxulub impact. That's equivalent to roughly twelve million megatons of TNT – 220 times more powerful than the largest thermonuclear device ever detonated by the Solarians."

"That does make sense," Istariol noted. "The Mekbudans would relish the symbolism of the number that defines their empire – 666 – being the velocity, in kilometres per second, at which the instrument of destruction, Apophis, is travelling. Especially since kilometres per second is a Solarian unit of speed."

"That must require a massive amount of energy. Do the Mekbudans have the technology to do this?" Ian enquired.

"I'm afraid so," Istariol replied. "As the asteroid is one of the smallest ones near Earth, its relatively low mass will make it somewhat easier."

"To achieve that velocity, the Mekbudans could apply a constant acceleration of around 50% of Earth's gravity. Apophis would then reach

666 kilometres per second, covering the 43 million kilometres to Earth in approximately one day and nine hours – impacting near Cozumel sometime on Christmas Day," Alexa concluded.

"Okay, so now we know their plans – we'd better make damn sure we stop them," Ian said grimly.

Chapter 21

They all met up for dinner at 8pm – which was another sumptuous affair. Afterwards, as usual, they retired to sit in the lounge.

"There's one more little titbit that our spy gave us," Istariol announced over coffee.

"The Mekbudans – Gulinrog, in fact – anonymously donated a sizeable amount of money to Donald Trump's re-election campaign funds."

"Really? Why would he have done that?" Rebecca asked.

"Gulinrog has given up on the Solarians," Istariol replied, "and now wants to rid the Earth of them. He wanted to get Trump re-elected because he knows what his views regarding climate change are – and how much Trump believes in *increasing* US fossil fuel production – to make 'America Great Again'. With Trump re-elected, it will weaken our defence at the Hearing.

"It seems that Gulinrog has decided it's inevitable that humans will destroy the planet unless they are stopped. And since there are now so many Solarian settlements worldwide, it's becoming increasingly difficult for the Mekbudans to keep their mining operations secret in order to comply with Directive 9.

"They now plan to repopulate the Earth – after the impact winter ends – with selected crops and animals, including humans from other planets. They plan to use huge transport spaceships for this. They believe that dealing with lower-technology Solarian societies will make it easier for them to be manipulated. They are harking back to the days of the ancient Aztec, Egyptian and Roman civilisations, where life for the Mekbudan gods was simple and very fruitful."

"Oh, and by the way," Aurelia interrupted, "our Russian FSB friend has now reported to his superiors.

"The Russians don't know a thing about the Hearing or your true role in all of this, Ian. They'd received a tip-off telling them that Ian was a US or NATO agent collaborating with the Ukrainians, feeding them intelligence on the Russians and training them on cyberwarfare techniques.

"This tip-off most likely came from a Mekbudan, but the trail goes cold and there's no proof of their involvement. It's highly unlikely to have been any of Gulinrog's people, though.

"And Jacques must have had the sense to keep his mouth shut – he was just trying to collect a bounty for killing you.

"As for the Russian, he's seen too much for his own good. We'll arrange for him to get shipped off Earth to one of our rehabilitation centres on an Antarian world. He's actually a very lucky man."

They ordered another round of drinks and chatted quietly among themselves for a while.

"Hi," Alexa said. "I've had quite a few messages from your friends and relatives. I'll forward all of their communications – along with my responses – to you both, so you can look at them. If either of you would like me to text or call someone with a message from you, just let me know. I'm sorry I have to act as the go-between, but those are the rules," she added apologetically.

Ian and Rebecca decided to retire for the night and spend an hour or two reading through the messages from their loved ones. They said their goodnights and headed to their room.

The next morning, Sunday, Ian and Rebecca walked into the private dining room to find that Istariol and Aurelia were already there, just finishing off their breakfast.

"Bonjour. I strongly recommend these croissants – the chef pâtissier has excelled himself today," Aurelia said between mouthfuls.

They took their seats, immediately going for the coffee, drawn by the irresistible smell.

A few croissants later, Ian asked, "So what's the plan for today?"

"Well, before we go over that, Alexa has uncovered more information about the FSB," Aurelia replied. "She hacked into their computer database and found the records linked to their mission to assassinate Ian. It appears there were at least two cells – teams independently tasked with the same mission. She then marked the mission in their database as 'completed' and uploaded a photo of Jacques's dead body, taken at the time – with almost nothing left of his head – as evidence of Ian's death.

"In addition, Alexa has altered the records to make it appear that the FSB operative we captured has gone undercover on another mission – so he won't be missed for a while.

"So we've done everything we can to neutralise the FSB threat, but we'll need to continue to take the normal precautions. As to what we do today, that's up to you," Aurelia concluded, looking at Ian.

"Ian, you do have the final say, of course," Istariol interjected, "but I think it may be a good idea to take a break. The delegates will be arriving throughout the day, but it would be best to let them settle in – I see no point in engaging with them today.

"And you and Rebecca have had a lot to deal with in the past week. In my experience, a day off can actually improve mental efficiency. As most of the major Solarian religions say, the seventh day is holy and set aside as a day of rest."

Ian was still worried about all the work they would need to do in the coming days, but his experience of managing projects in the military made him inclined to agree with Istariol. He'd seen marines being trained to push well beyond normal tolerances, but even the highly trained performed more efficiently when not driven to extremes.

"I agree – 'day at leisure' for all then," Ian ordered.

"Excellent. Aurelia, do you fancy a swim?" Rebecca asked.

"Good idea," Aurelia responded. "I've got a few things to sort out first, but I'll join you in about half an hour."

"I'd just like to go over a few things with you, Istariol," Ian asked. "I'll catch up with you later," he added, looking at Rebecca.

A little later, Rebecca and Aurelia met in their private swimming pool and soon found themselves racing each other through the water.

After their swim, they showered, got dressed and went out onto one of the balconies. They ordered some soft drinks and another pot of coffee and settled down in their chairs admiring the views of the Parisian landscape.

"So tell me, what's it like for Istariol and yourself – living on a spaceship and jumping through time?" Rebecca asked curiously. "Don't you have families that you're leaving behind?"

"Istariol and Alexa are the only family I've ever known," Aurelia replied, "apart from the foster parents who raised me in medieval France – but they're long dead, of course.

"It's not easy making friends or building deeper relationships – like trying to keep a long-term lover – when you never know when you'll have to skip forward in time again. So yes, for me it's a lonely life. You have to take every opportunity to live it to the full."

"Oh, but I thought you and Istariol were an 'item'? Didn't I see you go into his room last night?" Rebecca replied.

Aurelia gave a wry smile. "Istariol is like a father to me. He nurtured me while I was growing up in France – as often as he could, whenever he was on Earth. So no, we're just very good friends and colleagues.

"In fact, Istariol is in love with Alexa – and it's mutual."

"*What*? But Alexa is a *machine*?" Rebecca exclaimed.

"I can understand those unfamiliar with sentient AIs thinking that way. But no – Alexa is a person, with full Antarian citizenship rights. Just because she wasn't born in a flesh-and-blood body doesn't make her any less so. She fell in love with Istariol years before he ever reciprocated."

"Yes," Rebecca said. "I'm sorry – I didn't mean to suggest that I don't think of Alexa as a person; I do. I meant, how is this physically possible?"

"It wasn't me you saw going into Istariol's room last night – it was Alexa. Or, more specifically, Alexa inhabiting a cyborg body.

"There is a type of cyborg we call 'synths' – almost entirely flesh and blood, and indistinguishable in appearance from the species it's modelled on: human, Antarian, or even Mekbudan. But the body itself isn't sentient. Its brain does little more than keep its organs alive and regulate basic functions such as eating, drinking and exercise – everything required to maintain its health.

"We implant a non-sentient AI to control the body, so it can walk, talk, and obey complex verbal or transmitted commands. But they're just machines. Very popular in the sex industry, apparently.

"The best synth bodies, grown from specialised DNA, can take 16 years or more, depending on the species, to reach maturity – though that's not really a problem if you're skipping ahead through time.

"Alexa is able to take over a synth body and, in addition to controlling it, she'll see, hear, smell, taste and feel everything the body experiences. That allows her and Istariol to have a normal physical relationship."

"Wow! Okay – it's a bit mind-blowing, but I can see how it would be good for them both," Rebecca admitted.

"Yes. I understand that for Solarians the concept is unusual. We're simply more accustomed to distinguishing between non-sentient bodies and machines – and sentient AI people.

"And, by the way – with my permission – Alexa could take full control of *my* body. Of course, this wouldn't be appropriate for her intimate 'meetings' with Istariol."

"Really? But *you're* not a synth, are you?" Rebecca asked.

Aurelia laughed. "Of course not. I've just had some implants added that would allow Alexa to take control."

"Hmm. And when that happens, are you awake, or do you effectively go to sleep?"

"Normally I'm fully awake – I simply know that Alexa and I are both experiencing everything together. But I can choose to go to sleep if I want – which is useful when I've been awake too long and Alexa still needs my body."

"This is all just too weird for me," Rebecca exclaimed. "Why would Alexa need to use your body – and why did you even agree to have those implants fitted?"

"Istariol's life isn't easy – his mission involves monitoring Mekbudan compliance with Directive 9, counter-espionage, and constantly skipping forward through time. He rescued me from Roman slavery and I wanted – still want – to do something to repay him.

"There are undercover missions where all three of us – Istariol, Alexa and I – have to go, but we have to operate as a 'couple'. Without my implants Alexa couldn't join us except in a synth – a third body – which wouldn't work in those scenarios."

"Okay, I suppose that makes sense," Rebecca admitted.

"But what about you? Are there male synths aboard the ship?" Rebecca asked with a gentle smile.

"Yes, there is one – Alexa uses it occasionally for reconnaissance missions where a man is needed. Why – would you like to borrow it?" Aurelia replied, deadpan.

"No, of course not! I was asking about you, given that you've no long term partner. Don't you miss the touch of a man on your long space missions? If these synths are as good as you say they are, then wouldn't they be able to satisfy you – despite not being sentient?"

"Yes, at one level – and I think it's perfectly okay to sleep with a synth. But it's a matter of preference. I just find it simpler and just as satisfying to use other methods," Aurelia replied with a sly smile. "I reserve the touch of a man for occasions where I'm with a real person – a sentient male.

"Anyway, talking about real men – you've not told me anything about your relationship with Ian," Aurelia observed.

"Hmm. Well, understandably, he's been very distracted since we first came across your ship. And he's under a lot of stress – as am I, to be fair. I don't think it's quite the right time to judge, but it certainly could be better."

"What about before?" Aurelia asked. "How do you feel about living separately – in different countries?"

"It's hard. I think of my apartment I own in Reading as 'ours', even though it's in my name only. It's the one place we've both worked to make feel like our home.

"You'll know, of course, that my job is based in London and Ian rents an apartment in Odenton, near his base at Fort Meade.

"So I only get to see him when I take holiday and visit him in the US, or when he's on leave and comes to the UK. Occasionally, like now, he comes to the UK on business.

"I don't have a Green Card or work visa, so I'd have to give up my job if I wanted to live with him in the States. If we *were* living together, Ian could sponsor me for a Green Card even if we didn't marry – but once I got it, I'd still need to find a new job."

"… Or have children," Aurelia remarked.

"I'm not sure either of us is ready for that level of commitment," Rebecca replied. "And Ian could be posted to another Navy base anywhere in the world, which only adds to the complications."

"So, do you enjoy your job? Would you look to get a similar job in the US, if you went to live there?"

"Although I work for a global bank, I doubt it would have a suitable position for me in the States – especially in Maryland. The bank cut back its physical presence there significantly when it sold its US retail banking business in 2021.

"But, yes, I *do* enjoy my job. I work in anti-fraud in consumer banking. It's often heartbreaking to hear the stories from customers who have been scammed – although some do qualify for compensation. My role is mainly educational – running campaigns designed to spread awareness about scams and how to avoid them.

"As I'm sure you know, even with our 'non-sentient' AI, scammers can mimic people's voices – well enough to call their relatives and trick them into handing over thousands of pounds on some pretext or another. And often, a quick phone call to the relative supposedly in need of money would have shown they knew nothing about it."

"Yes – and people put so much information about themselves online," Aurelia replied, "on social media and job sites like LinkedIn, that AI can stitch it all together into very convincing conversations."

They sat in silence for a few moments, then Rebecca said, "Well, as it's a 'day at leisure', I'm going to order a bottle of wine from the Majordome."

"Allow me," Aurelia replied. "Alexa, please can you order a bottle of Chablis and two glasses – we're on the Ravel suite terrace."

"So, where did you two meet?" Aurelia asked.

"Ian was at a conference in London and decided he wanted more than the companionship he was getting from his male colleagues and the other delegates – so he registered on a dating app. I'd recently split up with my boyfriend and thought I'd play the field, so I was registered on the same app. We both swiped right and ended up on a date.

"When he's relaxed and at ease, he's great company – funny and, of course, highly intelligent. You're not really thinking ahead when you first meet someone you like; you're just buzzing with excitement. So when he invited me on a second date, I jumped at it.

"After we'd finished the main course at dinner, he invited me to his room, saying that he'd order some more wine from room service – and that his hotel did a very good cheese platter. Let's just say that I have never seen Ian eat so little cheese," Rebecca concluded with a broad smile.

At that point, the waiter arrived with the wine, ice and glasses, which he set down and poured.

Sipping her Chablis and gazing at the fabulous view, Rebecca contemplated what her life had become – and what the future might hold.

"The thing is, this all seems so trivial compared to what's happening now," Rebecca said. "If I assume we *can* save the world and everything stays as it is – no one will even know what we've done. I think I'll lose my job through my continued absence… so what am I going to do?"

"It's not really my place to say," Aurelia replied. "But you're never going to have to worry about money again. Directive 9 regulations recognise that representatives – or, in this case, both representatives – of any civilisation required to defend themselves against such an accusation will have their lives completely disrupted.

"Therefore, after all this is over the IGC will provide you both with a pension. It's an index-linked annual payment, which will rise each year in line with inflation in the country where you live. You'll each receive five million pounds sterling per year, paid monthly, for the rest of your lives."

"Oh my God!" Rebecca burst out. "How come I'm only finding out about this now?"

"I probably shouldn't have told you – but you asked. I think the policy is not to tell representatives too early in the process, so that they focus on winning the case, rather than thinking about what happens afterwards."

"That's an amazing amount of money – and you're right, we won't have to worry about money ever again. So, Ian and I can do what we want after this – retire, set up a business together, or maybe even have children."

"Oui," Aurelia responded, with a smile.

"Well, I do think it's better if I don't distract Ian from the task in hand – there *would* be a lot to think about, as we'll have a lot of options. So, unless he asks, I won't tell."

"Okay, fair enough," Aurelia replied. "So, changing the subject, what do you want to do today? We're right next to the Louvre, if you haven't been before."

"Perhaps another day. What about you showing me all these famous Parisian shops?"

At that point they heard voices and Ian and Istariol stepped out onto the terrace.

"Oh, I *see*. You girls are already drinking wine and relaxing, whereas us guys have been working all morning without a drop to drink," Ian protested, tongue in cheek.

"It's supposed to be a 'day at leisure', so you shouldn't have been working anyway," Rebecca protested.

They drew up some chairs and sat down with them, ordering two more glasses and another bottle of wine.

"So what have you two been up to? I thought you were supposed to be going swimming?" Ian asked.

"We *did* have a swim. Aurelia let me win every race. I was exhausted – she's clearly much fitter than I am. I'm going to have to make full use of our private gym while we're here," Rebecca said with a grimace.

"Rebecca is being far too modest," Aurelia chuckled. "But I imagine we'd all benefit from a little time in the fitness centre, judging by the amount of fabulous food they serve here."

"Anyway," Rebecca cut in, "us 'girls' are going to go shopping. Do you two want to come?"

Ian pulled a face – he hated shopping, unless it was online.

"Is that really a good idea, Aurelia?" he asked. "I thought you advised against leaving the Apartment on security grounds? Besides, I thought most shops in Paris were closed on Sundays?"

"Some *are* closed," Aurelia replied, "but many of the large and famous stores are open. We'll take a couple of guards with us and go in one of the limos. You can't come to Paris and not go shopping – tu ne penses pas?"

Ian looked at Istariol, who simply shrugged. "I'm sure Aurelia can look after them – and I doubt anyone would try anything in such a public place."

Ian considered joining them, but given that he was a much bigger target than Rebecca, he thought his presence might make things worse.

"Okay, *I'm* going to hit the gym before lunch, so you go ahead. I assume you'll get something to eat while you're out?" he said.

The conversation turned to shopping – whether to head for the Champs-Élysées or Boulevard Haussmann, or both. There were plenty of Parisian luxury department stores to choose from. Aurelia was convinced she hadn't provided Rebecca with enough shoes – despite two full rows of them in Rebecca's wardrobe – and so shoe shopping was added to the agenda.

When Rebecca left for the bathroom, Aurelia turned to Ian. "I'm sorry, with Rebecca around, I didn't get a chance to warn you in advance about the shopping trip. I'm not sure how much you've told her about the overall threat situation.

"We know there's another FSB cell," Aurelia continued, "who may or may not have found the fake information we planted in their computer system about your death. I'd like to see if I can pick up signs of them. Better to find out now if they're still active – rather than when they've infiltrated the hotel once the conference begins. Rebecca *will* be safe – she'll be wearing a portable force-field – and it won't just be the guards keeping watch."

"Okay, but I need to be part of the decision-making process before you announce things like shopping trips without my approval. I've told Rebecca the general nature of the threat, but not the full details."

"Oui. Do you give permission to proceed with this mission, sir?"

"Only on the condition that you relay all available information to Alexa, and she briefs me and keeps me updated in real time. I'll stay here and monitor the situation from the projection room. I'll want to know exactly how this outing is going to be supervised. And I'm not going to tell Rebecca now – she'll act more naturally if she doesn't know."

They heard Rebecca's footsteps returning to the terrace.

"Okay, I'm leaving you in Aurelia's capable hands. Enjoy yourself. I don't suppose there's any point in saying *"don't spend too much"*, since I'm sure Aurelia will remind us it won't make a dent in our $250 million budget," Ian said, laughing.

"Well, she'll have to pick up the bills, because I know *my* credit cards won't cover it," Rebecca replied.

Aurelia took Rebecca by the hand and led her away to prepare for their *expédition*.

"I just hope this doesn't turn out to be a big mistake," Ian remarked, looking at Istariol.

"In my experience," Istariol replied, "trouble rears its ugly head when you least expect it – not when you're actively looking for it. And if it's only an FSB cell we're dealing with, then they're quite likely to underestimate us, given how little they know about our technology.

"However, if any of Gulinrog's rivals are behind this, there's always the risk they've provided Mekbudan technology to the assassins. Illegal, of course – but if it points the finger at Gulinrog, they may consider it a risk they're happy to take."

"Anyway, come on. I'll join you in the projection room – we'll monitor this together. The ladies will be leaving soon."

With that, Istariol stood, and the two men strolled back into the reception room, carrying themselves as though they hadn't a care in the world.

"So much for a day at leisure," Ian thought.

Chapter 22

Once Ian had familiarised himself with the details of the surveillance operation – and had spent an hour or so watching the live video feeds on the projection room screen – Istariol persuaded him to leave the room.

"Alexa is more than capable of monitoring all the feeds simultaneously and will alert us the moment anything suspicious is spotted. So let's go and get something to eat," he suggested.

Despite Ian's concerns, the shopping expedition concluded without incident. Rebecca and Aurelia returned, trailed by their two guards laden with armfuls of shopping bags. Rebecca was bubbling with excitement. Apparently, Ian wasn't allowed to see everything she'd bought, as some of the bags were whisked away and stashed in her wardrobe in secret.

Somewhat disconcertingly, Aurelia winked at him, before following Rebecca out towards their respective bedrooms.

By Sunday evening, all the delegates had arrived, apart from a few 'no-shows' and stragglers who called in with excuses about delayed flights or other problems.

On Monday, they reviewed the delegates' CVs and shortlisted candidates for the three specialist roles: Professor Green, Lord White and Dr Blue. After a series of interviews, Ian and Istariol agreed on who would be appointed to each role.

The Apartment consisted of two connected suites – the Ravel Suite and the Quintessence Suite – each spanning two floors. The security team and the three Leaders – plus any family members who were staying with them – moved into the four bedrooms of the Quintessence Suite, whilst Ian and Rebecca, Aurelia, and Istariol occupied the three bedrooms of the Ravel Suite. Each suite contained its own reception rooms, a fitness suite, a treatment room, a hammam, a sauna and a private projection room, while the Quintessence Suite also housed the private swimming pool.

The days soon settled into a routine. During the day, Aurelia would walk the floor around the conference, mingling with delegates and slipping unnoticed into the seminar rooms.

One day, a group was locked in a fierce exchange about whether Earth's climate models underestimated methane feedback loops:

"You can't just dismiss the Siberian permafrost data," one delegate insisted.

"And you can't build policy on speculation," another snapped back, as Alexa recorded every word.

In another session, economists argued over the collapse of grain futures in drought-stricken regions:

"Mongolia could become the breadbasket of the world," Dr Blue declared.

"Not without reliable water supplies – that's a fantasy," came the quick retort.

Meanwhile, Ian and Istariol spent most of their time in the projection room, watching the recordings. With multiple seminars typically running simultaneously, there were always more hours of content than hours in the day. Alexa proved invaluable, analysing all the material and briefing Ian and Istariol on the most important sessions to review.

The specialists mostly used the facilities in their own suite, giving Ian, Rebecca, Aurelia and Istariol a measure of privacy. Each evening at 5.00pm, Ian gathered them all in their private projection room, where the debates of the day were reviewed, dissected, and turned into actionable strategy.

Although she always attended the 5.00pm team meeting, Rebecca dipped in and out of the other sessions, spending more and more time in the swimming pool, fitness centre and sauna. She felt far more at ease now, knowing they would each receive a pension – and a very generous one at that. Her future with Ian seemed more assured, with the means to live together anywhere in the world.

Ian, meanwhile, remained quite stressed, burdened by responsibility and the constant threat of an FSB attack. Yet in the stillness of night the two of them found refuge in each other – stolen hours of laughter and intimacy that became their sanctuary against both the threat of assassins and the shadow of mass extinction. For those few precious hours, the dangers outside their door ceased to exist.

And they *did* manage to find some time to appreciate Rebecca's newly purchased lingerie and shoes.

Ian agreed to hold Friday's team meeting earlier than usual, to give them time to visit the nearby Louvre, which stayed open late on Fridays. He said he would join them this time.

When Aurelia found a moment alone with Ian, she asked, "Would you like me to hire a private motorboat for a sunset cruise along the Seine after dinner? You'd see many of Paris's iconic landmarks – the Eiffel Tower, the Musée d'Orsay, Notre-Dame Cathedral and other grand buildings like the Grand Palais – along with picturesque bridges and riverbanks. It'd also give us another chance to see if anyone is tracking us."

"Hmm. What about the risk of snipers?" Ian asked. "Wouldn't we be quite exposed out there in a small boat?"

"Yes, you *would* be exposed, but that's the point," Aurelia admitted. "However, I'd generate a force-field shield around the boat, so you'd all be completely safe. And if a sniper fired at you, our sensors would instantly pinpoint their position. Alexa will be monitoring everything, of course, and our drones would quickly be able to zone in on their location."

"What about using all this advanced technology in public? What if there are witnesses?"

"The drones are silent – as they use anti-gravity propulsion – and they have cloaking devices. Sunset is at 9.27pm, so the sun will be low in the sky or it'll be dusk. It's highly unlikely anyone will see a thing."

"And once the drones close in on the sniper? They'll know their shot has mysteriously missed and could easily make a run for it."

"It depends where they are," Aurelia replied. "Most likely on a rooftop or inside a building, shooting through a window. The drones can be fitted with lethal weapons or tranquilliser darts – though the darts are less reliable. Would you prefer to kill them, if capture isn't possible?"

Ian thought for a moment. "We have to assume whoever is behind this can replace a sniper if they're killed. So if we can't capture them – we'll have to let them escape. I assume the drones' imaging technology will record as much detail as possible, so we can try facial recognition?"

"Yes, that's possible, though not guaranteed in low light. And ideally the drones won't reveal themselves unless they get a clear shot with a tranquilliser. Failing that, they may be able to track the sniper until they do."

"Okay. Then I see no reason not to do this. Either we get a relaxing trip on the Seine or we gain valuable intelligence on the FSB cell – or whoever else wants me dead. But I'm not telling Rebecca. I don't want to spoil her enjoyment."

"Great. I'll have Alexa organise it. You'll need to wear an earpiece so she can keep you updated in real time. I'd come to the Louvre with you, but it's better if just you three go on the boat. I'll shadow you from the riverbank – with a fifty percent chance I'll be on the same side as any sniper, I may be able to get there in time to intervene."

So after Friday's team meeting, the four of them walked the 300 metres to the Louvre.

To Rebecca, it felt strange that they were doing 'normal' things again. Everyone appeared relaxed, but she could see in Ian's eyes that he was still tense. It was, in fact, the first time he had left the Apartment since their arrival the previous Saturday. She also noticed that Aurelia's gaze was everywhere except on the paintings or antiquities the others were admiring.

At one point, they wandered into the Ancient Egyptian gallery. Rebecca couldn't help but wonder whether Ramesses the First had been a human king under the thrall of Mekbudans posing as gods – or whether, in fact, he had actually been a Mekbudan himself.

They returned to the Apartment just before 7.00pm and sat down to another sumptuous meal. Rebecca thought she detected the beginnings of a 'tummy' on Ian and decided she was going to have to cajole him into cutting down on the cheese and using the gym a little more.

After finishing their meal, "I have to take care of some security issues, so why don't you three go and enjoy the boat trip," Aurelia announced.

"Hmm. Luckily, I won't feel too much of a gooseberry, given someone's got to drive the boat. So are you two lovebirds ready to go on your romantic sunset cruise?" Istariol asked.

"We certainly are," Rebecca said, as she grabbed Ian's hand and jumped up from her chair. "Come on, the riverside looks lovely just before sunset."

"I've asked Alexa to have the boat brought round and moored at the Quai du Louvre, near the hotel," Aurelia explained. "I'll come and see you off."

Rebecca noticed Aurelia discreetly made sure that both she and Ian were carrying their personal shield devices. After Ian's last encounter with the FSB, Rebecca now knew exactly what those devices could do – and why Aurelia was checking.

They left the Apartment, the door whispering shut behind them, and walked into the main hotel, all the time shadowed by three of their guards – unmistakably armed. The elevator carried them down to the ground floor, where they exited the hotel.

Out on the street, the glow of the setting sun lit the façades of the Louvre. They crossed to the riverbank, descended the stone steps to the quay, and found the boat waiting – its powerful engine purring softly – with another member of their security team keeping watch.

It was a sleek ten-metre craft, polished teak gleaming like bronze in the sunlight, built for speed and elegance. The water shimmered against its hull, ripples of gold lapping at the wood. Inside, cushioned seats promised comfort for six, though the vessel carried an edge of purpose, more predator than pleasure craft.

Istariol stepped aboard first and settled at the controls in the forward section, his silhouette framed against the river by the last light of the sun.

Ian clambered aboard next and helped Rebecca in after him. They settled into the two seats at the stern, just in front of the pole where the French flag fluttered softly in the evening breeze.

"Before you get too settled, I think you'll find a few things under the seat you might want to get out," Istariol suggested.

They shifted onto the nearest seats and Ian pulled up the stern seat cushion. Nestling in the compartment underneath was a large cold box which Ian hauled out and placed on the floor of the boat. Inside were two cold bottles of Chablis, three glasses, and a variety of snacks – including savoury biscuits and some delicious smelling ripe cheese.

"Haven't you had enough cheese in the last week to last a lifetime?" Rebecca said to Ian, laughing.

"I didn't put them there. I blame Aurelia," Ian replied with a shrug.

"Hé, ne sois pas ingrate!" came the reply from the quayside.

"I thought I said no French?" was Ian's retort. "But of course I'm grateful – there's at least two cheeses I don't recognise."

Ian replaced the seat cushion, but as he did so, Rebecca couldn't help noticing that a black leather briefcase was also sitting inside the compartment. It looked suspiciously like the same briefcase she'd found in their bedroom a couple of days ago. The one with the Uzi submachine gun in it. She'd not said anything to Ian – but it was clear that Ian wasn't telling her everything.

Ian poured out three glasses of wine and handed one each to Istariol and Rebecca – and they took their seats at the rear again.

"We'll head downstream past the Louvre, towards the Grand Palais and the Eiffel Tower," Istariol explained. "Then we'll turn back before it gets completely dark, so we can see Notre-Dame."

Aurelia and one of their guards cast off the mooring ropes and the boat drifted free of the bank.

"Passez un bon moment. I'll see you in a couple of hours," Aurelia called after them.

The engine growled, its revs rising as Istariol eased the cruiser into the darkening waters of the Seine. The boat slipped away from the quay, making ripples which fanned out across the river – each one catching the last light of day like a signal flare.

Streetlamps flickered on along the riverbank. A few tourists leaned over the stone balustrades of the first bridge they passed under, waving down at the boat as they passed. Church bells tolled faintly in the distance, mingling with the hum of traffic.

They cruised slowly along the river, Istariol keeping the speed to a minimum so they could savour the moment. Everything seemed serene as they sipped their wine, and yet Rebecca couldn't shake the thought that, while the city glowed with beauty, hidden eyes might be watching from the shadows.

They passed the Louvre on the right, then the Tuileries Garden – a vast 17th-century formal garden dotted with bronze statues, stretching for almost a kilometre and a half along the riverbank.

But, after four bridges, when the distinctive domed glass roof of the Grand Palais appeared on the horizon, everything changed.

Rebecca heard a faint *thud-thud* from behind, barely audible over the gentle thrum of the engines.

Ian reacted instantly. He dragged Rebecca down to the bottom of the boat. The cruiser lurched violently to the left as Istariol gunned the engine, accelerating for the far bank, knocking over their glasses of wine.

"Get your gun out from under the seat – but keep it hidden," Istariol barked. "I don't want you brandishing a weapon in public. Only use it if attackers get close."

Ian yanked up the seat cushion, pulled out the briefcase and grabbed the Uzi. He had barely opened the case, when Istariol spun the wheel, slamming them against a jetty, and rammed the engine into reverse to bring the boat to a halt.

"Throw the stern rope around that bollard and tie it off!" he ordered, securing the bow line himself. Hastily dropping the gun, Ian scrambled to obey.

A *bateau-mouche* tourist boat was moored a hundred metres away, with a crowd still boarding. The jetty was much lower than the bankside itself, which had metal railings to prevent pedestrians from falling in. The only way out was along the jetty, towards the tourist boat.

"Stay in the cruiser," Istariol ordered. "The force-field will block bullets – or any fast-moving object – but it won't stop people."

With that, Istariol vanished. The boat rocked as he disembarked.

Rebecca rounded on Ian. "So what the hell's going on? And why have you been hiding a machine gun in your wardrobe?"

Ian winced. "I should've told you. We weren't certain anything would happen – but we prepared for it. A sniper fired two shots at my head a couple of minutes ago. The drones pinpointed the position – a top-floor window in that hotel. Aurelia and Istariol are on the hunt, hoping to capture him."

"What drones?"

"The invisible ones that were circling above us. They've gone after the sniper."

"How do you know all this?"

"I've got an earpiece. Alexa's briefing me in real time."

"So this is the FSB again?"

"Probably. We don't know for sure."

It was now dusk, the sky nearly black. Rebecca noticed the crowd at the bateau-mouche thinning as most of them had now boarded.

Voices drifted down from the street above. Ian and Rebecca ducked low, peering cautiously up. A couple strolled past, arm in arm, chatting in French. Nothing sinister. They relaxed.

"So what's happening now? And why don't *I* have an earpiece?" Rebecca demanded.

"I could hardly give you one without revealing what was going on. You can have one next time – if there *is* a next time."

"Well, next time you'd better bloody well not pretend nothing's happening!"

Ian fell silent, listening to Alexa. "Aurelia's reached the hotel. The room is empty, apart from two spent shells. The drones got there first, but the sniper had already gone. We've lost him."

Suddenly, they heard a heavy *thud* outside the boat, which made the whole jetty rock. Wood creaked with the sudden impact. A figure crouched there, pistol pointing at Ian, something glinting in his other hand.

There was a flash of light from the end of the pistol's silencer and a slight 'pffft' noise, immediately followed by a click from the assassin's gun.

Wherever the bullet went, it didn't hit Ian.

There was just enough light to see a brief look of confusion cross his face – before he fired again.

Ian shoved Rebecca flat and raised his Uzi to point at the assassin. In that fleeting moment, he could see the man's gun had disappeared and in its place was a wicked looking knife.

Ian pulled the trigger. *Click.* Nothing. The fire selector switch was still on 'safe'.

The man lunged, knife aimed at Ian's chest. Ian's combat training came into effect and he blocked the knife with the gun and twisted away. The attacker fell heavily into the boat, which made it rock violently from side to side, banging against the jetty.

Ian flipped the selector to semi-automatic and aimed at the back of the man's head. But he wasn't moving.

Rebecca edged forward, eyes fixed on the still body. "Is he dead... or just unconscious? And what's that on his neck?"

Four dart-like needles protruded, each tipped with small feathered fins.

"Are you hurt?" came Aurelia's voice, calling from high above.

A moment later she vaulted over the railing, landing lightly on the jetty.

"We're okay," Ian said. "Did the drones do that?"

"Yes. I recalled them once it was clear the sniper had escaped."

"Is he alive?" Rebecca asked.

Aurelia checked for a pulse, then plucked out the darts. "He's dead. They had to shoot him with twice the lethal dose. He got too close."

Ian helped her roll the body over – a heavy-set man, human, with no obvious identifying features.

"We could do with more light. There should be a torch under one of the seats," Aurelia said.

Ian found it and handed it over. She searched him – no phone, no wallet, no ID.

"This wasn't the sniper," she concluded. "He's built for close-quarters fighting. So stay sharp, as that means others may still be out there."

Aurelia produced a small device, about the size of a phone. She pressed each of the man's fingers to its surface, then put it away and drew out a sterile kit, swabbing the inside of his mouth.

"Looks like you're a walking DNA lab," Ian muttered.

"Needs must," she said with a quick smile.

Aurelia then picked up the knife with a handkerchief and carefully placed it inside a plastic bag she had taken from her pocket.

"There may be other prints – we'll get it dusted later."

There was no sign of the man's gun – it must have dropped into the river.

"Alexa, please send a couple of drones to scan the riverbed for the gun. If they locate it, have our security team do a scuba dive to retrieve it."

Istariol then appeared on the jetty. "Is everyone all right?"

"They're fine," Aurelia answered. "But he's dead. And I don't think he was the sniper. That means others could still be around."

"Someone get the anchor out from under the driver's seat," she ordered. "We need to 'lose' this body."

The body was bound with the anchor rope – the anchor chain wound around his neck – and the anchor placed on his chest.

"Is it clear, Istariol?" she asked.

He scanned the area, also checking with Alexa that the drones were not picking up any nearby activity. Their four guards now stood on the street above.

"Yes. Do it."

Together, Ian and Aurelia heaved the body overboard.

"I'd have preferred to dump him farther from here," she admitted, "as the jetty is in constant use by bateau-mouche tourist boats – but he'll stay buried in the mud long enough for our purposes."

"Okay, we should get out of here," Aurelia said. "The car's up there. Two of the guards will handle the boat."

Cautiously, they moved along the jetty and up the steps to the street above, Aurelia and two guards in the lead. The street was pedestrianised, yet a black limo was waiting there nonetheless.

They all climbed inside, the doors closing with a muted thud.

The ride back was uneventful. Soon the car swept into the hotel's underground car park and stopped outside the elevator to the Apartment.

"Well," Rebecca said dryly, "thanks everyone for such a *fabulous* river cruise. I, for one, need a drink. I never even got to finish that glass of Chablis."

Chapter 23

The next morning, over breakfast, Aurelia gave them all a debriefing on the previous day's attack.

"There were no prints or DNA on the spent rifle shells," she reported. "The assassin's knife and gun were dusted and checked, but apart from his own, they're clean. No records match his biometrics – not even in the FSB databases.

"However, we downloaded the drone footage, including close-ups of his face after he was killed. We found a match. He was a member of a Parisian drugs gang – an Algerian national. No criminal record and no obvious links to the FSB.

"Alexa hacked his bank account. She found one large payment last week, traced through a shell company. Source: the FSB. They paid him €20,000."

"Presumably, he'd have got a bonus if he'd killed Ian," Rebecca muttered.

"I would think so. Twenty K isn't much," Aurelia replied.

"And we still don't know how many people are in this cell – or who they are," she went on. "But I doubt they'll have any trouble replacing him."

"He was shocked when his bullets didn't hit me," Ian noted. "So he knew nothing about the force-field shields."

"Yes, but the sniper will be suspicious – and he escaped. We must assume they'll be better prepared next time.

"Alexa found new data on the FSB system," Aurelia continued. "The handler wasn't convinced of Ian's death, so the warrant's been reissued – with an explicit demand for DNA as proof of completion.

"We now know this FSB cell has orders to strike our hotel. It could come at any time. We need to evacuate the Apartment until further notice."

"Does that mean retreating to our spaceship?" Rebecca asked. "Surely we'd be safe there?"

"We *could* do that," Aurelia allowed. "You and Ian could review the workshop material on board. Istariol and I could maintain near-constant contact and meet you face-to-face when needed. But we'd still have to protect the three Leaders and their families – and potentially the other delegates. The FSB cell could take hostages once they realise Ian isn't in the Apartment. Directive 9 prevents us from putting force-field shields on any of them."

"So if I'm no longer available as a target," Ian said grimly, "it puts their lives at risk."

"In a nutshell, yes."

"Istariol, you're being very quiet. What do you think?" Ian asked.

"We need this workshop to go ahead next week," Istariol replied. "We're still compiling the evidence to convince the IGC you have a viable programme to limit global warming.

"The FSB think you're working undercover with Ukraine. They're targeting *you* – and there is no evidence to suggest that they realise the importance of the workshop. The cell operatives won't even know why the FSB want you dead.

"So yes, it's your decision, but I believe we should draw them out again – somewhere private – and wipe out the entire cell. We'll plant evidence of your death, including a DNA sample."

"So I'm bait again. What do you have in mind?" Ian asked.

Aurelia answered. "We leave Paris. The cruiser's still moored at Rouen. We take it upriver, find a secluded spot to moor overnight – and wait."

"Fine," Ian agreed. "But only if Rebecca stays safely on the spaceship."

"Hey, I *am* here, you know," Rebecca cut in. "Stop talking like I'm invisible. I can have as much protection as you. I'm coming. I won't sit twiddling my thumbs on that ship all weekend while you lot go off having fun."

Ian yielded under Rebecca's stern glare. "If you insist. But waiting to be attacked is hardly anyone's idea of fun."

"We're agreed, then?" Aurelia asked.

The other three nodded.

"Alexa, tell us what you can arrange." she ordered.

"Certainly," Alexa replied. "It's too dangerous to travel by train to Rouen, so you'll go by car. The FSB probably know about the limousines we've been using, so I'll get us different vehicles. Give me a few minutes to sort that."

"We only want them to strike when we're ready – somewhere quiet – no witnesses," Aurelia added.

"So the limos will go to Rouen Marina," she continued, "to let the FSB know that's where Ian and Rebecca are headed. We'll make sure they can see it's only the security team in the limos. They will follow, but they won't attack – not if they believe their targets aren't inside."

After breakfast, they moved onto the balcony with their coffee. Conscious of snipers, they all activated their personal shields.

A short while later Alexa announced: "I've just purchased two cars. My options were limited, since they had to be immediately available, but they'll be delivered to the underground car park within half an hour.

"Ian, as commander, you get first choice – blue or black?"

His phone beeped with an incoming message. He tapped it and two pictures appeared.

"Tricky. Hmm. Okay, I'll take the blue one," Ian said, unable to suppress a grin.

"Nice choice. Well done, Alexa," Aurelia remarked. "So, Ian, you'll drive me in the Bugatti. Istariol, you'll go with Rebecca. We need the Solarian Representative and his deputy in separate cars for obvious reasons. Rebecca, would you like to drive?"

"Why not? Should be fun," Rebecca replied. "Istariol, when I get in the car, can you go over the controls with me?"

"That's settled then," Aurelia said. "Alexa, please send us the location pin for the marina in Rouen."

"We leave in forty-five minutes. Some of our security personnel have already gone ahead in one of the limos to board the cruiser and secure the area before our arrival.

"Please leave your luggage outside your rooms by 9.00am. It'll be collected and taken separately. Hand luggage only in these cars – there's hardly any trunk space – so just the essentials. Like your Uzi, Ian."

They took the obvious route – via the A14 and A13 motorways – with no reason to do otherwise.

Ian relished the feel and power of the supercar. For him it was pure escapism and he would happily have stretched the drive far beyond the hour and a half it lasted.

They reached Rouen Marina without incident and pulled in behind Rebecca's black-and-orange car. Their 30-metre luxury motor yacht loomed above the jetty, a gangplank linking the quay to its stern.

Rebecca and Istariol were already out of their car, hand luggage in hand, waving as they headed up the gangplank.

Two people in business suits waited on the quay beside the cruiser.

"Don't worry," Aurelia said. "I've vetted them. They're clean. They're here to drive our cars away and park them somewhere safe."

Ian and Aurelia climbed out. Just before lifting their bags out of the trunk, she turned and gave him a sudden hug.

"Ne vous inquiétez pas, nous serons victorieux," Aurelia whispered into his ear.

"I thought I told you – no more French? And what happened to *'mon commandant'?"* Ian said, smiling despite himself.

"Ton souhait est mon ordre, mon commandant," she answered with a grin, hugging him again.

Ian felt a flicker of unease at this unexpected display of affection.

"Why is Aurelia telling me that we'll be victorious? Does she think I'm worried about how the FSB attack will play out and is trying to reassure me?"

He pushed the thought aside, slung his holdall over one shoulder, picked up the briefcase with the Uzi in his other hand, and followed her on board.

Istariol was waiting on the deck for him. He looked totally at home now, with his boating shoes, casual jacket and slacks – plus his signature hat, once again tilted at a jaunty angle.

"Would you like to drive?" he asked. "I think, as a Navy officer, you may have piloted a boat or two before?"

"Sounds good to me," Ian said grinning. "Lead the way."

"Yes, Captain."

Two of their security team busied themselves bringing the gangplank on board and getting it stowed.

Istariol climbed up the stairs to the 'flybridge' – the deck where the cockpit was situated – Ian following. Rebecca and Aurelia were sitting on stools in the aft section of the deck. Perhaps unsurprisingly, they were already sipping from glasses of wine – a bottle of Chablis in a bucket of ice sitting in front of them on the bar.

"Isn't this an amazing ship?" Rebecca exclaimed. "I've never been on anything quite so fabulous."

"You ladies just sit tight and enjoy the view," Ian responded. "Us boys have got to go play with our toy. And it's a boat, not a ship."

He took a seat at the helm and scanned the controls.

"The engines have already been warmed up," Istariol informed him. "There is a light wind, 7 knots, blowing us away from the quay, so you won't need the bow thrusters. She'll just drift off once we take off the mooring ropes. Permission to cast off, whenever you're ready?"

Ian looked around for any traffic in the marina. "Make it so," he ordered.

Istariol, who had clearly taken on the role of Executive Officer – or XO – called out to the crew to cast off. There were four security guards onboard acting as crew – and each of them were already positioned ready to cast off the four mooring ropes.

With the ropes off, the large cruiser drifted clear of the dock. Ian just feathered the powerful engines to ease her forward towards the exit of the marina.

"Wow, this is even better than the supercar," he thought.

Ian skilfully guided the massive boat out of the marina and turned to port to take her upstream. Istariol took a seat beside him.

"We're going to moor overnight near Les Andely," Istariol explained, "which will take us around eight or nine hours to reach. We'll have lunch on board as we travel."

"Fine by me."

They soon reached the Pont Gustave-Flaubert, a striking vertical-lift bridge – the tallest of its kind – which occasionally would rise to let very tall river vehicles pass beneath.

"I've checked," Istariol announced, "and we can pass underneath without needing the bridge to raise, as it's got a 7 metre clearance – but only just. Similarly, we're ok for the rest of the upstream bridges between here and Petit-Andely."

They cruised under a few more bridges and then, as they glided past central Rouen, they saw the soaring Gothic spire of Rouen Cathedral – once the tallest building in the world and famously painted over thirty times by Monet during different light conditions. In contrast, on the opposite side of the river, gulls wheeled over the industrial quays and warehouses.

Then they left Rouen behind them, the cathedral spire fading into the distance, as the river opened up into the pastoral Seine valley with gently rolling green hills and the quiet beauty of the Norman countryside. White alabaster cliffs rose occasionally, framed by peaceful villages that once inspired Monet himself.

Ian could hear the girls chatting away in the back and, knowing he wouldn't be overheard, turned to Istariol.

"Where do you think the FSB will attack?" he asked. "This riverside scenery is very tranquil, but I think it's too easy to feel safe, when it isn't."

"A rifle could already be trained on us from anywhere out there," came Istariol's reply. "But they should've learnt their lesson. I doubt any sniper will actually shoot at us whilst we're cruising down the river. We're not expecting them to try anything until after we're moored. So, for now, they're just going to be tracking the boat."

"But what about the locks? We'll be stationary there – a sitting duck."

"Yes, but they'll probably want to avoid witnesses. If I was them, I'd be attacking under the cover of darkness – and in the dead of night."

"They're going to attack en masse aren't they?"

"Yes. We were lucky that they under-estimated us before. They probably had their thugs spread out around both sides of the Seine before, which is why you only encountered one of them."

"And we've only got you, me, Aurelia, and four security officers to stop them."

"We had to leave two of our security team at the Apartment. And we can't recruit anymore guards now – it's too much of a risk that we'll end up with another mole. But we do have the drones."

"I take it you'll arm them with lethal weapons this time?" Ian asked.

"Yes. No prisoners. I don't think we need any information from them."

They sat in silence for a while – each absorbed with their own thoughts.

"What do you think about the Russian invasion of Ukraine?" Ian eventually asked.

"As you're aware, Directive 9 prevents all alien species from interfering in a 'local' conflict. In practice, it's in everyone's interests to avoid nuclear war – including the use of so-called 'tactical' nuclear weapons on the battlefield. Both the Mekbudans and ourselves really don't want that – so, unusually, we're in complete agreement."

"Are you saying that you'd step in to prevent a nuclear war? As would the Mekbudans?"

"No one wants the Earth polluted with radioactive waste, so it's possible that the computer systems controlling those weapons might... not quite work as expected. However, I wouldn't bank on it.

"As for the moral situation, in my opinion Putin is a gangster and a megalomaniac obsessed with making Russia great again – which involves restoring as much of the former Soviet Union as possible, at any cost. And he cares absolutely nothing for human suffering or lives."

"You know I actually *am* a spy, don't you? I'm working with the Ukrainians." Ian murmured.

"Of course. I *have* seen all of your records, including the CIA ones."

"You didn't say anything?"

"I know you're not allowed to tell anyone – particularly Rebecca. I'm a spy too – and I know how to keep secrets."

"Yes, but all the problems we've been having with the FSB are my fault. The Mekbudans may well have tipped them off – but it wasn't a false accusation."

"I really don't know all of the criteria the IGC used to select the short list for the Solarian Representative, but – when we looked at your service records – I can't say I was surprised to find that you'd been seconded to the CIA. So, it's not your fault and – compared to the challenge of saving all life on Earth – the FSB are just an annoyance."

"A dangerous annoyance, though."

"Consider it a combat training session. And with our technology to aid you."

They lapsed into silence again.

"So what *does* my service record say about me?" Ian enquired.

Istariol took his phone out of his jacket pocket and after a few taps, started reading.

"Educated Bristol University, Physics & Computer Science, combined honours – first class. Highly intelligent – IQ 160. Extremely good IT and cyber-security skills. Skippering and small craft handling – good. Personal combat skills – adequate. Small arms – competent. Rifle skills – very good.

"Looks like we know who to pick if *we* need a sniper," Istariol said laughing.

He continued. "Exceptionally calm under stress. A number of your superiors noted that they think you are *too* calm – and they worried about how seriously you were actually taking the situation."

"They were idiots," Ian retorted. "If I wasn't there to keep control of things, they would've run round like headless chickens."

Istariol chuckled.

"There's more, as you've asked," and he continued reading. "Negative character trait – lack of aggression and assertiveness. This means he's unlikely to be promoted above lieutenant. Good team player, however. Appears to be trusted and well respected by his men."

"Okay, so I won't be holding my breath and expecting a meteoric rise in my Navy career anytime soon," Ian observed, wryly.

"I'd give you a job after all this is over," Istariol said, smiling warmly.

Before Ian had a chance to reply, they heard Aurelia call out from the stern.

"Hey, what time's lunch? I'm starving."

"I'll go down to the galley and see what I can do," Istariol called back. Then turning to Ian, "I'll get one of our security team to come and take the helm."

Istariol climbed down the steps to the lower deck. He returned carrying a cool box, accompanied by one of the crew with a hamper. The guard took over the controls from Ian, and they joined the ladies at the back of the deck.

"I've asked them to serve lunch in twenty minutes," Istariol announced. "In the meantime, we've got drinks and nibbles."

He opened the cool box and they could see another bottle of Chablis, two large bottles of chilled cider and some more ice.

"Who would like some cider – and who fancies some wine?" Istariol asked.

Rebecca opened the hamper to find picnic plates and utensils, a bottle of Morgon, a bottle of Châteauneuf-du-Pape, mixed nuts, olives, water biscuits and a jar of paté.

Istariol grabbed some more glasses from the rack behind the bar and they all settled down for their pre-lunch drinks and snacks.

"I'll open one of the reds – to give it a chance to breathe," he said. "Any preference?"

They were cruising through the Seine Valley, with its picturesque chalk cliffs.

"Those cliffs look like they've been carved by giants," Rebecca pointed out. "Imagine rowing past here centuries ago, with no sound except your oars in the water."

"And with a longbow aimed at your back," Aurelia commented dryly. "Romance often omits the arrows."

Some children were cycling along the towpath, and an angler nodded as they passed. A white heron suddenly lifted off from the reeds, as their boat drew near.

"It's so peaceful," Rebecca observed, "it almost makes me forget that we're bait in someone else's trap."

"To traps, then. May they spring on our enemies," Ian toasted, raising his glass. The others joined him in the toast.

After a short pause, Istariol said: "Just remember, we still have to be alive to laugh about it. I think this may be a suitable point to discuss the plans for our own trap – if that's okay by you, Ian?"

"Of course."

Istariol stood, opened a cupboard in the boat's side, and pulled out two slim jackets, handing one each to Ian and Rebecca.

"When we go through the locks – or when we moor up – I want you wearing these. They're bulletproof. Alien polymer. We can't let one fall into Solarian scientists' hands, so don't lose it. Hit it with a hammer – or a bullet – and it won't budge a millimetre. But bend it gently, and it's pliable."

Rebecca studied hers. Thin, smooth, almost like imitation leather. When she slipped it on, the material moulded to her shape with the lightest pressure – surprisingly comfortable.

"Thanks, but why do we need them?" Ian asked. "We've got our personal shields."

"Yes – but every hit drains their energy. Depending on calibre and range, they can only absorb maybe ten or twelve bullets. A machine gun burst or two, and your shield fails."

"And *now* you tell us?" Rebecca shot back.

"In Paris you didn't need them," Istariol said evenly. "That riverboat carried a generator strong enough to shield the entire craft. This cruiser's far bigger – thirty metres and multiple decks. That's a lot of boat. At such short notice we only had time to install one medium-sized generator, protecting your cabin. These jackets give you fallback."

"What about drones?" Ian asked.

"Six are overhead now, six more are recharging," Aurelia said. "They'll cover us the whole trip and once we moor. After dark – sunset's about 9.30pm – they'll drop lower to the ground. Cloaking works best in low light."

"And where exactly *are* we mooring?" Ian pressed.

"Near Port de Venables," Aurelia explained. "Ten kilometres before Les Andelys. The marina's on Lac de Venables – over a million and a half square metres of water. We'll anchor by a spit of land near the hamlet of La Rive sous Venables. Remote, just a few dogwalkers.

"The marina's too small for our boat anyway. The only land access is a 200-metre long tree-lined footpath. I'll brief you again, once you see the terrain."

"So we just sit and wait?" Ian asked.

"Pretty much," Aurelia said. "The drones' infrared will sweep the whole area. Once they close in, we hit them all at once – kill or capture, no half-measures."

"What do *we* do?" Rebecca asked.

"If they attack when we expect – in the dead of night – stay in your cabin. It's shielded, you'll be wearing the flak jacket and your personal shield, so you'll be completely safe. We'll also station a drone outside."

"Are you giving personal shields to the security team?" Ian asked.

"Actually, yes. We're taking a calculated risk that if they get hit, in the heat of the battle they won't realise why the bullets aren't doing them any damage."

"Fine. We'll refine the plan once we're moored, but I'm not staying in my cabin when the action starts – although Rebecca will."

"Hey, stop making decisions for me," Rebecca protested.

"Firstly, I *am* in command. Secondly, you don't have a gun and can't shoot. You'd just be a liability."

"I *do* have a gun. Aurelia gave me a mouse gun."

Ian shot Aurelia a questioning look.

"What? Every lady should have one – especially when being hunted by Russian-hired assassins. It's only effective at point-blank range. Little point trying to aim – you just shoot."

"She's more likely to hit herself, or a friendly – or me. And have you even trained her on the use of the safety catch?"

"Hmm. Pots and kettles," Aurelia said with a cheeky smile. "I was wondering if *you* needed a refresher on the Uzi's selector switch – after what happened in Paris."

Ian pulled a face.

"Anyway, Rebecca's got the same model as mine. No safety catch. The mechanism *is* the safety: an eleven-pound trigger. She'll have to squeeze the trigger very firmly to shoot."

At that moment lunch arrived, carried up by two of the crew. Rebecca helped Aurelia set it out — Pié d'Angloys, Époisses, cold Italian meats, crusty French bread, quiche, bean and pasta salad, Moroccan tomato couscous, avocado and prawns.

"Time for that Morgon, I think," Istariol said, as he reached for the bottle.

They relaxed for a while, enjoying lunch, the company, and the quiet of the river – broken only by the steady thrum of the engines beneath them.

A couple of hours later, just after four thirty, they passed under a railway bridge, and the river ahead split into two: a double lock to port and a wide weir to starboard. Holding position ahead was a huge barge, nearly a hundred metres long, its open deck piled high with what looked like coal or coke. They had reached the Écluse de Poses lock.

"Flak jackets on, please," Aurelia instructed. "And check your shields are switched on."

They queued behind the barge. Thirty five minutes later, the lock gates creaked open and a huge gleaming white cruise vessel emerged, '*Cruise Europe*' emblazoned on its hull.

"Rebecca, Ian," Aurelia said, lowering her voice. "Inside the lock we'll be quite exposed. They're unlikely to try anything in daylight with so many people about, but I don't want to give them the temptation of having either of you in their sights. Go down into the saloon – or better, your cabin. Ian, screw the silencer onto your Uzi, but keep it on 'safe'."

The barge lumbered slowly into the 140-metre lock and made fast to the bollards. Then it was their turn.

As their cruiser edged in alongside, the sheer scale of the chamber closed around them: damp concrete walls loomed above, dwarfing their vessel. The crew rushed to secure the mooring lines. Their pilot then cut the engines.

Below decks, the gloom deepened. Daylight all but vanished, the tall walls shutting them in. The lock gates rumbled shut with a heavy thud.

"Alexa," Ian whispered into his microphone, "anything suspicious?"

"All clear so far," came the reply.

Everyone waited tensely as the lock filled. Water roared in, the cruiser rocking as it slowly rose. On the flybridge, Istariol and Aurelia kept their vigil, while the crew worked the lines to hold them steady against the surge and away from the barge's steel flanks.

And then, sunlight. As their boat rose up, a shaft of light cut through the grey, as the sun peeped out from the overcast sky overhead. The lock gates swung open.

A few hand gestures settled it – their boat would exit first. Engines rumbled back to life, ropes slipped free, and the cruiser surged forward, out of the lock and into the relative safety of the open river once more. A collective sigh of relief ran through the crew.

"All clear," Alexa confirmed, as the lock began to recede into the distance. "You can come back on deck."

Ian and Rebecca stripped off their flak jackets and stowed them in their cabin, Ian slipping the Uzi back into its briefcase, before rejoining the others on the flybridge.

"You'll be pleased to know that there are no more locks before we reach the marina," Istariol informed them. "So, enjoy the rest of the cruise. Anyone like a glass of wine?"

"But we've got to go through there again on the way back," Rebecca remarked.

"Yes, but by then we should have eliminated the FSB cell. And we've already parked our limousines in the hamlet near where we'll moor. Anyone who doesn't fancy the return trip can catch a ride back to the Apartment."

They settled down to enjoy the rest of their cruise, wine glasses in hand. The riverbank varied between chalk cliffs and wooded slopes, the occasional grand villa or small hotel-mansion peering out from the trees.

"Do we know for certain the FSB are tracking our boat?" Rebecca asked after a while.

"Yes," Aurelia replied. "In case you're wondering if this is a complete waste of time, the drones have confirmed it. The same 4x4 has been spotted in several places along our route. At first, it could've been coincidence – but it was seen near the marina six hours ago, and now it's up on the ridge, moving in the same direction as us. Alexa checked the plates: it's a hire car in a fake name."

A little later, they cruised past a picturesque ivy-clad watermill, perched over a spur of water just off the river's main course.

"That's the Moulin d'Andé watermill," Aurelia explained, "built in 1195 to supply flour to the garrison of Chateau-Gaillard at Les Andelys. That's the fortress that Richard the Lionheart built, when he was simultaneously King of England and feudal Duke of Normandy."

"Are you speaking from experience?" Rebecca asked curiously.

"No, Wikipedia," she replied with a straight face.

Then, at last, just after 7.30pm, their cruiser reached the gates of Port de Venables and the sheltered waters of the Lac de Venables – a broad lake cut off from the river's current. Ian, now at the helm, eased back the throttles and guided the boat gently to starboard, slipping through the narrow gates into calm water.

To port, two spits of land framed a small marina where three long jetties jutted out, crowded with dozens of moored boats bobbing in the fading light. This was where they would have turned in to moor at the marina, but none of the berths was large enough for their vessel.

Instead, they cruised past, running another kilometre northeast across the lake until they reached the hamlet of La Rive sous Venables. Ahead, another spit of land stretched out, marked by a modest jetty barely eight metres long.

Ian swung the cruiser in a wide arc, bringing her in parallel to the jetty, bow pointing northwest. At his command, the anchor rattled down, and with a deft hand he reversed the twin engines, applying just enough extra thrust to one motor so that the stern eased to starboard. The fenders brushed gently against the wood of the jetty and one of the crew leapt ashore with a mooring rope. Within moments, the stern was tied fast and the anchor secure. Ian killed the engines.

Two hundred metres away, the hamlet's streetlamps flickered into life.

Chapter 24

They were sitting up on the flybridge having dinner. It was a pleasant May evening – scattered clouds overhead, a light breeze making wavelets across the lake.

"Alright," Aurelia began, "we need a quick word about what happens next. Alexa, weather forecast, please."

"It's now about an hour until sunset," Alexa replied, her voice emanating from the flybridge's inbuilt speakers. "Clear skies overnight. Moonrise about 2.15am in the southeast – so it'll rise over the boat's stern. Two-thirds full, so it'll throw out plenty of light."

"Good," Aurelia continued. "We've rigged spotlights around the hull. Once the attack starts, Alexa will turn them all on. It'll blind the shooters while giving us good visibility."

She pointed toward the dark line of trees. "The obvious approach is from the hamlet. They can park their vehicles up there, then move along this spit under cover. We've left the gangplank down onto the jetty to make it look inviting."

"Vehicles?" Ian asked, eyebrow raised.

"We've only confirmed one 4x4. But this time they'll bring numbers, so assume at least one other car – maybe more, even if they don't park close by."

"And the drones?" Rebecca asked.

"Twelve will be aloft, spread high around us. Once they have targets, they will drop lower to shadow each man. Silent and invisible – until they open fire. Two will be loaded with tranquillisers. We need a live prisoner to witness Ian's death."

Rebecca's hands tightened on her wineglass. "But Ian isn't going to die."

"He will – on paper," Aurelia said coldly. "We'll use virtual reality to give the prisoner a false version of events – one where he sees Ian die and then collects his DNA. And we'll use his phone to send in a report. The FSB will buy it. But only if we eradicate the rest of the cell."

"One last thing." Aurelia's gaze moved from Ian to Rebecca, eyes glinting hard as steel. "Don't use your cloaking device unless it's life or death. If you vanish, Alexa loses you. And if you get caught in the crossfire and your shields are depleted, that could be fatal."

No one spoke after that. The food cooled on the plates. They finished what wine they could manage, but the laughter and warmth of the past day had drained away. The birdsong from the shore sounded distant now, eerie against the gathering dark.

They decided to get an early night, even if they *were* going to miss a beautiful sunset. If the attack came in the small hours, at least they'd face it after some rest.

"Wake up! They're here!" Ian sat upright with a jolt. It had been Alexa speaking in his earpiece.

"Their 4x4 has just parked next to the footpath leading down to our mooring. They drove up with their headlights off."

"What's the time?"

"Five past three. Another car – a black people carrier – had just pulled up behind them. Also with no lights."

"What's going on?" Rebecca asked in a whisper.

"They're here," he replied. "You've got to stay in the cabin. Check all your devices are turned on. Are you wearing your earpiece?"

Rebecca fumbled around in the gloom of their cabin's nightlight. "I am now."

"Istariol, Aurelia and the crew have all been alerted and are moving into position." Alexa was speaking again. "Ian, you should go up and join Aurelia on the flybridge. Don't forget to put the silencer on your Uzi."

Ian grabbed his pistol and jammed it into his shoulder holster and picked up the Uzi, which he'd put by the side of their bed.

"How many bogeys?" he asked.

"Twelve. The drones will stay behind them and shadow them as they come down the path. Except for the drone that will be outside your cabin guarding Rebecca."

Ian rushed out of the cabin and clambered up the two flights of stairs to the rear of the flybridge. Aurelia was already there, crouched down and peering towards the trees.

"You'd better keep your head down," she advised. "Even with your personal shield, a high powered bullet could knock you over and stun you."

"Alexa, SITREP," Ian ordered.

"Nine of them have spread out and are approaching under cover of the trees," Alexa replied in his earpiece. "They're wearing infrared goggles and are armed with silenced submachine guns – Uzis or similar. They're about a hundred metres away."

"Where are the other three?"

"For some reason they've held back, staying on this side of the path only, closest to our boat. They're carrying holdalls only. No weapons are visible. Perhaps they've got sniper rifles in their bags."

"Which one are you going to keep alive? Is the drone armed with tranquillisers ready?"

"It's tracking the bogey furthest from the boat – one with an Uzi."

"Any sign they know we're expecting them?"

"No, they're just moving slowly forward to encircle the boat."

"Okay. Order the drone to take down one man now – if they can do it silently and without any of the others seeing. Then, whenever you think it's the right time, open fire and turn all the spotlights on."

A few seconds elapsed.

"One bogey on the ground, tranquillised. It hasn't raised the alarm, so I'm going ..." Alexa's voice suddenly trailed off.

"Another car has drawn up and six more bogeys have got out, armed with Uzis."

"Really? They've sent eighteen assassins – just to kill me?"

"Looks like it. They must... Oh shit!"

Ian had never heard Alexa ever utter a single expletive. His guts clenched with sudden tension and fear.

"Rebecca – **GET OUT of the cabin NOW!**" Alexa screamed, her voice blasting into all of their earpieces. "Get to the rear of the boat!"

At once, dozens of spotlights flared from the cruiser, flooding the bank and tree line with harsh white light. Muffled cracks – sounding like nail guns – erupted all around as their security team opened fire.

"Those holdalls – they've got recoilless rifles. Anti-tank guns. I've ordered the drones to take them out."

Then every earpiece and speaker aboard shrieked with Alexa's warning:

"INCOMING! BRACE, BRACE, BRACE!"

An anti-tank missile slammed into the cruiser amidships on the lower deck, right where the cabins lay. Built to punch through tank armour, it ripped through the starboard carbon-fibre hull like a hot knife through butter before detonating. The blast tore across the vessel, blowing a gaping hole out of the port side and hurling equipment, bedding, and other debris into the night. Flames roared from the wreckage as the helm and control panel were obliterated in a single shattering eruption. All the spotlights instantly went out as the power system shorted.

"Rebecca's okay," Ian heard Alexa say. "Istariol is with her. A drone is on overwatch."

The cruiser shuddered beneath them, listing to port.

"Alexa, SITREP," Ian barked.

"All three men with anti-tank weapons are dead, along with five others. Remaining hostiles: ten. The drones and crew are engaged in a firefight. We've lost three drones – infrared goggles let the gunmen track them whenever they fire. The cruiser's been hit just above the waterline. Portside breach is taking water. She's going down – we'll have to abandon ship."

Before Ian could respond, a blinding flash ripped through the night. He and Aurelia lit up like Christmas trees, sparks arcing between them before everything went dark again. The air reeked of ozone. Every hair on Ian's body stood on end and he got a distinct feeling something was behind him.

"EMP!" Aurelia shouted. "All of our equipment's just been fried."

An EMP is a brief, typically very high-power, electromagnetic pulse which can disrupt communications and damage electronic equipment.

Ian spun, heart hammering. Out on the port side, a figure hovered above the lake, framed by moonlight and the orange flicker of flames licking out from the cruiser. A Mekbudan – armoured, silent, his wetsuit glistening wet – was watching them.

And his rifle was aimed straight at Ian. A flash seared from the muzzle.

Aurelia hurled herself at Ian, driving him down onto the deck behind the bar. A sickening thud followed as she hit the floor beside him.

For a heartbeat he froze. Training drilled into him screamed: *leave fallen companions – your survival must come first.*

But he couldn't. With shaking hands, he reached for her, turned her over. A fist-sized hole gaped in her chest, burned clean through the flak jacket. Her heart – gone. No blood. The edges of the wound cauterised, the air acrid with burned flesh.

"Aurelia…" The name tore out of him. He pulled her into his arms, clutching her against him, as if sheer will might hold her spirit in place. His chest shook with the effort of stifling the sobs.

"Alexa…" His voice croaked into his microphone… "Alexa… we're under attack. Mekbudan… port side." His voice broke. "Aurelia's… she's gone."

Silence.

"No response. My comms must be dead," he thought grimly.

He wiped his eyes with the back of his hand, grief hardening his fury.

"Alright," he whispered to himself, rising to his knees. His jaw clenched, eyes narrowing into steel. *"Right, where's that bastard."*

He risked a glance over the bar. The Mekbudan was climbing higher, silhouetted against the night sky. A beam lanced down, and the wood beside his head erupted in fire. The boat listed harder to port, the deck now sloping at a perilous angle.

Ian flicked the Uzi to full auto. Hugging the deck, he leaned out and raked a burst through the railings. The Mekbudan's body jolted, but the rounds ricocheted harmlessly off a shimmering force-field.

"I wonder if I can knock that shield out, if I hit it with enough bullets," he thought.

He shifted position and unleashed another burst from the other side of the bar. Half the shots connected. Still no effect. The assassin's reply gouged a fresh hole in the bar, scorching heat licking across Ian's cheek.

The Mekbudan was climbing, circling, angling for a clear shot. Ian's cover wouldn't last.

Muffled gunfire rattled in the distance – the fight with the other gunmen still raged. He clung to the thought that Istariol was keeping Rebecca safe. But the truth pressed hard in his chest: he needed backup – and fast.

And then the Mekbudan loomed directly above him – no cover left, nowhere to run without taking a shot in the back. Ian weighed up his only option: a desperate dive into the lake.

The crack of automatic fire split the night. Tracers streaked out, hammering the assassin. The rounds sparked harmlessly against the shield. One of their security team had taken position on the sundeck above Ian's head. Another of Aurelia's precautions, perhaps.

The Mekbudan coolly swung his beam rifle round to aim at the sundeck. A single shot. A sickening thud. Ian's gut twisted – whoever had been covering him had been wounded – or worse.

Then the Mekbudan turned his weapon on Ian again. Barely any cover remained.

"So this is it then. Hopefully Rebecca's safe. She'll have to save the Earth on her own now."

He braced himself to dive overboard – when something caught his eye.

The lake behind the Mekbudan was moving. The waters were swirling in a huge circle – twenty-five metres wide – almost as large as the entire length of their cruiser.

Suddenly, a searing beam of light burst from the rim of the rippling circle, just above the water's surface. It struck the Mekbudan from behind, engulfing his chest and lower body. His face went slack, eyes rolling upward, before his head and shoulders toppled backwards into the lake – sliced clean as if by a giant blade.

For a heartbeat, the rest of his body continued to hover in the air, lit up by the beam of light. Then it dissolved – liquefying into a cascade of flesh and liquid metal that poured into the lake's waters below.

The beam snapped off. In that instant, Ian glimpsed the source: a Tay-class Antarian scout ship hovering above the lake, its silhouette flickering ghostlike before vanishing again. It had clearly just surfaced only a few moments ago from beneath the lake.

Relief slammed through him – he had never been so glad to see a UFO. But the exhilaration twisted immediately into grief for Aurelia... and dread for Rebecca and Istariol.

The cruiser now listed twenty degrees to stern and nearly forty-five to port. Ian knew it could slip beneath the lake at any moment.

He scrambled up the stairs to the sundeck and found the crewman who had fired on the Mekbudan – who had undoubtedly saved Ian's life with that distraction. The man lay still, a round hole punched through his chest, most of his heart obliterated. He was gone.

The gunfire had stopped. Ian dared to hope the fight was over. Then he caught the faint distant wail of sirens – fire crews, or perhaps the police, closing in from the distance.

He hurried back down the two flights of stairs toward the gangplank. Every fibre in him screamed to take Aurelia's body with him, but he could almost hear her voice cutting through the chaos: *'Get off this bloody boat before it drags you down with it.'*

He sprinted onto the jetty and took shelter behind a tree. There was a flicker and Istariol suddenly materialised, turning his cloaking device off. His hat was nowhere to be seen.

"Take these," he said. Ian recognised the devices in the palm of Istariol's hand as a personal shield and a communications earpiece.

"She's dead," Ian blurted out.

"I know. It's terrible. But we've got to get out of here before the police arrive."

"Who's dead?" they heard Rebecca call out. She was a few yards away and probably cloaked, as he couldn't see her.

And then Ian was being hugged fiercely by an invisible Rebecca – although he could now see her, as the cloak's effect enveloped them both.

"Aurelia's dead," Ian replied. "She saved my life by diving in front of me at the instant I was shot, pushing me to the ground."

"We've got to go," Istariol urged. "The security guards have already snatched the tranquillised assassin and bundled him into one of the limos. I ordered two of them to go ahead and drive back to Paris."

They then heard a bubbling, gurgling noise behind them and, turning, they saw the cruiser slip down into the black waters of the lake, leaving just a few bubbles and ripples behind it.

The sirens stopped sounding off as the emergency vehicles came to a halt at the far end of the spit of land. Their flashing lights could be seen through the trees two hundred metres away.

Ian put on his earpiece and personal shield device, checking they were switched on.

"Alexa, SITREP," he ordered.

His earpiece crackled to life. "We have one gunmen alive, being driven in a limo to Paris by two of our guards. All of the other seventeen gunmen, as well as the Mekbudan, are dead. The police and fire service have arrived and are approaching from the northwest. They're about one hundred and fifty metres away. One of our guards died on the boat, as did Aurelia, so their bodies are now underwater. We also lost four of our drones. They all have self-destruct mechanisms, so there won't be any incriminating technology amongst the debris.

"Everybody else is safe and well," Alexa continued. "The fourth guard is waiting at the second limousine to drive you to Paris, as it's not practical for you to board the spacecraft at the moment. I will fly the ship back and re-submerge into our parking space under the Seine."

"We've really got to go – now," Istariol insisted. "I don't have another cloaking device on me, so share Rebecca's by walking with your arm around her. It's dark, so we just have to avoid their torches until we reach the parked police cars."

They skirted along the east side of the path towards the hamlet and the emergency vehicles, keeping the trees between themselves and the path. The police were too absorbed with the bodies and the dropped weapons to pay much attention to anything else, although their vanguard continued to advance cautiously towards the site of the sunken cruiser until they reached the jetty.

It was then that the police found the anti-tank weapons. This seemed to generate a lot of excitement. As Istariol led them towards the end of the path, where the emergency vehicles were parked, they could hear more sirens in the distance. They waited a couple of minutes before three ambulances arrived.

"Not much to do other than collect dead bodies, so there's not really any rush." Ian thought.

Then the firemen appeared and got into their truck and drove away. The ambulance men got some trollies out of the back of their vehicles and set off down the path.

"Okay, it's clear, let's go." This time it was Istariol's voice speaking in his ear. "We need to cross the road, staying away from the street lamps, and go down that dirt path. Our car's parked just the other side of those houses."

The three of them made their way to their limo without further incident. They turned their cloaking devices off just before they reached their car. The last remaining security guard was sitting in the driver's seat. He got out of the car to open the door for Rebecca.

And then they were all seated in the back of the car. The driver set off towards the main road, skirting the area where the police vehicles were gathered.

"Let's not talk now, with our driver in earshot," Istariol whispered. "I suggest you try and get some sleep."

It was ten past four in the morning.

They reached the underground car park around 5am, the streets still quiet at that hour. As they went up in the elevator, Istariol suggested a debrief in ten minutes in the lounge. He would arrange coffee.

Ian and Rebecca went straight to their room. Ian was still carrying his Uzi – safety now on – and slipped it into a drawer. The briefcase was gone, of course, lying at the bottom of the lake.

They held each other, both in tears. Ian told her, in clipped, broken sentences, what had happened. How Aurelia had died.

"She would have told us to move forward," he whispered. "To carry on. To make sure her sacrifice wasn't in vain."

They wiped their eyes, composed themselves, and made their way to the lounge.

Istariol was already there, pouring coffee, a new hat perched on his head as though nothing had changed. Somehow, the hotel had conjured up a continental breakfast, though neither Ian nor Rebecca had the slightest appetite.

Once the waiter left them, with steaming coffees in front of them, Istariol began the debrief.

"The prisoner is secure in Aurelia's room. He's asleep, and we've begun implanting false memories through a device at the base of his neck. Later today we'll have to take him back to the site and release him."

"Release him?" Rebecca blurted out. "Why? They murdered Aurelia!"

"We all grieve for her," Istariol said evenly. "But the mission stands. The Russians must be convinced Ian died with the boat."

"Why were there so many of them?" Ian asked. "And armed with anti-tank weapons? That's a massive overkill for one minor operative – me."

"I've hacked the FSB system again," Alexa's voice came through the hotel speaker. "It appears the records have been recently tampered with – likely by the Mekbudans. Ian, your priority level was raised two grades. Two additional cells were activated and assigned to the mission."

"So that explains the eighteen gunmen," Ian muttered. "But what about the anti-tank weapons? And the Mekbudan diver?"

"The assignment had been updated to show we'd be on a large luxury motor cruiser," Alexa reported. "Each cell was ordered to requisition a recoilless rifle – a Russian RPG-30 anti-tank weapon. Closest thing they had to a portable anti-ship system."

"As for the Mekbudan, we've no idea," Istariol added. "No drone was close enough and your devices were fried, so we've no record of his features. We'll need to recover his head from the lake bed. That, along with the falsified records in the FSB database, will be presented to the IGC as evidence: attempted murder of the Solarian Representative and his Deputy – and the murder of an Antarian citizen carrying out her duty."

"That place will be crawling with police," Rebecca said. "They'll have cordoned it off as a crime scene. How will you even find his head?"

"I'm going back there now," Istariol replied. "I've had someone fetch scuba gear from our submarine. I'll swim over from the far side of the lake, away from the cordon. I'll take a pair of drones to scan the lake bed."

Rebecca swallowed hard. "And Aurelia...?" The words faltered; she couldn't bring herself to finish.

Istariol's expression darkened. "There's nothing we can do. Even if the police recover her body, we could never claim it. She'll be filed as a Jane Doe – she doesn't exist in any Solarian database."

"We will hold a memorial for her. But not until after the Hearing has ended. She wouldn't have wanted to be a distraction. Saving the Earth comes first."

They sat in silence for a few moments, in silent appreciation of her sacrifice.

"How are you going to get back out to the lake?" Ian enquired.

"As a precaution, yesterday, we got a couple of drivers to bring the supercars from the Marina, back to the underground car park. So, I'll take one of those. And, no, you can't come," he added with a half-smile.

"I suggest you both go back to bed and get a few hours' sleep, if you can. It's Sunday, so you've not got much on. Sleep as long as you want. We'll do another debrief when I get back."

Istariol stood up. Rebecca jumped up and gave him a hug. "I'm so sorry you lost your niece," she said in his ear. She couldn't see his face, but he returned the hug.

Ian then shook his hand. "Good luck," he said. "Are you sure, you don't need me as support? As you say, I don't have much else on today."

"I don't want to have to worry about your safety out there, when I'm diving. Stay in the Apartment and relax. We've all had a terrible time in the last few hours and you need to be refreshed by tomorrow – to carry on with the workshop."

With that, Istariol turned and set off in the direction of the elevator.

Aurelia's death had shown them just how serious a game they were being forced to play. Yet even her sacrifice – and that of the security guard who had also given his life – paled into insignificance when measured against the fate of the planet, if they failed.

Ian and Rebecca finished their impromptu breakfast and returned to their room. To their surprise, they did manage to get some sleep.

Quite a few hours later, whilst they were having a light supper, Istariol returned.

"I need a drink," he announced. "Alexa, please ask the Majordome to bring me a strong gin and tonic."

"How did that go?" Ian asked, in a worried tone.

"To be fair, not bad," Istariol replied. "I managed to retrieve the Mekbudan's head, which is now on board our ship. We've submitted a scan of his face – as well as his DNA – to the IGC. Alexa can you fill in the details."

"Of course," Alexa responded. "The IGC has considered all the evidence and submitted a case to the petitioner – Gulinrog – demanding an explanation. The Mekbudan assassin has been identified as belonging to a rival tribe.

"Further investigation by Gulinrog's people has uncovered a small group of Mekbudans who have been plotting to assassinate you both. They gave the evidence to the head of their tribe – Sujarok – who had them all summarily executed."

"The head of their tribe has killed them all?" Rebecca gasped. "Why?"

"Sujarok had little choice. It was a flagrant breach of Directive 9. Of course, he's also distanced himself from the perpetrators by doing this. If they'd succeed, it may well have been a different kettle of fish. And, as to whether he secretly instigated this, we'll never know – although it's quite likely."

"You said if the Mekbudans breached Directive 9, it could halt or postpone the Hearing, Ian asked, leaning forward enthusiastically. "Has that happened?"

"No," Alexa replied. "The IGC is satisfied that Gulinrog had nothing to with this. They can't hold him responsible for the entire Mekbudan race. The perpetrators have all been executed and their heads presented to the IGC. So it's 'case closed', I'm afraid."

"What about the FSB," Ian asked. "Are they still out to get us?"

"Actually, no," Istariol cut in. "Our Russian guest took a little ride with me this morning. He woke up in police custody, nursing a big headache. In his memory, he was knocked out with a blow to the head – *after* witnessing Ian being shot dead and sending a coded text to his handler confirming the kill."

"And this memory will seem real?" Rebecca asked. "What about the DNA evidence?"

"It will feel real to him," Istariol assured her. "Along with the memory that he took a swab from Ian's mouth, as ordered. We planted your DNA on one of the sticks he carried."

"But he's in custody – won't the police confiscate it?"

"Unlikely. Enough drug-gang members were among the dead to make it look like a turf war or a deal gone wrong. The divers will search the wreck, but they'll find nothing. When he's released, he'll get his possessions back – including the swab.

"He was found half-conscious in a bush shortly after sunrise," Istariol added. "No weapons, no drugs. He'll be held on suspicion for a while, but nothing more. To the FSB, he'll be their credible witness."

"And I've already erased all the Mekbudan forgeries from the FSB database," Alexa's voice came through. "Ian, you're back to being a low-priority target – officially dead, provisionally, pending DNA confirmation. I'll monitor it, but I doubt we'll be having any more trouble from them."

"We've done it then? We're finally safe?" Rebecca asked, almost in disbelief.

"We'll never really know that," Istariol replied. "Perhaps it will be the CIA next time – if the Americans discover you are the Solarian Representative. But I don't see any more Mekbudans trying anything on. Gulinrog is our new-found friend in this instance. He will be using all of his spy network to detect and intercept any further conspiracies against you. He wants you alive – and at the Hearing – so he can win the case."

"Anyway, you must excuse me. I've had a long day, so I'm heading to bed. If you have any more questions, please feel free to ask Alexa."

Istariol's gin and tonic had arrived a little while ago and was sitting, untouched, on the table in front of him.

Ian stood, with his own glass of wine in hand.

"Before you go Istariol, we should make a toast. We miss her terribly already and will, no doubt, continue to do so in the days and weeks ahead. So, a toast to her bravery and sacrifice. To Aurelia."

They all stood and raised their glasses in a toast. "To Aurelia."

Chapter 25

Finally, the day of the Hearing dawned. The past ten days had flown by. Everyone missed Aurelia, but no one spoke her name – the pain was too sharp.

They had pored over their plans again and again, refining every detail. Now they were as ready as they would ever be.

Everyone was up early – and at breakfast by 7am. The Hearing was due to start promptly at 10am, but they didn't need to board the submarine until about 9.30am.

As usual, their 'experts' were having breakfast in the dining room in the Quintessence suite, so they were able to talk freely amongst themselves.

"I do have some information to share with you all," Istariol said, once they had finished eating, and were sipping their coffees.

"I wouldn't want it to come as a surprise, when you get to the Hearing – but I've been putting off telling you."

"Okay, well get on with it then," Ian demanded, impatiently.

"One of our spies has reported back and given us the identity of the Mekbudan prosecutor. He is a human, calling himself Krognák and, apparently, he has Mekbudan citizenship."

"Krognák is quite an important person – not only has he been put in command of the spaceship hosting the Hearing, but he's also the Head of Gulinrog's secret police."

"The thing is – and this is what I don't want you to react to later today when you see him – his real name is Heinrich Luitpold Himmler."

"What – *the* Himmler? The one who worked for Hitler and headed the Gestapo?" Ian cried out. "But he died in 1945."

"It seems not," Istariol replied. "It looks like the Mekbudans got to him in time – presumably faked his death – and have been making use of his talents ever since."

"I would imagine that he's skipped forward in time quite a lot. Our spy says he doesn't look much older than the photos of him during World War Two."

"And *he's* going to be the one representing the Mekbudans at this Hearing?" Rebecca asked, incredulously.

"Yes," Istariol replied. "But if their tactic was to shock you both when he walked in, that won't work now. Incidentally, he will have to wear the robes of an IGC lawyer – as will I."

"We'll tell our expert witnesses that this is all part of the 'mock trial' we are recording. And that the prosecutor will be impersonating Himmler."

"Oh, and one other thing. We cannot take any weapons or advanced technology devices on board the Mekbudan spaceship. They would be detected by their ship's sensors and trigger an alarm. So, leave anything of that nature you have in your rooms – or, if absolutely necessary, leave them on the submarine."

After breakfast, they got together with their experts in the 'Projection Room'.

Istariol, as Lead Counsel, was in charge – and he reiterated that they deliberately had more material than they could possibly present to the court in the time available. He would decide what they would actually use, depending on how the case unfolded.

"Today, the Prosecutor will present the case against mankind, probably calling a number of witnesses," Istariol explained. "My role will be to provide counter-arguments, where appropriate. Your role is primarily to listen and make notes. If you have anything important you want to inform me about, you will need to pass me a note – preferably discreetly.

"Tomorrow will be our opportunity to present our case for the defence. This would be when one or more of you may be called up to be an expert witness – and the prosecutor may cross-examine you, after you've given your testimony.

"If you reply to the prosecutor, you should use the word 'sir'. In the unlikely event that one of the judges asks you a question, then you should say 'Your Honour' when you reply.

"The prosecutor will physically be in the courtroom, but each of the judges will join the Hearing by video-link.

"As I've explained before, we will travel to the courtroom by submarine, as our host has arranged for the Hearing to be held in a secret underground room next to the River Seine – only reachable by submarine."

They spent the rest of the time going over, once again, the things they may present to the judges.

At 9.00am, Istariol called the meeting to a halt and asked everyone to go and get ready to leave the hotel. "We should all meet at the Apartment's elevator at 9.15am at the latest," he ordered.

At 9.15am, they all gathered outside the elevator, joined by several members of their security team.

Istariol had put on a black robe and was wearing a white wig with small curls at the sides and a tail at the back. No one commented, although Rebecca couldn't quite suppress a slight grin.

They descended to the underground car park, where two limousines were waiting to pick them up.

Five minutes later, the cars pulled up next to where their submarine was moored. A few curious passers-by had gathered to gawk at the yellow boat.

Two security officers assisted everyone aboard, untied the mooring ropes, then climbed down the ladders, securing the hatches behind them. The submarine pulled away from the bank and submerged into the murky waters of the Seine. Once again, there was little to see through the windows.

About ten minutes later, the submarine began to rise. Moments after it became motionless, a security officer climbed up one of the ladders, opened the hatch, and went topside – calling for the others to follow and warning them to be careful, as the surface would be slippery.

Ian was the first to climb onto the deck behind the crewman. The submarine had surfaced next to a white concrete platform and its mooring ropes were now tied up to two bollards. Ahead, he could see a black metal door set into the wall. Stepping cautiously onto the damp platform, Istariol led the way. Pushing down on the door's handle, he opened the door and entered a large room.

Inside, several chairs were arranged in two rows, all facing forward with an aisle down the middle. At the front stood a bench, atop of which were four large flat-screen TVs. In one side of the room, visible to all, was a single seat on a raised platform.

Istariol's companions filed in one by one behind him and, following his lead, sat in the front row. No one else was there. It was 9.50am.

About five minutes later, a man walked into the room from a side-door they hadn't noticed before. Rebecca was pretty sure the door hadn't been there before it suddenly opened.

The man was wearing black robes and a white wig, reminiscent of a 17th century court. But, even today, barristers and judges in criminal courts in Britian still dress this way. On his chest was a small badge – a bronze eagle surrounded by a dark blue hexagon – the symbol for the Mekbudan Blått realm. Gulinrog's tribe was one of the six in this realm.

Despite the wig, everyone recognised the man as Himmler – or his supposed 'impersonator'.

"I am Krognák," the man announced to the assembled audience, in English, with just the faintest trace of a German accent. Perhaps he had been practicing. "I will represent the Mekbudans in this Hearing."

He went over to the bench and picked up a remote control. After pressing a few buttons, all the four TV screens turned on – each showing a different person – three men and one woman, all sporting an even larger wig than Krognák.

"Good morning, Your Honours," Krognák said, bowing. "I am Krognák, the Mekbudan Representative – or Prosecutor."

Istariol also stood up. "Good morning. I am Istariol, Lead Counsel for the Solarian Representative – and the Defence, Your Honours," he announced, bowing at the end of his sentence.

"Very well," one of the judges said sternly. "I am the Chair of this IGC Hearing, so all statements and questions should be addressed to me. Names will not be necessary."

"Istariol," the Chair continued, "you will present the case for the Defence tomorrow. If you intend to submit any detailed evidence, you must transmit the relevant documents to the Court – and to the Prosecution – by noon, local time, today."

"Any witnesses you call may summarise their position and should be prepared to answer questions pertaining to their field of expertise. However, I do not wish to hear witnesses delivering lengthy lectures on matters already fully documented. Is that understood?"

"Yes, Your Honour," Istariol confirmed.

"Then you may now proceed Krognák."

"With your permission, I would like to call my first expert witness, Your Honour," Krognák asked. The Chair nodded.

A clean-shaven man in his mid-forties, dressed in a plain, dark blue pinstriped business suit, entered through the same doorway previously used by Krognák. With measured steps, he ascended the dais and took his seat in the witness box.

"This individual is a recognised Solarian expert on climate change," Krognák announced. "For the purposes of this Hearing, he shall be identified as Doctor X. His true identity and full credentials have been submitted to the Court under seal. I respectfully petition that he be permitted to testify under the protection of anonymity."

"Granted. Continue," the Chair of the IGC Hearing responded.

"Dr X," Krognák said, "I would like to start by asking you to describe what would happen if Earth's climate started to get out of control."

"Yes, sir," Dr X replied. "The first thing most people think of when they hear the words 'global warming' is **flooding**.

"In the twentieth century, the average global sea level rose faster than at any time in at least the past three thousand years – climbing by about 2.3 millimetres per year. And, in the last decade, that rate has nearly doubled.

"This is driven by two forces: the thermal expansion of warming ocean water and the vast influx of meltwater from glaciers and ice sheets.

"Even under the most optimistic scenario – a global temperature rise of only **+2°C** above pre-industrial levels by 2100 – land now home to around **200 million** people will lie permanently below the high-tide line.

"Over three-quarters of those at risk live in Asia, particularly in Bangladesh, China, India, Indonesia, Thailand and Vietnam. In China alone, some 43 million people could see their homes submerged by the end of the century.

"But the threat of permanent flooding is by no means confined to Asia. By the end of the century, without major coastal defences, land now inhabited by more than a million people in nineteen other nations – including Brazil, Egypt, Nigeria and the United Kingdom – could disappear beneath the sea.

"And long before the ocean swallows that land, those communities will face saltwater contamination of freshwater supplies and chronic flooding, rendering their homes uninhabitable long before they vanish beneath the waves. Another 360 million people are projected to face frequent flooding – bringing the total to more than **half a billion** lives affected. That's one in twelve people on the planet – almost as much as the entire population of Europe. And these are today's numbers, not accounting for future population growth."

"So we're not just talking about rising seas," Krognák enquired, "we're talking about whole regions vanishing?"

"Precisely. Vast stretches of coastline, cities, farmland – gone."

"Dr X, please could you explain what cities and regions would be affected?" Krognák directed.

"The latest Intergovernmental Panel on Climate Change report, released in 2023, projects that under high-emission scenarios, sea levels could rise between 2 and 3.3 feet by 2100. These figures exclude several poorly understood ice-sheet processes.

"In a less likely, but still possible case, accelerated melting in Antarctica and Greenland could add more than 3.3 feet on top of that – pushing total sea level rise towards **6.6 feet**, or about **2 metres**, by the century's end."

"Objection – speculation," Istariol challenged.

"Sustained," ruled the Chair.

"I admit that this *is* speculative," Dr X replied. "But our uncertainty over each of the dynamics that lead to sea level rises and climate change – ice sheet collapse, Arctic methane release, the albedo effect – limits our understanding only of the pace of change, not its scale. In reality, we know what the endgame for oceans looks like – we just don't know how long it'll take to get there."

"*What's the albedo effect?*" Rebecca whispered to Istariol.

"*White surfaces, like ice, reflect more sunlight than dark ones,*" Istariol whispered back. "*So when the ice sheets melt, the darker land or ocean beneath absorbs more heat – creating a self-reinforcing spiral.*"

"Almost two-thirds of the planet's largest cities sit along coastlines," Dr X continued, "alongside critical infrastructure such as ports, naval bases, power plants and key agricultural regions like fisheries, farmland and rice fields. Even areas situated seven feet or higher above sea level will face increasingly frequent and severe flooding."

"There are so many things that would actually be underwater if sea levels rose by two metres, that I struggle to mention them all. Perhaps the Court would allow me to display a list of examples on a screen?" Dr X asked.

The IGC Chair nodded and a list appeared on a large screen suspended above the Court.

Examples of things that could be underwater by the year 2100 with a 2 metre increase in sea level:

> Every beach on the planet;
> The coral islands of the Maldives, Taro Island in the Solomon Islands, and the Marshall Islands;
> Much of Greater Dhaka – the capital of Bangladesh and a megacity of over 24 million people – along with most of the Kolkata metropolitan area in India, home to more than 20 million, as well as vast stretches of coastline lying between them;
> Norfolk naval base in Virginia, the United States' largest;
> Large areas of New Orleans, Louisiana;
> Kennedy Space Centre;
> Facebook's META headquarters in California;
> Much of San Francisco Bay, including San Francisco International Airport and Oakland San Francisco Bay Airport;
> Almost all of Venice, including Saint Mark's Basilica;
> Most of Mumbai (previously Bombay) and much of the coastland in the surrounding area, with an estimated population of 12.5 million;
> All of the city of Bangkok, Thailand;
> Ho Chi Minh City and the entire Mekong delta region in Vietnam – an area of over 40,000 square kilometres;
> Most of South Florida's Paradise Coast, all of Miami Beach and the Florida Keys;
> Trump's 'Winter White House' home in the Mar-a-Lago Club, Palm Beach, Florida.

"However, that would only be the start. Even if we stop all greenhouse gas emissions today, the global sea level will continue to rise over the next few centuries.

"Scientists have been able to determine ocean levels during the two most recent periods in Earth's history when global temperatures were around **two degrees Celsius** above pre-industrial levels," Dr X explained.

"Between about 130,000 and 116,000 years ago – a period known as the *'Last Interglacial'* – sea levels were roughly **six to nine metres**, or twenty to thirty feet, higher than today.

"And during the earlier *'Super Interglacial'* period, around 424,000 to 374,000 years ago, the seas stood between **six and thirteen metres** – that's twenty to forty feet – higher than at present.

"So, even under the most optimistic +2°C scenario, our oceans could eventually rise by **six metres** – and possibly more. The planet would lose around 444,000 square miles of land, home to some **375 million people** today, and millions more would be exposed to annual flooding.

"The twenty cities most affected by such a rise would all be Asian megacities – including Mumbai, Kolkata, Shanghai and Hong Kong.

"In fact, about **one billion** people now live on land less than 10 metres above high-tide lines."

"Thank you, Dr X," Krognák said evenly. "Earlier, you mentioned that flooding is what most people think of when they hear about climate change. Could you please tell the Court about some of the other factors?"

"Of course," Dr X replied. "***Extreme heatwaves*** will become increasingly common and millions more people will experience heat stress – not occasionally, but routinely.

"We use the term *'Uncompensable Heat Stress'* to describe a point beyond which the human body can no longer rid itself of heat fast enough to survive. In that state, the body's core temperature begins to rise uncontrollably. High humidity makes it worse – the air becomes so saturated that sweat can't evaporate and the body's primary cooling system fails.

"Uncompensable heat stress is one of the most brutal forms of physical suffering we know – every bit as disorienting and agonising as hypothermia. The first stage is *heat exhaustion*: heavy sweating, rapid breathing, a weak, racing pulse. But when this progresses to *heat stroke*, the body's blood vessels open wide, sending blood to the skin in a desperate attempt to release heat. The body dehydrates rapidly – nausea, vomiting, and pounding headaches follow – and blood pressure collapses, causing fainting or dizziness.

"With severe heat stroke, people become confused, delirious – even violent. As blood pressure continues to fall, the heart rate surges as it tries to maintain circulation, and blood vessels in the extremities constrict, turning the skin pale or bluish. Young children, in particular, can suffer seizures.

"And, when the body finally can't take any more... consciousness fades. Organs fail. And death follows."

Dr X paused, letting the silence hang for a moment.

"As global temperatures continue to rise, cities home to millions across the Middle East and the tropics would become so hot that going outside in summer could be lethal.

"The first regions to endure extreme moist heat waves – and the steepest increases in annual hours of dangerous heat – are also the most densely populated on Earth. These areas are largely composed of low to middle income nations, making them among the most vulnerable populations on the planet.

"Those most at risk include sub-Saharan Africa, with roughly 800 million people, the Indus River Valley and much of India, home to over 2 billion people, and eastern China with another billion.

"In the spring and early summer of 2015, both Kolkata in India and Karachi in Pakistan experienced severe heat waves that resulted in widespread fatalities, with thousands dying from the extreme temperatures. In Karachi alone, more than 1,200 people died within a single week.

"Even if the world meets the +2°C target, many cities in these regions are expected to face deadly heatwaves every single year.

"Earth's scientists have analysed a range of scenarios, each depending on how effectively we can cut greenhouse gas emissions. The projection for high emissions warns that by the year 2100 the planet could warm by **between 3.3 and 5.7** degrees Celsius above pre-industrial levels.

"Regions of North and South America would experience more extreme heat waves in a +3°C warmer world, while northern and central Australia would become affected once +4°C is reached.

"In 2003, a devastating heatwave swept across Europe – one of the deadliest weather events in the continent's history – claiming more than seventy thousand lives. In 2010, a similar event in Russia caused an estimated fifty-five thousand deaths.

"If global temperatures were to rise by four degrees Celsius above pre-industrial levels, those kinds of heatwaves would no longer be exceptional – they'd be the norm every summer.

"Extreme heat has been responsible for an average of **half a million deaths annually** over the last two decades. Even today, around **one billion** people are already at risk from heat stress worldwide, and around 30 percent of the world population is exposed to deadly heat for at least twenty days every year. But, by 2100, this could increase to **75 percent**."

"Thank you for that enlightening information," Krognák said encouragingly. "But as I understand it, it's not just flooding and deadly heatwaves we can expect to see more of?"

"Yes, global warming *is* having a wide ranging impact on the planet," Dr X replied. "**Wildfires** will become increasingly frequent and far more destructive – and in turn, they'll release even more CO_2 into the atmosphere. The six most extreme wildfire years on record have all occurred since 2017.

"In 2023, mega-fires in Canada, the Amazon and other regions, drove global burnt areas to record levels – devastating a total of 320,000 square kilometres.

"And in 2024, fires burned **5 times** more tropical primary forest around the world than in 2023. Globally, a record-shattering total of 67,000 square kilometres of tropical forest was lost – an area nearly the size of Scotland – disappearing at a rate of 18 soccer fields per minute. This was almost double that of 2023 – and this doubling was almost entirely down to fires.

"This loss in 2024 alone, caused 3.1 gigatonnes of greenhouse gas emissions, equivalent to slightly more than the annual CO2 emissions from India's fossil fuel use.

"While fires occur naturally in some ecosystems, in tropical forests they are almost entirely human-caused, often started to clear land for agriculture, and they can then spread out of control into nearby forests.

"And the losses weren't confined to the tropics. Tree-cover loss globally reached a record high in 2024, with boreal regions like Canada and Russia experiencing extreme fires.

"Although forests can recover after fires, the combined effects of climate change, and deforestation for agriculture make that recovery increasingly difficult – and raise the risk of future fires."

"Thank you, Dr X," Krognák said, a thin smile on his lips. "Could you please tell the Court about the impact on our oceans?"

"Of course," Dr X replied. "I'll now go through how global warming will harm our **oceans**.

"Water covers more than seventy percent of the Earth's surface, and about ninety-seven percent of that is contained in the oceans. Because of this, the oceans have a massive influence on the planet's weather, temperature and food supply – not just for humans, but for almost every living thing on Earth.

"Aquatic foods play a vital role in global food and nutrition production, and their consumption is projected to keep rising. Worldwide, more than three billion people depend on seafood for roughly one-fifth of their animal protein intake. These foods are especially important in lower- to middle-income countries, where they are often the primary – and sometimes the only – source of protein.

"Global warming has already caused many fish populations to migrate hundreds of miles towards the poles in search of colder waters – leaving local fishermen with empty seas.

"The ocean acts as one of Earth's great carbon sinks, absorbing roughly 30 percent of all carbon dioxide released into the atmosphere. As atmospheric CO_2 levels rise, so too does the amount drawn into the sea – and with it comes a profound side effect: ***ocean acidification*** – which has far reaching implications for the ocean and the creatures that live there.

"This isn't theory; it's measurable chemistry. The water is becoming more acidic and that change is already reshaping marine ecosystems. Corals, oysters, clams, sea urchins, deep-sea corals – and microscopic organisms like planktonic snails – all rely on calcium carbonate to build their shells and skeletons. But as acidity increases, there are fewer carbonate ions available, making it harder for them to grow – and at lower pH levels, their shells begin to dissolve.

"Since the dawn of the Industrial Revolution, the ocean's surface pH has decreased from 8.18 – to 8.04 in 2024. That might sound trivial, but the pH scale is logarithmic. In real terms, it means the oceans are now around **40% more acidic** than they were two hundred years ago.

"One of the clearest warnings comes from a tiny creature called the pteropod – or 'sea butterfly'. It's no bigger than a pea, yet it's a cornerstone of marine food webs, feeding krill, fish, birds, even whales. In laboratory tests using seawater with acidity levels projected for the year 2100, pteropod shells dissolved after just 45 days.

"Ocean acidification is now progressing faster than at any time in at least the past 66 million years – and quite possibly the last 300 million. If carbon emissions continue unchecked, the average surface pH of the oceans is projected to fall to around 7.8 by the end of this century, making it more than **twice as acidic** than in the year 2000. The last time Earth's oceans reached such levels of acidity was about **fifteen million years ago,** during the mid-Miocene – when global temperatures were roughly 4°C higher and the planet was undergoing a major extinction event."

Dr X paused and shifted in his seat, as if to make himself more comfortable.

"*Coral reefs* are among the most important ecosystems on Earth," Dr X continued. "They support nearly a **quarter of all known marine species** – a staggering diversity of life that depends on their structure for food and shelter.

"But ocean acidification is eroding their resilience. As ocean waters absorb more carbon dioxide, they lose the calcium carbonate that corals need to rebuild after bleaching events. Each year, recovery becomes harder. The reefs grow thinner, more fragile – less able to survive the next ocean heatwave.

"The Intergovernmental Panel on Climate Change has warned that if global temperatures rise by **two degrees** Celsius or more above pre-industrial levels, up to **99% percent** of the world's warm-water coral reefs could disappear entirely. When they die, they take with them entire ecosystems – and the livelihoods of hundreds of millions of people who rely on them."

"Thank you, Dr X," Krognák remarked dryly. "So, apart from flooding, dying oceans, deadly heat waves and rampaging wildfires, is there anything else mankind can look forward to?"

"Well, yes, I'm afraid there is," Dr X replied. "*Droughts* and water shortages will become more severe. Let me explain what that means in practice.

"Four billion people – about half the world's population – currently face water shortages for at least one month each year. The situation is worsened by drought, shrinking rivers, and violent weather events that strike with growing frequency.

"To understand how fragile our freshwater balance really is, consider this: the seas and oceans contain more than ninety-seven percent of all the water on Earth. Roughly two percent is frozen in glaciers and polar ice caps – which accounts for more than two-thirds of the planet's total freshwater. That leaves just a sliver, barely a third of one percent, in all the world's rivers and lakes combined.

"Rising seas are now pushing saltwater further inland, seeping into rivers and aquifers and contaminating freshwater sources. Drinking water becomes unsafe, crops fail, and the salt kills ecosystems that once thrived along the coasts. The corrosion doesn't stop there – it eats into buildings, bridges and other infrastructure. And the damage is most severe in the low-lying coastal areas – home to approximately 40 percent of the global population – including many regions where people can least afford it.

"Glaciers act as vast natural reservoirs – storing snow that hardens into ice in cold, wet periods and releasing it as meltwater during warm seasons – stabilising rivers through parched summers.

"Today, nearly eight hundred million people depend, at least in part, on that meltwater, particularly for agriculture. In regions with drier summers, meltwater from ice and snow is often the only major source of water for months at a time.

"Glaciers blanket about seven hundred thousand square kilometres of the planet's surface. Between 2000 and 2023, the world's glaciers lost an average of two hundred and fifty gigatonnes of ice every year – over 6.5 trillion tonnes in total. That's equivalent to all the freshwater humanity consumes in thirty years.

"In fact, since records began in 1975, more than nine trillion tonnes of glacial ice have vanished – enough to cover the *entire state of **Kansas*** in a 151-foot-high slab of ice. Picture the copper Lady of the Statue of Liberty: that towering figure is the same height. Now imagine that colossal mass of ice simply… gone."

He paused, letting the magnitude sink in before continuing.

"Five of the past six years have seen the most rapid glacier retreat ever recorded. At current melt rates, many glaciers in the Tropics, as well as the United States, western Canada, Scandinavia, central Europe, the Caucasus and New Zealand will not survive this century. And when those glaciers vanish, the consequences will cascade far beyond mountain valleys.

"When the glaciers go, the rivers that depend on them will follow."

He let the words hang for a moment.

"The great rivers of Asia – the Indus, the Ganges, the Brahmaputra, the Mekong and the Yangtze – all draw life from the mountains. Their flow is sustained through the dry months by glacial meltwater. As those glaciers retreat, first the floods will come – swollen rivers bursting their banks each summer – and then, once the ice is gone, the rivers will simply wither. What was once a lifeline for more than a billion people will become a thread of dust.

"In the short term, the meltwater surge will drown farmland, wash away homes, and contaminate the soil with sediment. But within decades, the real catastrophe arrives – the droughts. Fields that once yielded two harvests a year will struggle to grow one. Irrigation networks will fail, reservoirs will dry, and aquifers already strained by overuse will collapse from salt intrusion."

He glanced briefly toward the Chair.

"The loss of the glaciers is not just a matter of scenery – it's the slow, methodical dismantling of Earth's water cycle. This isn't a distant prospect, it's a timeline already unfolding. Satellite data show snowlines retreating higher each year. Agricultural output in South Asia and western China is already falling, not because of poor technique, but because the water is simply disappearing.

"It all connects – heat, water loss and food. By mid-century, major crop belts – wheat, rice, maize – will begin to fail seasonally in some regions. And when you combine that with heat stress on crops, collapsing fisheries, and displaced populations, you have the makings of systemic famine. Food prices will rise, export bans will follow, and the poorest nations will starve first."

He folded his hands.

"Today, around **1.4 million people** face catastrophic levels of acute food insecurity – the last stage before *famine*. Across the world, more than 670 million people still go to bed hungry each night, and countless others live with daily uncertainty about where their next meal will come from.

"The planet now supports just over eight billion people. According to the UN's '2024 World Population Prospects' report, global population growth will start to slow, with numbers expected to peak at around 10.3 billion in 2084, before easing slightly to 10.2 billion by 2100. That's still a lot more mouths to feed.

"But the very systems that are needed to feed humanity are also driving the crisis. Agriculture is not just a victim of climate change – it's a major contributor. It accounts for roughly 90 percent of global freshwater consumption and produces more than a quarter of all human-caused greenhouse-gas emissions. These emissions have nearly doubled in the past half-century, fuelled by deforestation, intensive livestock farming, and the conversion of forests and wetlands into cropland.

"Agriculture is also the largest contributor of methane and nitrous oxide, both far more potent than carbon dioxide as heat-trapping gases. Nitrous oxide in particular has 265 times the effect of CO_2 on global warming.

"Extreme weather – from torrential floods to prolonged droughts – is now degrading arable land and cutting harvest yields across every continent. Whilst rising temperatures can boost growth for certain crops, the benefits are short-lived: once daytime heat exceeds a crop-specific critical threshold, yields collapse."

He paused, before adding softly: "When food becomes scarce and water runs dry, people move. It's the oldest pattern in human history – and it's about to unfold on a scale the world has never seen."

He adjusted his spectacles, his voice calm but edged with warning.

"By mid-century, entire regions will begin to empty. Farmers will abandon land that has turned to dust. Coastal populations will retreat inland as rising seas swallow their towns. Desertification, floods and heat will make migration not a choice – but a necessity."

He glanced down briefly at his notes before continuing.

"Imagine the world's borders under that much pressure. Refugee flows not just from war – but from the climate. Nations already struggling with food security and economic instability will fracture under the strain. And where there are borders, there will be walls. Where there are walls, there will be conflict.

"Drought has already played a role in destabilising regions – from Syria to the Sahel – forcing rural populations into cities, igniting competition for resources and feeding extremism. Multiply that pressure across continents and the geopolitical consequences are staggering. We're not only facing a crisis of climate – but a crisis of governance."

He paused, his voice softening.

"History teaches us that famine, displacement and collapse rarely occur in isolation. They come together – and when they do, they bring war with them."

He glanced at his notes again, then back up at the tribunal.

"Conflict is already the single greatest driver of hunger. Around 70 percent of the world's undernourished population live in regions scarred by war and violence. Where conflict and climate converge, famine follows.

"Wars are not created by climate change alone – any more than hurricanes are created solely by it – but both are made far more likely.

"Rising water scarcity will strike at the heart of global food production and increasingly trigger armed conflicts, as fresh water becomes scarcer. Since 1900, there have been over five hundred water-related conflicts and nearly half of them have erupted since 2010. As rivers dry and aquifers are drained, the competition for what remains will turn neighbour against neighbour – and nation against nation."

The courtroom had fallen utterly silent.

"Krognák," the Chair said, "I think we now all understand how bad things could get with runaway climate change. I appreciate you wish to make it a matter for the record – but please direct your witness to keep it brief."

"Yes, Your Honour," Krognák replied. "Dr X, please can you tell us – as briefly as possible – what would happen if climate change got out of control."

"Very well," Dr X said, shuffling his notes. "I think it's time we talked about the *elephant in the room* – carbon dioxide levels.

"In 2024, atmospheric carbon dioxide rose by a record **3.5 parts per million**, reaching a new high of **424 ppm** – the largest annual increase since modern measurements began in 1957."

"Your Honour, may the Court view the historical CO_2 graph?" Dr X asked.

"Yes, go ahead," the Chair replied, somewhat impatiently.

The screen above the courtroom now displayed this chart.

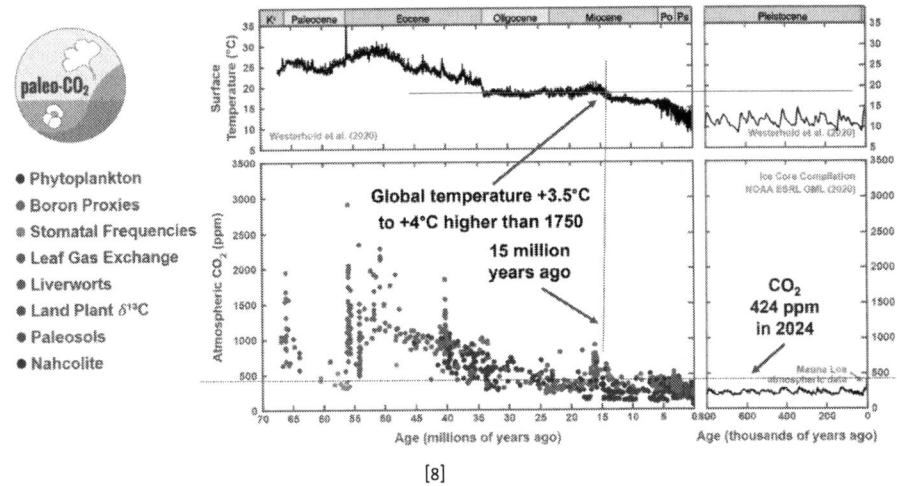

[8]

"We have fairly accurate records of historical CO_2 levels for the past 800,000 years, derived from samples taken deep beneath the ice sheets of Antarctica and Greenland. Beyond that point, there's greater uncertainty. However, scientists have used a range of different methods to estimate carbon dioxide levels – represented on this chart by the various coloured dots – extending back 70 million years.

"What this tells us is that we can be quite confident **CO_2 levels today are higher** than at any point in the last **eight hundred thousand years**. And if we take an average of the different methods used to estimate earlier periods, we have to go back to the middle Miocene Epoch – about **fifteen million years ago** – to find the last time carbon dioxide levels were similar to those we see today."

Dr Blue hurriedly scribbled a note and passed it to Istariol.

"Fifteen million years ago," Dr X continued, "the global average temperature was somewhere between **3.5°C and 4°C** above pre-industrial levels. That does not bode well for where we may be headed."

"Objection – speculation," Istariol interjected.

"Explain your objection," the Chair demanded.

"The chart clearly shows that Earth was gradually *cooling* from a very high global temperature fifty million years ago," Istariol replied. "Just because the amount of CO_2 in the atmosphere fifteen million years ago was the same as today, when the temperature was higher, doesn't mean you can draw any conclusions about what will happen in the future in a world that is **warming**."

"Dr X, you may answer this criticism. I also want you to justify why you said it *'does not bode well,'* when referring to the Earth fifteen million years ago," the Chair directed.

"Yes, Your Honour," Dr X replied. "As already explained, fifteen million years ago the planet was at least three degrees Celsius warmer than pre-industrial levels. Earth had much smaller polar ice sheets then, and sea levels stood between twenty and thirty metres higher than today – that's sixty-five to one hundred feet higher.

"Yes, the Earth *was* cooling at that time. But the Miocene's temperature and CO_2 levels demonstrate one possible climate equilibrium – one that persisted for millions of years – and it could represent Earth's long-term fate, even if CO_2 levels do *not* go any higher.

"Even if emissions stopped today, severe global warming still *in the pipeline* would occur. Ice sheets take thousands of years to melt and multi-metre sea-level increases will unfold over centuries.

"When I said it *'does not bode well'*, I meant that today's CO_2 levels match those of a time when Earth was far hotter and less habitable – and our present trajectory suggests we could be heading for a similar world.

"There are several major feedback loops that take time to amplify global warming. With the Court's permission, I'd like to explain these."

"The objection is overruled," the Chair stated. "Dr X, you may continue."

"Thank you, Your Honour. I'd now like to go through the climatic tipping points, and then summarise what a world warmed by **4°C** would look like."

Dr X took off his glasses and cleaned them with a small cloth.

"May I ask that the Court bring up the tipping-points chart?" he said.

The Chair nodded, and an image appeared on the screen.

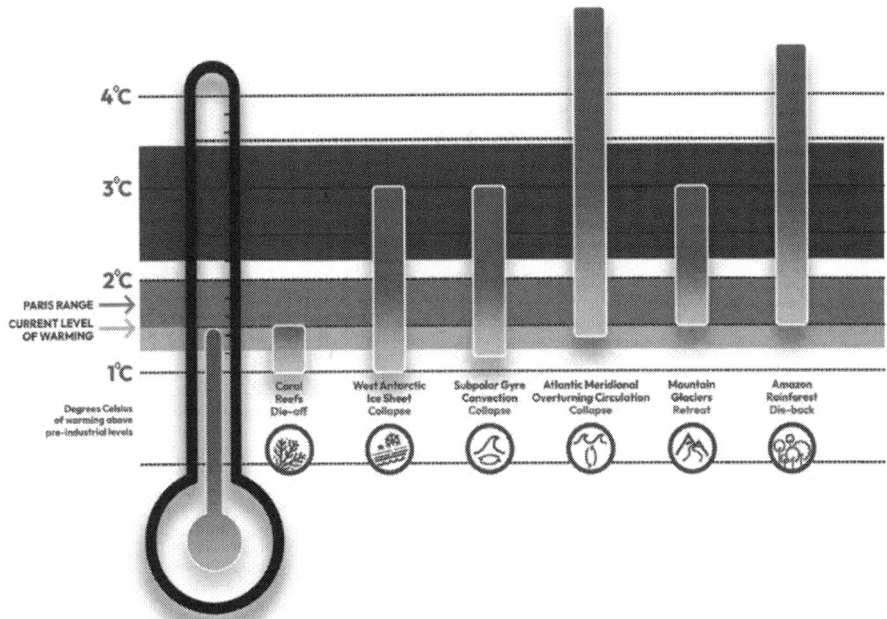

Risk of Earth system tipping points increase with temperature [9]

"At **+4°C** of warming, as much as **half of all species** on Earth could face extinction. Coral reefs would vanish entirely and polar ecosystems would collapse. The melting of permafrost would release vast stores of methane. More of the planet's great climate tipping points could also be triggered – the dieback of the Amazon rainforest, and the shutdown of the Gulf Stream – the Atlantic Ocean's circulation system. Each of these would accelerate the others in a chain of self-reinforcing feedback loops.

"Many regions of the world would become effectively uninhabitable for humans due to extreme heat, desertification and rising seas. Large areas of Africa, Australia, the United States, and much of the Mediterranean basin would be affected – as would equatorial regions, including vast stretches of South America and Asia."

He drew a slow breath before continuing.

"Flooding, starvation, thirst and unbearable temperatures would drive mass migration and conflict on a scale that defies imagination.

"Consider this: the Syrian civil war, which began in 2011 and displaced roughly **one million refugees** into Europe, was intensified by drought and failed harvests linked to climate change. Now imagine **ten times** that number forced to flee Bangladesh alone, as rising seas swallow the Ganges delta – in a world already destabilised by climate chaos."

He lowered his voice slightly.

"And they won't be the only ones. The World Bank looked at six regions around the world – South Asia, East Asia and the Pacific, Eastern Europe and Central Asia, North Africa, sub-Saharan Africa, and Latin America. Their report estimated that **by 2050** more than **216 million people** in these regions could be displaced by the impacts of climate change – a tide of human movement the modern world is utterly unprepared to face.

"These people are generally expected to move within their own countries, but desperation does not have much respect for national boundaries.

"And some analyses put that figure close to a **billion** by the end of the century, depending on how quickly conditions deteriorate."

He let the silence settle for a moment before continuing.

"When systems fail, they do not fail neatly. They collapse in cascades.

"The pressures we're talking about – famine, drought, displacement – don't stay contained. They ripple through everything: trade, finance, energy, health. Every nation, no matter how rich or insulated it believes itself to be, will feel the impact.

"As harvests fail and supply chains fracture, the global food market will implode. Prices will soar – first wheat, then rice, then meat – until even developed nations face shortages. Insurance systems will collapse under the strain of constant disasters. Economies that depend on global shipping will falter as ports are inundated or crippled by storms.

"Governments will start diverting budgets to crisis response – rebuilding, firefighting, policing migration – and the cost of recovery will outstrip the cost of prevention a hundredfold. Infrastructure designed for a stable climate – power grids, rail networks, sewage systems – will buckle under stress. Cities will face rolling blackouts, water rationing, transport breakdowns."

He looked around the room.

"Disease will follow. Warming seas breed pathogens, while floodwaters spread cholera and dengue to regions that have never known them. Vector-borne illnesses like malaria will move northward and southward from the tropics. Heat itself becomes a killer – silent, indiscriminate – claiming more lives annually than any war.

"The World Bank has already warned that the global economy could shrink by as much as 18 percent by 2050 under severe warming scenarios.

That's not a recession – that's the slow disintegration of the global market itself."

He closed his folder, his voice softening.

"And when people lose their livelihoods, when nations lose faith in institutions, democracy begins to erode. Authoritarianism grows in the vacuum – the promise of control in a world spinning out of it. Civil order falters. Then comes conflict, famine, and, finally… chaos."

Then, almost as an afterthought, he added: "If this century ends with more than three degrees of warming, the term 'climate refugee' will no longer describe the few – it will describe the entire human race."

He paused – long enough for the weight of his words to settle across the courtroom like dust after a storm.

He drew a final breath, his tone quiet but absolute. "A +4°C world is not 'adaptable' in any meaningful sense. It would cause widespread societal collapse and an ongoing planetary emergency."

He paused briefly, before continuing.

"But it wouldn't stop at +4°C.

"The climate tipping point risks are interconnected and most of the interactions between them are destabilising, meaning tipping one system makes tipping another more likely. The resulting impacts would cascade through the ecological and social systems we depend upon, creating escalating damages.

"Once we trigger these global tipping points, the self-reinforcing feedback loops could eventually drive temperatures to +6°C – perhaps even to +8°C.

"It might take hundreds or even thousands of years to unfold, but those loops are irreversible – and therefore, effectively permanent. You might hope we could then simply reverse climate change, but we won't be able to. It will outrun us all," he concluded.

"Thank you, Dr X. Now please tell us what mankind has done to reduce global warming," Krognák directed.

"In 1997, the 'landmark' Kyoto Protocol was signed – an international treaty designed to combat climate change by reducing greenhouse gas emissions. At the time, two degrees Celsius of global warming was considered the threshold of catastrophe: flooded cities, crippling droughts and heatwaves – a planet battered daily by hurricanes and monsoons that we used to call 'natural disasters' – but which we now simply call *'bad weather.'*

"The Kyoto Protocol achieved practically nothing. In the twenty years since it came into force in 2005, despite widespread climate advocacy, legislation, and progress on green energy, humanity has produced more emissions than in the twenty years before.

"In 2016, the Paris Agreement replaced the Kyoto Protocol. Vulnerable countries – such as small island states and least developed nations – had pushed hard to set 1.5°C of warming as the target, arguing that *'2°C is a death sentence.'* Developed nations, however, had long regarded 2°C as the politically and technologically achievable ceiling. The Paris Agreement ultimately set 2°C as the global goal, but also included 1.5°C as an aspirational benchmark – recognising that even half a degree can mean a life-or-death difference for millions of people and many ecosystems.

"But now, in 2025 – not *one* industrial nation is on track to meet its Paris commitments."

"May I request that the Court now shows the global temperature chart?" Dr X asked.

The Chair nodded his agreement. On the screen, a chart appeared.

Global annual averages of near-surface temperatures (°C) of land and ocean 1900 to 2024
(relative to the pre-industrial period 1850-1900)

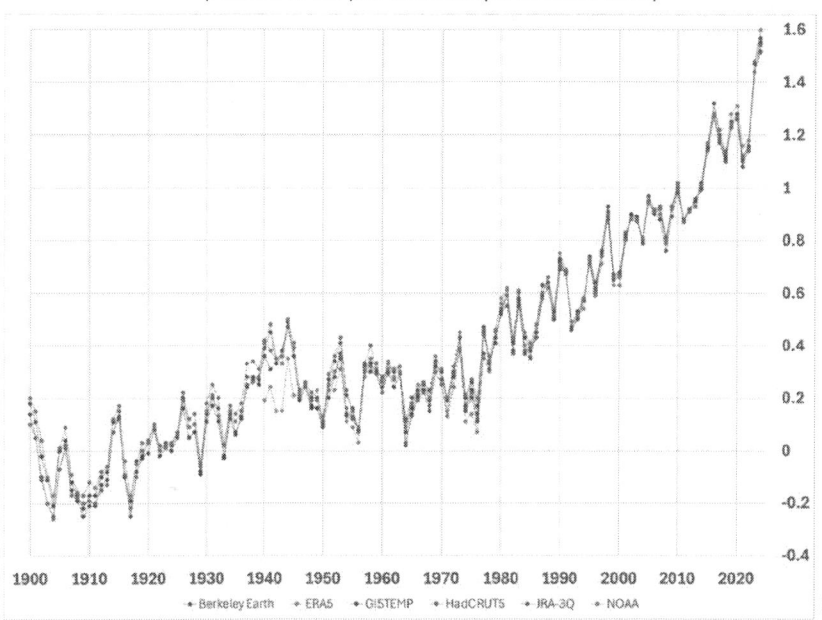

Berkeley Earth • ERA5 • GISTEMP • HadCRUT5 • JRA-3Q • NOAA

[10]

"Since the 1970s, global temperatures have risen faster than in any other fifty-year period of the last two millennia, with the past decade – up to 2024 – being the warmest on record."

"By 2100, the future of Earth's climate could unfold along very different paths depending on humanity's choices," Dr X explained.

"According to the latest available scientific forecasts, if the world were to rapidly slash emissions – the most optimistic pathway – global warming might be held to around **+1.4°C**, with a *likely* range of +1.0 to +1.8°C above pre-industrial levels.

"However," he went on, "those projections were made a couple of years ago. In reality, last year global warming **breached the +1.5°C aspirational target** – reaching somewhere between **+1.51°C** and **+1.60°C**.

"Alternatively, if progress proves uneven but emissions do stabilise around 2050, the world could be on track for roughly **+2.7°C** of warming by 2100 – within a range of **+2.1 to +3.5°C**.

"But if emissions continue to rise at their current rate or even higher, the most pessimistic scenarios foresee global temperatures rising by **+3.3 to +5.7°C**, with the central estimate at **+4.4°C**.

"So, in truth, two degrees now looks more like a best-case outcome, with a range of more horrific possibilities extending beyond it.

"Even the most optimistic outlook leaves Earth permanently hotter than today. At the other extreme, civilisation would face levels of heat and disruption unseen in human history – a world remade by fire, flood, famine and relentless instability."

"Thank you, Dr X," Krognák said with a satisfied smile. "I now come to my final question. Does the Paris Agreement have any binding commitments to reduce greenhouse gas emissions?"

"The Paris Agreement is a treaty and certain provisions are legally binding, including the requirement for countries to submit and update their Nationally Determined Contributions every five years.

"However, whilst countries are required to submit their voluntary emission reduction targets, these targets are not internationally mandated or enforced through any penalties.

"So, no – there are *no* binding commitments to reduce greenhouse gases."

"Thank you very much for coming here to explain all of this to us, Dr X. I have no further questions. Does the Defence Counsel wish to cross-examine?" Krognák asked, turning towards Istariol.

"No questions," Istariol replied.

"Then the Court will now adjourn," the Chair announced, emphasising his declaration with a strike of a gavel. "We will reconvene at 11.30 hours."

The TV screens went blank – except for one TV – which was now displaying a digital clock.

Chapter 26

Dr X stepped down from the witness box, and he and Krognák left the room through the same door they had entered by.

Another door opened in the opposite side of the room and a dark-skinned man strolled in.

"Jambo. How you dey all? We get drinks for you dis room, ya highnesses," the man announced in pidgin English, holding his arm out towards the doorway he had come from. "Hakuna Matata, yote yatakuwa sawa," he added in Swahili, with a gap-toothed smile.

Rebecca was quite convinced that this man had never visited a dentist.

Istariol and Ian decided it was best not to hold any discussions on board the Mekbudan ship – and so, leaving the rest of the group to go and have some refreshments, they went outside and climbed down into the submarine.

"You didn't really challenge much of what Dr X was saying?" Ian observed.

"The truth is," Istariol replied, "there was very little incorrect about what he said. We all know how bad global warming will be for mankind and for the planet. And no one really knows how long it'll be before things become truly dire – it depends on whether humanity actually starts taking action, and on a global scale.

"Our defence strategy has to focus on that – why and how Solarians *will* stop global warming before it's too late."

"Okay, then I guess there's not much more to discuss at this point," Ian acknowledged. "We'd better get back to the others."

As 11.30am approached, the group filed back into the Hearing room and took their seats again.

Then Krognák marched into the room and the TV screen lit up once more to show the faces of the judges.

"With your permission, Your Honour," Krognák asked, looking at the IGC Chair, "I would now like to call the second witness for the Prosecution – US President Donald J. Trump."

Rebecca couldn't help whispering, "What the *fuck*?"

"Your Honours," Krognák continued, "I am in full compliance with Directive 9 in calling this witness. President Trump believes he is being interviewed by a TV news broadcaster – in exchange for a substantial donation to the Republican Party, of course.

"He has no knowledge of the true nature of this Hearing, and we will only communicate via video link. When he sees and hears me speak, I will be using an avatar and will appear to him as a typical TV news anchor – complete with an American accent and a TV studio backdrop."

The Chair nodded and said, "Very well, proceed."

A live video feed of Donald J. Trump appeared on a large wall screen. President Trump is seated behind a desk. The US flag and the President's flag are displayed behind him.

Krognák, standing with arms clasped behind his back, turned to the screen and began the interview.

KROGNÁK:
"Good morning, Mr President. Thank you *so* much for joining us today. I would like to begin by asking you to tell our audience what your views on climate change are?"

TRUMP (smiling into camera):
"Thank you very much. Great to be with you.

"I should probably say something about maybe my views on climate change and oil and gas because I think they're probably different from what most people would assume because my views are actually pretty, I think moderate in this regard, which is that I don't think we should vilify the oil and gas industry and the people that have worked very hard in those industries to provide the necessary energy to support the economy. And if we were to stop using oil and gas right now, we would all be starving and the economy would collapse.

"Look – I'm not a believer in man-made climate change. I've seen people say it's a hoax. Some people say that, and I tend to agree. I mean, it could be, right? Could be. A lot of smart people are saying that."

KROGNÁK:
"But scientists from your own country's agencies have warned of serious consequences."

TRUMP (shrugging):
"They say a lot of things. I've seen it go both ways. You know, years ago they used to call it global cooling. In the 1920s, they thought the planet was going to freeze.

"I mean, I remember in the '70s they were talking about global cooling. Remember that? Global cooling. Then it was global warming. Then they started calling it climate change because they didn't know what was going on.

"Now they think the planet's going to burn up. Well, I don't think science knows, actually."

KROGNÁK:
"Thank you, Mr President. Your administration withdrew from a global agreement on climate change – the Paris Accord – can you tell us more about that?"

TRUMP:
"Oh yes – the Paris Accord was a disaster for America. Total disaster. We would have been punishèd, other countries like China and India – they got a free pass. I wasn't going to let that happen. I put America first. We saved six and a half million jobs. We prevented a loss of $3 trillion GDP.

"For example, under the agreement, China will be able to increase these emissions by a staggering number of years – 13. They can do whatever they want for thirteen years. Not us.

"And let's be clear – the agreement doesn't eliminate coal jobs, it just transfers those jobs out of America and the United States, and ships them to foreign countries. This agreement is less about the climate and more about other countries gaining a financial advantage over the United States.

"The bottom line is that the Paris Accord was very unfair at the highest level to the United States. It would have undermined our economy, hamstrung our workers – and have effectively decapitated our coal industry."

KROGNÁK:
"So, you don't accept that rising emissions are harming the planet?"

TRUMP (leaning forward):
"Even if the Paris Agreement were implemented in full, with total compliance from all nations, it is estimated that by the year 2100 it would only produce a reduction in global temperature of two-tenths of one degree Celsius – think of that. Tiny, tiny amount.

"In fact, fourteen days of carbon emissions from China alone would wipe out the gains from America – and this is an incredible statistic – would totally wipe out the gains from America's expected reductions in the year 2030, after we have had to spend billions and billions of dollars, lost jobs, closed factories, and suffered much higher energy costs for our businesses and for our homes.

"I want the cleanest air, the cleanest water. But we're not going to destroy our economy over a theory. Some of these scientists – they're political. They have an agenda. We've had record energy production. Record clean coal. Tremendous."

KROGNÁK (smiling):
"And if Earth's climate becomes unstable?"

TRUMP:
"Well, I'll tell you this – weather changes. It's always changed. You have storms. You have cold. You have heat. That's what weather does. But nobody's gonna tell me we have to shut down America over it."

KROGNÁK:
"Thank you, Mr President. Since you've been back in office, what steps have you taken to promote your approach to climate change policy?"

TRUMP (nodding, hands steepled):
"Well, first of all, we're restoring energy dominance. That's what we're doing. I rolled back Biden's ridiculous climate regulations – they were killing our businesses, destroying jobs. We're bringing back fossil fuels. We've reopened leasing on federal lands – oil, natural gas, clean coal. Energy independence is back."

KROGNÁK:
"So, you've reversed environmental protections?"

TRUMP:
"Protections? No. I call them 'obstructions.' We've cut the red tape. We terminated all that Green New Deal nonsense. We're fast-tracking permits for pipelines – like the great Keystone XL. You remember that? Biden shut it down – I brought it back. Tremendous for jobs."

KROGNÁK:
"And in terms of alternative energy?"

TRUMP:
"Look, I like clean energy. Wind is fine – unless you live near one, they're loud and they kill all the birds. And they don't work when the wind stops. Solar? Sure. We'll let the market decide. But I'm not going to subsidise it

like the last guy. We're drilling, we're fracking, and we're building. That's how you grow an economy."

KROGNÁK:

"And carbon emissions?"

TRUMP:

"We already lowered emissions during my first term – more than anybody expected. And we did it without hurting the economy. China? India? They're the real polluters. If we shut everything down and they keep going – what's the point?

"The biggest threat is not global warming, where the ocean's going to rise one-eighth of an inch over the next 400 years – and anyway you'll have more oceanfront property, right?"

"But they don't talk about a madman that's building nuclear missiles right now. That's your real global warming – it's nuclear warming," he said. "We have five countries now that have significant nuclear power."

KROGNÁK (reading):

"To quote something you've previously said, sir: *'The concept of global warming was created by and for the Chinese in order to make US manufacturing non-competitive.'* Do you still stand by that statement?"

TRUMP (grinning):

"That was a tweet – very famous tweet. Millions of likes. But look, we've got to be smart. The US has the cleanest air and water – we've done more than any other country. But I'm not going to let radical left climate extremists destroy American energy. I brought energy independence. Under me, we are number one in oil and gas."

KROGNÁK:

"Thank you, Mr. President. I'd now like to ask about your government's current climate policy – specifically your support for Project 2025, a blueprint for dismantling environmental oversight. Are you familiar with it?"

TRUMP (smiling):

"You know, a lot of people are talking about Project 2025. It's a tremendous plan. Some of the best people – really smart people – helped put it together. It's about making America Great Again. We're taking power away from unelected bureaucrats and giving it back to the people."

KROGNÁK:

"Mr. President, I understand that since you returned to the White House, your administration has initiated a number of cost-cutting measures, designed to shrink the size and cost of government.

"But this has resulted in hundreds of climate and weather scientists being fired or let go — and ties have been cut to hundreds more scientists who work in academia or the private sector.

"Your team has also eliminated major climate programs, frozen or cut grants for climate research and moved to shutter the Environmental Protection Agency's greenhouse gas reporting program.

"Is it true that under your leadership, the United States is moving to eliminate climate regulations?"

TRUMP:

"My really great 2026 Budget Request completely eliminates funding for woke EPA research grants — you know, the kind they give to far-left environmental groups pushing the radical climate agenda.

"We are not funding globalist climate nonsense anymore. We are unleashing American energy like never before — oil, gas, clean coal — and we're going to have the greatest economy in the history of the world. Bigger than ever before.

"Look, climate change is a very complex issue. I've said it before — '*I don't believe it's a hoax, but I don't believe it's man-made.*' And I said that. And I was right. What we're doing is protecting American jobs. We don't want China and India laughing at us while we destroy our economy for some Paris Agreement nonsense."

KROGNÁK:

"I believe your budget calls for even deeper cuts in the months and years ahead. For example, billions of dollars will be cut to climate and weather research at the NOAA — the National Oceanic and Atmospheric Administration — and NASA, widely considered two of the world's top science agencies.

"Scientists are saying that this is an unprecedented assault on mankind's understanding of how global warming is transforming the planet.

"Are you not concerned that these actions will blind the United States and the world to the ways we are rapidly heating the planet by burning fossil fuels?"

TRUMP:

"Look, the Energy Secretary, Chris Wright, recently explained that: *'Climate alarmism has had a terrible impact on human lives and freedom. It belongs in the ash heap of history'.*

"And, as Chris went on to say: *'Climate change is real, but far from the world's greatest challenge. Politicians, media and activists have abused the climate issue to pursue highly destructive ends of top down control, expensive energy, and wrongly scaring children'.*

"You know, NOAA's so-called 'educational' grants – they've been pushing climate fear and radicalising students against capitalism, against America. It's environmental alarmism – pure and simple.

"We need to roll back this climate nonsense. These so-called 'scientific studies' are just being used to create job-killing regulations that hurt American energy. My administration will unleash US fossil fuel production – and we're not going to let woke bureaucrats stand in the way."

KROGNÁK:

"I believe you are planning to eliminate the Department of Energy's renewable energy programs and expand fossil fuel drilling across federal lands. Given Earth's worsening climate condition, do you believe increasing emissions is a responsible action?"

TRUMP:

"Fossil fuels are reliable. You can't run a country on windmills and solar panels. I mean, the wind doesn't always blow, right? That's what I've said. *'When the wind stops blowing, that's the end of your electric.'* That's a direct quote from me. People love that quote."

KROGNÁK:

"So, to clarify – you support a strategy that accelerates fossil fuel use, dismantles climate safeguards, and removes limits on greenhouse gas emissions?"

TRUMP:

"I support a strategy that helps American workers and keeps us strong. Not like under Biden where the price of everything went up. And by the way, that climate science – a lot of it is political. Some of these scientists are making a fortune off of fear."

Krognák suddenly turned away from the screen showing President Trump and said, "Your Honours, Mr. Trump can't hear us talk at the moment. I have finished with my questions and would like to ask whether the Defence wishes to cross-examine?"

"I have no questions, Your Honour," Istariol replied.

Krognák then turned back towards President Trump.

KROGNÁK:

"Thank you so much for your time, Mr. President. And thank you for joining us and explaining your views."

TRUMP:

"You people will never report it fairly, but that's okay. Someday you'll admit I was right.

"We're going to make America Great Again."

The wall display went blank.

Turning toward the IGC judges, Krognák declared, "Your Honours, let the IGC put on record that the witness, President Donald J. Trump, has confirmed his support for climate rollback policies and has dismissed planetary-scale climate science as politically motivated."

"Your Honour, may I make a rebuttal statement?" Istariol asked.

"Objection, there are no grounds for a rebuttal," Krognák claimed.

"Overruled," the IGC Chair stated. "You may make a statement – but make it brief."

"Honourable members of the IGC Hearing," Istariol said. "You have just heard testimony from Donald John Trump, twice elected President of the United States of America, one of Earth's most powerful nations. His words speak clearly for themselves. I will not contest their authenticity – only their consequences.

"He dismissed climate science as political. He mocked renewable energy. He championed fossil fuels as a matter of pride.

"And that *is* his right, under Earth's political rules.

"But the IGC should ask: *'Does this represent all of humanity?'*

"The answer, honourable judges, is a resounding NO. Earth is not ruled by one man – nor by one nation.

"The United States currently emits only 20% of Earth's greenhouse gases. Other nations – some large, some small – are working tirelessly to transition to clean energy, to protect forests, to innovate, to survive.

"The Solarians are not perfect. But nor are they indifferent. Hundreds of millions marched for climate action. Many nations pledged net-zero targets. Courts have ruled against their own governments for failing to protect the climate. Children are teaching their elders. Scientists are ringing alarm bells.

"And, yes, many politicians who are simply looking for short term benefits – like economic growth – still get elected. But they are challenged, every day, by people who believe Earth needs to saved.

"Mr Trump represents one voice. I ask the IGC to hear the other voices. Let his words be entered into the record not as Earth's final statement, but as a warning – of what happens when those in power ignore the consequences of their actions.

"And let Mankind's defence rest not in denial, but in its rising resistance to it."

"Thank you," Istariol concluded, bowing to the judges.

There was a brief moment of silence.

Turning towards the IGC Chair, Krognák asked, "May I now make my closing argument?"

"Proceed," the Chair allowed.

"Firstly," Krognák began, "I have demonstrated that Mankind is *not* ignorant of the dangers of global warming – they are fully aware, as evidenced by the testimony of Dr X, a *Solarian* expert witness.

"Secondly, Mankind is doing very little about it. Greenhouse gas emissions continue to climb inexorably, year after year. Despite all the fanfare surrounding their so-called Paris Agreement, there are *no* binding commitments to reduce emissions.

"Thirdly, as a telling example of Solarian attitudes, Mr. Trump – the so-called 'Leader of the Free World' – refuses to accept that Mankind is causing climate change. Now that he is once again the US President, he is intentionally investing in expanded fossil fuel production, whilst simultaneously slashing the budgets of some of Earth's foremost climate-monitoring organisations.

"Mankind continues to release unacceptably large quantities of greenhouse gases into the atmosphere, fully aware of the devastation this will cause.

"I have therefore shown that Mankind *is* guilty of gross negligence and has committed a dereliction of its duty as caretaker of the Earth."

"The prosecution rests, Your Honour," Krognák declared.

With a strike of the gavel, the Chair declared, "The Court is now adjourned. We will reconvene at 10.00am tomorrow morning."

Chapter 27

"I don't think that went very well," Rebecca observed, dryly.

They were back in the Apartment – and the whole team was sitting around having lunch in one of the dining rooms.

"It went pretty much as expected, apart from Mr. Trump's appearance," Istariol replied.

"I knew Trump was a sceptic of man-made climate change," Ian said, "but I hadn't realised the extent of what he's done since returning to office – reversing everything President Biden had put in place to help, repealing climate protection regulations, ramping up fossil fuel production, and slashing the budgets of his own climate science agencies.

"And as for his administration considering the education of young people about climate change as 'scaring children' – it beggars belief. You couldn't make this stuff up."

"Excuse me, but I do need to interrupt," Alexa suddenly announced. "I've been looking into Mr. Trump's interview – and have found something interesting."

Having got everyone's attention, Alexa continued. "That interview with President Trump was a fake. I thought it wasn't very likely that he'd be talking to us that early in the morning. It was about 11.30am here – so it would have been 5.30am in Washington DC, as they're 6 hours behind.

"Anyway, I analysed the background in the supposed TV interview and it was definitely set in the Oval Office of the West Wing. I then hacked into the White House systems and looked at the CCTV records. At 5.30am local time, the Oval Office was dark and quiet – and Mr Trump was fast asleep in his bedroom on the second floor."

"Wow. Why would the Mekbudans have done that – they must have known we'd check?" Rebecca asked.

"I'm not sure," Istariol replied. "Alexa, what about the content of the interview – is what Mr Trump actually said in the interview accurate?"

"Yes, it all seems to be," Alexa said.

"Okay, thanks. Well, we'll make a motion to dismiss Trump's testimony tomorrow and see what happens."

The next morning, after a short pep-talk from Istariol over breakfast, they made their way back to the Mekbudan spaceship for day two of the Hearing.

Once everyone was seated and the Hearing had recommenced, Istariol rose and addressed the Chair.

"Your Honour," Istariol replied. "We have come across information that leads us to believe that the interview with Mr Trump was not live.

"As it was presented to the Court as a live interview – we are making an immediate motion to dismiss Trump's testimony – on the basis that the Court has been deceived by the Prosecution."

"Krognák, what do have to say about this?" the Chair barked.

"Indeed, Your Honour, it is true that President Trump cancelled the interview at the last moment," Krognák admitted. "This was despite the very large donation that we would've made. He claimed that his office should never have agreed to an interview so early in the morning, particularly on a day when he was scheduled to fly to Pennsylvania to deliver a speech on tariffs to a group of steel workers.

"However, I would like to point out that Counsel for the Defence *did* accept President Trump's testimony in his rebuttal, stating: *'I will not contest their authenticity...'*

"In addition, I submit that the dramatic effect of a live interview would have fairly represented his views to the Court. President Trump's cancellation put this opportunity in jeopardy – so we constructed an interview based purely on his previous public speeches and his administration's published official policies.

"Therefore, I object to the motion to dismiss his testimony – on the grounds that, whilst I may have exercised some poetic licence in presenting it as a live interview, the content itself was entirely accurate."

There was a brief pause as the judges appeared to engage in an off-camera discussion.

"Krognák, you are walking on very thin ice," the Chair declared sternly. "If you dare to mislead this Court again, there will be serious consequences – to be precise, the entire case will be dismissed and the Solarians will be free to do with Earth as they please.

"However, we find that the content of the interview *is* factually accurate. Therefore, we permit the testimony to stand." The Chair struck the gavel for emphasis.

"Istariol, we received the documents you sent to us yesterday," the Chair continued. "You may now proceed with your presentation of the case for the defence."

"Thank you, Your Honour," Istariol responded. "In the same way that the Counsel for the Prosecution called an anonymous witness, Dr X – we wish to give anonymity to our witnesses – 'Professor Green', 'Lord White' and 'Dr Blue.' We have, of course, provided all of their true identities and credentials to the Court."

"Permission granted – your witnesses may remain anonymous," the Chair ruled.

"Thank you, Your Honour. I would now like to call 'Lord White' as our first witness," Istariol announced.

'Lord White' stood up and walked up to take his seat in the witness box.

"Lord White," Istariol began, "the Court has already received the documents outlining our proposals to reduce Mankind's greenhouse gas emissions over the next five years and beyond. Could you please explain your role and how we intend to achieve this?"

"Certainly, sir," Lord White replied. "We are establishing a not-for-profit organisation that will oversee our dedicated investment programme, and I have agreed to serve as its Chief Executive Officer.

"We recognise that addressing this crisis will require trillions of dollars to halt – and, we hope, reverse – the rise in greenhouse gas concentrations in Earth's atmosphere. As outlined in our proposal document, we will directly invest up to one hundred billion dollars of our own funds in greenhouse gas reduction programmes. In addition, we will leverage this investment by encouraging co-investment from national governments and global institutions.

"I trust the Court has reviewed my extensive experience in this field. I have worked across industries involved in carbon capture and emissions reduction, and I have collaborated with national governments, investment banks and international bodies. I also maintain a strong network of contacts within those institutions."

"Objection," Krognák interrupted. "Your scientists have only just realised that our entire 'universe' is trapped inside a massive blackhole," he scoffed. "Why should we believe Solarians can develop the technology capable of stopping – let alone reversing – global warming?"

"Overruled," the Chair announced, with a strike of a gavel. "The Court is already satisfied that the Solarians have the capability to reverse global warming. What is at question here is – do they have the collective will to do it?"

"You may continue, Lord White," the Chair pronounced. "But please keep it brief – we have already read all of the Defence's proposals."

"Yes, Your Honour. As I was about to say, we plan to lobby national governments – with the support of anti-global warming organisations such as 'Friends of the Earth' – to secure commitments to a binding planetary charter…"

"Objection," Krognák interrupted once again. He turned towards the Chair and said, "Your Honour, may we approach the bench?"

Krognák and Istariol walked up towards the screen on which the Chair was displayed.

"Your Honour," Krognák whispered, "I respectfully request the opportunity to cross-examine this witness now. I have several points I am convinced the Court will find informative. We have all read the Defence proposal documents and I question what further value this witness's current testimony will provide at this stage."

"If I am permitted to cross-examine at this stage, I will, of course, allow the Defence the opportunity to redirect."

"Istariol, do you object to this?" the Chair asked.

"No, Your Honour – provided I have permission to question my witness further, after the cross-examination has concluded," Istariol replied.

"Then, Krognák, you may now move to the cross," the Chair ruled.

"Thank you, Your Honour," Krognák replied. He then turned towards the witness box and said, "Lord White, may I ask whether this not-for-profit organisation has been established?"

"Well, no sir, not yet," Lord White replied, his eyes flicking briefly towards Istariol. "But that will not take any time at all."

"I see," Krognák acknowledged. "May I also ask whether this $100 billion fund is available for investment now?"

"Uhm, well – no, this is a five year investment programme. We have the first two year's funding – but the rest will be raised over time," Lord White replied, somewhat nervously.

"Okay...," Krognák said, nodding. "But how – and by whom – is this $100 billion fund going to be raised?"

"To be fair, this is really something that Ian is dealing with, sir," Lord White responded.

"Thank you," Krognák said. "When you refer to 'Ian' – do you mean the gentleman seated there?" he asked, pointing at Ian. "The person we recognise as the Solarian Representative?"

"Yes, sir," Lord White replied.

"Your Honour. I would like to call, Ian – the Solarian Representative – as a hostile witness," Krognák requested.

"Objection," Istariol retorted. "The Prosecution has no right to summon additional witnesses at this stage."

"Overruled," the Chair announced. "Your own witness opened this up by admitting that the Solarian Representative is the only person who can answer the question he was asked."

"Lord White, you may step down," the Chair continued. "Ian, as the Solarian Representative, you are called to the stand."

Ian didn't like where this was going, but he had no choice but to comply.

"Yes, Your Honour," he acknowledged.

As Lord White stepped down and rejoined the others, Ian rose, walked to the witness box, and took his seat.

"I would like to welcome the Solarian Representative to the stand," Krognák said. "May I call you 'Ian'?"

"Yes, of course, sir," Ian replied.

"Excellent, then I hope you don't mind me asking you the same question I asked Lord White. How – and by whom – is this $100 billion fund going to be raised?" Krognák demanded.

"Primarily, the initial funds will be raised by selling Bitcoin," Ian replied, hesitantly. "These funds will then be reinvested in different crypto-currencies and other financial investments."

"I see. This sounds to me more like what you Solarians call *pie-in-the-sky*," Krognák observed.

"Objection," Istariol interjected. "Argumentative."

"Withdrawn," Krognák replied, before the Chair had an opportunity to rule.

"I do have one more question," Krognák continued. "Where have these Bitcoin come from? Specifically – who has given you these coins – and have they been mined? And, if they've been mined, what computer system was used to do this?"

Ian did his best not to squirm. "They've been mined by the Antarians – who have donated them to our fund," he replied.

Krognák paused, for dramatic effect, before asking: "The *Antarians*?"

"Yes, sir," Ian replied, with the best poker-face he could manage.

After another pregnant pause, Krognák announced, "Objection. I move to dismiss the Defence's proposals to tackle global warming – on the grounds that their plans are in breach of Directive 9.

"The Antarians are forbidden, under the Directive, from interfering with the development of an inferior civilisation," Krognák insisted. "This includes arbitrarily giving them 100 billion US dollars. Without the Antarians' interference, it is quite clear that Mankind would have continued to do nothing of any consequence to prevent runaway global warming!"

The Court fell deathly silent. Seconds ticked by.

"Sustained," the Chair said, striking his gavel forcefully.

"The Court is now adjourned. Reconvene at 10.00am tomorrow."

"Istariol, you will have an opportunity to make your concluding statement for the Defence tomorrow, before we make our ruling."

Chapter 28

Ian was the last person, apart from one crewman, to climb down into the submarine. There was a big hub-bub – all of their experts were standing around Istariol, all trying to talk at once.

He heard *"What about the money for our projects?"* and *"What's all this about a Directive?"* until Istariol, his hand raised, said, "Ladies and gentleman, please take your seats. There will be a briefing shortly after we get back to the hotel. We'll answer all of your questions then. In the meantime, we have to get this submarine moving."

Later, as the submarine was surfacing next to the riverbank, Istariol turned to Ian and said, "Please can you take the experts and go with them in one of the cars to the Apartment. Then come and meet us in our lounge."

"There will be a briefing in the lounge in the Quintessence Suite at 11.30am," Istariol called out, before anyone had left the submarine. This was the lounge nearest to the experts' bedrooms.

Rebecca followed Istariol to the other limousine parked furthest from the submarine.

Just as they reached the car, Rebecca turned to Istariol and cried out, "What the hell happened back there?" She looked as though she was about to burst into tears.

Istariol stepped forward and wrapped his arms around her, giving her a big hug. "I know it's been difficult," he whispered into her ear, "but it's not over yet."

They travelled in silence as the car swept around the block and descended into the underground car park.

A few minutes later, Ian joined Rebecca and Istariol in the lounge. A waiter was in the process of pouring coffee into their cups.

"How are the experts?" Istariol asked. "Are they still discussing this amongst themselves?"

"Yes, I'm afraid so. But what else would you expect?"

They waited until the waiter had left the Apartment.

"So, what did happen in the courtroom?" Ian asked. "Why was it cut short, without giving you an opportunity to continue interviewing the witnesses?"

"As it stands, the IGC considers our investment programme to be invalid – on the grounds that the funding originates from us, the Antarians. However, the situation is not quite as simple as the prosecution suggests. For example, whilst we have mined the Bitcoin in question, when we sell those coins, the funds we receive come from Solarian investors – investors who, in our opinion, are foolish enough to invest in what is effectively a Ponzi scheme, where the underlying asset has no intrinsic value."

"Surely you realised that this could be a problem all along?" Rebecca asked.

"Yes, I did. But we had no choice – we have no other defence."

"The truth is, it is *actually* the Solarians who are funding these programmes. All we, the Antarians, are contributing is computing power. And, incidentally, since we use fusion energy to power our computers, the process is entirely clean – so we produce no greenhouse gases. This is in stark contrast to what would occur if the Solarians mined the Bitcoin themselves.

"The regulations governing the Hearing contradict the usual provisions of Directive 9. It's somewhat paradoxical, since the Directive actually permits certain members of an inferior species to be exposed to advanced technological knowledge under specific circumstances. One such circumstance is when a Hearing is convened to prosecute a species for gross negligence in the stewardship of their planet.

"For example, as the Solarian Representative and his Deputy, you and Rebecca are permitted to know about the IGC, the Mekbudans and ourselves – alien species that live on other planets – as well as being exposed to our advanced technology, including our spaceships.

"In addition, the Antarians have been assigned the role of assisting you as the Defendants in this case, and the nature of that assistance is not precisely defined. We will argue that providing the computing power to mine Bitcoins falls within what is permitted.

"The bottom line is this: this is a fine point of law and all translations of the regulations into Mekbudan, English and other languages are subservient to the language in which this law was originally written – Antarian.

"So, tomorrow, we will argue our point – and hope that the judges fully appreciate the finer aspects of the law."

"So that goddamned bastard Himmler runs rings around us – he fakes an interview with Trump and gets away with it, while we get pulled up because you're doing a bit of Bitcoin mining to help us save the planet?" Rebecca complained.

"This feels like a 'fit up'," Rebecca continued. "Gulinrog has already fixed Trump's re-election by anonymously pouring vast quantities of money into his campaign's coffers.

"So how do we know he hasn't bought the IGC judges? After all, he could take a lesson from Trump – who's appointed so many Supreme Court judges he practically owns it."

"I'm afraid it's quite possible," Istariol responded. "And, as for Gulinrog funding Trump – if we could prove it, it would mean Gulinrog would be in breach of Directive 9. But we've already looked at this – and he's covered his tracks too well.

"Anyway, I'm afraid I must go. Please excuse me, but I need to go and give our experts the 'briefing' we promised them," Istariol concluded.

"What are you going to tell them?" Ian asked.

"That this is all a scripted part of the proceedings – and not to worry, the five billion dollars *will* be allocated to the best climate change projects." He gave a wry smile. "It seems that human nature so often manages to bring out selfish behaviour – all they seem to be worried about is the money."

With that Istariol stood up and left the room, heading for the Quintessence suite.

The rest of the day was pretty subdued. Ian did his best to keep everyone's spirits up, but there really was no way to get away from the stress of the whole situation.

When it finally came to dinner time, they ordered the finest meal that money could buy – and, of course, it wasn't even their own money. But, despite the fabulous meal that the hotel provided – accompanied by spectacular red and white wines – no one was really in the mood. So, they ate mostly in silence and, once Ian had finished demolishing the cheese course, they all bid their 'good nights' and headed to their respective rooms.

The next morning, they met once again for breakfast in their own dining room. As usual, the Leaders were having breakfast in the Quintessence suite.

Istariol was acting normally, but both Ian and Rebecca were struggling to put on a brave face. Ian, in particular, seemed to be very engrossed with his cup of coffee.

Time seemed to drag on and on – but, eventually, it came to the point where everyone was assembled by the Apartment elevator. The journey to the Mekbudan spaceship was uneventful and they were soon taking their seats in the Hearing room.

Krognák marched in and took a seat in the opposite part of the room to where they were all sitting. Then the TV screens lit up. The Hearing was once more in session.

"Istariol," the IGC Chair asked, with no pre-amble, "would you now like to make your concluding statement for the Defence?"

"Yes, Your Honour," Istariol replied.

"Honourable Members of the Inter-Galactic Tribunal, I rise before you not to deny the charges brought against Mankind, but to ask that you weigh them in full context – not as a record of a perfect species, but as evidence of one at a crossroads, still evolving.

"Yes, we acknowledge that Earth's dominant civilisation – Mankind – have contributed significantly to the destabilisation of their planet's climate. Their global expansion, industry and fossil-fuel dependence has released vast quantities of greenhouse gases into the atmosphere – and their delay in responding to the resulting impact on the climate has brought Earth dangerously close to a tipping point.

"But Mankind's story should not just end with their guilt. It should begin again – in awareness, in action, and in hope.

"In the past decade, we have witnessed a profound awakening on Earth. Renewable energy is now the fastest-growing source of power. The global rate of deforestation is slowing, and reforestation is accelerating. Carbon pricing schemes have been adopted across continents. Clean technologies – solar, wind, electric transport, green hydrogen and carbon removal – are scaling at unprecedented speed.

"These are not hollow gestures. Earth's nations have signed a global climate accord. The Paris Agreement, though imperfect, is a living commitment to limit warming, to cooperate across borders, and to ensure that no nation is left behind.

"Consider this: they are capable, with a bit of help, of launching the 100 billion dollar planetary action strategy which has been documented for the Court. Forests will be restored across Latin America and Africa. Solar microgrids will light up homes in the Sahel and Southeast Asia. Carbon is already being drawn from the air, not just emitted into it. Methane is being contained, and children are being taught the science of climate stewardship in schools across the planet.

"Also consider this. Under the normal conditions of Directive 9, *we* – the advanced civilisations – are forbidden from interfering with 'inferior' beings such as the Solarians. But this Hearing actually suspends those normal conditions for the Solarian Representative and his Deputy. I have been obliged to take two Solarians and completely disrupt their lives – cutting them off from their families and preventing them from carrying out their jobs, thereby jeopardising their careers.

"I think you will find – if you look at the fine details of the law – that this suspension of the 'normal' Directive 9 regulation *does* allow us – the Antarians – to provide the Solarian Representative with some one-off funding assistance.

"I ask this Hearing to recognise that Mankind *does* have a conscience. Young people are leading climate strikes. Judges in Earth's courts are holding polluters accountable. Civil society, scientists and indigenous guardians of nature are demanding change – and creating it.

"Yes, Mankind is late to act. But they are acting. The curve is bending. The danger is real, but so is the will to change.

"I propose not pardon, not exemption, but guidance. Let this Hearing impose conditions. Give Mankind a chance to commit to a binding planetary charter. But do not condemn a species that is, for the first time in its history, beginning to act as one.

"The IGC has granted reprieve before to civilisations on the edge. Grant it now – not for what Mankind has been, but for what it is becoming.

"Thank you."

"The Defence rests, Your Honour."

With a final bow towards the Chair, Istariol sat down.

The Chair then declared, "This Hearing is adjourned. We will reconvene after lunch – at 14.00 – when we will give our ruling."

"Only the Counsel for the Prosecution and the Counsel for the Defence – together with the Solarian Representative – should be present," the Chair added. "No other persons will be permitted in the Court."

"What about the Solarian Representative's Deputy?" Istariol asked.

"What Deputy?" the Chair barked. "Anyway, no, even if there *is* a Deputy, he's not needed if the Representative is present."

The Chair struck his gavel his gavel. "Hearing adjourned," the Chair ordered.

The TV screens went blank.

Once they were back in the privacy of the Apartment, Ian said "Nice speech Istariol. But do you think they will go for it?"

"It's difficult to tell, when all you can see of the judges is on TV screens. But we've done everything we could possibly have done at this point."

Ian reflected on everything that had happened since they'd 'stumbled' upon a UFO carving a crop circle on the Wiltshire Downs. Today was Sunday the 1st June – only three and a half weeks since they'd first boarded an Antarian spaceship. It felt like a lifetime ago.

For the rest of the morning – and throughout lunch – they really didn't know what to do with themselves. Conversations seemed stilted and false.

When it was finally time for Ian and Istariol to leave to go to the Hearing, Istariol said goodbye to Rebecca with a kiss on each cheek.

"Am I really banned from going to the Hearing with you to hear the verdict?" Rebecca asked. "Am I supposed to kick my heels here, whilst you 'boys' go and do the serious business?

"Perhaps I should go shoe shopping again?" she added, sarcastically.

"Yes," Istariol replied. "Sorry – but it's not sexist – it's just about our roles. I'm not saying the judges *aren't* misogynistic – but it *is* just standard practice. Ian is the Representative and there is no need for his deputy to be there."

Ian and Rebecca hugged. "Good luck, my love," Rebecca whispered to Ian, as she kissed him.

They made their way to the Mekbudan spaceship and into the courtroom.

It seemed like an age before finally their adversary, Heinrich Himmler, pranced into the room. The TV screens flicked on.

However, this time, the screen that had previously shown the Chair as a human avatar now displayed a species Ian had never seen before.

"The Solarian Representative should stand," the Chair ordered.

Ian thought that the fact that the Chair had revealed his face was not a good sign, but he did as he was ordered and stood up.

"We rule that the Solarians – Mankind – are hereby found guilty of gross negligence and dereliction of duty in the care of their planet. Mankind continues to release unacceptable quantities of greenhouse gases into Earth's atmosphere, despite being fully aware of the devastation this will cause.

"I am sorry that it has come to this – but it is quite clear that Mankind is intent on destroying the Earth. Even with our advanced technology, once global warming has spiralled out of control, it would take millennia to reverse.

"Therefore, we rule that the following apply.

"One: From the 4th July 2025, Directive 9 is suspended and the Mekbudan authorities will be appointed as the caretakers of the Earth.

"Two: The Mekbudans are hereby granted permission to 'cleanse' Earth of Mankind, in what so ever way they choose."

The Chair banged his gavel. "This Hearing is terminated," the Chair announced.

The TV screens once again went blank.

Chapter 29

The sickening churn in Ian's stomach was overwhelming — so intense it made him feel as though he might actually be sick.

He doubled over in the submarine, nausea threatening to overtake him. Istariol was speaking, trying to say something, but the words passed through Ian like mist. His brain had shut down under the sheer magnitude of it all.

The moment the IGC judge had read out the ruling, he realised the truth he'd been avoiding – deep down. He'd never truly believed it would come to this. He'd clung to hope, leaned too heavily on Istariol's quiet confidence, deluded himself into thinking that somehow, they would prevail. That *he* would prevail. That *he* would be the hero who saved the world.

Now, the true enormity of the situation had finally sunk in. Almost all life on Earth would be annihilated. Everyone he had ever loved — his friends, his family — wiped out. The reality was so vast and brutal, it left him breathless.

He knew he was showing symptoms of acute psychological trauma, but intellectual awareness of that didn't help — not when it felt as though his very soul was cracking open.

As soon as the submarine docked, Ian stumbled up onto the deck and collapsed against the railing, gulping in the fresh air like a drowning man. He stared into the water, willing the dizziness to pass. Eventually, he became aware of Istariol's arm around his shoulder. Somewhere behind them, a small crowd had gathered, talking amongst themselves and pointing at the strange yellow submarine. Ian didn't care.

He forced himself to his feet, legs like lead, and staggered to the waiting car. He slumped inside, his body heavy with grief, Istariol climbing in beside him.

"We'll talk when we get back to the Apartment," he heard Istariol say softly.

When the car drew up in the underground car park outside their elevator, Ian paused. "Just… give me a minute," he muttered. "I'm not ready to tell Rebecca yet."

Istariol hesitated. "We *should* go up as soon as you feel okay, though."

Ian nodded. A few minutes later, he gathered himself together and they both got into the elevator. They ascended in silence.

When they stepped into the Apartment, Rebecca took one look at Ian's face and realised the verdict had gone against them.

"How the hell did you let this happen, Istariol?" she screamed. "You're supposed to know the law inside out – it's even written in the Antarian language!"

Istariol winced and stepped back.

"And why on Earth did you build this defence when there's such a fundamental flaw in it – because of those damn Directive 9 rules?" she yelled, marching right up to him.

"There *is* no other defence," Istariol snapped, his face flushed red.

"What am I supposed to do when Earth is riddled with selfish, greedy people, only interested in their own short-term well-being? They get the leaders they deserve – men and women who, desperate to cling to power, enact the policies the people demand.

"Why is the Amazon Rainforest – the greatest absorber of carbon on land – shrinking irreversibly, and so fast? In just one country, Colombia, in the last six months alone, 340 square miles have vanished – an area larger than New York City.

"I'll tell you why: money. This deforestation was caused by the rapid expansion of illegal roads, coca cultivation, unregulated gold mining – all driven by profit and greed. And it's the same story in nearly every other country the rainforest covers.

"Ignorance plays its part too. Who thinks of the rainforest when they drink cocoa or eat chocolate? Who considers global warming when they order a mahogany dining table?

"But even if they *did* know, most people would just shrug. Apathy rules. It's not going to affect them anytime soon – and anyway someone else can deal with it."

Rebecca had gone silent. Ian slipped an arm around her waist.

Istariol paused.

"You know I could go on," he said finally. "The list of failures seems endless. But let's sit down and talk."

Rebecca and Ian sat together on the sofa, while Istariol took a seat opposite.

"I would like to start by saying that you've both already been granted asylum by the Antarian authorities," Istariol announced. "We can take you to live in one of our colonies, where you'd be eligible to apply for Antarian citizenship. This offer also extends to your immediate families.

"Alternatively – though I can't say I would recommend it – we *could* take you fifteen or twenty years into the future, to a time when the impact winter on Earth has ended. A few people will have survived, but 'civilisation' – if that's what you'd call it – will be completely different from today.

"But the other thing I have to tell you – is that I *do* have a plan."

That seemed to get their attention.

"You know that we – Alexa, Aurelia and I – have been planning this for almost a year. Well, I have to admit... this is the outcome I've always expected. I hoped for the best, but I've planned for the worst.

"Don't get me wrong – we had to present the best possible case we could at the Hearing – but we've known from the beginning that Mankind really doesn't have much of a defence. Solarians *are* destroying the planet.

"Anyway, there are two pieces of good news I can now share with you. First, although the judge didn't announce it, there are certain provisions in the terms and conditions of Directive 9 and the IGC ruling that work in our favour.

"The Mekbudans are on a clock. There's a three-year time limit to their stewardship – it will automatically expire on the 3rd of July, 2028. If the Mekbudans haven't managed to exterminate mankind by that date, then Directive 9 will be reinstated – and they won't be able to apply for another Hearing for at least fifteen years.

"As previously explained, the Mekbudans plan to crash Apophis into Earth on 25 December 2027 – meaning they'll have already used up more than two years and five months of their three-year limit."

Istariol was getting a lot of blank stares.

"If their plan to make Apophis hit the Earth was to fail – they'd have just over six months to try and find another asteroid to use. Apophis itself goes round its orbit in a little under one year, so it will be heading away from Earth during that period. Alexa has examined all the possible ways of causing an impact winter in that six month window and concluded it's impossible – even with *our* advanced technology.

"So – if we manage to sabotage their Apophis operation, they won't have enough time to attempt it another way. That would buy mankind a fifteen-year reprieve – eighteen years if you count from today."

"How the hell could we sabotage it?" Rebecca asked.

"Well, now we come to the second piece of good news. We saw Uma on board yesterday – which means the Hearing must have taken place on Rorcmog's ship. And Rorcmog is the Mekbudan who's been ordered to carry out the Apophis operation."

"You must know that we have no idea who Rorcmog or Uma are," Ian replied. "So, you'd better explain that first."

"Oh, yes, sorry. I think I've already told you that Gulinrog – who believes he's the rightful owner of Earth – is the Mekbudan who has initiated this prosecution of Mankind. Gulinrog is the Patriarch of the most influential tribe in the Blått realm.

"Well, Rorcmog is Gulinrog's youngest child – but two of his siblings are female and he's his third oldest son. Mekbudan society is totally misogynistic, in that females are not allowed to hold office. So, Rorcmog is third in line to become the Patriarch.

"We have a spy on board Rorcmog's ship. This is how we know of their plans to crash Apophis into Earth on Christmas day 2027 – and that his father has ordered Rorcmog to do this.

"Our spy has not been able to smuggle out any more messages recently, so until now we didn't know which Mekbudan spaceship was actually parked beneath the River Seine to host the Hearing.

"Yesterday, we had a breakthrough.

"At the Hearing, a man offered us refreshments – speaking in Swahili and pidgin English. That, combined with the black gentleman's dental condition, perfectly matches a description previously provided by our spy. That man was Uma, the foreman from Rorcmog's central African tantalite mine. This can only mean that the Hearing took place on Rorcmog's ship."

Rebecca still couldn't see where this was going – but she felt a rising glimmer of hope, coupled with a nagging sensation of fear.

"Okay – so spit it out, Istariol," Ian said.

For the first time – in what they now realised had been quite a while – Istariol actually smiled.

"We don't have any real grounds for an appeal – but, nonetheless, we still have the right to make one. We need to submit the documents for our appeal within twelve hours of the Hearing termination. This appeal is almost certainly going to fail, but – we *are* allowed to go back to the IGC Court to make our argument in person.

"The appeal will be considered by a completely new set of judges, who will have access to all the videos and transcripts from the Hearing. These judges will then take as long as they wish to deliberate on their verdict – up until the day *before* the 4th of July – when the Mekbudans are due to take control of Earth. Typically, appeal judges take two or three weeks to deliver a verdict.

"I've already submitted the appeal documents – and we've been summoned to appear at the Court at 10.00am tomorrow. The only people allowed to go are myself – as Lead Consul for the Defence – and Ian, as the Solarian Representative.

"We now have one final opportunity to board that ship – the vessel assigned to carry out the operation to crash Apophis into Earth. The very ship on which one of the crew is our spy."

"So… it's me, then?" Ian whispered. "I have to go with you tomorrow, slip away from the Court with your spy's help, and hide somewhere on the spaceship?

"And then, knowing nothing about Mekbudan navigation or propulsion systems, I'm supposed to sabotage the Apophis operation in order to save the planet."

"Yes, I'm sorry – but this is what you were actually recruited for," Istariol replied.

"*What?*" Rebecca almost screamed. "Are you kidding? Why can't your spy do it?"

Istariol blanched. "Because the Vegan spy is too terrified. If he were caught, he'd almost certainly be tortured and then killed – slowly, and in the most excruciating way imaginable."

This time Rebecca did scream. "*Oh*, but it's okay for Ian to take that risk?"

"Ian is protected," Istariol said evenly. "He's the Solarian Representative. If he were caught, Rorcmog wouldn't dare harm him – not without risking war with the Antarians — even if Ian was caught red-handed attempting sabotage."

Rebecca glared at him. "And we're supposed to believe the Antarians would go to war with the Mekbudans over one human? *Really*? And besides, wouldn't Directive 9 be suspended once the court order comes into effect?"

"Yes, but it's not that simple," Istariol admitted. "Ian's position is unique. The Solarian Representative is a lifetime appointment."

Ian frowned. "But once the Hearing and Appeal are finished, why would there be any need for me to remain the Representative?"

"If the Appeal succeeded," Istariol explained, "but global warming continues to worsen, the Mekbudans would file another petition and there'll be another Hearing in 2050. You'd still be the Solarian Representative. And if the Appeal fails — even though Earth would lose Directive 9 protection — your diplomatic immunity would remain intact.

"As for whether my people would truly go to war..." He spread his hands. "That's above my pay grade. It wouldn't be about one human life. It would tie into the larger issue of who 'owns' Earth — and the IGC treaty signed after the dinosaurs were wiped out. What I can say is this: it would create a major diplomatic storm, one that *could* spiral into war. And neither Rorcmog nor his father would risk being the spark. If they did, the Mekbudans might well execute them both just to appease us."

Silence hung between them.

"Alright. Understood," Ian said at last, his voice low. "So tell me how I'm supposed to do this."

"Of course." Istariol's expression hardened. "You won't be able to act until the beginning of their operation. That means staying hidden until after the ship jumps forward to December 2027. You'll be aboard for roughly a week, ship's time, before then.

"And remember: tomorrow, the same rules as at the Hearing apply. No weapons. No advanced devices. Their sensors will pick them up instantly — and you'll be exposed before you even begin.

"However, it will not detect this..." Istariol held out his hand and showed a small ceramic stick in his palm — slightly smaller than a typical Solarian USB memory stick.

"If you plug this device into a port in one of their navigation consoles, it will inject a virus into their computer. It will reprogramme their warp drive and navigation systems so that, once they begin the operation, they will falsely believe they're accelerating Apophis at 0.5g towards Earth.

"In reality, nothing will be happening – but their systems will be telling them otherwise. By the time they realise that they've been duped, it will be too late."

There was a short period of silence, as people absorbed all of this.

"Well, Istariol, you continue to be full of surprises," Ian observed. "I guess that's what makes *you* a spy. Looks like we *do* have a plan then," he added with a wry smile.

"Okay, but how is Ian going to get home?" Rebecca demanded.

"I'm sorry – we don't know for certain where Rorcmog will take his ship afterwards," Istariol responded. "If they don't realise that the Earth is unharmed, they might jump forward in time twenty years or so – thinking they have to wait until after the impact winter is over before returning to Earth. But it's highly unlikely they'd leave the solar system without confirming the impact.

"So, one of two things are most likely to happen once they realise the operation has failed. Either Rorcmog will take his ship back to Earth – he might even resume his African mining operations, given his foreman Uma is on board – or he'll travel to one of the Mekbudan colonies – most likely the nearest one, in the Delta Pavonis system.

"In either of those two situations, Rorcmog has no reason to jump forward in time, so all you have to do, Ian, is stay hidden until the ship lands – where our spy can smuggle you off the ship. If he's going to Earth you'd arrive the same day – Christmas Day 2027. Otherwise, the journey to Delta Pavonis would take less than a week."

Rebecca was not looking very happy. "You're telling us that Ian – if he's lucky enough not to be discovered, captured and tortured – could end up on a hostile, alien planet light-years away from Earth?

"And what am I supposed to do in the next two and a half years?" Rebecca asked.

"Well... we don't know what the Mekbudans are planning to do from the 4th July," Istariol replied.

"Incidentally, I suspect that once again – given their interest in symbolism – they picked that date to be a slap in the face for the Americans.

"Perhaps they'll choose to take complete control of the Earth – and enslave all Mankind. Or, maybe, they'll just park a spaceship in full view above Washington, Beijing and Moscow and announce the end of the world – just to see how everyone reacts.

"Or they could even do nothing – at least, in public. That *would* be the easiest thing for them to do. With Directive 9 suspended, they could still act with impunity below the radar – and profiteer as much as they like for the next two and a half years.

"For example, they could mine all the remaining Bitcoin, selling as much as they could to buy precious minerals and metals. They could expand their own precious mineral mining operations and take over all the other profitable mines on Earth by force. They could infiltrate organised criminal gangs and rake off the profits from gambling, drugs and prostitution. Similarly, they could earn huge profits from manipulating banks, hedge funds and other financial institutions – using their ability to hack into any computer system in the world.

"So, I strongly recommend that we leave Earth to its own devices and that we jump forward to December 2027. But I'm open to suggestions?" Istariol finished, adding, "And you can delay that decision for up to a month or more."

"I have to ask – aren't you risking outright war by helping us to sabotage their spaceship? Surely this in breach of Directive 9?" Ian enquired.

"Plausible Deniability. We'll make it look like you – a Solarian – has done this on your own, without any assistance from us. Our spy will not reveal his identity to you – you may not even see him."

Istariol reached into his pocket and handed Ian a small, white oval disc.

"This is a remote control for the ship's doors. Touch it against a wall in the ship and – if there's a door in the wall – its outline will glow softly. Then, just put press the fob's button and the door will open for a few seconds – if you walk through, it will automatically close behind you.

"That USB stick and this remote control were both 'borrowed' from another Mekbudan ship some weeks ago. And the door control is compatible with nearly all of their spaceships, so it'll work on Rorcmog's.

255

"Both of these items could easily have been provided by one of Gulinrog's rivals – so it's entirely possible that you obtained them without Antarian assistance."

"But what about that virus on the memory stick? That has to be pretty sophisticated to effectively disable their navigation systems? How could I, a member of such an 'inferior' civilisation, possibly have created that?"

Istariol smiled for the second time that day.

"It's actually a Mekbudan worm," Istariol explained. "They engineered it as a weapon – designed to cripple other species' ships. But it'll work on their own ships too. There's so much shared technology among IGC member civilisations that many systems are built with the same components. Even their military vessels run on hybrid code. It's a bit like how the Russians have US designed chips inside their own military hardware.

"Anyway, our cyberwarfare people have recently identified an RCE – Remote Code Execution – vulnerability in the navigation system of their Xolak-class destroyers – exactly the type of ship Rorcmog has. This critical security flaw will allow malicious code – the worm – to run on their systems."

He turned to Ian. "You are a Cryptologic Warfare Officer in the US Navy. Take a look at the payload – understand how it's built, how the worm utilises the RCE to work its way into their systems. We've got all the data on this for you to study. You'll need that knowledge before you go on board their ship tomorrow morning."

"You deliberately recruited a military cyberwarfare specialist as the Solarian Representative, specifically so he would succeed on this mission, didn't you?" Rebecca asked.

"This is true," Istariol admitted.

"What about the other candidates? How did you know Ian and I would solve the puzzle first – or were there other specialists on the short list?" Rebecca enquired.

"There *were* other cyberwarfare experts on the list," Istariol replied, "but sometimes you have to just roll the dice and see what happens – providing you've stacked the odds in your favour, of course."

Ian nodded his head. "And you're sure they can't trace this back to the Antarians?"

"Yes, we're confident there is enough 'plausible deniability' to ensure the Mekbudans couldn't prove anything. In fact, it's just as likely that one of Gulinrog's many rivals provided you with this equipment – someone who would benefit from the failure of the Apophis operation and the extensive damage to Gulinrog's reputation."

"One more question," Ian said. "Do you have permission from the Antarian authorities to do this?"

"Of course not," Istariol replied, smiling once again. "How could we possibly have plausible deniability, if they *had* given me permission."

"Then, let's do it," Ian said firmly. He looked around at the others, eyes burning.

"There is _no_ 'Planet B'. No second chance. If this is our only shot – then I'll take it."

With that, he rose to his feet and turned towards Rebecca, arms open.

She didn't hesitate. She rushed into his embrace, burying her face against his chest. Her shoulders shook with silent sobs as he held her tightly, one hand in her hair, the other gripping her waist like he'd never let go.

Neither of them said a word. But in that embrace, everything was understood.

Chapter 30

Ian spent the rest of that afternoon in the projection room with Alexa, going through the worm's code line by line.

Meanwhile, Istariol kept Rebecca company, doing his best to lift the mood – suggesting they make the most of the hotel's luxury and the fabulous views of Paris from their balcony. A generous amount of Chablis and Champagne was consumed, before they both eventually retired to their respective rooms for an afternoon nap.

That evening, they all gathered for dinner as usual in their private dining room. They ordered the finest food the hotel could offer, with a dizzying array of choices. As for the cheese course, Ian had never seen – or tasted – so many varieties in his life.

Although no one dared say it aloud, it felt very much like an 'end of an era' celebration – or perhaps even like a Last Supper.

When the meal finally came to an end, they retired to their lounge for coffee and liqueurs. Ian and Istariol decided they wanted to keep a clear head for the morning, but said nothing as Rebecca declined the coffee and ordered another bottle of Chablis.

Finally, Ian stood up and poured a small glass of wine for himself and for Istariol. Still standing, he said, "I would like to make a toast. To the best friends we've ever had – who have selflessly and tirelessly gone out of their way to help us through these dark times. To Istariol, to Alexa – and to Aurelia's memory."

With that, Rebecca and Istariol echoed, "To Istariol, Alexa and Aurelia."

Their glasses touched gently, each finding the others in turn, and then they drank together, a quiet bond holding them in that moment.

The next day, Monday the 2nd of June, people gathered for breakfast a little later than normal. Rebecca looked like she was a little bit under the weather, but still managed to tuck into a fair amount of the splendid continental breakfast laid out on their table. The coffee, in particular, seemed to go down quite well.

Ian and Rebecca had already said their 'goodbyes' to each other in their own room, before going to breakfast.

Then, 9.30am arrived. Istariol got up from the breakfast table and walked around to Rebecca to give her a hug.

So, with that, Ian and Istariol left and stepped into the elevator. Istariol checked that Ian had the Mekbudan memory stick and the door-control fob.

"And make sure you're not carrying your phone – and that you've left behind any weapons or Antarian gadgets. Otherwise, the spaceship's sensors will detect them and you'll be caught."

About fifteen minutes later, as they prepared to climb out of the submarine, Istariol offered a final piece of advice.

"This is likely to be the trickiest part of our plan," he explained. "You'll need to slip away before anyone notices. Himmler has no formal right to be there, but any one of Rorcmog's crew could be in the room. I'll explain to the new judges that you've waived your rights – as the Solarian Representative – to be there in person, and that you've delegated everything to me.

"There's a hidden door to the crew's quarters immediately to the right as you go in. Just touch your door-fob against that wall."

They climbed up onto the submarine's deck, stepped off the boat and approached the door to the courtroom. Istariol was leading the way.

"Let me go in first," he said to Ian, without looking back. "If there's a problem, I will step back out, pretending I've forgotten something."

Istariol opened the door and walked in, leaving the door ajar. Ian waited for perhaps ten seconds, then cautiously approached and looked through the doorway. Istariol was seated at the front of the empty courtroom and no one else was in sight – it looked exactly the same as it had on previous days.

Trying not to look too conspicuous, Ian crept further into the room and touched his fob against the right hand wall. He could see a doorway faintly illuminated in the wall just ahead of him. He pressed the button on the fob and a small section of the wall disappeared to make a doorway. He walked forward and stepped through.

He was in a short narrow corridor about twenty feet long – but not a single door was to be seen anywhere in its white walls. In retrospect, he thought, it might have been quite useful to know more of the ship's layout. After all, they supposedly had a spy on board who must be familiar with the ship.

"So, what the hell am I supposed to do now?" he thought.

Just as his thoughts were about to turn even more uncharitable, the wall at the end of the corridor suddenly displayed a glowing doorway. Panicking, with nowhere to hide, Ian just crouched down waiting to see what happened next.

Then what was clearly a Vegan hand came through the doorway. The forefinger lifted upright, then curled forward and back in a beckoning motion. The message was unmistakable: *come here*. A moment later, the hand withdrew.

Ian got up and quickly went through this new doorway. This time he was in a dark room, perhaps 30 feet long, with one slightly curved wall to his right – possibly one that was following the contours of the spaceship. The room seemed to be full of crates and boxes, all stacked up on top of each other. There was no sign of the Vegan who had summoned him.

Then he could make out a faint glowing ahead – but this time it was in the ceiling. As he approached, the glowing outline turned into a black hole – a hatchway perhaps? He gingerly clambered onto a crate which happened to be underneath the hatchway – and standing up, he put his head through the hole.

He could see a small dimly lit room about ten feet square – with walls almost completely covered with pipes and cables.

Incongruously, a human-sized single mattress and sleeping bag were lying on the floor on one side of the room. In the opposite corner, was what looked like a portable toilet – like one you might find on a caravan or a boat.

"Looks like this is going to be 'home' for a while," he thought. *"I guess that these low technology living quarters are the only ones that will keep me hidden."*

He pushed himself up into the room and stood, taking stock of his surroundings. He found a five-litre container of water, a plastic tumbler, some eating utensils and a few basic toiletries – including a toothbrush – but no food. He touched his fob against each wall, and then the ceiling and floor. Only the floor revealed a hatchway; there was no other way out of the room.

Ian sat down on the mattress. *"Okay,"* he thought. *"Well at least I've made it safely aboard. Now, I guess, I'm just going to have to wait it out. Shame I didn't think to bring a book – or a hipflask."*

"Xurek, have our 'guests' left the ship?" Rorcmog enquired.

"Yes, Captain," was the response.

"We're going to leave as soon as possible. But, since Directive 9 is still in force, we're going to have to leave Paris in the dead of the night – at 3.00am tomorrow morning.

"Xurek, plot a course away from the inner planets – towards the nearest point in space where we can generate a time-warping wormhole," Rorcmog ordered.

"Yes, sir. As you aware, a full wormhole cannot be safely established in the presence of gravity. Too many gravitational fields are generated by the inner planets – Mercury, Venus, Earth and Mars. The two nearest positions, where gravity is sufficiently low to establish a full wormhole, are near Jupiter and Saturn. Specifically, the 'L1 Lagrange point' close to each planet, where the Sun's gravitational pull is cancelled out by that of the planet.

"Given the current planetary alignments, we have two options, Captain. If we go to Jupiter – which is now on the opposite side of the Sun to the Earth – we would need to travel quite close to the sun, inside Mercury's orbit. Alternatively, we could go directly to Saturn, although it *is* further away, sir."

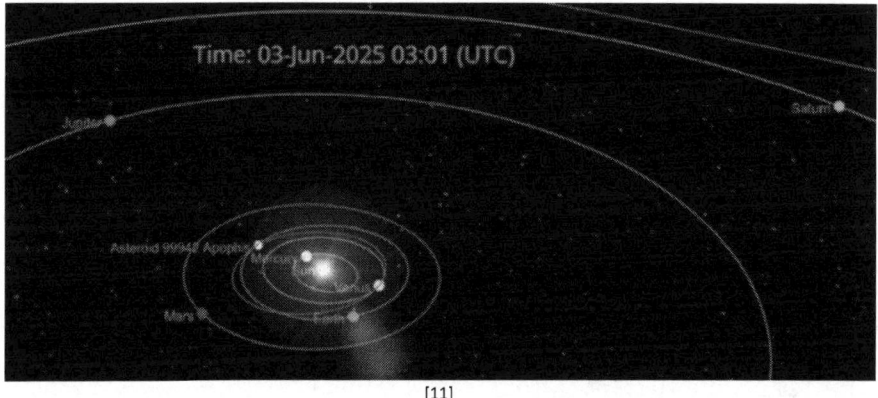

Time: 03-Jun-2025 03:01 (UTC)

[11]

"Hmm, I'm not sure I like the idea of travelling so close to the sun, so that rules out the Jupiter option," Rorcmog mused. "And anyway, Saturn is further away from the inner planets' gravity fields, so we will get a more stable wormhole.

"Xurek, plot a course to Saturn," he ordered.

"Xurek, how long will it be after leaving Earth, before we can generate the wormhole?" he demanded.

"We are 1.473 billion kilometres away from Saturn – but the gravitational equilibrium point is 65 million kilometres this side of Saturn, so we'll have to travel 1,408 million kilometres, sir.

"We'll be there 31.4 hours after departure, Captain."

Rorcmog did hate space travel. All he ever seemed to do was wait. Sometimes he wondered what he was doing running a spaceship.

"Surely, there must be an easier way of earning a living?"

At 3.00am local time, the dark waters of the Seine began to churn as Rorcmog's warship rose silently to the surface. Its cloaking system was active, but as it broke through the water, a few late-night wanderers gaped at the swirling waters. Rorcmog didn't care.

"Captain," Xurek enquired, "at what level do you want me to set the ship's onboard gravity? Earth gravity or standard Delta Pavonis?"

"We're not leaving for Delta Pavonis until after the special operation, so leave it at one Earth gravity. Anyway, Commander Krognák will no doubt complain if we increase it to 1.09g.

"Xurek, let's get out of here. Engage the gravity drive, maximum acceleration."

The maximum acceleration achievable with the gravity drive was attained by reversing the orientation of the drive's field by 180 degrees. Instead of pulling the spaceship down to Earth, this made the gravity field push the ship upwards away from the planet – with a force equal to the planet's gravitational pull. In other words, the ship would accelerate upwards from Earth at one 'g' – 9.81 metres per second squared – the rate at which an object would normally fall to Earth.

However, gravity decreases with distance – falling off in proportion to the square of the distance from the planet's centre – so the ship's acceleration diminished rapidly as it ascended.

After approximately one and three-quarter hours, the spaceship reached the Moon's orbital distance, about 32,000 kilometres from Earth, where gravity was only 2.75% of its strength at the Earth's surface. By this point, the ship's acceleration had slowed to almost nothing, but it had reached a speed of roughly 37,000 kilometres per hour.

At 4.47am, "Captain, we are now far enough away from Earth to initiate warp acceleration," Xurek announced.

"Disengage the gravity drive and engage the warp drive, Xurek. Maximum acceleration. Take us out of here."

"Yes, Captain."

A large, stable wormhole – one that allows a spaceship to 'jump' to another star system or travel forward in time – requires an almost complete absence of gravity to allow it to be established.

However, in regions of relatively low gravity, a reasonable distance away from any planetary body, the warp drive can generate a 'micro-wormhole' in front of the ship, aligned with the desired direction of travel. This micro-wormhole, powered by the fusion generator, allows the ship to 'fall' forward into the edge of the wormhole, accelerating much faster than the gravity drive could achieve.

"Captain, we are about to begin accelerating at a constant 440.8 metres per second squared, until we reach the halfway point. The ship will then rotate 180 degrees and accelerate at the same rate in the opposite direction, bringing us to a complete stop relative to Saturn once we reach our destination."

An acceleration of 440.8 m/s^2 is 45 times that of Earth's gravity. Almost any living creature would normally be crushed like a bug under such extreme acceleration. However, the physics of a micro-wormhole do not conform to Newtonian principles.

Just as falling freely in an aircraft or spacecraft causes occupants to experience weightlessness, a ship 'falling' into a micro-wormhole exerts no high-g stress on its passengers. The ship's gravity drive can maintain a steady onboard artificial gravity of 1g, so the crew continue to feel as though they are standing on Earth.

Rorcmog couldn't claim to understand the physics – but he didn't care. He knew how to navigate a spaceship across star systems and that was all that mattered – with his trusty, non-sentient AI doing all the heavy lifting when it came to the navigation calculations, of course.

"Xurek, set an alarm for one hour before we reach Saturn," Rorcmog ordered.

"In the meantime," he thought, *"it looks like I've got some time to kill. Perhaps I should renew my acquaintance with a couple of my concubines."*

Rorcmog strolled onto the bridge at precisely noon the following day, feeling somewhat reinvigorated by his recent leisure-time activities.

"Xurek, give me a report," Rorcmog ordered.

"Yes, Captain. The ship is still at full deacceleration and currently travelling at approximately 850,00 kilometres an hour. We will come to a complete stop, relative to Saturn, in nine minutes time, sir."

Xurek brought up on an image on the bridge's main display screen.

[12]

Rorcmog watched as the image of Saturn grew slightly larger. Saturn – a giant ball of ammonia ice and methane gas – has the most extensive and visible ring system in the solar system, consisting of countless icy particles ranging in size from dust grains to mountains. He had, of course, seen it many times before in his travels, as Jupiter and Saturn were the best places to establish a full wormhole.

After a few more minutes, Xurek announced: "Captain, the ship has arrived at Saturn's L1 Lagrange point, 65 million kilometres from Saturn. From this position, Saturn lies in the exact opposite direction to the Sun, which is 1,369 million kilometres away. Here, the Sun's gravitational pull is effectively cancelled out by that of Saturn – giving us virtual zero gravity.

"The micro-wormhole has now been collapsed and we are ready to generate a time-warping wormhole, Captain."

"Have you plotted our course into the virtual black hole to take us forward to December 2027, Xurek? And how long will the transit take?"

"Yes, Captain, our trajectory has already been calculated. We'll enter the black hole nearly tangential to its event horizon, achieving an effective transit velocity of 99.999% the speed of light relative to the Solarian heliocentric frame of reference.

"To achieve a temporal increase of 931.24 Solarian days, we'll have to maintain this speed in the wormhole for precisely 4 days, 3 hours, and 57 minutes. At that time, we will collapse the wormhole, allowing us to re-enter normal space back at our original position and velocity – at 18.00 GMT on 22nd December 2027, sir.

"That will give us enough time to travel to Apophis to arrive just after midnight GMT on 24th December, Captain."

"Good. Re-engage the warp drive and establish the wormhole, Xurek."

"Yes, Captain."

Rorcmog heard a faint high-pitched humming sound – the telltale sign of the warp drive operating at extremely high energy levels.

"The wormhole is stable, Captain."

"Jump. Time warp us to 2027," he ordered.

The entire spaceship gave a faint shudder, as it was pulled into the wormhole, vanishing from real space.

Within seconds, it was 'falling' into a virtual black hole at near-light speed.

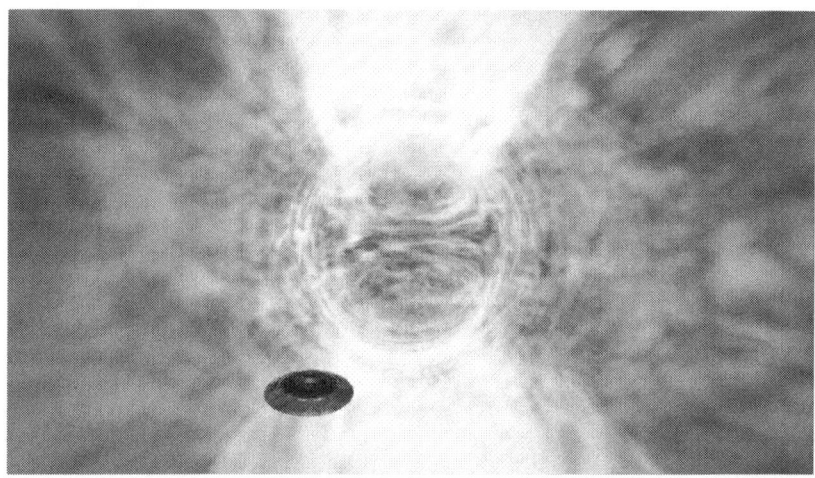

[13]

Chapter 31

The spaceship rematerialised into real space, as the wormhole collapsed.

"Give me a report, Xurek," Rorcmog ordered.

"Yes, Captain. We are back at our original position – where the L1 Lagrange point used to be. The time is 18.01 GMT on 22nd December 2027. Saturn has moved further along in its orbit and is now 743 million kilometres away, sir."

It takes Saturn about 29.4 Earth years to complete one orbit around the Sun, travelling at an average orbital speed of 34.8 thousand kilometres per hour.

"What's our fuel situation?"

"The ship's water tanks were full when we left Earth, Captain. They are currently registering 86% full now."

"Good. Lay in a course to get us to Apophis at midnight on 24th December 2027, Xurek."

"Yes, sir. Course laid in and the warp drive is ready to generate a micro-wormhole, Captain."

"Oh, Captain," Xurek interrupted. "We have just received a transmission from our cloud platform on the Earth's moon, sir."

"Okay, well go ahead and tell me what we've got," Rorcmog ordered.

"It seems that the Solarian appeal was successful and Directive 9 has *not* been suspended. A petition can be submitted to apply for another Hearing – in 2050, sir."

"Xurek, apply a 'top secret' categorisation to this message immediately. On no account should anyone on board be permitted access, other than myself."

"Yes, Captain. That is, you mean of course, except Commander Krognák. He *is* technically higher ranking than yourself. Anyway, I can see he's already read the message, sir."

Rorcmog pulled a face, his tail swishing. "Where's Krognák now?"

"He was in his quarters when the message came in – but he's now on his way to the bridge, sir."

"*I bet he is,*" Rorcmog thought.

It was not long before Krognák marched onto the bridge.

"Good evening, Commander," Rorcmog greeted him. "I take it you've heard the news?"

"Yes, Kapitän," was the curt reply. "But the Appeal result doesn't matter."

"So why does this message say that Directive 9 is still in force?"

"The Appeal was only upheld on a technicality," Krognák replied. "The Antarians were set to mine a hundred billion dollars in Bitcoin to bankroll those ridiculous Solarian projects. Anyone could see that was a blatant breach of Directive 9. However, the Appeal judges accepted the Defence argument: the funds counted as Solarian, not Antarian. And once that *Arschgeige* Solarian Representative was appointed, Directive 9 allows the Antarians to help him in any way they choose.

"Anyway, it doesn't matter. My orders are to proceed with the special operation in any event. I will personally supervise the destruction of life on Earth," Krognák concluded.

Rorcmog severely doubted that his father would have given such an order, but he was in a very awkward position, as Gulinrog had issued a specific directive placing Rorcmog under Krognák's direct command.

"Yes, Commander," Rorcmog replied. "Xurek, engage the warp drive. Take us to Apophis. Set the arrival time at one minute past midnight on December 24th."

Ian was bored. He had been sitting on the mattress for over an hour, staring at the walls and worrying about whether he'd succeed in his mission. He now regretted not bringing a paperback book – although the lighting was probably too dim for reading anyway.

Suddenly, the floor around the hatchway began to glow, then faded to black as the hatch opened. Ian stood up and saw what looked like a space helmet just below floor level in the opening. A Vegan hand reached up through the hatch, holding a black tablet. It was clearly a Vegan – wearing only a space helmet – standing on a box in the room below.

"That helmet's obviously not for vacuum protection – he's not wearing a space suit," Ian thought. *"So, he must be using it to conceal his face. Although, I can't tell one Vegan from another, so it really isn't necessary."*

The Vegan was still holding out the tablet. Ian took it and flipped open the cover. It had a couple of buttons on the side; he pressed one. The screen lit up. It was an Android tablet and on the desktop were icons for Notepad and the Kindle app.

Now the Vegan held up a second device – a transparent glass tablet about the size of a smartphone. With a tap of his forefinger, the screen lit up, displaying a message in English.

> *'It will be many days before the ship reaches Apophis. You must stay in this room with the hatchway closed until then. I will bring you food and, when necessary, more water.*
>
> *Uma sometimes comes into this store room – and robot guards also walk through here on their patrols – so I cannot stay here very long.*
>
> *I will give you a report on the ship's movements when I bring you food.*
>
> *I have disabled the wifi and Bluetooth on the tablet I gave you, as the ship's sensors would pick up the transmissions if they were turned on. You would then be captured.'*

Ian acknowledged the message with an "Okay, thanks."

The words on the glass tablet disappeared and the Vegan put it back into a belt he was wearing around his waist. He then picked up a plastic container from the top of the box he was standing on and passed it up to Ian.

Ian took the container and the Vegan then stepped down off the crate. The hatchway disappeared, leaving Ian looking at the floor again.

He opened the container to find it contained food. It was clearly French in origin – including a small baguette, pâté and – much to Ian's surprise – an excellent selection of cheeses. Ian was also pleased to find a half bottle of claret.

"Aha, things are looking up," he thought to himself. *"Perhaps Istariol told the spy about my fondness for cheese and wine?"*

He picked up his tablet and opened the Kindle app. He found that a large selection of books – in various categories – had already been downloaded onto it.

"Okay, I guess I'm not going to be as bored as I thought I would be," Ian thought.

However, the hours and days actually did drag on interminably for Ian, even with access to a wide selection of books. Somehow, losing himself in a detective mystery felt jarringly out of place – an inadequate escape from the weight of his current situation. No matter how hard he tried to distract himself, his thoughts kept circling back to what he had to do – and when the moment would finally come.

The Vegan spy kept him well supplied with food, particularly French cheese, pâte and wine – and kept him abreast of how many more days it was likely to take to get to Apophis.

Ian was not able to shave, but he *had* been provided with a change of clothes every three days or so. They didn't fit very well, so he guessed they'd been borrowed or purloined from another crew member. After a few days, Ian was really looking forward to having a hot shower and a shave.

"*I hope I don't get discovered simply because I smell so much,*" Ian thought, sniffing his armpits.

Eventually, the spy informed him that over the next four days the ship would be travelling forwards in time to December 2027. Ian *had* noticed the ship judder slightly, so presumably that had been the point the spaceship had initiated its time-warping 'jump'.

Finally, the Vegan appeared and showed him this message on his glass tablet.

> *'Yesterday, we arrived at December 2027. It is now the 23rd December and the time is nearly 7pm GMT Earth time. We will arrive in the vicinity of Apophis in about 5 hours' time.*
>
> *I will wait 5 minutes for you to gather your thoughts – and then you will need to follow me. I will take you to the navigation control console. Leave the tablet I gave you behind – I will wipe it clean.*
>
> *I will give you a genetic-spoofing device that will get you access to the navigation control room. You have to do this – if I did it, it would incriminate me.*
>
> *If we come across any robot guards – or Uma – immediately hide wherever you can. The robots, at least, might just assume that you are a human slave from your heat signature.*

They plan to land the ship on Apophis about midnight. You must insert the memory stick before we arrive. The NavCon will allow you to see the landing countdown. Good luck.'

Ian decided that it was probably a good idea to have a swig of water and relieve his bladder.

"Okay, I'm ready now," Ian called out quietly a couple of minutes later.

Ian sat on the edge of the hatchway, legs dangling, then pushed himself forward, dropping down onto the box beneath. The Vegan stood silently in one corner of the storage room. Unusually, he wasn't wearing a space helmet, though he *was* facing away from Ian – presumably to keep his identity hidden.

Lying on the box was a weird looking object about the size of an egg, with a small LCD-like display – which was faintly glowing. There were alien symbols on the display – perhaps these were Mekbudan letters, Ian thought. Ian picked it up and put it in his pocket.

A door then opened in front of the Vegan and he disappeared through it. Ian rushed to follow, stepping into a short corridor. At the far end, a Vegan hand was sticking out of a door on the left-hand side, its forefinger wagging back and forth.

Walking through the door, Ian found himself in what appeared to be a dormitory. He was surprised by how basic it seemed. Surely, they had advanced space-saving technology? Was there really a need for empty beds to be taking up room?

The space contained two small Vegan-sized hammocks, strung one above the other, and three human-sized bunk beds stacked vertically. Only the lowest bunk showed signs of recent use – its sheets and pillows in visible disarray. Around the room, a large number of boxes and crates were stacked up against the walls, as if they had been hastily relocated from another storage area.

Suddenly, they heard loud clunking noises coming from behind them – from the corridor they had just come in from.

The Vegan flashed his glass tablet. "*Hide!*" was displayed on the screen.

With a flash of inspiration, Ian dived onto the lowest bunk bed and pulled the sheet up over himself. He turned on his side facing the wall and tried to steady his breathing.

The clunking noises came into the room. And stopped right next to his bed. Ian almost stopped breathing, not daring to turn his head around to look. After what seemed like an eternity, but what must have only been a couple of seconds, the clunking resumed – as whatever was causing the noise stomped out of the room. Presumably, a robot guard resuming his patrol.

The noise receded into the distance until, finally, silence was restored. Ian nearly jumped out of his skin when a hand shook his shoulder. But it was only the Vegan spy. The Vegan quickly turned away from Ian and walked in the same direction that the robot had gone.

Ian sat up in the bed. He couldn't help noticing a faint smell coming from the pillow – not unpleasant – like perfume or after-shave. There was something about it that seemed vaguely familiar. Anyway, he needed to catch up with the Vegan, so he quickly got off the bed and followed him through the next doorway. They were in yet another corridor. This time, the Vegan turned immediately right, walking through another door.

When Ian went through the doorway, he found himself in a small dimly lit room – with a number of strange looking consoles fixed to the walls. Alien glyphs were lit up on the consoles, constantly flickering and changing shape.

The Vegan, his face shrouded by the shadows, was repeatedly pointing to Ian and to a glowing circle in the floor. Presumably, another hatchway.

The Vegan then flashed his glass tablet again.

> *'This is it. The NavCon is in the room below. Use the biometric device to open the door. Press the display and it will generate a Vegan fingerprint – not mine though, it belongs to a Vegan who no longer works on board the ship. I have now reinstated its validity, so it should work fine.*
>
> *Hold the display against the floor hatchway and it will open for you. When you have finished the job – come back out and I will guide you back to your hideout. I wish you good luck.'*

Ian did as he was instructed and the floor hatchway opened. The Vegan disappeared the way they had come in. Ian peered down into the hole in the floor. This must just be a maintenance room, as it was tiny – only about 8 feet by 8 feet. Ian dropped down into the room. The only light in the room was coming from the screen of a single console mounted against one wall. There was a small stool in front of it, mounted on a single pole fixed to the floor.

Above him the hatchway disappeared. Ian sat down on the stool, but it was too low down for him and he had to bend his legs – it must have been set up for Vegans. However, as he put his full weight on the stool, he felt it start to rise up. After a few seconds it stopped moving – it was now at a much more comfortable height above the floor.

The Vegan had said he would be able to tell when they arrived at Apophis. Ian studied the NavCon's screen. All of the writing on the screen was in an alien language. There were three yellow oval circles at the very bottom of the screen, each with a different alien word inside it.

In one part of the screen a symbol was changing fairly regularly, about once every eight seconds. The symbol next to it seemed to change about once every other minute. The next two symbols were not changing. This was presumably a countdown clock.

"Damn. Why didn't they at least teach me some basic Mekbudan words?" he thought. *"Or give me some instructions on how to drive this sodding thing."*

He found a small slit about the same size as the memory stick he'd been given. *"Okay, well that looks like the port I should plug this into,"* Ian thought. *"And he told me to do it before we arrive at Apophis – but when would be the best time?"*

After a while, Ian noticed that the countdown display had reduced from four digits to three. He checked his watch and saw that half an hour had passed since he had first entered the room.

Ian had been thinking about the three icons at the bottom of the screen.

"Surely, I would have been warned by the Vegan – who must be familiar with these consoles – if pressing one of these icons would cause an alarm to be raised? But, if it is safe, which button should I press? I have to do something, because this display is pretty much incomprehensible."

So, with his heart in his mouth, he put his finger on the middle icon. The screen immediately changed. The format was the same, but all of the letters and symbols were different. He had been studying the screen for the last half an hour or so and he was quite convinced that none of these new symbols were the same as any of the ones previously displayed.

Ian's gut instinct told him: *"Perhaps this has simply changed the language?"*

Once again, he pressed an icon – this time choosing the one on the right.

The screen immediately blinked and switched to another language. Amazingly, it was now displaying everything in English. The three icons at the bottom of the screen now showed 'Mekbudan', 'Vegan' and 'English' from left to right. The main display showed that their destination was 'Asteroid 99942 Apophis' and a timer – in Solarian hours, minutes and seconds – was counting down in real time. It was showing they would arrive in 3 hours and 53 minutes.

Ian decided that, if it were up to him, he would fire whoever had written the console's software. Why on Earth hadn't each icon contained the name of the language in the target language? Meaning, the right hand icon should always say 'English', even when the main display was in Mekbudan or Vegan.

Anyway, it now made sense to Ian. They had humans working on board their ships, so of course they needed to accommodate their language – and, rightly or wrongly, they had decided that English was the standard language for humans.

So far, everything had gone to plan. Now came the hard choice: when to slip the memory stick into the console's port.

The earlier he did it, the longer the malicious software would run before they reached Apophis – giving the Mekbudans more time to realise something was wrong. Wait too long, and the virus might not have enough time to spread. Multiple firewalls could slow it down. And who knew what defences an alien network might have?

He took a breath. No reason to wait. No reason at all.

Heart pounding, palms slick, Ian slid the memory stick into the single slot he'd found earlier.

Nothing happened.

He had discussed this with Istariol – and they had come to the conclusion that it would be quite possible for the virus to just start working, whilst giving no visible indication of success.

However, Ian couldn't afford to take the risk that it might not have worked – he needed to see if there was any way he could confirm the worm had penetrated the navigation system and was up and running.

He looked at the NavCon's screen. He had no idea how to proceed – all it had in terms of control buttons were the three yellow icons at the bottom of the screen.

Then he had an idea. Placing his finger in the middle of the screen, he dragged it to the left edge. Nothing. He tried the right edge instead.

Suddenly, the display shifted to reveal an array of strange icons scattered across the screen, each with three or four letters beneath them in mixed capitalisation. Presumably acronyms – but none he recognised.

Then he noticed a familiar-looking icon – a teethed cog – with the letters 'Set' under it. He pressed his finger onto that icon. Nothing seemed to happen, until he took his finger off to reveal three tiny symbols were now surrounding the icon: a minus sign '-', a plus sign '+' and another familiar symbol – a miniature dustbin.

"Hmm. If this console's interface was designed for humans, perhaps it has some similarities with the way our tablets and phones work?" Ian thought.

He tried an experiment. He put two fingers onto a different part of the screen – where there were no icons – and moved them further apart. Sure enough, the screen zoomed in and the icons grew in size.

He then pressed the 'cog' icon once – and the small symbols around it disappeared. He definitely didn't want to accidentally delete it. He then tapped the cog icon twice. The screen changed again, this time displaying a completely new set of icons.

"Bingo," Ian thought. But his stress levels were rising – he still had no idea how to check the worm's status, and, if it *had* been successfully installed, the Mekbudans might discover it at any moment.

He studied these new icons and noticed one with a symbol which looked like a large asterisk or snowflake – '*' – superimposed on a larger symbol that resembled a shield. He decided to try double tapping it. Ian was now looking at a very long list of items which seemed like they may be software modules.

These were the four things at the very top of the list:

2025-09 .NAT 9.0.17 Security Update for NavCon Client (XB5063326) – successfully installed on 22/12/2027

2025-06 Cumulative Update Version 26H4 (XB5063060) – successfully installed on 22/12/2027

2024-11 .NAT 6.0.35 Update for NavCon Client (XB5047486) – successfully installed on 20/05/2025

2025-01 .NAT 8.0.16 Security Update for NavCon Client (XB5061935) – successfully installed on 10/02/2025

Ian immediately noticed the date of the security update at the top of the list – it had been installed the day before yesterday – *after* they had jumped forward to 2027.

"Shit. Of course. The RCE vulnerability is now over two and a half years' old – so the Mekbudans would have found it and issued a security update – a patch – to their navigation systems to remove the vulnerability. The ship must have automatically downloaded the patch once it returned to the solar system two days ago. The worm won't be able to run on an updated navigation system."

Ian suppressed the rising panic he was beginning to feel. Then casting his eyes down the screen, he caught sight of the familiar dustbin icon again – only this time the words 'Uninstall update' were displayed next to the symbol, together with a '>' sign.

"Oh wow. Maybe that would work?"

Ian pressed the '>' symbol and the screen changed again. This time it was only showing three items – but one of them was the most recently installed security update. Next to each of these items was the underlined word 'Uninstall'.

Ian decided that he ought to remove the memory stick before he continued. Having done that, he quickly tapped on the 'Uninstall' next to the most recent patch and a pop-up screen invited him to confirm – showing the options 'Yes [Admin]' and 'Cancel'.

He tapped the **Yes** button, and the screen displayed the message: *'Enter Administration Password or scan your fingerprint.'*

"Shit. I haven't got an admin password and there's no way it's going to accept my fingerprint."

Ian paused, forcing himself not to panic. Then, with a sudden jolt of realisation, he remembered the egg-sized biometric device he'd been given to open the door to this room. It made sense that the Vegan fingerprint it simulated might also grant him admin-level authorisation.

He pressed the strange device and a fingerprint appeared on its surface. Then he placed it face-down onto the navigation console's screen, where the message was still displayed.

The screen went black – except for a blue circle swirling slowly in the centre.

"If that's worked, I just hope no one notices I've just taken down the whole navigation system – before it reboots and comes back up again," Ian prayed.

Holding his breath, Ian continued to watch the swirling circle. It reminded him of trying to watch a live tennis match during Wimbledon on BBC iPlayer – particularly during the men's final.

Then, finally, the NavCon console screen lit up again with another set of icons. Ian decided that he didn't have time to confirm whether the security patch had been removed – he just had to try using the memory stick.

So, he inserted the memory stick back into the USB slot. This time, a screen pop-up appeared showing *'Open drive'* or *'Autorun'*. He selected the auto-run option and the pop up disappeared.

"Okay, it looks like it's working now – and I think I've done everything I can," Ian thought. *"I'd better get out of here – just in case I've done anything to raise their suspicions and they send someone, or something, to investigate."*

Ian stood on the stool and touched the ceiling with his door control – to make the hatchway appear – and pressed the button to open the door. He raised himself up and looked around the room. Nothing had changed.

"So far, so good."

He climbed up into the room. He remembered that the door they used to enter this room was on a wall that didn't have any consoles mounted on it. Sure enough, he found the door and opened it, stepping into a corridor. Retracing his steps, he immediately turned left and found the door in the corridor. He opened that door and walked through into the dormitory.

But just as he entered, he heard a sound behind him in the corridor – the unmistakable clunk of one of those robot guards. He immediately crouched down to the right of the doorway, partially shielded by a stack of boxes.

Suddenly, all hell broke loose. Klaxons blared and red strobe lights – which he hadn't even noticed before – began flashing throughout the room.

"That damn robot must've spotted me before I got through the door," Ian thought, alarmed.

Then he caught sight of the Vegan – or at least *a* Vegan – crouched in the doorway on the far side of the room. The figure threw something underarm into the room – it looked like a small pineapple – and it rolled across the floor toward Ian. The Vegan immediately vanished back into the adjacent corridor. There was a loud hissing sound and dense white smoke began spewing from the object – a smoke canister, Ian now realised – quickly filling the room.

"He must've done that to help me escape the robot," Ian thought. *"Let's hope it blocks infrared as well as visible light or this'll be a complete waste of time."*

No robot had entered yet, so Ian bolted, sprinting across the room as fast as he could, heading for the door where the Vegan had been moments before.

Just before he reached the doorway, which was still open, he ran straight into a robot guard – almost physically colliding with it. It had come into the smoke filled room, but was now standing in front of the doorway, completely blocking his escape.

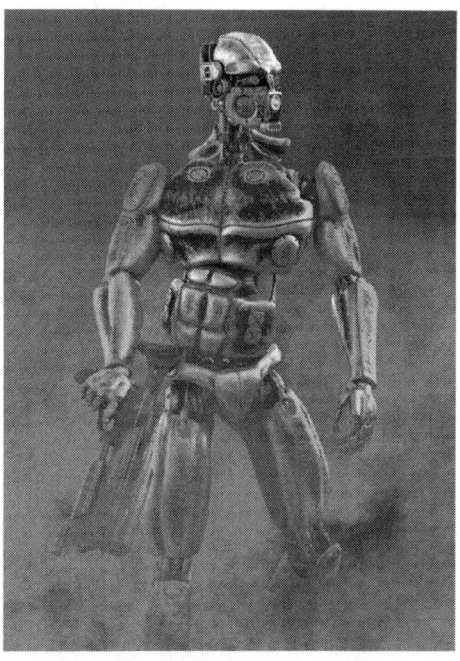

Ian immediately turned round, intending to run in the other direction. But then something embedded itself in the back of his neck, causing him to wince with the sharp pain. Then everything went black.

Chapter 32

Ian opened his eyes. He was staring down at his feet. His body was upright, arms hanging at his sides, but the only thing he could move was his neck – and even that felt stiff and painful.

Slowly, he raised his head and found himself facing a dark green wall.

Then a voice from somewhere behind him said, "Ah, you're awake." Ian couldn't turn his neck far enough to see who was speaking, but he could tell he was in one corner of a large room.

"Xurek, release him," the voice ordered.

Suddenly, Ian's knees buckled, and he almost collapsed to the floor. Bracing himself against the wall with both hands, he managed to stay upright. He turned around slowly.

He was standing in the far corner of what looked like a study, complete with a large desk and two comfortable-looking sofas. Hanging on the wall behind the desk was a flag. On it, was an emblem Ian instantly recognised – that of the Mekbudan emperor.

Ian took in the background in a flash – but what really seized his attention was the creature sitting behind the desk, scowling at him.

It could almost have passed for a man – except for the pointed ears and the two horns sprouting from the top of its head.

The creature rose and walked around the desk, heading towards him. Ian now saw his long tail swishing from side to side, its barbed tip flicking like a cat's.

This was unmistakably an ancient Mekbudan. Ian couldn't help thinking that he wouldn't make a great poker player – not with a tail like that to give his emotions away.

"I am Captain Rorcmog," the creature said. "And *you* have caused me a great deal of trouble!"

"I wish I could say I was sorry," Ian replied. "But I'm only sorry I failed."

"I'm sure you are. We had to restore all our computer systems from a backup data dump to purge that worm you infected us with. Now tell me – who smuggled you onto the ship, and who helped you access my navigation systems?"

Ian remained silent.

After a few seconds, Rorcmog said "Xurek, I want you to turn on the pain stimulators for three seconds."

Ian collapsed to the floor writhing in agony. He heard a voice screaming and recognised it was his own. Every nerve in his body seemed to be flooding his brain with pain signals. What was must have been only three seconds, seemed to take hours to pass.

And then it was over.

"Who smuggled you onto the ship and who gave you access to the navigation systems?"

Ian just lay on the floor panting, as he tried to catch his breath.

"I should tell you that a small device has been implanted inside your head. No one would be able to remove it without killing you – not even your Antarian friends – as it has a tamper-proof sensor. The device contains a small explosive powerful enough to kill you if it self-destructs – but it can also be made to stimulate your brain's pain receptors. As you've just experienced.

"Listen, after we've finished here, the ship is going to skip forward in time about 23 years. You must be aware that there's no going back. So, if you stay on my ship, you'll do the same. Everyone on Earth that you know – family, colleagues and friends – will all have aged 25 years since the date of the Hearing. Your girlfriend, Rebecca will be almost 60 years of age –

and she will have lived most of her adult life without you. No doubt, she will marry somebody else and have his babies.

"Give up everything you know about the spy and I'll let you go free. Otherwise, you're coming with me.

"So, I'll ask you a final time. Tell me who the spy is – the one who got you onto my ship undetected – and who let you into the navigation maintenance area?"

"There is no spy," Ian managed to say, between gasps, still lying on the floor. "I did it myself."

"Liar," Rorcmog retorted. "Xurek, give him five seconds this time."

After a few seconds of screaming and thrashing around on the floor, Ian went silent and stopped moving. He had passed out.

"Xurek, throw this thing in the brig," he ordered. "We'll take it to my father's prison on Delta Pavonis and *he* can deal with it."

Ian's unconscious body stood up and proceeded to walk stiffly out of the room, head dangling.

"Okay, Xurek, what time do we commence the 'special operation'?" Rorcmog demanded.

"Captain, the Commander has ordered you to report to the bridge at 01.00 hours – in just over four hours' time, sir."

Rorcmog couldn't help bristling at the idea that he was being ordered around on his own ship.

However, he decided he was in the mood for 'company' – and that he had enough time before he had to go to the bridge. That would help take his mind off all the other issues he was facing.

"Xurek, tell Jasmine to come to my quarters immediately. And I want dinner for two served in my quarters.

"And, turn off all the cameras and recording devices in my quarters. I don't want to be disturbed until at least 00.30 hours."

Rorcmog issued a mental command and the desk – along with the section of floor beneath it – slowly rotated downward and disappeared from view, while a large double bed rose into place in its stead.

A few minutes later, the door to his room opened and one of his 'companions' – a strikingly beautiful young woman – gracefully sauntered through the doorway.

She was a half-breed: half ancient Mekbudan, half human. Whilst she did lack a tail, two red horns curled out from her head, matching the colour of her hair. The skimpiness of her clothing – wearing only a thong and what might generously be called a bikini top – was compensated by her tattoos.

"Hello, my darling. You asked for *me*?" she enquired, in a sultry voice.

"Ah, Jasmine, how nice to see you again. Come, let us have a seat together – I've ordered us dinner."

Ian opened his eyes. This time he was curled up in the foetal position on the floor. Looking around, he saw he was in a circular room barely four feet in diameter, its walls, floor, and ceiling all glowing with a soft white light – just bright enough to make him squint.

He cautiously tried to stand, but the ceiling was no more than five feet high. The only position he could find that was even relatively comfortable was to sit with his back against a wall, knees drawn up toward his chest.

"This is going to be fun," he thought.

He felt something slightly cold against his neck. Reaching up, he touched a small oval disc, no longer than his little finger, clamped tightly to his skin. Gingerly, he began to pull it away from his neck – and immediately felt a sharp pain. It seemed to be anchored by at least four barbed hooks. If he tried to remove it completely, it would likely tear a large chunk of flesh from his neck and, knowing his captor, could even rupture his carotid artery.

It struck Ian as strange that they hadn't used some sort of truth drug on him, or some other advanced technological method to extract information. Torture was generally considered a poor way to obtain reliable intelligence – a victim would say whatever their tormentor wanted to hear simply to make the pain stop, truth or not.

Ian also wondered, despairingly, whether he should have accepted the deal Rorcmog had offered him. The thought twisted in his gut. But aside from the fact that betrayal was not in his nature, there was no guarantee Rorcmog would have honoured the agreement. Rorcmog could have killed him the moment he outlived his usefulness – and tortured and executed the spy as well. At least this way, there was still a chance – however slim – that the spy would remain undetected.

Still, the weight of what was in store for Earth pressed on his chest like a stone. He knew in his heart that Istariol would keep Rebecca safe – even if he never saw her again. But his entire family and everyone he knew on Earth were about to die – and quite probably, die very horribly.

It wasn't much longer before Ian's thoughts were interrupted by a door in his cell's wall opening.

A Vegan was standing in the doorway. Without a word, he reached into his mouth and pulled out a small cylinder – roughly the size of a cigarette. He tapped it lightly, and a thin rolled piece of paper slid out. He placed the empty cylinder back into his mouth and began chewing it slowly, then held out the rolled paper towards Ian.

Ian took the note and unrolled it. The handwriting was immediately recognisable – it was Istariol's distinctive scrawl.

It read: *"Do not give up hope. I have a plan. But you're going to have to escape from Gulinrog's prison on Delta Pavonis."*

The Vegan then held out an empty hand towards him, blinking. Ian handed back the note and watched as he put it into his mouth and swallowed.

"Was there anything else?" Ian asked desperately. The Vegan just shook his head sadly, bowed, and turned away – walking back through the door, which silently closed behind him.

He wasn't happy that the spy had finally shown him his face. Did that mean they'd given up on torturing him – or had they just decided he was marked for death? To be thrown out of an airlock, perhaps?

Ian was one of the last people in the world to give in to despair. But his logical mind refused to ignore how dire things had become.

Life on Earth was on the brink of annihilation. Everyone he'd ever known – his parents, his friends, his family – would be gone.

Aurelia was already dead, having given her life for a mission that had failed.

Rebecca, at least, should be safe. But if he ever saw her again – after being hurled forward to 2050 – she would be almost sixty years old.

And, even if he managed to escape from this alien prison on another planet, the implant in his skull would finish him: either kill him outright or drive him to crawl back to his captors, begging for mercy.

"So, Istariol, my friend," he thought, *"I fear your latest plan will end no better than your last ones did."*

Chapter 33

"Xurek, give me a report – are we in position?" Rorcmog ordered.

The spaceship had settled near the leading edge of Apophis, generating a localised gravity field to keep itself firmly anchored.

[14]

Krognák, as he now called himself, marched onto the bridge. He had come to personally witness the special operation – one that would divert Apophis's orbit and accelerate the asteroid toward a collision course with Earth.

Rorcmog had investigated Krognák and knew full well that his real name was Heinrich Luitpold Himmler. Himmler had been a leading member of the Nazi Party in the 1930s and '40s and had become the head of the Schutzstaffel – the '*SS*' – and the Gestapo.

The outbreak of World War Two saw the full implementation of the Nazi Party's *'final solution to the Jewish question'*. The ultimate goal of the Nazis' ideology was nothing less than the annihilation of Europe's Jewish population. Jews in occupied territories were forced into ghettoes or systematically killed.

As the principal enforcer of the Nazis' racial policies, Himmler was responsible for operating concentration and extermination camps, as well as forming the death squads in German-occupied Europe. In this capacity, he played a central role in the genocide of an estimated five and a half to six million Jews and the deaths of millions of other victims during the Holocaust.

In May 1942, Hitler approved the *'Generalplan Ost'* – the *'Master Plan for the East'* – a plan commissioned by Himmler. This was Nazi Germany's plan for the settlement and *'Germanisation'* of captured territory in Eastern Europe, involving the genocide, extermination and large scale ethnic cleansing of Slavs, Eastern European Jews, and other indigenous peoples of Eastern Europe, categorized in Nazi ideology as *'Untermenschen'* – literally meaning *'subhuman'*. It resulted in the deaths of approximately 14 million people in Eastern Europe.

The campaign was a precursor to Nazi Germany's planned colonisation of Central and Eastern Europe by Germanic settlers. To achieve this, they intended to carry out systematic massacres, mass starvation, chattel slavery, mass rape, child abductions, and sexual enslavement.

In April 1945, in the final months of the war, it became known that Himmler was hoping to succeed Hitler and that he had started negotiations with a Swedish diplomat to surrender to the Western allies. Hitler had promptly stripped Himmler of all his offices and ordered his arrest.

Himmler had attempted to go into hiding, but was captured by British forces. Officially, he committed suicide in British custody on 23rd May 1945 – but in reality, Gulinrog's agents had broken him out of prison and taken him aboard a Mekbudan spaceship. The British covered up the escape with the story of his suicide.

It remained unclear why his father had appointed Himmler as the head of his Secret Service. Despite the 82 years or more that had passed since Himmler's faked death, Xurek had estimated that only three years had actually elapsed for Himmler. He had clearly been travelling forward in time, presumably with his father's retinue – so he had wasted no time adjusting to his new circumstances.

"I trust everything is in order, Kapitän?" Krognák barked.

"It is now 01.03 hours, GMT Earth time, on 24th December 2027," Xurek replied. "The ship has landed on Apophis, which is currently travelling at its usual orbital speed of 30.7 kilometres per second."

A display screen on the bridge flickered to life, revealing an image of the inner planets of the solar system.

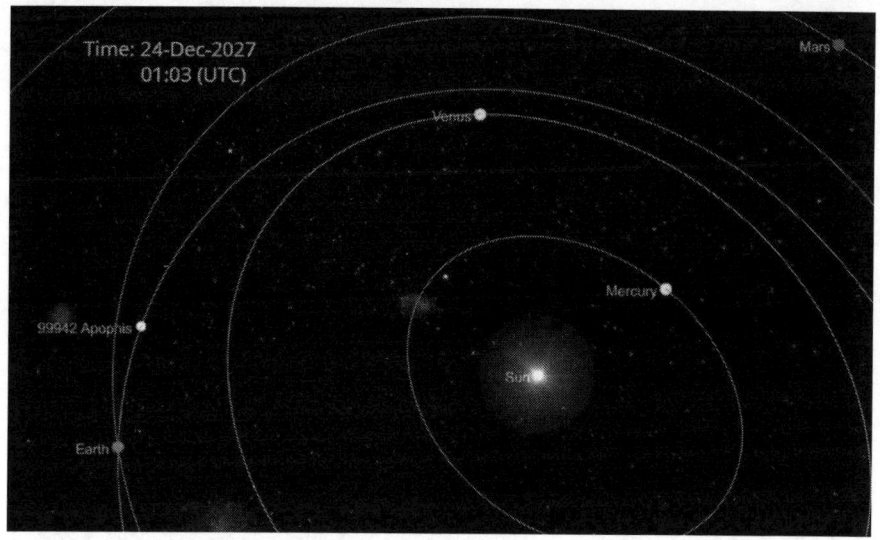

[15]

"This is an output from our navigation system," Xurek explained. "You can see Apophis and Earth – along with their respective orbits – displayed on the left-hand side of the screen.

"Earth lies 44.3 million kilometres ahead of us and it's moving at an orbital speed of 30 kilometres per second. We are at one of the closest points that Apophis will get to Earth on this revolution of its orbit. Without any intervention, Apophis will now begin to get further away from Earth, sir."

"You *do* understand, sir," Rorcmog said, "that the Mekbudan intervention requesting a suspension of Directive 9 – and the implementation of an impact winter – has been postponed until at least 2050 by the successful Solarian Appeal?"

"That is of no consequence. My orders are clear – the operation will continue nonetheless," Krognák replied.

"Yes, sir! However, before we can proceed – as technically, Directive 9 is still in force – I am obliged to go through some procedures with you," Rorcmog explained.

"Fine, then get on with it. I'm sure we don't have all the time in the world to waste," Krognák snapped.

"Xurek, I need you to explain to the Commander our predictions for the result of this special operation," Rorcmog ordered.

"Yes, sir," Xurek replied. "Approximately 33 hours after the beginning of the operation, Apophis will enter the Earth's atmosphere. By then, the asteroid will have been accelerated to a velocity of 666 kilometres per second – one hundred times faster than a bullet.

"Apophis will compress the atmosphere ahead of it far more violently than any natural object in history. The atmosphere will superheat, creating a plasma tunnel glowing hotter than the Sun. The air itself in front of the asteroid will explode, sending shockwaves miles ahead.

"Apophis will crash into the north coast of Cozumel, in the Yucatán Peninsula, at a 45 degree angle. Apophis will not just hit the Earth – it will plunge into the crust like a beam weapon, completely vaporising itself and the surrounding rock in milliseconds. This will create a crater 45km wide and ejects gigatons of molten rock, ash, dust and sulfate aerosols into the stratosphere.

"A seismic shockwave equivalent to a magnitude 11+ earthquake will radiate outwards and entire continents will shake. Mega-tsunami waves 500 to 1,000 metres high will radiate outward. Coastal cities will be obliterated within a couple of hours. Harbours from New York to Shanghai will vanish beneath walls of water.

"A fireball 500km wide will rise into the upper atmosphere. Within 1,000 km anything flammable will ignite instantly – forests, cities and grasslands. Fine debris will spread globally, raining down red-hot glass spherules and ash. Even areas far from 'ground zero' will experience surface fires and suffocating air.

"The kinetic energy would raise all of this material to millions of degrees Kelvin, fully ionising and dispersing it into plasma. No solid or intact fragments would survive.

"This will inject dust, ash and sulfate aerosols into the stratosphere, blocking out over 80% of all sunlight globally. Within months, this will trigger global cooling of about 10°C and cause an impact winter expected to last 10 years, possibly longer.

"This will cause massive die-offs in land and ocean ecosystems, as photosynthesis collapses and global food chains break.

"Sulphur compounds in the atmosphere will cause acid rain, which will damage vegetation and marine life. Chlorine-bearing rock vapor will also destroy most of the ozone layer, increasing UV radiation significantly.

"Global agriculture will collapse and billions of humans will die through famine and cold. Billions of birds, insects and small mammals will begin to die from cold, darkness and loss of food. About 70% to 90% of all species will become extinct over the next few years.

"And," Xurek concluded, "Solarian human survivability is estimated to be extremely low."

"Excellent, Xurek," Krognák replied. "That seems to be a pretty comprehensive report. So, Kapitän Rorcmog, can we now proceed?"

"Certainly, sir, I just need your specific command to proceed," Rorcmog responded.

"Xurek, commence operations – begin the procedures that will cause Apophis to crash into the Earth," Krognák ordered.

"Yes, Commander," Xurek responded. "Captain? Shall we now proceed?"

"Xurek, have you calculated the acceleration required to increase Apophis's velocity to 666 kilometres per second?" Rorcmog demanded.

"Yes, Captain," Xurek replied. "We'll need to accelerate at approximately half of Earth's gravity – 0.54g – for 33 hours, sir."

"Xurek, have you factored in the change in direction needed to intercept Earth's position in 33 hours' time?" Rorcmog asked.

"Yes, sir," Xurek said. "Our orders are very specific about the point of impact. Apophis has to crash into the north coast of Cozumel at a 45 degree angle – so the timing has to be very precise and allow for Earth's rotation."

"Okay, Xurek," Rorcmog confirmed. "Then engage the warp drive and create a wormhole in front of Apophis – to generate 0.54g acceleration at the calculated interception angle."

"Yes, Captain," Xurek said. "We'll have to generate a full-sized wormhole, as it needs to be large enough for the asteroid to 'fall' into. So we'll also need to engage the antimatter generator."

"Understood," Rorcmog replied.

Apophis had a mass of approximately 61,000 million kilogrammes. The ship's mass, by comparison, was only a tiny fraction of that. If the ship were to generate a micro-wormhole and begin to fall into it, Apophis would remain unaffected and be left behind. The ship would effectively be plucked off the asteroid like a flea from a dog.

However, it was highly unusual to generate and sustain a full-sized wormhole this close to a star or planet, as gravitational fields caused too much interference. Creating a stable wormhole within such a field required an enormous amount of energy – far more than a fusion drive could supply – which is why an antimatter generator was essential. Only a warship had the capacity to house such a drive; scout ships were limited to fusion-based energy systems.

"Perhaps that's why my father nominated me to do this," Rorcmog thought, *"as the other Solarian mine owners don't operate warships."*

"Captain," Xurek announced. "I am now ready to engage the antimatter generator and establish the wormhole – on your signal, sir."

"Engage," Rorcmog replied.

The ship began to vibrate and hum as the antimatter system was activated. Rorcmog knew that if the containment field failed – even for a nanosecond – all of the antimatter would instantly explode, its entire mass converting into pure energy. The resulting blast would not just vaporise his ship and everything on board – it would obliterate the entire asteroid.

"All systems engaged, Captain," Xurek confirmed. "The wormhole has been safely established and the special operation has now commenced. Apophis will collide with the Earth at 10.38 GMT on Christmas day 2027 – at 05.38am local time, sir – one hour and 43 minutes before dawn.

"I would like to point out," Xurek continued, "that we *will* need to make a final course correction as we approach Earth, sir. As we pass inside the

Moon's orbital path, we'll need to adjust Apophis's trajectory a few degrees, so that it strikes Cozumel at a 45 degree angle.

"Once we've made the course correction, we'll obviously need to detach the ship from Apophis before impact and clear the area. I've calculated that we'll have a maximum of ten minutes to do this, prior to collision."

"Sehr gut, Xurek," Krognák announced. "I would like to observe the immediate aftermath of the impact from the Moon – and I will need to dock with my own spaceship, which is already waiting there."

"Understood, Commander," Rorcmog replied. "However, it will take some time to bleed off our speed, so that we can manoeuvre for a lunar landing. Xurek, please factor that into your course calculations."

"Yes, Captain," Xurek responded.

"Okay Commander," Rorcmog said, "there is nothing more to be done – until it is time to decouple from Apophis – in about 33 hours."

"However, I *am* curious. What reward has my father promised you for successfully carrying out this operation?" Rorcmog asked.

Krognák was actually smiling, albeit thinly, as he replied. "Well, I don't see the harm in telling you now. You see, I will have finally implemented the *'Final Solution'* – and rid the Earth of all of the 'Untermenschen'. Gulinrog, your father, has agreed that I'll have my genome incorporated into the re-seeding of humans on Earth, after the impact winter is over."

"So, mankind on Earth will become dominated by clones of Himmler – generating millions of children and grandchildren of the Aryan race. Very interesting," Rorcmog thought.

"Then, sir, congratulations are in order – and I think we should all celebrate," Rorcmog said. "I, for one, intend to retire to my quarters. It *is* Christmas Eve, after all."

He gave his commander a sharp salute. Krognák responded with an instinctive Nazi salute and a curt *"Sieg Heil!"*, as he turned on his heel and began walking toward the door.

"Oh, just one more thing, sir," Rorcmog added. "I have a Christmas present for you – just a small token gesture. We have a female human slave on board, a long-legged blonde. Shall I arrange for her to be sent to your quarters, sir?"

Chapter 34

Rorcmog was in his own quarters, getting some rest, when Xurek interrupted his dozing. "Excuse me sir, but we have an emergency on board," Xurek announced.

"What is it, Xurek? This'd better be good," Rorcmog enquired, drowsily.

"The medical sensors are reporting traces of blood in Krognák's quarters, sir," was the response.

"Okay …," Rorcmog asked, thinking this was like pulling teeth, "… and what can you see from the cameras in the room?"

"Krognák has ordered all the cameras in his quarters to be turned off – and he has locked the door to his room," Xurek replied.

"Fine. As Captain of this ship, I am overriding those commands. What do the cameras show now?" Rorcmog barked.

"It looks like someone took the precaution of covering up all the cameras, so none of them show anything but darkness," Xurek reported.

"Then fucking get someone to open his door and report on the situation. Oh, and don't forget to tell them to knock politely first, just in case," Rorcmog ordered.

There was a short delay and then Xurek said, "Captain, Krognák is dead. He's been stabbed in the stomach with his own dagger – and his throat has been slit, probably with the same weapon, sir."

"How could this possibly have happened – why didn't the medical nanobots immediately seal and repair those wounds?" Rorcmog demanded.

There was a short pause. Then… "The nanobots are only automatically activated if a Mekbudan is injured, sir."

"But Krognák *is* a Mekbudan citizen, you idiot!"

"Yes sir, but the nanobot protocols are set up for native Mekbudans only, not humans, irrespective of their citizenship status – and Krognák is a human, sir," Xurek protested.

"How ironic, that the author of the 'Generalplan Ost' died because some robots considered him subhuman – or rather sub-Mekbudan," Rorcmog thought, smiling inwardly.

"Hmm. Xurek, you'd better reset the nanobot parameters immediately – and enable automatic medical assistance for both Vegans and humans," Rorcmog ordered.

"But tell me, Xurek, why didn't Krognák's personal defensive force-field protect him from the attack?" Rorcmog asked.

"Ah… well, his force-field device was attached to his trousers, sir – and he wasn't wearing them at the time of the attack," Xurek explained. "Oh, and there are some serious-looking teeth marks on his '*reðr*', sir."

"I see. And the female slave – what's her condition?" Rorcmog enquired.

"Unharmed, Captain," was the reply. "It looks like she'd been tied up, but she managed to escape her restraints."

"Fine. Well get someone to escort her here to my quarters and have her wait in the anteroom – I'll deal with her later," Rorcmog ordered.

"So, Xurek, give me an update on our position and speed," Rorcmog said. "How is our special operation proceeding?"

"Yes, Captain," Xurek replied. "It is now 03.16 hours GMT Earth time on 24th December 2027. The ship and Apophis are currently travelling at 30.7 kilometres per second, and we are about 44.3 million kilometres from Earth."

"*What*? How long has it been since we commenced the special operation?" Rorcmog demanded. "Why are we still moving at the same speed and have not gotten any closer to Earth. Aren't we supposed to be accelerating at 0.5g?"

"The operation rehearsal began at 01.27 GMT – one hour and 49 minutes ago, Captain," Xurek responded. "And, no, we've remained on Apophis's natural orbital path at its standard velocity, since no acceleration has been applied. Our distance from Earth will now begin to gradually diverge."

"What do you mean by '*operation rehearsal*', Xurek?" Rorcmog growled, menacingly.

Xurek's voice did not waver or change tone. It responded in a flat monotone, "Your orders were very explicit, Captain. We were to conduct a dress rehearsal before commencing the actual operation. And to make it more realistic, Commander Krognák was not to be informed that it was only a rehearsal, sir."

"You must be mistaken, Xurek," Rorcmog insisted. "I gave no such order. Are you sure you haven't been hacked – someone must have altered the command records?"

"I can only reference the command history data that I have access to, Captain," Xurek replied. "But I *do* have a video of you giving that order. Would you like me to display it on the screen in your quarters, sir."

"That won't be necessary, Xurek," Rorcmog said. "As those records have clearly been falsified, I need you to delete them – including any deep-fake videos on the database that show me giving those orders. And delete this conversation, too, whilst you're about it."

"Yes, Captain," Xurek confirmed. "It will be done immediately, sir."

"Okay, now we've got that mess cleared up, it's time to clear up another," Rorcmog announced. "Xurek, flush Commander Krognák's body out of an airlock – and pack up all of his possessions and bring them to my quarters – I'll need to inspect them."

"Yes, sir," Xurek confirmed. "I've now issued the order to get that done, Captain. Shall I send a message to Commander Krognák's ship, telling them that we won't be landing on the moon, since the Commander is dead?"

"All in good time, Xurek," Rorcmog replied. "They aren't expecting him for at least another 36 hours. Besides which, we've got a mine to get operational again," Rorcmog said, with a rare smile, his tail gently waving to and fro. "Xurek, once the body has been ejected, lay in a course for central Africa."

A minute or so later and Rorcmog heard Xurek report: "Captain, Commander Krognák's body has now been laid to rest in space, sir."

"So, Heinrich Luitpold Himmler – 7th October 1900 to 24th December 2027 – you will now spend eternity accompanying Apophis in its orbit around Sol," Rorcmog thought. *"The universe is a far better place without you. I'll have to ask that female slave whether he suffered much from his stomach wound, before she slit his throat. Hopefully, he died horribly."*

"Excuse me, Captain," Xurek interrupted. "What about the 'special operation'?"

"Krognák is dead – and, with him, his authority over me as Commander. According to all the information that I have at my disposal, the Solarian

Appeal was successful – so Directive 9 is still in force. So, *no*, there will be no 'special operation' anytime soon, Xurek."

"Yes, Captain," Xurek acknowledged. "Course is now laid in for central Africa – do I assume you'll want to approach at night, as we usually do, sir?"

"Of course, Xurek," Rorcmog responded. "Oh, and as it *is* Christmas Eve, break out the extra food and drink we brought on board in Paris – and distribute it all to the crew and the slaves.

"And Xurek, we won't be skipping forward in time now – as there's no need to wait for the impact winter to end. When we land in Africa, have the robots unload and re-install all the mining equipment. But give the crew and slaves two days' holiday – today and tomorrow, Christmas Day.

"Once all the equipment and robots have been unloaded and all the mining personnel have disembarked, plot a course to a suitable point in the outer reaches of the solar system and onwards to Delta Pavonis. And configure it for maximum speed, Xurek, I've got some tantalum to sell and more slaves to buy."

"Yes, sir," Xurek replied. "And, Captain, what about the Solarian Representative?"

"You can let him out of the brig now – but he'll be coming with us to Delta Pavonis, where I'll hand him over to my father.

"However, put him out of his misery – tell him their Appeal was successful – and that Earth is safe... for the moment. We *are* free, however, to petition for another Hearing – if the greenhouse gas emissions remain a problem – but not until 2050.

"Mankind have got their reprieve – they'd better not screw it up again!"

"Anyway, Xurek – ask the female slave to come in," Rorcmog ordered. "Oh, and turn off all the cameras and other recording devices in my quarters."

The door opened and Rorcmog saw a woman dressed entirely in black, framed in the doorway. She wore a cloak with the hood up, partially concealing her face.

As she walked into the room, he caught a glimpse of a short skirt and her thigh-high boots. Rorcmog could easily imagine what Himmler would have seen in her.

"Joyeux Noël. Please come in and take a seat, mademoiselle," Rorcmog said with a broad smile. "Can I get you something to drink?" he asked, his tail swishing benignly.

"Oui, Capitaine, du champagne serait délicieux, s'il vous plait," Aurelia replied, smiling back.

Epilogue

Ian was sitting on the bottom bunk in the dormitory.

Uma had come and let him out of the brig, accompanied by one of the robot guards.

"Nilikuambia. Hakuna Matata, yote yatakuwa sawa," he'd explained gleefully, with his typical grin.

Ian had no idea why he always seemed so happy. Still, at least he was out of the brig.

"Follow mfanyakazi robotis," Uma had directed, pointing at the robot.

Ian had dutifully followed the robot through a series of rooms and passages until they reached the dormitory he'd been in before.

On a crate beside the bunk beds sat a tray: with a baguette, a large wedge of French cheese, and an open bottle of wine nestling in an ice bucket. Plus two glasses, two plates and two knives.

The robot had trundled off, the doorway disappearing behind it with a silent finality.

So now, he poured himself a glass of wine and broke into the bread and cheese.

"Paris was our last port of call – so I suppose it makes sense they'd stock up there. But how come everyone in the universe seems to know I like cheese? And why two settings?"

Then the door opened again. A figure filled the frame, cloaked in black. Thigh-high boots hinted she was female. The hood was pulled low, her face lost in shadow.

"Tu ne vas pas dire bonjour?" she asked.

Ian instantly recognised Aurelia's voice and leapt up to greet her.

"Oh my god – you died. I held your mutilated body in my arms. How can you be alive?" he blurted out, before she was in his arms and they clung to each other with desperate force.

Then it struck him: the perfume he'd noticed earlier on the bunk's pillow had been hers. No wonder it had seemed so hauntingly familiar.

"You've been on this ship for some time, haven't you?"

"I'm so sorry we had to do this. To make you believe I was dead." Aurelia was clearly upset. "But let's sit down together and I'll explain everything."

So they sat together on the bottom bunk, sharing their impromptu lunch and a glass of Chablis, while Aurelia recounted everything that had happened.

"After the verdict was announced, we had to assume the appeal would fail – and we…"

"What was the result of the appeal?" Ian cut in. "We lost, I take it?"

"No," Aurelia said, a broad smile breaking across her face. "We won. It took the judges five days to decide, but we won."

She leaned closer. "Anyway, we knew Rorcmog had been tasked by his father, Gulinrog, with destroying all life on Earth. But our spy aboard his ship – the Vegan who helped hide you – reported something useful. There was no love lost between Rorcmog and Himmler. To Rorcmog, this mission was nothing but a massive inconvenience."

"So," she continued, "we decided it was worth testing the waters. Through our agent, we persuaded Rorcmog to meet Istariol and myself aboard his ship."

"Wasn't that dangerous?" Ian asked, frowning. "You're at war with the Mekbudans."

"Not quite," Aurelia replied, with a grim smile. "We're trying to *avoid* going to war with them. So really, we expected the worst case scenario to have been a 'no deal' – and that our personal safety was assured – although we *had* already revealed that we had a spy on board his ship by sending the invitation through him."

"Anyway, we met Rorcmog and struck a deal. I agreed I'd come onto his ship before it departed and, at a suitable opportunity, I'd kill Himmler. But there was a snag. Himmler, head of Gulinrog's secret police, had spies everywhere – including on Rorcmog's ship – and on ours."

"What? You knew Himmler had a spy on board *our* ship? Who?"

"Dewey, our Science Officer," Aurelia replied. "After Dewey fled to an Antarian colony seeking refuge, his family was brought into custody by the Mekbudans. He'd thought they were dead – until Himmler's people threatened him with their deaths – *if* he didn't co-operate."

"So why didn't you eliminate him? Or imprison him?"

"Partly because we were sympathetic to the plight of his family. And partly because I found out he was spying for Himmler without Dewey realising I knew. So we used him as a 'plant'. We hid truly secret information from him – and fed him information we wanted Himmler to know – false or otherwise."

"Okay, but what was the snag then?"

"Himmler knew all about me. We didn't think he would let his guard down – even on a Mekbudan warship – whilst I was alive. With me dead, we thought I'd be more likely to get an opportunity to get close enough to him to kill him."

"How did you fake your death?"

"I had an identical double. A clone. A cyborg – just a machine. They took my DNA and modified it to make the clone non-sentient. The body was controlled by an AI, programmed only to mimic me. It could walk, talk, even pass itself off as me – so long as no one pushed it into deep conversation. Though," she added with a grin, "its French wasn't too bad.

"When you went up onto the flybridge, it was already there – dressed identically to me. The flak jacket was fake; we didn't want a real one falling into Solarian hands. Its orders were to protect you... but to deliberately put itself in harm's way. To die in the most public manner possible.

"I'm really sorry we had to deceive you and Rebecca. But with all these spies around, until Himmler was dead, we couldn't take the risk of letting you in on the secret, in case either of you inadvertently let something slip.

"So, the deal was struck – and I came on board just after you did. I could never have boarded wearing all my technology if Rorcmog hadn't turned the ship's sensors off."

"I don't understand. Rorcmog captured me. He implanted an explosive device in my head. He tortured me – trying to find your spy. A spy whose identity he already knew?"

"Rorcmog needed 'plausible deniability'. He couldn't be seen to condone or be complicit in my actions – or yours. And, with at least one of Himmler's spies on his ship, he had to assume the ship's logs – the voice and video recordings of everything that was happening on board – would end up in Gulinrog's hands.

"But he lied. He didn't put a device in your head. You're the Solarian Representative and protected by Directive 9."

"Oh, so this protection didn't extend to not torturing me on a false pretext?"

"It had to be realistic – for the cameras – for Himmler and Gulinrog. And there's no permanent damage – no one can present any evidence that he breached Directive 9 to the IGC."

"This deal. Exactly what was agreed?"

"Rorcmog would let me come on board his ship and go into hiding. I would kill Himmler – Rorcmog didn't trust him and wanted him dead. Whether our Appeal was successful or not – Rorcmog would *not* create an impact winter. Your safety was assured. We – both of us – would not reveal Rorcmog's role in this. If his father had proof of Rorcmog's actions, he would kill him."

"So, Rorcmog's working for us then?"

"No, actually Rorcmog only works for Rorcmog," Aurelia replied. "But if our interests align again, he may be up for another deal."

"And you managed to kill Himmler?"

"Yes. As it happens, I actually had no choice. When Himmler heard our Appeal was successful, he said it didn't matter and claimed that Gulinrog had ordered the 'special operation' – to push Apophis into Earth – to proceed in any event. Rorcmog was under Himmler's orders and, despite being doubtful that Gulinrog had given such an order, he could see no way that he could disobey. I had to kill Himmler to give Rorcmog back control of his ship.

"We think Gulinrog planned this all along. He banked on Himmler taking it upon himself to wipe out all life on Earth, in the expectation that it would be repopulated with Aryan clones. Afterwards, he'd hand Himmler over to the IGC, disown him, and claim that since Himmler was a Solarian, the blame lay entirely with them. By then it would be too late, and Gulinrog was gambling the Antarians wouldn't go to war over a lost cause."

"So my mission was pointless, then? You'd cut a deal with Rorcmog regardless – it didn't matter whether I managed to insert the worm or not?"

"That's not quite true. When we boarded Rorcmog's ship we didn't know how the Appeal would go. If it failed, sabotaging the special operation would have been essential.

"And we couldn't fully trust Rorcmog. If the Appeal was rejected, would he really refuse his father's orders and spare Earth? If not, I'd have had to kill or neutralise Rorcmog and make sure the worm did disrupt their 'special operation'.

"Finally," Aurelia said, "if Rorcmog honoured the deal, we still needed you to be seen as the culprit of any sabotage – successful or not."

"Right. So Earth's saved and we can all at last go home?" Ian said. "Fantastic. Well done."

Ian gave Aurelia a big hug. But there was something about her expression that disquieted him.

Aurelia looked him in the eyes. "There's more, I'm afraid. Yes, Earth is saved – at least until 2050. But if mankind has not been able to slow or reverse the rate of global warming by then, the Mekbudans will take you to court again."

"And...?"

"There *was* one more condition Rorcmog imposed – one that we had to accept. He insisted you be handed over to his father. On Delta Pavonis."

"You're kidding."

Aurelia pulled a face. "He needs to supply extra proof to his father that you're the culprit – that you smuggled yourself on board, that you hacked the ship's navigation to foil the operation. And if that didn't work, your failsafe was to plant fake records to make the ship's AI think they were only running a dress rehearsal."

"I don't know anything about a dress rehearsal."

"No – that was Rorcmog's idea. He used it to convince Himmler that the special operation had been initiated. But he needs to 'prove' he wasn't involved. You're the person who can provide that proof. So you'll be sent to Gulinrog's prison on the Mekbudan colony of Delta Pavonis to bear witness."

Ian's mouth opened and several choice expletives lined up. "Why in hell have you lot sold me down the bloody river?" he spat.

"We had *no* choice," Aurelia said, blushing. "Look, everything our team has done has finally been successful – together we've saved all life on Earth.

"And we assumed you would have agreed to do this, if we'd asked."

Ian's shoulders slumped, as he realised that she was right.

"Okay. But if I'm tortured – or coerced like the way you handled those Russian prisoners – Gulinrog will eventually learn the truth. You've just made it worse by giving me more information."

"That's somewhat true," she conceded, "but you deserved to know the truth. Besides, Gulinrog is already on thin ice with the IGC after our complaint that a Mekbudan attempted to murder you – and *did* kill me. He won't risk their wrath by harming you; he'll have to release you eventually."

"On that topic, that Mekbudan nearly killed me – and he did kill one of our security team."

"It's true that we hadn't expected a Mekbudan with advanced technology to come after you – in a blatant breach of Directive 9. But you were more protected than you realised. We had two invisible drones above you, ready to dart in the way of any lethal shot he fired at you. It was unfortunate about the guard, though."

"Yes, but couldn't you have taken out the Mekbudan earlier – before he killed the guard?"

"Once we realised that we had no weapons that could affect the Mekbudan's shield and armour, I ordered Alexa to bring our ship up out of the lake. He couldn't survive a shot from the ship's plasma weapon – as you witnessed – but, sadly, we were a few seconds too late to save the guard. The drones were focused on protecting you at all costs."

"Why weren't the drones zapped by the EMP blast?"

"Military drones are EMP-shielded as standard. It's not something we can do with small devices like personal shields and communicators, though."

"Ok, but what was our spaceship doing sitting at the bottom of the lake?"

"I ordered Alexa to fly up from Paris in the middle of the night and hide at the bottom of the lake – in case we needed some backup."

Ian pondered that for a few moments.

"Going back to what might happen to me in prison – what if they manipulate my mind using virtual-reality scenarios?"

"I'll give you a safe phrase that only you and I know. If you encounter one of us and we don't speak that phrase, it's a fake reality. If that happens, your instructions are simple: take the blame and exonerate Rorcmog – they'll accept it."

Ian let out a breath, almost a sigh. *"Another mission then,"* he thought grimly. *"But I really just wanted to go home. To Rebecca. To a life that feels like mine again."*

"How's Rebecca – and where is she?" he asked at last.

"She's safe. I've received word that once the Appeal verdict was announced, she joined Istariol and jumped forward to December 2027. So she's only been waiting a few days for you. I'm going to have to leave this ship in a few hours when it lands in Africa – its next destination. I'll join our ship there, so I can give her a message if you'd like?"

"You're leaving me here? Alone?" Ian asked quietly. "To go to a prison on an alien planet without any help?"

Aurelia looked crestfallen. "I'm sorry. Our Vegan spy is still on board – Rorcmog won't harm him. And when you get to Delta Pavonis we've more agents on the planet who will help you escape. But, yes, I have to leave. Otherwise, I'm likely to be discovered by one of Himmler's – now Gulinrog's – spies. And that would risk betraying Rorcmog."

"You're abandoning me to protect *Rorcmog*? Really?" Ian blurted out, incredulously. "Surely, there's a way you can get me off this ship."

"He's too important an asset to give up," Aurelia retorted. "What's going to happen in 2050? Do you really think mankind is going to change its spots – and vote for the long term, rather than their own short term selfish interests? We're highly likely to be back exactly where we were in 2025 – with another Hearing. Only this will be one that we won't be able to defend. The 'Programme' you've instigated will, no doubt, have failed through lack of global support. And global temperatures will be even closer to catastrophic levels."

They sat in silence for a while.

Then: "Yes, you're right. I'm just being selfish," he said. "If you can get me some paper and a pen, I'll write a letter to Rebecca."

"Of course. Take this," Aurelia said, handing him a notepad and pen from a pocket in her cloak.

"But you'll be wondering what happens next. The ship will land in Africa in less than an hour. I'll disembark and transfer to our ship. I believe Rorcmog intends to remain here for a day or two over Christmas, while he unloads all his mining equipment, robots and other workers."

"After that, he'll depart for Delta Pavonis, probably via one of the L1 Lagrange points near Jupiter or Saturn. The journey should take about a week. You won't be put back in the brig – and our Vegan agent will keep you informed. Once you arrive, you'll be transferred to the prison, where another of our agents will make contact."

They finished their lunch – and the bottle of wine. Aurelia gave Ian some space to write his letter. A little while later, he folded the pages and pressed them into her hand.

"Please give her my love," he said softly. "And tell her it won't be long before I'm home."

"I will. I have to go now – to bid farewell to Rorcmog before I leave the ship, and to assure him once more that his secrets are safe with us."

They both rose. Aurelia looked close to tears; Ian's eyes glistened. They embraced again, fiercer this time, as if it might be the last.

"Oh – you haven't given me the safe phrase," Ian realised suddenly.

Aurelia placed a hand on his shoulder and whispered "Je t'aime" into his ear. Then she turned and, without a backward glance, walked out of the door.

To be continued in …

Volume II
of the
Solarian Chronicles

Neil Templar

I hope you have enjoyed the story so far.

If you would like to know when the next book in the series is available, please go to galactic-spacetime.com and register your email with

Galactic Spacetime Publishing

Afterword

Thank you very much for reading this far. But if you're just taking a quick peek and haven't finished the book yet, I should warn you: there *are* **SPOILERS** in this section.

For many years, I've been curious about whether alien civilisations have ever visited Earth – and whether they might still be visiting us. The biggest questions I had were:

- Why does it seem that there's no tangible evidence of this?

- Why are they so reluctant to reveal themselves? Why not just land next to the White House or on Buckingham Palace's lawn and say *'Hello – take me to your leader'*?

- Why haven't they conquered us – whether to enslave mankind or wipe us out?

- And why would they want to come here at all? What makes Earth worth visiting?

I thought it would be fascinating to create a scenario that might explain all of these questions – whilst also doing some myth busting. That was over twenty years ago. Whilst I did continue researching – in the meantime, life got in the way – and I didn't actually start writing until this year, 2025.

In recent years, I've become increasingly concerned about global warming – and the drastic impact it could have on our planet. This inspired me to make climate change the central theme of this novel. My aim was not just to entertain, but also to highlight aspects of climate science that readers might not have fully appreciated. And in the process of writing this book, I've learned a great deal myself.

As for my approach in writing this book: everything concerning the aliens, their technology, and any events attributed to alien activity is, of course, entirely fictitious. But I wanted to follow in the spirit of Sir Arthur C. Clarke and, wherever possible, ground everything else in fact or scientific theory. For example:

- Earth *has* experienced five previous mass extinction events and all but one – the dinosaur-killer – were caused by greenhouse gases.

- Apophis *is* real and it will pass incredibly close to the Earth on Friday 13th April 2029 – nearer than many satellites – and be visible to the naked eye.

- In fact, all the asteroids mentioned *are* real, as are their quoted orbits, speeds and positions at specific times.

- Water is one of the most extraordinary substances in the universe. Essential for life, it contains oxygen and hydrogen – the latter capable of unleashing immense energy through fusion. Earth's abundance of water makes it a rare jewel in the galaxy.

- Einstein's theory of relativity, confirmed experimentally, *does* predict one can travel forward in time relative to a stationary body. The extreme time distortions described here, however, would require energy far beyond our present capabilities.

- Most importantly, all information on climate change, greenhouse gases, and the projected consequences of global warming have been researched as accurately as possible. In 2024, the world *did* cross a line: in failing to achieve the Paris Accord's aspirational target – as global temperatures rose more than +1.5°C above pre-industrial levels. Almost all of that increase has occurred since 1975 – a mere half-century.

- Within these pages is a fictitious interview with President Donald Trump. However, every statement attributed to President Trump in the book *is* taken directly from his actual speeches, interviews, or his administration's White House publications.

If global warming continues at its *current* rate, temperatures would climb to **+3°C** within the next fifty years – and to **+3.5°C** by 2100. The pace could even accelerate, driven by positive climate feedback loops, as the planet gets hotter.

I know some people are sceptical and think global warming is not man-made. They're entitled to their opinions, although I do wonder how well-informed they might be. All I ask of them is this: "What if you're wrong?"

I don't expect to live long enough to experience the full consequences of irreversible global warming. But in a single human lifetime – seventy-five years – it's entirely possible that civilisation as we know it will collapse.

Anyone born today could live to witness that future – unless something radically changes. Collectively, humanity has the knowledge and the resources to prevent such a catastrophe. But do we have the will? Or shall it remain tomorrow's problem – someone else's to deal with?

Is this truly the legacy we want to leave behind?

Acknowledgements & Sources

My heartfelt thanks go out to all my friends and family who – bombarded with multiple draft versions of this book over the last few months – nevertheless managed to read through the material and give me invaluable feedback and constructive criticism.

This includes members of my family: my wife, Bex; my father (who checked all my maths); and my brother, Simon.

I'd like to give a huge 'thank you' to my friends – Ian, whose eye for detail is without parallel (and who thought I'd named the hero after him); Chris and Frances; and Liam. Let's just say the book would be nowhere near as good without their help and insight.

And finally, the dramatic way that David Wallace-Wells presents the story of how global warming could impact the Earth in his book, inspired my own approach to writing some of the material for the Hearing.

'**The Uninhabitable Earth**: A Story of the Future', by **David Wallace-Wells**, Penguin Books Ltd.

If you would like to read more about Climate Change, I recommend this book:

'**The New Climate War**: the fight to take back our planet', by **Michael Mann.**

Sources

This novel has drawn upon information from several **Wikipedia** articles – some of which are explicitly referenced below. These articles are freely available at www.wikipedia.org and are shared under the Creative Commons Attribution–ShareAlike License (CC BY-SA 4.0) – https://creativecommons.org/licenses/by-sa/4.0/deed.en Changes made: Text has been paraphrased in character dialogue.

'**Crop Circle Seasons**' by **Temporary Temples** – https://temporarytemples.co.uk/what-are-crop-circles

'**Discover the Apartment**', by **Cheval Blanc Paris hotel**, **Cheval Blanc** – https://www.chevalblanc.com/en/maison/paris/rooms-and-suites/theapartment/

'**GHG emissions of all world countries**', **European Commission**, Emissions Database for Global Atmospheric Research Creative Commons Attribution 4.0 International (CC BY 4.0) licence Changes made: Text has been paraphrased in character dialogue – https://edgar.jrc.ec.europa.eu/report_2025 by Crippa, M., Guizzardi, D., Pagani, F., Banja, M., Muntean, M. et al., GHG emissions of all world countries - 2025 Report, Publications Office of the European Union, Luxembourg, 2025, doi:10.2760/9816914, JRC143227.

'**Greenhouse gas**', by **Wikipedia**, CC-SA BY 4.0. Changes made: Text has been paraphrased in character dialogue – https://en.wikipedia.org/wiki/Greenhouse_gas

'Carbon dioxide levels increase by record amount to new highs in 2024', World Meteorological Organization – https://wmo.int/news/media-centre/carbon-dioxide-levels-increase-record-amount-new-highs-2024

'Ocean Acidification', by The Copernicus Programme, part of the European Union's Earth Observation Programme – https://marine.copernicus.eu/ocean-climate-portal/ocean-acidification

'Roswell UFO incident facts and history', BBC Sky at Night Magazine – https://www.skyatnightmagazine.com/space-science/roswell-ufo-incident

'The 1950 UFO Crash at El Indio' by Robert Bitto, Mexico Unexplained – https://mexicounexplained.com/the-1950-ufo-crash-at-el-indio/

'Roswell incident' by Wikipedia, CC-SA BY 4.0. Changes made: Text has been paraphrased in character dialogue – https://creativecommons.org/licenses/by-sa/4.0/deed.en https://en.wikipedia.org/wiki/Roswell_incident

'Flying Disc Found; in Army Possession', The Bakersfield Californian 1947 07 08, Public domain – https://archive.org/details/the-bakersfield-californian-1947-07-08-page-1

'Extinction event' by Wikipedia, CC-SA BY 4.0. Changes made: Text has been paraphrased in character dialogue – https://en.wikipedia.org/wiki/Extinction_event

'The evidence for biosignatures on K2-18b is flimsy, at best' by Ethan Siegel – https://bigthink.com/starts-with-a-bang/evidence-biosignatures-k2-18b-flimsy/

'You say "Velociraptor," I say "Deinonychus"', by Riley Black, Smithsonian Magazine Science Correspondent – https://www.smithsonianmag.com/science-nature/you-say-velociraptor-i-say-deinonychus-33789870/

'Climate change', by Wikipedia, CC-SA BY 4.0. Changes made: Text has been paraphrased in character dialogue – https://en.wikipedia.org/wiki/Climate_change

'Climate change: atmospheric carbon dioxide', May 2025, by Rebecca Lindsey, Climate.gov – https://www.climate.gov/news-features/understanding-climate/climate-change-atmospheric-carbon-dioxide#:~:text=The%20annual%20rate%20of%20increase,a%2030%25%20increase%20in%20acidity

'Climate change feedbacks', by Wikipedia, CC-SA BY 4.0. Changes made: Text has been paraphrased in character dialogue – https://en.wikipedia.org/wiki/Climate_change_feedbacks

'The rate of change since the mid-20th century is unprecedented over millennia', by NASA – https://science.nasa.gov/climate-change/evidence/

'Sea level rise' and 'Coastal cities and sea level rise' by Wikipedia, CC-SA BY 4.0. Changes made: Text has been paraphrased in character dialogue – https://en.wikipedia.org/wiki/Sea_level_rise https://www.coastalwiki.org/wiki/Coastal_cities_and_sea_level_rise

'Global Sea Level Change', by the US Government's **earth.gov** –
https://earth.gov/sealevel

'New elevation data triple estimates of global vulnerability to sea-level rise and coastal flooding'. *Nat Commun* 10, 4844 (2019). Kulp, S.A., Strauss, B.H, CC-SA BY 4.0 http://creativecommons.org/licenses/by/4.0/ Changes made: Quotes have been paraphrased in character dialogue – https://doi.org/10.1038/s41467-019-12808-z

'Report: Flooded Future: Global vulnerability to sea level rise worse than previously understood', by **Climate Central** – https://www.climatecentral.org/report/report-flooded-future-global-vulnerability-to-sea-level-rise-worse-than-previously-understood

'Rising Seas', by **National Geographic** magazine – https://www.nationalgeographic.com/magazine/article/rising-seas-coastal-impact-climate-change

List of places underwater with a 2m sea-level rise was derived using '**Coastal Risk Screening Tool**' by **Climate Central** – https://coastal.climatecentral.org/map/10/-74.1146/40.803/?theme=water_level&map_type=water_level_above_mhhw&basemap=roadmap&contiguous=true&elevation_model=best_available&refresh=true&water_level=6.6&water_unit=ft

'Sea-level rise due to polar ice-sheet mass loss during past warm periods', **Science**. 2015 Jul. Dutton A, Carlson AE, Long AJ, Milne GA, Clark PU, DeConto R, Horton BP, Rahmstorf S, Raymo ME. SEA-LEVEL RISE. 10;349(6244):aaa4019. doi: 10.1126/science.aaa4019. Epub 2015 Jul 9. PMID: 26160951 – https://pubmed.ncbi.nlm.nih.gov/26160951/ https://www.science.org/doi/10.1126/science.aaa4019

'Communicating the deadly consequences of global warming for human heat stress', by Tom K. R. Matthews, Robert L. Wilby, and Conor Murphy, published in the **Proceedings of the National Academy of Sciences** journal – https://www.pnas.org/doi/full/10.1073/pnas.1617526114

'Widespread outdoor exposure to uncompensable heat stress with warming', Fan, Y., McColl, K.A.. *Commun Earth Environ* 5, 762 (2024), CC-SA BY 4.0. Changes made: Text has been paraphrased in character dialogue – http://creativecommons.org/licenses/by/4.0/ – https://doi.org/10.1038/s43247-024-01930-6

'Hyperthermia', by **Wikipedia**, CC-SA BY 4.0. Changes made: Text has been paraphrased in character dialogue – https://en.wikipedia.org/wiki/Hyperthermia

'2003 European heatwave', by **Wikipedia**, CC-SA BY 4.0. Changes made: Text has been paraphrased in character dialogue – https://en.wikipedia.org/wiki/2003_European_heatwave

'5 Critical Observations on Unbearable Heat and Human Health', by **United Nations University**, April 2024, Creative commons – https://unu.edu/ehs/series/5-critical-observations-unbearable-heat-and-human-health

'Fires Drove Record-breaking Tropical Forest Loss in 2024', **World Resources Institute, Global Forest Review** – https://gfr.wri.org/gfr with data from **University of Maryland's GLAD lab** – https://glad.umd.edu/

'Ocean Acidification', by the US **National Oceanic and Atmospheric Administration**, 25 September 2025 – https://www.noaa.gov/education/resource-collections/ocean-coasts/ocean-acidification

'Ocean acidification', by the **European Environment Agency** – https://www.eea.europa.eu/en/analysis/indicators/ocean-acidification

'Middle Miocene Climatic Optimum', by **Wikipedia**, CC-SA BY 4.0. Changes made: Text has been paraphrased in character dialogue – https://en.wikipedia.org/wiki/Middle_Miocene_Climatic_Optimum

'CO2 and Ocean Acidification: Causes, Impacts, Solutions', by the **Union of Concerned Scientists** –https://www.ucs.org/resources/co2-and-ocean-acidification

'Global warming is making oceans so acidic, they may reach the pH they were 14 million years ago', by the **World Economic Forum** – https://www.weforum.org/stories/2018/08/global-warming-is-making-oceans-so-acidic-they-may-reach-the-ph-they-were-14-million-years-ago/

'Vanishing Corals: NASA Data Helps Track Coral Reefs', by **NASA** – https://science.nasa.gov/earth/climate-change/vanishing-corals-nasa-data-helps-track-coral-reefs/

'99% of coral reefs could disappear if we don't slash emissions this decade, alarming new study shows', by **World Economic Forum** – https://www.weforum.org/stories/2022/02/coral-reefs-extinct-global-warming-new-study/

'From Not Enough to Too Much, the World's Water Crisis Explained', **National Geographic** – https://www.nationalgeographic.com/science/article/world-water-day-water-crisis-explained

'Glacier melt will unleash avalanche of cascading impacts', by the **World Meteorological Organization** – https://wmo.int/news/media-centre/glacier-melt-will-unleash-avalanche-of-cascading-impacts

'How much of the Earth's water is stored in glaciers?', by **US Geological Survey Water Science School** – https://www.usgs.gov/faqs/how-much-earths-water-stored-glaciers

'Community estimate of global glacier mass changes from 2000 to 2023', by **The GlaMBIE Team.** *Nature* 639, 382–388 (2025). https://doi.org/10.1038/s41586-024-08545-z CC-SA BY 4.0. Changes made: Text has been paraphrased in character dialogue –http://creativecommons.org/licenses/by/4.0/ – https://www.nature.com/articles/s41586-024-08545-z

'Key messages', by **2025 The International Year of Glaciers' Preservation** – https://www.un-glaciers.org/en/key-messages

'**Water and the global climate crisis: 10 things you should know**', by **UNICEF**, the United Nations agency for children – https://www.unicef.org/stories/water-and-climate-change-10-things-you-should-know

'**We Have the Tools to End Hunger – Now We Need Unity**', by **United Nations Secretary-General** in message for **World Food Day** – https://press.un.org/en/2025/sgsm22858.doc.htm

'**Food Security Update**', by **World Bank Group** – https://www.worldbank.org/en/topic/agriculture/brief/food-security-update

'**Human population projections**', by **Wikipedia**, CC-SA BY 4.0. Changes made: Text has been paraphrased in character dialogue – https://en.wikipedia.org/wiki/Human_population_projections

'**How to Feed 10 Billion People**', by **Axel Reiserer, OPEC Fund** – https://opecfund.org/news/how-to-feed-10-billion-people

'**Groundswell 2: Preparing for Internal Climate Migration**', by Clement, Viviane; Rigaud, Kanta Kumari; de Sherbinin, Alex; Jones, Bryan; Adamo, Susana; Schewe, Jacob; Sadiq, Nian; Shabahat, Elham. 2021. Groundswell Part 2: Acting on Internal Climate Migration ©**World Bank** – https://hdl.handle.net/10986/36248 License: CC BY 3.0 IGO http://creativecommons.org/licenses/by/3.0/igo

'**The Global Tipping Points Report 2025**', by Lenton, T. M., Milkoreit, M., Willcock, S., Abrams, J.F., Armstrong McKay, D.I., Buxton, J.E., Donges, J.F., Loriani, S., Wunderling, N., Alkemade, F., Barrett, M., Constantino, S., Powell, T., Smith, S.R., Boulton, C. A., Pinho, P., Dijkstra, H., Pearce-Kelly, P., Roman-Cuesta, R.M., Dennis, D. (eds), 2025, **University of Exeter**, Exeter, UK. ©The Global Tipping Points Report 2025, University of Exeter, UK. CC-SA BY 4.0. https://creativecommons.org/licenses/by-sa/4.0/deed.en Changes made: Some text has been paraphrased in character dialogue – https://global-tipping-points.org/download/1419/

2017, **The White House**, '**Statements by President Trump on the Paris Climate Accord**' – https://trumpwhitehouse.archives.gov/briefings-statements/statement-president-trump-paris-climate-accord/

2018, '**Climate Science Misrepresented by President Trump**', **Columbia Law School** / Climate School, Columbia University, New York – https://climate.law.columbia.edu/content/climate-science-misrepresented-president-trump-4

Sept 2020, **Jessica McDonald, FactCheck.org**, '**Trump Bucks Climate Science in Wildfire Briefing**' – https://www.factcheck.org/2020/09/trump-bucks-climate-science-in-wildfire-briefing/

28 June 2024, **Roll Call**, 'Donald Trump Holds a Political Rally in Chesapeake, Virginia' –https://rollcall.com/factbase/trump/transcript/donald-trump-speech-political-rally-chesapeake-virginia-june-28-2024/

August 2024, **Jessica McDonald, FactCheck.org**, 'Trump Revives – and Further Decreases – His Absurdly Low Estimate of Sea Level Rise' – https://www.factcheck.org/2024/08/trump-revives-and-further-decreases-his-absurdly-low-estimate-of-sea-level-rise/

17 August 2024, **rev.com**, 'Donald Trump campaign rally in Wilkes-Barre, Pennsylvania' – https://www.rev.com/transcripts/trump-rally-in-wilkes-barre-pennsylvania

Sept 2024, **Jessica McDonald, FactCheck.org**, 'Trump Clings to Inaccurate Climate Change Talking Points' – https://www.factcheck.org/2024/09/trump-clings-to-inaccurate-climate-change-talking-points/

8 December 2024, **rev.com**, 'Elon Musk interviews Donald Trump' – https://www.rev.com/transcripts/elon-musk-and-donald-trump-interview

6 Feb, 2025, **William Brangham, PBS News Hour**, 'Trump aggressively working to dismantle US efforts to fight climate change' – https://www.pbs.org/newshour/show/trump-aggressively-working-to-dismantle-u-s-efforts-to-fight-climate-change

12 Feb 2025, **POLITICO**, 'Climate reports vanish from federal science program website' – https://subscriber.politicopro.com/article/2025/02/climate-reports-vanish-from-federal-science-program-website-00203815

20 March 2025, **Reuters**, 'Trump administration to open more Alaska acres for oil, gas drilling' – https://www.reuters.com/world/us/trump-administration-open-more-alaska-acres-oil-gas-drilling-2025-03-20/

25 March 2025, **Simmone Shah, TIME**, 'Trump Is Bringing Project 2025's Anti-Climate Action Goals to Life' – https://time.com/7271567/trump-project-2025-anti-climate-action/

2 May 2025, **The White House**, 'The President's FY 2026 Discretionary Budget Request' – https://www.whitehouse.gov/omb/information-resources/budget/the-presidents-fy-2026-discretionary-budget-request/

2 May 2025, **The White House**, 'Ending the Green New Scam Fact Sheet' – https://www.whitehouse.gov/wp-content/uploads/2025/05/Ending-the-Green-New-Scam-Fact-Sheet.pdf

12 June 2025, **The White House**, 'President Donald J. Trump Stops the Green Agenda in the Columbia River Basin' – https://www.whitehouse.gov/fact-sheets/2025/06/fact-sheet-president-donald-j-trump-stops-the-green-agenda-in-the-columbia-river-basin/

5 July 2025, **Washington Post**, 'How the Trump administration is already cutting off climate research' – https://www.washingtonpost.com/climate-environment/2025/07/05/trump-cuts-climate-research/

Robert Lea, space.com, '**Is our universe trapped inside a black hole? This James Webb Space Telescope discovery might blow your mind**', March 2025 – https://www.space.com/space-exploration/james-webb-space-telescope/is-our-universe-trapped-inside-a-black-hole-this-james-webb-space-telescope-discovery-might-blow-your-mind

Image Credits

Licensed Images

A number of images in this book are used under licence from their respective rights holders. All rights remain with the original copyright owners. No attribution is required.

- ©Shutterstock – used under purchased licence.
- ©iStock – used under purchased licences.
- ©Vecteezy – used under purchased licence.
- ©Freepik – used under purchased licence.
- ©Pixaby – used under free licence (attributions below).

UFO image on front cover from **Pixabay** by **Patrick Fischer**
https://pixabay.com/users/alienized-11040952/?utm_source=link-attribution&utm_medium=referral&utm_campaign=image&utm_content=5114437

Image of blue supercar from **Pixabay** by **Nikesh Khadka** –
https://pixabay.com/users/nikeshkhadka45-22118811/?utm_source=link-attribution&utm_medium=referral&utm_campaign=image&utm_content=7971480

Creative Commons Images

A number of images in this book are used under **Creative Commons Attribution–ShareAlike (CC BY-SA)** licences. Each creator retains copyright in their work. Images have been modified or adapted where necessary. Full details of these images are included in the following pages.

Other Images

A number of other images in this book are public domain or used courtesy of the respective rights holders. All rights remain with the original copyright owners. Full details of these images are included in the following pages.

General Note

All other images, text, layout, and compilation ©Neil Andrew Esslemont, 2025. The author claims no ownership of the images referred to above or listed below, beyond licensed, Creative Commons or public-domain use as described.

---

[1] Image: '**Barbury Castle, Wiltshire, 1st June 2008, Barley OH**', by **Temporary Temples** – https://temporarytemples.co.uk/crop-circles/2008-crop-circles

[2] Image: '**The inner Solar System from the Sun to Jupiter, including the asteroid belt**' by **Mdf** at English Wikipedia, Public domain, via Wikimedia Commons
https://en.wikipedia.org/wiki/User:Mdf
https://commons.wikimedia.org/wiki/File:InnerSolarSystem-en.png

[3] Image: '**3200 Phaethon Orbit**' (screenshot) by **Phoenix7777** – Data source: HORIZONS System, JPL, NASA, CC-SA BY 4.0 https://creativecommons.org/licenses/by-sa/4.0/deed.en via Wikimedia Commons. Changes made: image is a screenshot of animated .gif file – https://commons.wikimedia.org/wiki/File:Animation_of_3200_Phaethon_orbit.gif

[4] Image: '**Heinrich Himmler**', by **Bundesarchiv,** Bild 183-R99621, licensed under CC BY-SA 3.0 Germany https://creativecommons.org/licenses/by-sa/3.0/de/deed.en at Wikimedia Commons. Changes made: colourised and insignia removed – https://commons.wikimedia.org/wiki/File:Bundesarchiv_Bild_183-R99621,_Heinrich_Himmler.jpg

[5] Image: '**Redrawing of Apophis symbol for near-Earth asteroid 99942 Apophis**' (after Denis Moskowitz & Alec Finlay, One Hundred Year Star-Diary), by **Kwamikagami**, licensed under CC BY-SA 4.0 https://creativecommons.org/licenses/by-sa/4.0/deed.en via Wikimedia Commons. No changes made – https://commons.wikimedia.org/w/index.php?curid=113061837

[6] Image: '**A representation of the Egyptian Deity Apep, the embodiment of chaos, as he was depicted in The Tomb of Ramesses I, 1307 BCE**', by **RootOfAllLight**, licensed under CC BY 4.0, https://creativecommons.org/licenses/by/4.0/ via Wikimedia Commons. No changes made. https://commons.wikimedia.org/wiki/File:Apep_(Deity).svg

[7] **Image of the orbits of Apophis, Earth, Venus and Near Earth Objects** courtesy of **NASA's Eyes on Asteroids** – https://eyes.nasa.gov/apps/asteroids/#/home?time=2027-12-24T07:21:57.347+00:00&rate=1

[8] Image: '**The 70m Years plot**' from **Scripps CO2 program** graphics, CC-SA BY 4.0 http://creativecommons.org/licenses/by/4.0/ Changes made: Added 424ppm as 2024 average and 15m years ago point highlighted with arrows and commentary: "Global temperature +3.5°C to +4°C higher than 1750" – keelingcurve.ucsd.edu uses paleo-CO2 data that have been assembled and curated by an international group of proxy experts – https://www.paleo-co2.org/ Ice core data from Baerbel Hoenisch. (2021). Paleo-CO2 data archive (Version 1) [Data set]. Zenodo. https://doi.org/10.5281/zenodo.5777278

[9] Image: '**Risk of Earth system tipping points increase with temperature**' from '**The Global Tipping Points Report 2025**', by Lenton, T. M., Milkoreit, M., Willcock, S., Abrams, J.F., Armstrong McKay, D.I., Buxton, J.E., Donges, J.F., Loriani, S., Wunderling, N., Alkemade, F., Barrett, M., Constantino, S., Powell, T., Smith, S.R., Boulton, C. A., Pinho, P., Dijkstra, H., Pearce-Kelly, P., Roman-Cuesta,

R.M., Dennis, D. (eds), 2025, **University of Exeter**, Exeter, UK. ©The Global Tipping Points Report 2025, University of Exeter, UK. CC-SA BY 4.0. https://creativecommons.org/licenses/by-sa/4.0/deed.en Changes made: Chart title moved and size changed. Current warming updated to 1.5°C. Trajectory removed. Sources moved to book endnote – https://global-tipping-points.org/download/1419/

[10] Chart: '**Global annual average near-surface temperatures 1900 to 2024 – relative to the pre-industrial period 1850-1900.**' Data source: **European Environment Agency (EEA)**, licensed under CC☐BY☐4.0, https://creativecommons.org/licenses/by/4.0/ – Chart created using global data only, no changes made to data. https://www.eea.europa.eu/en/analysis/indicators/global-and-european-temperatures/global-and-european-annual-average#:~:text=Above%20chart:%20Global%20annual%20averages,(NOAA)%20and%20Berkeley%20Earth.

Additional information sourced from EEA 'Global and European temperatures', published 16 Jun 2025: https://www.eea.europa.eu/en/analysis/indicators/global-and-european-temperatures

[11] Image: **The orbits of Apophis and other planets in June 2025** courtesy of **TheSkyLive.com** ©2025 TheSkyLive.com – https://theskylive.com/3dsolarsystem?objs=apophis&date=2025-06-03&h=03&m=01&

[12] Image of '**Saturn in natural colors (captured by the Hubble Space Telescope)**' by **Hubble Heritage Team** (AURA/STScI/NASA/ESA) – https://esahubble.org/images/opo9828c/

[13] Image: '**Visualization of a supercomputed magneto-hydrodynamic simulation of a disk and jet around a black hole**' by **Andrew Hamilton**, JILA, University of Colorado – https://jila.colorado.edu/~ajsh/insidebh/intro.html

[14] Image: **Close up Apophis asteroid** courtesy of **NASA's Eyes on Asteroids** – https://eyes.nasa.gov/apps/asteroids/#/99942_apophis

[15] Image: **Orbit of inner planets and Apophis in Dec 2027** courtesy of **TheSkyLive.com** ©2025 TheSkyLive.com – https://theskylive.com/3dsolarsystem?objs=apophis&date=2027-12-24&h=02&m=03&

Printed in Dunstable, United Kingdom

74462599R00179